Corrupt

Ed Adams

a firstelement production

Ed Adams

First published in Great Britain in 2021 by firstelement
Copyright © 2021 Ed Adams
Directed by thesixtwenty

10 9 8 7 6 5 4 3 2 1

A CIP catalogue record for this book is available from the British
Library.

ISBN 13: 978-1-913818-14-2

eBook ISBN: 978-1-913818-15-9

Printed and bound in Great Britain by Ingram Spark

rashbre
an imprint of firstelement.co.uk
rashbre@mac.com

ed-adams.net

Edge, Red

For the vigilant

Thanks

A big thank you for the tolerance and bemused support from all of those around me. To those who know when it is time to say, " step away from the keyboard!" and to those who don't.

To Julie for that kind of understanding that only comes with really knowing me.

To thesixtwenty.co.uk for direction.

To the NaNoWriMo gang for the continued inspiration and encouragement.

To Topsham, for being lovely.

To John, for his uncompromising readthroughs.

To Elizabeth, Georgina, Roger, John, Caroline, Richard and other cover reviewers.

To the edge-walkers. They know who they are.

And, of course, thanks to the extensive support via the random scribbles of rashbre via
http://rashbre2.blogspot.com
and its cast of amazing and varied readers whether human, twittery, smoky, cool kats, photographic, dramatic, musical, anagrammed, globalized or simply maxed-out.

Not forgetting the cast of characters involved in producing this; they all have virtual lives of their own.

And of course, to you, dear reader, for at least 'giving it a go'.

Books by Ed Adams include:

Triangle Trilogy		About
1	The Triangle	Dirty money? Here's how to clean it
2	The Square	Weapons of Mass Destruction – don't let them get on your nerves
3	The Circle	The desert is no place to get lost
4	The Ox Stunner	The Triangle Trilogy – thick enough to stun an ox
		(all feature Jake, Bigsy, Clare, Chuck Manners)
Archangel Collection		
1	Archangel	Sometimes I am necessary
2	Raven	An eye that sees all between darkness and light
3	Card Game	Throwing oil on a troubled market
4	Magazine Clip	the above three in one heavy book.
5	Play On, Christina Nott	Christina Nott, on Tour for the FSB
6	Corrupt	
		(all feature Jake, Bigsy, Clare, Chuck Manners)
Stand-Alone Novels		
1	Coin	Get rich quick with Cybercash – just don't tell GCHQ
2	Pulse	Want more? Just stay away from the edge
3	Edge	Power can't be left to trust
4	Now the Science	the above three in one heavy book.
Blade's Edge Trilogy		
1	Edge	World end climate collapse and sham discovered during magnetite mining from Jupiter's moon Ganymede.
2	Edge Blue	A human outcome, after a doomsday reckoning, unless…
3	Edge Red	An artificially intelligent outcome, unless…
4	Edge of Forever	Edge Trilogy

About Ed Adams Novels:

Triangle Trilogy		About
1	Triangle	Money laundering within an international setting.
2	Square	A viral nerve agent being shipped by terrorists and WMDs
3	Circle	In the Arizona deserts, with the Navajo; about missiles stolen from storage.
4	Ox Stunner	the above three in one heavy book.
		(all feature Jake, Bigsy, Clare, Chuck Manners)
Archangel Collection		
1	Archangel	Biographical adventures of Russian trained Archangel, who, as Christina Nott, threads her way through other Triangle novels.
2	Raven	Big business gone bad and being a freemason won't absolve you
3	Card Game	Raven Pt 2 – Russian oligarchs attempt to take control
4	Magazine Clip	the above three in one heavy book.
5	Play On, Christina Nott	Christina Nott, on Tour for the FSB
6	Corrupt	
		(all feature Jake, Bigsy, Clare, Chuck Manners)
Now the Science Collection		
1	Coin	cyber cash manipulation by the Russian state.
2	Pulse	Sci-Fi dystopian blood management with nano-bots
3	Edge	World end climate collapse and sham discovered during magnetite mining from Jupiter's moon Ganymede
4	Now the Science	the above three in one heavy book.
Blade's Edge Trilogy		
1	Edge	World end climate collapse and sham discovered during magnetite mining from Jupiter's moon Ganymede.
2	Edge Blue	Endgame, for Earth – unless?
3	Edge Red	Museum Earth – unless?
4	Edge of Forever	Edge Trilogy

Ed Adams Novels: Links

Triangle Trilogy		Link:	Read?
1	Triangle	https://amzn.to/3c6zRMu	
2	Square	https://amzn.to/3sEiKYx	
3	Circle	https://amzn.to/3qLavYZ	
4	Ox Stunner	https://amzn.to/3sHxlgh	
		(all feature Jake, Bigsy, Clare, Chuck Manners)	
Archangel Collection			
1	Archangel	https://amzn.to/2Y9nB5K	
2	Raven	https://amzn.to/2MiGVe6	
3	Raven's Card	https://amzn.to/2Y8HLgs	
4	Magazine Clip	https://amzn.to/3pbBJYn	
5	Play On, Christina Nott	https://amzn.to/2MbkuHl	
6	Corrupt		
		(all feature Jake, Bigsy, Clare, Chuck Manners)	
Now the Science Collection			
1	Coin	https://amzn.to/3o82wmS	
2	Pulse	https://amzn.to/3qQlBvL	
3	Edge	https://amzn.to/2KDmYOW	
4	Now the Science	https://amzn.to/3iG5Nc2	
Edge of forever Trilogy			
1	Edge	https://amzn.to/2KDmYOW	
2	Edge Blue	https://amzn.to/2Kyq9au	
3	Edge Red	https://amzn.to/2KzJwjz	
4	Edge of Forever	https://amzn.to/3c57Ghj	

TABLE OF CONTENTS

Wise Monkeys

The three wise monkeys "see no evil, hear no evil, speak no evil". They are:

- **Mizaru,** who sees no evil, covering his eyes
- **Kikazaru,** who hears no evil, covering his ears and
- **Iwazaru,** who speaks no evil, covering his mouth.

The phrase is often used to refer to those who deal with impropriety by turning a blind eye.

PART ONE

Beauty and Terror

"Let everything happen to you
Beauty and terror
Just keep going
No feeling is final."

Rainer Maria Rilke

Setup

Clare sensed that her iPhone would ring. She was looking out across River Thames from the Triangle's office in Hays Galleria. It still startled Clare when she saw Amanda's name come up on the screen.

"Clare Crafts," she said, "Hello Amanda! It's been a while."

Clare knew that if Amanda Miller was calling from SI6, the UK's Secret Intelligence Service, then it must be something significant. Amanda wasn't one to waste words.

"Hello, Clare, yes, it has been a while. I've another interesting situation developing here!"

"Okay Amanda, can you explain by phone, or do we need to meet?"

"I can give you the outline by phone, but yes, we should also meet," answered Amanda, "And this time it's you I need help from!"

Clare was puzzled; usually Amanda contacted Jake if it was a general request. After all, she had known Jake the longest, from that time when he'd been incarcerated by the security services, while she, Bigsy and Chuck Manners had been chasing around the deserts of Arizona. Such a long time ago...

"Ok, tell all," asked Clare.

"Well, it's once again the nature of you being 'off the radar' that could prove so useful. Clare, I'd like you to spend a little time working alone the river at the Houses of Parliament."

"Really? You know my sister Sam is there?" asked Clare.

"We do, and as a matter of fact that is one of the reasons that this is such a good fit," answered Amanda, "Samantha Crafts, Research Assistant to Mary Crestwell, Conservative MP for Darland Totteridge, in Surrey."

"She calls her Mary," answered Clare, "And seems to think she's all right, if somewhat tough."

"Yes, she has a sterling reputation. No expense wheezes, no house flips, no dirty laundry in the cupboard – Samantha struck luck with Mary!" answered Amanda.

"We are hoping you'll be able to take on a similar role, also for a Conservative MP. After all there's more of them to choose between."

"And why would I do that?" asked Clare, intrigued.

"The situation you discovered based upon that listening station out at Greenwich Peninsula hasn't gone away. There are more MPs being caught out now and it's by a mix of corruption, both sleazy and slushy."

"What? They are still trying to use the system to corrupt MPs, as a cheap way to bypass lobbying procedures?"

"Yes, although we got that Minerva listening station place by the Dome shut down just after our actions the last time."

"They must have been on to a good thing, if they have started it up again," said Clare.

"That's what we want you to find out, and who you think is involved. We've kept this from the nosey parkers in the press and overtly from the loose jawed MPs. We think there is still someone - we think it is probably the Russians - trying to exert moral suasion over some of our MPs."

"Moral suasion? You mean blackmail?" asked Clare, "Like the last time with Bernard Driscoll? I seem to remember it ended catastrophically for him. Killed in a car crash on the way to Norwich."

"Yes, and it is because you have the knowledge of this and access to your very talented friends, that I am asking you to help us. I could offer some remuneration too, but I somehow sense that your organisation has sufficient funds already."

Clare thought carefully; Amanda was referring to the substantial funds that had come to the Triangle team from past endeavours, and Clare knew that Amanda had turned a blind eye to the source of the funds. Not that Amanda was trying to exert any direct pressure on Clare.

"Of course we'll help," said Clare, "There is never a dull moment around you, Amanda. You must tell me what I need to do!"

"It'll be working for an MP called Andrew Brading; Secretary of State for Internal Affairs; you might not know so much about him at the moment, but they tip him for the top in a few years. You must read up on him before you go to their offices. Get someone to test you too.

"The next thing will be to talk to your younger sister about working in Parliament - it'll be a much better briefing than anything that I can provide! I'll take it that this is settled then? I'll make sure the path is cleared to get you inserted into an appropriate role in Parliament. One thing, I suggest you'll need to move from your apartment for this. It will be better if you are with some other researchers - that way you'll pick up the news and gossip more readily."

"Great," said Clare, "And do I get paid for this work - like as a civil servant?"

"Not enough to live on," answered Amanda, "Barely enough to buy your food every day. Most of these posts go to people with connections, usually heavily supported by Trust Funds or The Bank of Mum and Dad."

"Okay - no need to sell it," smiled Clare into the phone, "I'll get on to Sam to find out what's what."

"Excellent," said Amanda, "We'll talk again in a few days when I've set this up."

Clare heard the phone click.

Bigsy looked over, "What breaks you from staring out of the window?" he asked.

"You'll never guess what! That was Amanda - she wants me to work at the Houses of Parliament - some kind of surveillance gig!"

"What about the rest of us?" asked Bigsy.

"Oh, I'm sure we'll all be involved!" answered Clare., "If not, I'll request it from my Member of Parliament."

Cellarium

Clare had arranged a lunchtime meeting with Samantha at the Cellarium by Westminster Abbey.

"Hi Clare, we can't get much closer than this!" said Samantha, referring to them being opposite the Palace of Westminster.

Samantha had breezed in, wearing business attire. A dark trouser suit with a white blouse buttoned to the top.

"Very business-like!" smiled Clare.

"You soon get used to it, but you'll need several of this type of outfit to fit in! Dress for success but don't upstage the politicians!"

Two gin and tonics later, Clare had ordered the pumpkin gnocchi and Sam had caramelised onions and quiche. The Abbey continued the ancient benedictine tradition of providing hospitality to visitors and presented its food with panache. The Cellarium was part of the 14th century fabric of Westminster Abbey, where in olden times the monks kept their stores of food & drink. Now the

Cellarium café kept the tradition of hospitality alive, albeit at London prices.

Clare looked at Samantha, "Are you still with that Stewie Fosdick?" she asked.

Samantha looked startled, "It was Stuart Fosdyke and no, I'm not - he was a dweeb. All watermelon sweet but then I heard he was making out with some other girl. It hurt me for a while but I've moved on, I am so over it - over him."

Clare looked at her sister. She seemed clear-eyed and not in the least put out by the recent turn of fortunes.

"I hope she doesn't need to fake it like I did."

"But that took you two years?"

"Yes, it took two long years to call it quits. But forget that boy, I'm over it. Babe - Clare - I'm cool by the way."

"From what I remember you seemed fond of him...I always wondered if he was right for you - and he always scowled at me."

"I noticed - both his scowls and your looks of displeasure. And I didn't I love him, anyway. So, I decided I'd live my life... It's my life...Not following around a two-timer."

"Better without him, right on sister!"

Sam continued, "He thought he was quite the man, and he tells his friends he made my heart break. It shows he knew nothing."

"Urgh. He sound like a right head case. The big 'I Am.'"

"Yes, I did the right thing - breaking from him. Deleted all his pictures from my phone. And the sexts. Blocked him dead. He won't ever bring me down again. He is gone."

"Whoa." Said Clare, "But you still need a hug then?"

"Hugs are still good," said Samantha.

"And what about you? Any boys, or girls in your life? Who was that last one? Olivia? "

"Aurora actually. No, it didn't last. But we were both in it for the spree!"

"And you are still hanging around with that Triangle gang? I think Jake and Bigsy must be your secret boyfriends? I can see that Jake is kinda hot."

"Strictly professional. Maybe I'll meet someone in Parliament - If I was looking, that is."

Clare asked, "Tell me about working in Parliament. What will the first week be like, Ms. PPE from Oxford?"

"Are you sure you'll get the role? I mean, it is difficult to get into a Parliamentary Researcher role and quite competitive. Not to mention the awful pay. Oh, and thank you very much for helping to keep me afloat. It seems strange getting subsidies from my older sister!"

"I guess I've been lucky with 'That Triangle gang' as you put it, and we've been able to charge some impressive fees along the way. And, of course, you are tax deductible!" Clare grinned at her sister.

Samantha began, "When I sent my CV to an MP's office after graduation, I never dreamt that a few months later I would work at the heart of British politics in one of the most beautiful buildings in the world.

"Nor did I imagine that I would pound the streets during a general election campaign, sneaking into media soirees at party conference or sweating in the gym next to politicians but I have, thanks to this role, which has given me the chance to get my foot firmly in the door - and thank you, Clare - I really mean it- when I say thank you for your moral and financial help to get me started."

"Well, it's family - isn't it - not quite Bank of Mum and Dad, but along those lines!"

Samantha continued, "In Westminster, internships are common and most MP's offices will take on interns to help ease the workload. It's why I'm worried whether you'll get the job - and it's a direct jump to Researcher too. Normally it is a rite of passage to be an intern first, as MPs are wary of taking on staff without knowledge of how Parliament works.

"For some, this extra hoop to jump through is seen as a selection process, but Clare, as you know, it prices out those who can't afford to live unpaid in London.

I remember when I was going for an interview. It was with the MP's office manager and a researcher. They were both testing me, but not too formal.

They asked me about my experience and how much I knew about the MP and why I wanted the role. Of course, I had my Philosophy, Politics, and Economics degree from Oxford to wave around, plus I had done my research. So I got this six-month internship which although unpaid, includes expenses to cover my travel and food every day.

"It's really like slavery then?" confided Clare, "They all grab enormous expenses budgets and then pay you in potato crisps?"

"Don't say that during the interview," said Samantha, looking serious, "You pretend that you like the working conditions,"

"To be honest, I'll still be getting paid by Triangle, so the food money really is for food -er - or drinks."

"That's the spirit. I remember my first day clearly, trying hard not to stare as MPs I had spent three years studying stood next to me in the queue for lunch.

"I also remember how hard it was to adapt to the demands of an MP's office and the realisation that in Westminster the working day never ends at 6pm as business in the House can go on late into the night. Be prepared for that.

"As a result, my first week was one of the most exciting yet draining of my life, and I remember leaving work on Friday and wondering how I was going to make it through the next six months.

"Being an intern in such a busy office meant that for the first few weeks I was bottom of the heap and they gave me tasks such as opening the post, filing letters and emails and answering the phone. Later, they gave me more responsibility as I proved myself to the team and they trusted me.

"Sam, it always looks like you've got a glamorous job and

you never give away that there are some drudgey parts!"

"I know, and I thank you for saying that. Case in point: I remember meeting my MP for the first time and her turning to me as she strode down a corridor, me running along behind. Then she looked me dead in the eyes and asked why I wasn't a member of the party."

"What did you say?"

"A bit wishy-washy - I offered that I didn't feel able to become a member of any party as I agreed and disagreed with elements of them all. Then I watched nervously, wondering if I had just blown my chances as she studied me closely, smiled, and carried on walking."

"I'd better get some stock responses ready!"

"Yes, I learnt very quickly that you have to have an answer for every question asked, even if it's not the right one, as it might be your only opportunity to offer an opinion and people make their minds up quickly."

"So, they can make decisions then?"

"Stoppit. I know you are only doing it to worry me. The same day I went into the House of Commons for the first time (it's much smaller than you think)."

"I remember visiting it on a school trip once."

"Yes, I forgot that. But as well as the exciting things, being an intern means I also had the more mundane office responsibilities too, such as making tea, doing the washing up and stuffing envelopes. You are somehow hoping to bypass all the mundane stuff? It might be more difficult than you think."

"I'm hoping for some sponsorship from a friend."

"It'd have to be a friend in a very high place. Do you know someone in the Cabinet or Secret Service or something?"

"I couldn't possibly comment," answered Clare, smiling.

"Oh, I see you are doing Civil Servant speak now. There's more to you than meets the eye, sister dear. One of the best things about being a researcher, is the varied nature of the job.

"That first week, as I was walking to the kitchen to make a cup of tea, I met the Prime Minister, standing alone pouring out a cup of tea. He poured a second one and handed it to me. I was slightly star-struck and somehow managed to garble a thank you.

Clare smiled at the thought of her kid sister meeting the Prime Minister without a word to say.

Samantha continued, "Perhaps not the best first impression, but the opportunity to make it at all means that hundreds of cups of tea later, it's still worth it!"

"I'm sold," said Clare, "And I'm determined to get the role."

"Who is it with?" asked Samantha, " I promise I'll keep schtumm!"

"Andrew Brading," answered Clare, studying Samantha's face for a reaction. She didn't need to study it.

"Unbelievable!" said Samantha, "You've hit the jackpot there. He's tipped for the top. He's also, how shall I say 'photogenic', regardless of whether he's wearing a shirt."

"I thought he looked quite smart in the photos"

"Yes, and everyone that is around him always says he has a wonderful personality too. I can't believe it. You get one of the hotties in Parly and I get a female dragon. And I'm the one with the PPE(Oxon)"

"I'm quietly philosophical," answered Clare.

"And I'm quietly late!" answered Samantha looking at her watch. She stands. They hug.

"Does this mean I'm picking up the bill?" asks Clare.

"Ooh, would you, thank you! It means I can just be back in time!" smiles Samantha. She skips to the outside of the Cellarium. Then across the road to enter Parliament via the Old Palace Yard.

Clare paid and was walking back to Westminster tube when her phone rang.

"Hi, It's Bigsy. What you said got me thinking. Remember that Pete Burr? He was observing us at the Triangle. I remembered that I sent him some minor viruses so that we could keep tabs on him. I've just called him for a meeting!"

The Rose

Bigsy had been busy. He had tracked down Pete Burr, who had worked at the old listening station called Minerva, along the Thames at Canada Water. It had been run by dubious sorts before it was closed down. Pete had become tangled up in something involving The Triangle and seen the business end of several weapons. He'd have been traumatised except, Bigsy remembered, he was wearing a ludicrous sailor costume at the time. Bigsy wasn't sure if he'd been the one who was more traumatised by that incident.

They met upstairs at The Rose, a pub on Albert Embankment, which also has a good view across to the Houses of Parliament. Bigsy had also invited Christina Nott along, because he felt sure Pete would remember Christina from their last encounter.

Clare, Bigsy and Christina arrived together. They could sense that Pete was nervous. They worked out that he sensed that the three of them together spelled trouble.

Christina smiled, "How's business Pete? Are you still working for the Americans?"

"Hello Christina, sorry if I seem jumpy, but well - you

know. The last time I saw you there was a lot of guns involved and then we got stormed by the police. Nothing like that planned for today, I hope?"

"Everything is cool. Nothing to worry about. We were simply wondering if you still had contact with any of your old buddies from that place by The Dome?"

"What the US-operated listening station called Minerva?" he replied, knowing that they both knew all of this, but he wanted to frame it accurately.

"That's right, I guess some of the folk there would like to see their jobs continue even after Minerva got shut down."

Pete nodded, "Very astute. Actually, several of the old team moved to a new job when it was set up. As a matter of fact, I'm also still in contact with two of the Americans - you might remember them - Emily Karankawa and Anne-Marie Bristow, who were also at that traumatising event at the Lanchester."

"Did they also move with the job - I don't mean with that dubious agency- I mean with the other dubious Agency?" asked Clare.

"Ah yes, I even got paid by the Miel Doux Agency after all of that. I assume Jennifer Sussex wanted us to keep silent about everything. And, if you remember, Emily and Anne-Marie were quite junior agents, trusted for overseas work, from the CIA. Neither of them wanted to rock the boat and - remarkably - they were both awarded medals for their part in the capture of Turgenev and Yegorin - even if it didn't go quite as planned after their capture.

"Are they secret medals?" asked Bigsy, remembering something he'd seen in a spy movie on television.

"No, they were regular medals and presented in a ceremony. I can tell you that their boss Olivia was spitting nails though. She'd ignored what we'd told her, and wasn't even along for the operation."

"Operation?" asked Bigsy

"Oh yes, we had to repackage the whole event as if it had been a perfectly planned CIA operation, after the fact," said Pete, "Of course, we here all know what really happened."

Pete continued, "I decided I was well out of it after that little session. I applied for another helpdesk role. Well, I'm a small fish for some sharks at a Chinese Bank. I'm not allowed to call myself a Financial Advisor, so I'm a financial services executive. I phone people, get them interested in investments and then pass them on to someone genuinely qualified to sell them financial instruments."

"Hmm," said Bigsy, "This sounds quite on the edge?"

"Yes, it is really. It's not chop stock, microcap or pump and dump, though. The Chinese want people with good British accents to sell their financial services, We are the front line. The financial people behind us have all been poached from other British banks but then the real machinery of their banking system is run by Chinese."

"Anyway, my ex-colleagues are based in a new place, not far from here, as I explained to Bigsy when we spoke by phone. The new centre is a block of apartments opposite the Nine Elms Market at New Covent Garden. It's called

Riverside Quay."

"In other words, it is but a stone's throw from the American Embassy?" asked Clare.

"Yep, and it has line of sight to the Houses of Parliament," added Pete, "And a view along the Thames - especially from the higher floors."

"Almost a clone of the setup you had in East London, then? Asked Clare.

"It even has a similar name to Minerva - Medusa," added Pete.

"Medusa and Minerva?" weren't they sisters?" asked Clare.

"It didn't end well for Medusa," said Bigsy, "She was the one who could turn people to stone with a single glance, but then Perseus came along and chopped off her head."

"I wonder if they knew that when they were thinking up names?" mused Clare.

"Well, and according to my contacts, it is the same scam. They are once again targeting Members of the Cabinet - to short circuit the normal lobbying processes. Catch people with their trousers down or their fingers in the till and then ask them to assist passage of some highly profitable legislation."

"I think there will be more to it than that," observed Clare, "After all they are so close to the American Embassy, I'm amazed no-one has worked it out."

"That is the brilliance of staffing it with the CIA, hiding

in plain sight," said Christina.

"Okay, well, it has been great to meet you all," said Pete, arranging his backpack and looking ready to leave. He gulped the last quarter of his pint of beer.

"So soon?" asked Clare.

"No disrespect, but I don't want to get roped into another dressing-up show with firearms," said Pete.

"Okay, but thanks for coming here and being so open with us," said Bigsy. Clare and Christina smiled.

Pete stood and walked towards the door.

Christina looked at Bigsy, "He knows more than he was telling," she observed.

Minerva and Medusa

Medusa was once a beautiful woman, her beauty rivalling that of her Gorgon sisters Sthenno and Euryale.

Minerva found the god Neptune and Medusa were kissing in Minerva's own temple. In a rage, Minerva turned Medusa into a monster, replacing her ringlets of hair with hissing. From then, Medusa turned any living creature she looked upon into stone.

When the hero Perseus is sent to destroy Medusa, he used her reflection in his shield to avoid contact with her eyes, and then beheaded her. He delivered the severed head to Minerva, who placed Medusa's image on the centre of her own shield to thwart enemies in battle.

Zoom call to Amanda

This time Clare was seated in the Triangle Offices, waiting for a Zoom videocall from Amanda.

"Hello Amanda," smiled Clare, "How are things progressing?" She could see Amanda against a neutral background. It looked more like a hotel room than Amanda's office.

"Hi Clare, I'm in Paris today. But let's talk about you. You must attend an interview, just like any other Researcher. Check your inbox - I've just sent you an email. We've created your CV. It is an adjustment of your actual one but should see you through without any trouble. It still focuses on your media and graphics background, but then we have been somewhat creative with your subsequent period at the Triangle. We've said you were a lifestyle influencer, working for several high-profile companies. They will interpret that as lobbying skills."

Clare was looking through the email that Amanda had just sent her.

"No. This makes me look like a bubblehead. I'm not sure that this will do at all. She read some of it out loud.

"Listen to this...

'Having studied professional arts and music theatre in college, Clare Crafts has taken her love of being in front of a camera to becoming an online vlogger. To date, she has accumulated thousands of followers across her social media platforms, where she updates fans on her varied projects, as well as giving them sneak peaks of her day-to-day life.

'Her YouTube videos consist of fashion and clothing hauls, makeup hauls and tutorials, storytimes, relationship talks and more. She keeps her relationship with her fans as authentic as possible, as she often opens up about her personal experiences regarding her health and her opinions on various social concerns.

'Clare's empowering attitude towards female identity has become her watchword and she often takes to Instagram to exhort her values.

'Her influence throughout the online world has prompted various brands and businesses to collaborate.

'More recently, Clare has shown an interest in ethical politics and has successfully taken this to her many followers.'"

Amanda replied, "That sounds perfect. Just what they will be looking for. Someone to advise on appealing to the metropolitan female market. And we'll have put in a few good words about you too. As long as you don't say anything too upsetting during the interview, then they should snap you up!"

"Oh yes, one other thing. You'll need to find somewhere

to live. Ideally with other interns or researchers. It wouldn't look right with you living in your apartment and if you can get in with some other like-minded spirits then it should help us short circuit some of the investigation."

"Okay, I'll ask my sister where I should start looking, she seems to know her way around. When is the interview?"

"I guess you'll have Andrew Brading's office call you about that. Oh, and good luck!"

There was a gentle click as Clare realised Amanda's Zoom session had been terminated. It looked as if it was really happening- she was going to Parliament.

"Bigsy! Jake!" - She called, "I'm going to need some help!"

Clare needs digs

Clare called Samantha again, this time about accommodation.

"I'll get on to it. We have a system here that tells us about flat shares. It's on the Parliamentary intranet. I'll send you some over when I've had a look."

Soon enough a message pinged onto Clare's phone. It was a WhatsApp group Clare shared with Samantha.

"You could be very lucky...My friend Tessa is looking for someone to move into their flat. She shares with a couple of other girls, but one is moving out. This is so hot that it smokes! - See the attachment. I can put in a word if you like. S. x x x"

Intrigued, Clare clicked on the attachment link provided.

It opened.

AVAILABLE: DOUBLE ROOM TO RENT IN FLAT W/GARDEN, LIVING ROOM

Enquire here:
https://www.sparespace.co.uk/flatshare/london/bermondsey/1 667081321

Hey everyone – We're in an amazing house in Bermondsey and need a new third person to take the last room.

Price: £630, bills probably around £70, deposit is one month's rent (housing benefit should be fine, references not needed etc)

About us: 2 women in our mid-twenties, both working in politics. We're both sociable and enjoy going to the pub, watching trash tv, sitting around reading and getting out and about.

We'll both be working from home for a while and will be using the living room as a work from home space. We're generally tidy people and hope everyone will pitch in but won't expect everything to be perfect all the time, as we all have busy lives and more interesting things to do at times. Generally easy-going and love a good political discussion from time to time.

About you: we're looking for a friendly person who is up for socialising (but obviously we'll all be doing our own thing at times as well). If everything above sounds good to you then I'm sure we'll get on fine.

About the room: A small double. The smallest of 3 rooms which is reflected in the price. It has a built-in wardrobe and storage with a raised bed and storage underneath.

The house: the house is honestly amazing with a beautiful open plan kitchen living room. There's lots of hidden storage including under the window seat, cupboards in the hallways etc. There's also a sofa bed in the living room for people to stay over. There's a small garden with loads of plants, a table and seating area. It is south facing so would be amazing in the summer. There's 2 bathrooms, 1 ensuite, so you'd only be sharing with 1 other person.

Accessibility: flat is on the first floor with a small staircase up and then another down to the garden area (about 10 steps). The room also has a raised bed.

There's no lift in the building, unfortunately. There is an intercom.

Send us a message and we'll arrange a chat to get to know each other/ answer your questions about the house.

Clare forwarded the email to Jake, Bigsy and Christina.

"What do you think?" she asked.

Bigsy came back first, "It looks ideal for what you will be doing. Two women who work in Westminster, political connections, and it's so cheap for London. £700 pcm all in. Say Yes."

Then Jake, "No brainer - say yes."

Christina's reply was more circumspect, "Three single females living in a flat share in central London - what could possibly go wrong?"

Clare buzzed her WhatsApp back to Samantha - "Yes - It'd be great! I'm in if they'll accept me!"

A few seconds later Samantha replied, "This has got to be the fastest ever room grab! They will want to meet you before they agree, though. I'm with Tess at the moment."

"Okay - How about tonight? Topolski's 18:30?"

"Tess is nodding. Do you mind if I come along as well?"

"Excellent see you all at 18:30!"

Topolski's to meet the Flatmates

Clare decided it would be simplest to take a cab to Topolski's, but to stop it around the corner from the venue. She didn't want to let on that she could afford random cabs until she had met her potential flatmates.

For Clare, this was going backwards a step or two. Ever since she had made the initial money from the Triangle, she had been living in her own small but fairly luxurious apartment. No sharing, except for when she had guests and a kind of freedom which fitted very well with her lifestyle.

She was seated in the bar, looking at the drinks menu, when her new flatmates arrived. Samantha guided them over and winked. Clare knew that Sam would have 'bigged her up' for the occasion, but she had no idea what stories Sam would have told.

"Hi, I'm Tessa," smiled the short-haired one, "I work for Anne Reeves, Labour MP for West Shields"

"She's the shadow minister for something, isn't she?" asked Clare.

"Environment," answered Tessa, "I hear you are more of a Conservative?"

"Well - it looks as if that's who I'll be working for," answered Clare, "Andrew Brading, MP for Ranmore Grenville."

"Is that even a place?" asked Tessa.

"You lucky lady," said the other one, "My name's Lottie and my MP is the rather wandery-handed Duncan Melship, MP for Knutsford North."

Lottie continued, "Compared with Duncan, your MP Andrew is an absolute angel. I know I shouldn't say this of the Tories, but he's a dream come true. You watch as he rises from the pack."

"Have you been accepted yet?" asked Tessa, "Sam said you still needed to go for the interview."

"That's right," explained Clare, "This has all happened in something of a rush - but they know I've been waiting for an opening."

"Well - you sounded convinced about our flat share," said Lottie, "At least according to your sister. I'm not sure about this...sibling influences in Parliament." She smiled and Clare could see she was teasing.

"How did you know about this bar?" asked Tessa - "I mean, we live in Bermondsey - Only a short walk away - yet neither of us knew about here."

"You have to know some of the wrong people!" joked Clare.

Tessa started, "Well let's talk first about the flat. Our friend has moved out. She wants to go live with her boyfriend. It is all very torrid. That has opened up her double room, which could therefore be yours. There's a double bed, storage, a desk, a decent window with street view and access to the other rooms like the shared kitchen/diner and a lounge with the communal telly. We've decent high-speed Wi-Fi and it has been given a certificate by the House of Commons security people."

Lottie added, "It's actually only 4 stops from Westminster to Bermondsey on the Jubilee line. They are about every three minutes. TfL keeps the line open during disputes and outages, because of its strategic significance."

Clare nodded, she didn't want to say that she was a regular user of the line to get to London Bridge, and then onward to the Triangle offices in Hays Galleria. Her subterfuge was proving increasingly difficult.

"I know this area of London pretty well," she ventured, "I've worked around here too."

"Ah, that would explain your choice of here for cocktails!" said Tessa.

Clare noticed a slight accent when Tessa talked. It was well-honed London but had a slight hint of somewhere European - maybe Germany.

Lottie's accent was It-girl London. Close to Samantha's chosen voice.

"So - how did you get the flat - and the jobs?" asked Clare, " I know about my sister, but surely everyone can't be like that?"

Samantha had been able to get her appointment via a friend of the family, plus her First-Class degree, plus the funding of somewhere to live which Clare was supporting.

"Daddy knows Sir Hugo Petheridge, and they came up with a placement for me," answered Lottie.

"I was recruited to help with the positioning of DNS Industrie into the opposition Agenda," said Tessa, "My father is a President of the company in Hannover and was able to get me this sponsorship. Technically, I'm supposed to look out for sales opportunities. Land and Expand."

Clare could see that Lottie and Tessa were too highly attractive female assistants, operating in what was still seen by many as a boorish men's club even despite the increase in female MPs to around 220, or around one third of the House.

"So, tell me what it is like to be an intern or Research Assistant?" asked Clare.

"It's all about the poodles," said Lottie.

"And the labradoodles," continued Tessa.

"But never the dachshunds," added Samantha - looking towards Tessa.

"Nein, niemals der Dackel," said Tessa.

Lottie continued gesturing as if answering a phone, "OK, so you've got a problem with your neighbour. Sorry yes, with your neighbour's dog. Your neighbour's dog is jumping up at your fence and damaging your roses? Yes I do understand, it's just I'm actually in Westminster and we're quite busy at the minute so it might be difficult to come and have a look. Yes, of course we have time for you, I'll call you back."

The other two nodded. "This is top-flight research," added Samantha, "Knowing which dogs can to the most damage."

"To sanity," added Lottie.

"That's a typical constituent call, could be by phone. Now they all want to use Skype or Zoom or even Teams - but Teams buggers up everything on the intranet, so we'd rather not."

"...and Skype sounds like its underwater half the time," added Samantha.

Lottie continued, "There's a set of constituents - they are like regulars and we think they phone us more to chat than anything else. After a few calls it becomes a case of laughter as the best way to stay sane as we deal with so many similar calls, sometimes 20 a day, and hundreds of letters and emails.

"So where's the Research part of this?" asked Clare, intrigued.

Lottie answered, "Well, it sounds as if you are skipping the intern part of the process and being bumped straight up to researcher. That goes beyond casework and leads to other things. We'll all be there too someday, and the reason we get given support - like Tessa has - from DNS Industrie is because they all know how influential a trusted Researcher can be."

Tessa nodded, "We all start by making the tea and dealing with constituents, but in the course of it we meet so many other people and build amazing networks. Plus, our quiet backroom networks of intern-to-intern and among the researchers.

Samantha said, "It's like I told you, Clare - There are various aspects to casework; from answering the phone, writing letters and emails on behalf of constituents and attending advice surgeries with the MP to meet local people."

Lottie added, "It's hard to keep emotions in check as problems range from the serious or sad to ridiculous. Dealing with the correspondence is the best and worst part of an intern's job. All constituents believe their problem is important and we should drop everything else to solve it."

Samantha continued, "In some cases, we stop everything else. They often call us upon to help constituents with immigration issues, domestic violence, addiction and depression."

Tessa spoke, "Yes, what many people don't realise is that most times an MP's office is a last port of call for those who have fallen through the cracks of civil society. Often constituents start a phone call with: 'I'm sorry to call you but there's no-one else left'."

Samantha added, "Remember Clare, to help, you need patience, good people skills, the ability to stay calm and think logically. Hmm. Maybe as your sister I know too much about your skills in those departments."

The other laughed, and Clare joined in, "Ouch," she said.

Lottie added, "And remember that working for an MP gives you an insight into just how powerful a name can be; I remember my first 'don't you know who I am' moment when I used my MP's name to get through to the top immigration official at a national airport after being passed from pillar to post for an hour. I felt a mixture of pride and achievement as I got through to the right person and helped our constituent get where he needed to be."

"Okay, I'm getting the lay of the land now," said Clare, "But there's still one thing you haven't told me about..."

"What's that?" asked Tessa.

"The Boys," answered Clare, to raucous laughter.

"We'd better get some more cocktails," said Lottie.

Portcullis House Interview

Clare had another session booked in the House of Parliament. She arrived at the visitors' gate but was directed across the road to Portcullis House. There, after the formalities of being photographed, badged, and processed, they then took her to a small side area where she met two other people.

"Hello, my name is Serena McMillan, I'm the office manager for Andrew Brading, and this, here, is Maggie Shannon; she is one of the other researchers for Andrew."

Clare shook both their hands, resisted the overwhelming temptation to curtsey and said, "Hello, yes I'm Clare Crafts and I'm hoping for the Researcher Post here working for Andrew."

They had some general questions, said that her CV looked very strong, and that she appeared to have some great references including from a James Cavendish, who worked for the security services. Clare realised what Amanda had done - she'd substituted James as a referee, instead of herself. It provided some distance but meant that Clare had to think on her feet.

"Yes, James (or Jim) is a friend of my father, I suspect he may have had a hand in my sister's hiring as well."

"It is always wheels within wheels," observed Serena, "Do you also know Sir Stafford Peters, by any chance?"

Clare remembered that Sir Stafford Peters had been involved in the incident with Maximovich, Yegorin and Turgenev - but she wasn't sure how much to admit. She knew that Sir Stafford would remember her, though.

"I did briefly meet Sir Stafford Peters once," replied Clare, "We were along at the same event. I can't say I really know him though,"

This answer seemed to satisfy Serena, who scribbled something onto a corner of Clare's CV. Then it was Maggie's turn to ask a few questions. The combination of Samantha's briefing and then the questions that Bigsy and Jake had invented meant that Clare was able to answer just about everything. She was even asked if she was a member of the Party. Clare remembered Samantha's reply.

"I didn't feel able to become a member of any party because I agree and disagree with elements of them all - I hope that my time as a Researcher with Andrew Brading will help me decide."

Clare realised she had said 'with' instead of 'for' and watched nervously in case it would get picked up.

Serena smiled, " I notice you said 'with' rather than 'for' Andrew Brading. A good sign of an intelligent and free-spirited candidate. Andrew is most insistent that the surrounding people will think for themselves and bring him fresh ideas."

Clare smiled, "I think I should ask you a few things as well?" She hoped that by doing this she would push the interview beyond the tipping point. She could also see how they responded to questions.

The most obvious one is what will I be expected to do in my first few weeks as a Researcher?"

Serena answered, "Political issues are often at the front and centre of news bulletins, and the unpredictability of the field means every day will bring new challenges and obstacles to overcome.

"You'll be making and implementing change that will have an actual effect on the lives of those on a national scale. If you feel passionately about the issues, you'll experience a great deal of job satisfaction seeing plans and policies put into action that you've helped to bring together."

Maggie added, "Working as an MP's assistant is often the first step in a political career. Moving to parliament may be your next career move. The skills and experience you'll gain could see you working for high-profile politicians, working internationally, or embarking on your own political career."

"Is that what is driving you, Maggie?" asked Clare.

Maggie smiled, "For political jobs, MPs typically hire a team of people, rather than a single assistant. They usually split the team between the MP's constituency office and the national political offices in Westminster. We are all parts of a team together. However, as MPs hire their staff directly, the structure of their teams, whether they hire full or part-time staff and where their team is based, can vary.

"I started as a caseworker in the constituency office, where I provided advice and support on issues in the local community such as immigration, housing and benefits, and liaising with government agencies and local media outlets. I had to attend local and national events and help to solve problems in our local constituency community."

"Then, when I moved to Westminster, I found the jobs were more directly related to assisting MPs with their workload.

"My responsibilities (and I assume yours too) may include:

- keeping your MP up to date on key issues and policy developments
- drafting and writing speeches, articles, and correspondence
- overseeing media coverage of your MP
- liaising with the constituency office team on local and national issues
- general diary management."

Clare said, "Well, I've done similar things in the Private Sector, particularly with media coverage as a facet. My skill with graphics and social media mean that I've a head start over some more inky types."

Clare decided she wanted to push it a little to see whether the people she was to work with could be flexible.

Serena cut in, "The role of a politician's assistant can be demanding. Because of this, you'll need a well-developed skill set, including (she looked down at a sheet of paper)

- the ability to cope in high-pressure situations
- adaptability at short notice
- excellent written and verbal communication
- high levels of organisation, including the ability to multitask
- firm but fair debating skills.

And you are right to surmise that it's your work experience and enthusiasm that will make you stand out."

"This is where I give my tears in rain speech?" joked Clare, testing their reaction. She could see that Maggie understood it immediately, but Serena looked more lost.

Maggie rescued her, "C-beams glittering in the dark near the Tannhäuser Gate. Did you know it was one of Andrew's favourite quotations?"

"I had no idea," answered Clare, imagining her clenched fist and a yelp of 'Yes!"

"Okay, " said Serena, "I'll need to talk this over with Maggie in a moment and then we will be able to let you know the outcome. We should be able to advise you this afternoon, maybe by 18:00. Do you have other questions?"

Clare said she didn't, and Serena asked Maggie to show Clare how to get out of Portcullis House. They walked along side-by-side.

"I have to show you out, it's to discourage loiterers and nosey parkers," she said, "You did fine by the way, I should think you'll get the role, especially with that CV and those references."

They reached the exit. Clare shook Maggie's hand again and then departed. A little burst of joy rippled through her body.

Stepping Out

I'm stepping out

Don't you talk to me of no responsibility
Don't you go and pull that little pout
It ain't no use giving me your abuse
Because tonight I'm stepping out

I'm stepping east
I'm stepping west
I'm gonna put my
Toot-toot-tootsies
To the test
I'm gonna do what
I do best
I'm stepping out

Michelle Shocked

Day One at the House

Day One in Parliament for Clare. She'd been through the rigmarole of getting badged and given an email account. She now felt like she was a proper Researcher sitting with Maggie in the cramped office.

Then it happened.

A commotion in the corridor. Serena first into the office.

"Oh, hello - new girl - Welcome to the team. I must do the proper walk-around and introductions tomorrow. We've a minor crisis on our hands today."

Serena walked out of the office again, and Maggie walked across from her desk crammed in the corner.

"It can be like this sometimes," she said, "Andrew made a speech in the House today. He accidentally said something that has been picked up by the media."

"Was that the thing he said about 'I don't want to single out the BAME workers in this discussion?' " asked Clare. She had listened to the Today Programme on her way into the office.

"Yes, that's right; now the Media are twisting it to imply that Andrew doesn't care about BAME workers at all, they are sending in the Pomps to cover it."

"The Pomps?" asked Clare.

"Yes, the pompous Cabinet ministers, who will run defence for the story. Defend Andrew."

"But isn't it a storm in a teacup? And won't the so-called Pomps make it worse?" asked Clare.

"Yes, but it is running interference across the really big story about the Identity Bill First Reading," explained Maggie, "Andrew has become the unwitting sacrificial goat to distract attention from the main news agenda. You remember when we were negotiating Brexit? We kept bringing the fishing rights to the fore."

"Yes - a red herring," said Clare.

"Precisely, but it was something that everyone could get behind. And we could wave a Union Flag over the fishing waters too. Remember Rees-Mogg speaking to the empty House about 'British Fish and happier for it'? - honestly!" continued Maggie, "Look, it will get lively around here for the next couple of hours. Why don't you find some pro-BAME speeches by our MP? - That'll be like a simple test for you as a researcher."

Clare tapped into her keyboard:

"Something like this?" she asked almost immediately.

"Andrew Brading, (Cons) Member for Ranmore Grenville, speaking at the Westminster Business Development Circle,

said, 'There is a perception that certain ethnic groups are not interested in politics which I disagree with. Just because I am white, middle income and come from a certain perceived class, does not mean I am not sympathetic. BAME Politicians - that's Black, Asian and Minority Ethnic - are starting to overcome the barriers to getting to those places that are really difficult, although they have to be extremely resilient.

'I will always acknowledge the trailblazers. Bernie Grant, Diane Abbott and Paul Boateng. They were the first black MPs, all elected in 1987. These were household names growing up. They spoke up on issues I guess many people wouldn't normally talk about, like stop and search. Then we saw James Cleverly appointed as Co-chairperson of the Conservative Party, something that was inconceivable when I started taking an interest in politics. Now we need to tackle the need to get BAME representation into FTSE100 Companies, along the lines supported by the CBI.'"

"Wow, that was fast," said Maggie, "But can you tell me what's wrong with it?"

"No soundbites," answered Clare, "But give me a minute and there will be one."

Clare clicked on the text, deleting most of it.

Conservative MP Brading speaks out for Black Lives at Westminster: White conservative MP Andrew Brading notes that, "It's time to get BAME representation into the top of the biggest companies in Britain. Black Lives Matter."

Maggie said, "That's not bad at all, and it hasn't even been through the Press Office yet."

"I know - *'Brading backs blacks for big business'* is more their kind of thing," answered Clare, "Now we need to get a couple of externals to endorse the quote and there's the story. I suggest Microsoft, Linklaters and hell, the CBI itself. There's your boxout-ready copy."

"Wow," said Maggie, "Put that into an email, send it to me and copy it to Serena. You'll get a gold star on the first day!"

Clear smiled, she was earning her keep, but it somehow all seemed simple compared with things she had to handle at The Triangle.

Maggie added, "I don't want to burst your bubble, but this latest scuffle is just that. It is a dawn patrol - looking for lighted cigarettes over the trenches. A warning exchange of fire, which the generals are pleased to see happen so the two sides remind each other they are still there."

"Two sides?" asked Clare, "I see it as five: the clergy, nobility, commoners, media and fifth estate,"

"Oh - philosophical too?" asked Maggie, amused.

"Well, the fifth estate won Trumpi his victory," added Clare, "and the fourth estate was mighty peeved."

"It's great to have you here, but you'll soon find out that with this lot we are more into reactive tactics rather than strategic offensives. Deception over Depth," added Maggie.

Serena came back into the room speaking on her phone, "Yes - it was the Westminster Business Development Circle," she hung up, "Clare, thank you for that counter-offensive to support Andrew. The news cycle has shifted now, and we are talking about that Labour MP who ordered a pizza and chips as a substantial meal. Andrew will be in the clear."

Clare smiled, "But isn't this all reactive? And diversionary? What about the big stories?"

"It's our job to bury them, or to obfuscate them," explained Serena, "To be honest Andrew doesn't like this fuzziness, but for The Party, it works well and is a way to keep Power. Give the flag-wavers something they can get their heads around. Scotch eggs, caravan parks, level playing fields. All the fancy statistics are wasted on most people. The average person in the street has lower-high-school math skills. They don't want bases, decimals beyond percentages, let alone stacked graphs. Listen to the X-Factor, it's 1000 percent true!"

Clare laughed at Serena's cynicism.

"Honestly," `Serena said, "You really have to break it down for the toddlers. The Daily Mail has it on point - its why I liked your alliterative headline. The Sun or Mail could run it right down the page."

Serena grabbed a handset and flipped on a television in the room's corner. It was tuned to BBC News. An Outside Broadcast showed a pizza and chips with 2269+996= 3265 calories written across it.

"See how fickle the news can be - the story about the pizza is more of a runner than Andrew's stumble over words. And they are gunning for that Labour MP in any case- ever since he slagged off the Daily Mail in a speech."

Another person enters the room.

"This is Douglas, he's the 'MP next door' and a friend of

Andrew. Duggie, this is our new researcher - Clare Crafts - who has just been saving Andrew's reputation on live television."

Douglas smiles towards Clare; she thinks she recognises him, but then realises it is from television, rather than real life. She needs to break the reflex to want to curtsey to everyone.

"Yes, whoever came up with that soundbite needs an instant promotion! And Andrew made a mistake! One mistake! After years of dutiful shit-eating during Brexit and then twenty-hour days and sleeping in his office for half a year to get a question slot! This can be a rough house. Delighted to meet you, Clare!"

Douglas turned around, grinned wolfishly, then pulled forward a woman in a flatteringly feminine salmon-coloured suit who looked like a young Nicole Kidman.

"This is my researcher, Hannah- I'm sure you, Clare, and Hannah will get to know one another, and Maggie and Hannah can surely show you the ropes."

Hannah beamed across to Clare, "Yes, and we can tell you of some hazardous areas too, maybe over a glass of wine?"

Clare grinned, "Or a bottle?" she replied, and Hannah and Maggie both nodded.

"We must go," said Douglas, "And yes, you can call me Duggie!"

They left and Clare looked back towards Maggie and Serena. Maggie commented, "Yes he's a good one - although he nearly always has the hottest researchers.

I'm not sure how he selects them."

Serena suggested to Maggie, "Why don't you take Clare to the lobby? Show her the aftermath and make sure she gets seen a bit?"

"Good idea, I can point out a few people too,"

They walked down the shallow stone steps to the landing overlooking Westminster Hall. Clare sensed a change of mood. The Victorian gothic fantasy was replaced with the austere grandeur of the oldest part of the parliamentary estate. A vast space the length of a football field, its hammerbeam roof a masterpiece of fourteenth-century engineering. Clare remembers it now. A school trip to see Parliament. A rainy day so they could eat their picnic lunches inside this very hall.

Maggie says, "Guy Fawkes and Nicholas the First were both sentenced to death here. It's been a shopping arcade, a courtroom, a church, a concert hall, a feasting chamber. It is full of ghosts."

'Even one of mine,' thought Clare.

A sudden burst of activity.

"Maggie! How are you?"

"Rachel, and how are you?"

Rachel Crosby. A lobby journalist for The Post - one of the many papers who have just been attacking Andrew Brading, his party and his leader. Maggie suspects that Rachel is not as loyal to the party in power as her bosses believe. Rachel keeps her reports factual, and even calls for comment before she runs something. She is also a very careful gossip. Clare spots that Rachel is wearing TV make-up, which makes her look ten years younger under TV lights.

Rachel replies, "Yeah, like you care. And try no more of those print ready soundbites. You are so goddam lucky that the rags wanted to get at Philip Clarke-Smythe as our pizza-eating knight in pound-shop armour today."

"So, Maggie, are you off for one of your walks? And aren't you going to introduce me to the new girl? I'll keep you company to the edge of the estate."

"Fine. This is Clare, a new researcher for Andrew Brading. She might have been the source of that soundbite too!"

They walk down the steps together and the ceiling rises above them. Clare notices Rachel is wearing trainers. A lot of women in parliament switch into heels for any time the cameras are nearby, with trainers handy for the rest of the time when they are wandering the endless corridors, chasing division bells, bills, stories.

"So when did you join the gang?"

"Today, actually!"

"Okay, I'll go easy - Kudos though; you produced a good line to bail out Brading. You are probably wondering why I'm chatting to you too?"

"It crossed my mind, but I assume that's how you get a lot of the informal stuff? From the back-room people? It was the same for me when I was in the Private Sector."

Clare had thrown a mild swipe with her own sword. Not

the cutting edge, but the side. Enough to alert Rachel that she might think she was the cat playing with the mice, but that at least some of them could roar.

Rachel looked at them both, "I'm giving you a heads-up. And you'll owe me one. The Labour Party leadership is launching an anti-BAME investigation."

Rachel looks at them both as if she is giving away a big secret.

"A slightly tawdry freelancer called Roger Slater has whipped the editors of the Chronicle into a frenzy with the prospect of a damning expose. Your leadership might want to get out in front of the story. That piece about Brading could make for a great attack."

Clare looks at Maggie, "Here we go again," she thinks, "More noise to clog up the arterial messages. Nothing like a spat to sell Mainstream Media."

They go out through the doors and into the diesel-fumed rainy air. Three steps out onto the tarmac, Rachel puts a hand on Maggie's arm.

Maggie watches Rachel for her next move, "There - but remember me first when Brading wants to run his story. I know there is more to it."

Now they are on the tarmac forecourt, the echoing space of the ancient hall is replaced by traffic noise, the smell of the roast chestnut vendors, the chants of a small cluster of protestors with the view obscured by a line of red buses.

Day One at the flat

It was still raining when Clare left the office at around 7pm. She felt as if she'd had more than a day's worth of experiences in her first working day inside Parliament. Now she would hit the tube and get back to her new flat share in Bermondsey.

She arrived at the flat before 7:30pm and climbed the stairs. She opened the door and there was a whooping sound and party poppers exploded, covering her with thin paper streamers.

Tessa and Lottie had arranged an impromptu celebration. Three glasses of Bollinger Special Cuvée Brut were speedily poured and then Lottie proposed a toast.

"To Clare, fragrant but unbeaten on Day One!"

Clare laughed, and Lottie and Tessa cheered.

"Group Hug," said Clare, and they all wrapped arms around one another.

"We heard about your news report too. A classy piece of action to get something out on Day One and also able to defend your MP like that! - Incredible!"

Clare signed, "But you know what. I'm pooped. The day veered from adrenaline to ennui in a few minutes."

"Who did you meet?" asked Tessa.

"Oh, I still haven't actually met my MP yet - Andrew Brading, but I met Serena and Maggie, who work in the same office as me - and the office - it's tiny!"

"We all know Maggie Shannon. Serena McMillan has a bit of a reputation as a hard case though. Be glad she is on your team. Don't be surprised if it's more than a week before you meet your MP. They move around in wildly unpredictable ways.

"I met a lobbyist too," said Clare, "Rachel something - Ah yes Rachel Crosby - she seemed to know something about what was going on around the place too."

"Oh yes, we know Rachel, but it is amazing that you met her so soon. She usually loiters around the lobby and then targets people with an eye for a good story," said Tessa.

Lottie nodded and continued, "Her paper, The Post, is a bit of a muck-raker, so you need to have your wits about you when you talk to her. She can come across all friendly, but she is looking for the angle or the lead. I guess today it was because you had put that one-liner into circulation, and she wanted to know its actual source."

"Ah yes, I met another M.P. Douglas Lessiter, and his assistant Hannah. They literally just stuck their heads around the door."

"Duggy is a charmer, but Safe in Taxis. He always picks amazing women assistants - did you think that Hannah looked like a film star? She is smart too. We'll have to give you some of their phone numbers. We think that Douglas is gay, by the way, although he's not 'out' and no-one seems to be that interested in following the story."

"I learned something in the private sector about having a stash of stories which could be ready to be used, rather than already out there," answered Clare, "Usually mild indiscretions, but if played at the right time the could be hurtful. It was all in the interests of business."

"We've heard that there could be something like that operating around Parly too," said Lottie, "Although the stories are mainly innuendo and they are very difficult to pin down."

Tessa nodded, "Except when those MPs were caught at that club - for - you remember - a Gentleman's Evening or something,"

Clare realised that Tessa was talking about the very event that she had been directly involved in, with Jake, Bigsy, Christina Nott and Chuck Manners. She wouldn't be owning up to it and thought it best to let it slide.

"But what about you two? Have you ever been approached by anyone shady?" asked Clare.

"Shady? That's about half of them!" joked Lottie, "No, I'm kidding, but there are sometimes things that make you question how the system works."

"That's right,"" said Tessa, "For example, in the Register of Interests most of the Researchers show up as having

'Interests: None'. I did disclose my link to DAS Industrie, so I show up as a 'Consultant, digital communications' on the Register. The reality is that Researchers or others close to them may well be paid through a lobbying group."

"It will take you a few days to realise, but the lobbying system is rife around the Halls of Westminster.

Clare made a mental note to get Bigsy to chase down and provide a briefing for her on lobbying. But now she was employed, she would need to think how and when she could get to the Triangle Offices. The question from Tessa arrived next and was ideally suited to Clare's situation.

"What about you, Clare, are you seeing anyone?"

Clare suddenly realised that this was the answer - an imaginary boyfriend.

She found it coming out of her mouth before she'd really had a chance to think, "Yes, his name is Jake and he's a journalist."

Lottie said, "Alarm bells. Some of what we deal with is Secret or Top Secret. You'll have to be careful what you talk about."

Clare was thinking, 'Perfect - an excuse to visit the Triangle offices and even to go back to my Apartment - I can say I'm visiting Jake's.'

"No Jake isn't interested in politics and he writes for a lifestyle magazine. They write about billionaires, fast cars and fancy places to eat."

"Well, if you need someone to test somewhere, then I'll

be up for it," said Tessa.

"I don't mind testing any of those categories: billionaires, fast cars or nice places to eat," added Lottie.

"As a matter of fact, I'll be with him tomorrow evening," Clare lied. She thought that she could visit The Triangle and get Bigsy digging in to help her research.

Bigsy describes the Lobby

"It's lucky we start late," joked Jake as Clare arrived at just after seven in the evening. She had been working in Parliament for a week now and had started to get a routine.

"Bigsy tells me you've asked him to pull some info about the lobbying system. We decided - including Christina - that we'd all like to hear about it and about your first days in Parliament"

Christina walked over; she was carrying a bottle.

"I thought we should make this a more relaxed session," she said, as she unscrewed the metal top from a bottle of Burgundy. Then Bigsy arrived with four wine glasses and a bottle of Vouvrey.

"We kept it in the fridge. I can get some nibbles too, if anyone is hungry."

Clare started her explanation of the last couple of days. She included her impressions of the people she met, but also noted that they had all seemed to be friendly and quite open with her. She told them about her flatmates and then got to the part about her deception.

"I've had to invent an imaginary boyfriend to get away to here - and for that matter, to go back to my apartment. I told Lottie and Tessa that my boyfriend's name was - er - Jake.

Jake guffawed. The others smiled.

"It's the most logical," said Bigsy, "They saw me when I helped you move in and I introduced myself as a 'helpful friend'; luckily we didn't talk about Jake at all. You are also unlikely to get caught out if you must describe Jake or anything. And we can call you as long as we say it is Jake."

Clare looked to Jake, "Are you okay with this?" she asked.

"Clare - after the craziness we've been through, this is just the next stage of our grand adventure," answered Jake, "and I guess it is simpler than having Aurora as your current fling!"

Clare smiled, stood, walked around the table and hugged Jake.

"Thank you," she smiled and then Christina poured everyone a glass of the chilled white wine.

"We'll let the red breathe for a moment," she said, "Now we've heard all about Clare - even her love life - we need to hear what Bigsy has found out about lobbying."

On cue, Bigsy switched on a TV flat screen to present a few slides.

He began: "Lobbying in the United Kingdom plays a significant role in the formation of legislation and is used by a wide variety of commercial organisations. There are lobby groups for particular policies and decisions by Parliament and other political organs at national, regional and local levels"

"I could see, even in my quick walk through Westminster Hall, that there were many people hanging around. And they looked like they were dressed for Westminster rather than casual tourists," added Clare.

Bigsy continued, "Yes, Lobbying is a massive industry now and the professional lobbying industry has been rapidly growing since as long ago as the mid-1990s. The last in-depth report estimated it to be worth £1.9 billion, employing 14,000 people. The report also suggested that some MPs are approached over 100 times a week by lobbyists."

"We were approached in the lobby, but it was by a journalist, rather than a lobbyist," said Clare.

Jake spoke, "At least, they said they were a journalist, could you be sure?"

"Oh yes, I was with another researcher and she already knew the other person, a Rachel Crosby."

"Journo," said Jake, "I've run into her before, she writes 'colourful' pieces for the red tops."

"She seemed to know things too. Stuff that wasn't out in

the open," added Clare.

"She is very good at her job," said Jake, tapping into his laptop. Here we are - her CV -

Rachel Crosby is a British journalist and writer. A few years ago, she was an editor on ITV News. Earlier, she worked for four years as a political editor on BBC Two's Newsnight. She has co-presented a Sunday news programme for a couple of years. State school in west London and then onto Emmanuel College, Cambridge.

"She's also been a producer for the BBC, on the foreign desk at The Times and wrote for The Independent and the New Statesman.

A significant player to meet on Day One, Clare. But Bigsy, back to your story..."

Bigsy was waiting patiently, the next slide already projected onto the screen, "The original phrase "lobbying" comes from the gathering of Members of Parliament and peers in the hallways and lobbies of the Houses of Parliament before and after parliamentary debates. Nowadays - mainly because of the old free-for-all system there are also formal procedures to enable individual members of the public to lobby their Member of Parliament.

"It means most lobbying activity centres have become subtle. Nowadays there are each of corporate, charity and trade associations lobbying, where organisations seek to amend government policy through advocacy."

"I'll need to be careful then, it sounds as if they are everywhere," said Clare.

"Companies and individuals who operate in this sector commonly use the terms 'public relations', 'public affairs', 'political consultancy' or 'corporate affairs' to describe their activities. I'd say that their methods are often suspect and the new terms to describe them are partially a reaction to the negative publicity surrounding the word 'lobbyists' after the old 1994 cash-for-questions affair."

Jake added, "Yes, I remember in my journalism work. I'd run into professional public affairs agencies, representing multiple clients. They would undertake significant lobbying activity beside individual organisations conducting lobbying on an in-house basis."

Jake screwed up his face "It was all a bit shonky actually, and the companies were often taking their clients for a ride too. A case in point: The tobacco lobby - which would try to stop restrictions on ciggy advertising - they'd talk about 'sticks' - meaning cigarettes - and were quite used to being advocates for several firms at once. I interviewed a 'fast boy' who had made money from this and he said, quite seriously, that they kept a lobby presence in the UK, but that most of the action had moved out of Europe. He was part Chinese, and said China was one of the biggest growth markets and he was running his efforts there now, 'Follow the money,' I think he said it had risen from $160 billion in 2012 to around $225 billion now. I remember him saying it was around ten times the size of the biggest European market - The Germans."

Christina nodded, "It's the same with Russia - over half the men still smoke. Lung cancer is a national problem. Women less so, although it isn't fashionable compared some countries. Of course, the cigarettes are still cheap too," added Christina.

Bigsy looked back at the projection, "Since 1994 there have been various complaints by MPs about unacceptable lobbying and several police investigations. It's a corrupt picture overall. I'd characterise it as hired guns with expensable inducements."

"And quite amoral, judging by the cigarette scenario described by Jake," added Clare.

"And what about the police investigations? Was anything done about it?" asked Jake.

Bigsy replied, "You'll see in a minute; very little, just a few people caught with their hands in the till."

"What a few being made examples of?" asked Christina, "That's how the Russians do it - well maybe their methods are a little more strong-armed."

Bigsy nodded, "Yes in the UK it is very understated. Current levels of lobbying are 'causing concern' as is the so-called 'revolving door' by which industry professionals move rapidly between legislative and commercial roles in the same sectors, creating potential conflict of interests.

"Tired of being an MP? Been voted out? Thrown out even? Become a lobbyist, or even a broker for lobbyists. We all know of politicians who have jumped ship to a lucrative role in the private sector."

"I can remember we had some 'hired-gun' approach us when I worked at the media company," said Clare, "He was a suited old duffer who had 'revolved out' of Parliament and was offering to get us introductions at the upcoming party conferences season - Cash for introductions - totally legal, especially because he was now a officially a parliamentary outsider. My boss agreed to pay him a finder's fee, but then he booked himself and his female helper into a swish hotel at the Birmingham conference but none of the rest of us were allowed into any of the sessions. It was truly shocking and a total rip-off."

"What happened to the 'clear blue water clause?" asked Jake, "You know when someone couldn't work for a conflict of interest for six months or a year?"

"It was unenforceable in most cases. The argument was that it was preventing people from taking further legal employment," answered Bigsy.

He continued, "That brings us up to the current period when ministers appoint Special Advisors (SpAds) who are staff members employed by the minister personally but paid for from the public purse - like Dominic Cummings was. They are often selected from related private sector industries and have sometimes criticised for engaging in campaigning while still on the government payroll or for moving directly between lobbying roles and the advisor role."

"Like those firms that employ someone who then becomes a civil servant who can then hire their old firm to help out?" asked Jake, "Jobs for the boys? I can think of a few examples of that."

Bigsy continued, "Curiously enough, the House of Commons Public Administration Select Committee recommended creation of a statutory register of lobbying companies and activities similar to the one required in the United States, but the government rejected that recommendation."

"I guess they could see which side their bread was buttered?" asked Jake.

Bigsy continued, "Then, in 2014, Parliament passed the Transparency of Lobbying, Non-Party Campaigning and Trade Union Administration Act, requiring statutory registration of professional lobbyists. The Office of the Registrar of Consultant Lobbyists (ORCL) maintains the register as an independent statutory office.

Bigsy flipped another PowerPoint slide and added, "In June 2015 the Chartered Institute of Public Relations launched the UK Lobbying Register to replace a joint voluntary register previously run in conjunction with The Public Relations Consultants Association and the Association of Professional Political Consultants."

"We are, by now, drowning in the alphabet soup," said Jake.

"I agree, all the various regulatory bodies - yet run by the people they are trying to regulate. Like 'It's my football, so my game and my rules.'"

"None of this is new, though," said Bigsy, "For example, in 1923, Winston Churchill acted as a highly paid lobbyist for Burmah Oil (now BP plc) to persuade the British government to allow Burmah to have exclusive rights to Persian (Iraqi) oil resources, which were successfully granted. No heads turned over that little arrangement."

Bigsy flipped another slide, "Or in 1994, The Cash-for-Questions Affair reported by the Guardian when parliamentary lobbyist Ian Greer of Ian Greer Associates bribed two Conservative Members of Parliament in exchange for their asking parliamentary questions on behalf of Mohamed Al-Fayed. Various people were criticised for these deeds."

Bigsy added, "Then, shortly before the 1997 general election Bernie Ecclestone as head of Formula One donated £1 million to the Labour party; after Labour's victory and after a meeting between Tony Blair and Mr Ecclestone, the Department of Health sought exemption for Formula One from the United Kingdom's proposed ban on tobacco advertising."

Clare said, "Wow, Bigsy"

Another slide and Bigsy continued, "Save your wows, Clare. Next, we have Jonathan Aitken, previously Minister of State for Defence Procurement under John Major in 1992. He was jailed in 1999 in relation to the Arms-to-Iraq scandal. Prior to becoming minister, he had been a director of an arms company BMARC, and after losing his seat at the 1997 election he was appointed as a representative for the arms company GEC-Marconi."

"That's a whole other thing, when the politicians can have a finger in the pie," said Jake.

"You should hear about Russia," said Christina, "The politicians sold off the state in a fire sale and conveniently bought up everything themselves with money that they loaned to one another from their newly acquired ex-state banks. The rise of the oligarchs. Thank you, Vladimir."

"That explains the rich oligarchs with so much cash," said Clare.

Bigsy projected a cover picture of a book, showing a USAF helicopter on the cover,

"And I had a look at an interesting little reference work called 'Fuel on the Fire' by Greg Muttitt.

"Muttitt argues that disclosed minutes from 2002–2003 (leading up to the war in Iraq) showed that many oil companies lobbied towards a war in Iraq to seize Iraqi oil reserves.

"For example, BP plc allegedly said in their minutes that they 'are desperate to get in', describing Iraq as 'the big oil prospect'.

"'This won't be the last resource war,' says Muttitt, 'The legacy of Iraq and the many blunders of the US and UK hangs over NATO's conflict in North Africa, and the way the Western nations are pursuing their agenda in another oil-rich state.' Muttitt's book should trouble even the most ardent liberal interventionist."

Bigsy flipped another slide, "Or, more mundanely, we could also mention the fundraisers for the parties, including the Cameron 'Leaders Group'. In March 2007 the Select Committee on Standards and Privileges published a report investigating a series of fundraising events which allowed donors to meet Cameron."

Jake added, "Nowadays, of course, it is all about games of tennis with the Prime Minister."

Bigsy picked up, "The investigation concluded that it was improper to employ parliamentary staff for fund-raising purposes and that it was 'ill-advised to link directly, in promoting the Leader's Group, the issues of access to his office and party fund-raising.'

Clare nodded, "Whiffle-waffle," she said, "Weasel words

that let everyone off the hook with a gentle tap on the knuckles for a minor indiscretion."

Bigsy continued, "Lord McNally, a member of the Lords Committee, said that this was 'yet another example of how pressure on political parties to raise ever larger sums from private sources pollutes our politics'."

"So, the river is polluted - no mention of fixing it then?" asked Jake.

Bigsy grimaced, "No - everything is quite slippery around this point and there's so many vested interests. Like the London runway for Heathrow. I can't pin anything specific on the Freedom of Information request showing that Heathrow Airport Holdings (BAA) executives met the Department for Transport 117 times between 2002 and 2007, including 24 meetings with the Secretary of State. Maybe that one still needs time to mature?"

Bigsy continued and flipped another slide, "But also in October 2007 Lord Hoyle, a member of the House of Lords, was paid an undisclosed sum to introduce an arms lobbyist, a former RAF officer who worked for BAE Systems, to the Defence Minister, Lord Drayson. The lobbyist had also a security pass as a "research assistant" from another MP. Accepting money for introductions is 'frowned on', but not illegal."

Bigsy flipped a further slide, "Then, in January 2009, The Sunday Times claimed that when a reporter had posed as a lobbyist that Lord Snape, Lord Moonie, Lord Taylor of Blackburn and Lord Truscott had offered to influence legislation in return for payment. The Metropolitan Police said that no action would be taken, noting that 'The application of the criminal law to members of the

House of Lords in the circumstances that have arisen here is far from clear,' and 'there are very clear difficulties in gathering and adducing evidence in these circumstances in the context of parliamentary privilege.'"

"Ha - 'Adducing,' lawyer-speak and then a word in someone's ear maybe?" said Jake.

Bigsy nodded, "A deal more like. The House of Lords voted to suspend Lord Taylor and Lord Truscott for all of six months in the first such action since the 17th century."

"Wow," said Clare, again, "Bigsy - you have been busy and several of these are pretty major events. A war, funding an election campaign, cash for introductions, cash for legislation, using civil servants to promote a specific party."

"Oh, I haven't finished yet," said Bigsy.

"You'd better send me that PowerPoint deck," asked Clare.

"My pleasure," said Bigsy, "Let's continue, from 2010, there were several, separate developments:

"The Department for Transport were being investigated by the Information Commissioner's Office and could face a criminal investigation over allegations it had deleted, or concealed records related to Heathrow to prevent them from being disclosed under the Freedom of Information Act. The investigation followed a complaint by Justine Greening MP."

"But does it end up in the long grass?" asked Jake.

Bigsy nodded and continued, "Andrew MacKay, a conservative MP and previously a senior advisor to Cameron's team was reported to be joining the lobbying firm Burson-Marsteller after quitting parliament at the next election with a salary of more than £100,000; His wife, Julie Kirkbride, also an MP, was reported to be looking for a lobbying job as well at a similar salary. The couple were both stepping down at the next general election following their part in the MP's expenses scandal during which they had claimed second-home allowances on separate houses. They had been ordered to repay £60,000."

"A fall from grace and a grab at the scraps?" suggested Jake.

Bigsy added another slide, "Labour MP Tom Watson complained of 'unprecedented and relentless lobbying' around the Digital Economy Bill sponsored by Lord Mandelson. He suggested that over 100 people were probably working full-time to bounce it through parliament and possibly only two people representing the interests of the nation's youth. He observed that it was difficult when being lobbied by people you respect and admire. Lord Puttnam accused the government of attempting to push through the legislation without allowing for proper discussion, and that the bill as it stands was not fit for purpose."

Jake grimaced, "The aftermath from that was exposed three years later during the pandemic which showed parts of the country and population still didn't have fast access and that the reach of digital education to school kids was highly inefficient."

"Yes - and that was after the Bill became an Act," added Bigsy

Bigsy pressed the slide advance again, "David Cameron, the conservative leader, predicted that this lobbying corruption was 'the next big scandal waiting to happen. It's an issue that crosses party lines and has tainted our politics for too long, an issue that exposes the far-too-cosy relationship between politics, government, business and money'."

"What happened to that golden sound bite?" asked Clare.

Bigsy added, "Cameron suggested he would shine 'the light of transparency' on lobbying so that politics comes clean about who is buying power and influence. Ironically, Cameron himself had moved from the role of ministerial special adviser to become Director of Corporate Affairs at Carlton Communications when the company bid successfully with Granada television for license to launch the world's first Digital terrestrial television service (ONdigital - later branded ITV digital)."

Jake laughed, "So Cameron was trying to outlaw something he had been directly involved with?"

Bigsy continued, "It's murky. Cameron resigned as a director of Carlton to run for parliament, but he remained on as a consultant to the company. During a roundtable discussion on the future of broadcasting, he criticised the effect of overlapping regulators on the industry."

"It could be construed that he still had an interest in the outcome?" asked Jake.

"It's really difficult to figure that one out," answered Bigsy, "Just like that Jeremy Hunt situation with BskyB."

Bigsy reminded them all, "The then Labour leader, Ed Miliband, called for the resignation of the culture secretary, Jeremy Hunt, over allegations he set up a private back channel to Rupert Murdoch's News Corporation when he was charged with making a quasi-judicial decision on whether to allow its takeover of BSkyB."

"I remember that, accusations of fingers in the pie?" said Jake.

"Hmm, not so much in the pie as hands around it," said Bigsy, "Miliband said the Conservative MP Hunt was 'standing up for the interests of the Murdoch's rather than those of the British people, after it was alleged in evidence to the Leveson inquiry that he had provided detailed information to James Murdoch on the state of the bid, and the thinking of the media regulator Ofcom."

"Sounds like a spy in the camp?" stated Jake, "It was incredibly untidy behaviour for a Minister. I won't be surprised if it gets selected in Uni classes as a case study."

"Strangely enough, that's where I found some of the information - In the London School of Economics Media Policy Planner website!" Bigsy snickered, "Hunt said that he had asked Lord Justice Leveson to bring forward his appearance before the inquiry and was 'confident that when I present my evidence the public will see that I conducted this process with scrupulous fairness'.

"He said: 'We've heard one side of the story today, but some evidence reported meetings and conversations that simply didn't happen.'"

"Hunt implied someone was lying?" asked Clare.

"Yes, or that he was being set up." answered Bigsy, "During the appearance by James Murdoch, News Corp's deputy chief operating officer, before Lord Justice Leveson the inquiry was shown extracts from 163 pages of email correspondence from Fréd Michel, News Corp's director of public affairs for Europe during the Sky takeover bid, to Murdoch marked "Confidential", detailing communications with Hunt, often via Hunt's special adviser, Adam Smith."

"This was a master class in obfuscation, " said Bigsy, " Use of 'I don't recollect', missing pages, you name it ..."

Bigsy continued, "Cleverly, Hunt's aides suggested Michel had wildly exaggerated the level of his knowledge and contacts with Hunt's Department for Culture, Media and Sport (DCMS) during the decision-making process between June 2010 and July 2011. However, the Michel emails published by the Leveson inquiry revealed that sometimes half a dozen confidential texts and emails a day would fly back and forth between the culture secretary's Cockspur Street office just off Trafalgar Square in central London and the News Corp team promoting the Sky takeover bid."

"That's not easily forgotten or denied," said Clare.

"Murdoch, in his evidence to the inquiry, steadfastly defended Michel's relationship with Hunt's office, saying it was 'active public affairs engagement' and 'legitimate advocacy'."

"Does the gun smoke?" asked Jake, "...But wasn't that bid ultimately scuppered?"

"Yes, but because of another reason - phone hacking -

another Leveson enquiry. It finally saw the Murdoch empire off the table," answered Bigsy,

"And there's still more, and by the way, I didn't have to dig too deep for this stuff. In March 2010 Dispatches and The Sunday Times recorded four Members of Parliament offering lobbying in return for influence with the Cabinet. Stephen Byers, a former member of the cabinet was recorded as saying he would work for up to £5,000 a day and was like a "cab for hire".

"And a real fun one," said Bigsy clicking another slide on the PowerPoint, "Also in March 2010 the Advisory Committee on Business Appointments revealed that Tony Blair, who had resigned as prime minister and MP had acted as a paid business consultant to an oil firm with interests in Iraq just 14 months after leaving office. He had requested to the committee that his relationship with UI Energy Corporation should be kept secret for reasons of 'market sensitivity' and the committee agreed to postpone publication for three months against normal procedures.

"The committee then had to then 'chase' Blair and send a formal letter to his office, which he responded requesting continued secrecy. "

"I see, extending it until the public are no longer interested? - Long grass tactics again?" said Jake.

Bigsy said, "Yes, but this time the committee chairman Lord Lang disagreed, and the information was published on their website with the note 'Publication delayed due to market sensitivities'. The news raised concerns that Blair had profited financially from contacts he made during the Iraq war. Blair also earned money from the ruling family in Kuwait for whom he produced a report on the oil state's future over the next 30 years for a reported £1,000,000 fee. "

"I see, puff pieces for royalty - good fees though," said Jake.

Bigsy nodded, "A 2009 investigation by The Guardian found that Blair had put his multimillion-pound income through 'an obscure partnership structure called Windrush Ventures, which enabled him to avoid publishing normal company accounts'. Blair later went on to close down his empire established after he stepped down as Prime Minister in 2007. He used £9 million of funds from his companies to create a new non-profit called the Tony Blair Institute, aimed at making globalisation work for everyone by combating poverty."

Bigsy added, "Blair's business empire proved highly controversial in the approximately ten years he ran it. His companies provided strategic advice on economics and politics but often worked with controversial clients such as the authoritarian government of Kazakhstan and oil companies. The Sunday Times claimed Blair was involved in a secret 'cash for contacts' deal with PetroSaudi to help broker oil deals and advised the Kazakh leader on how to present the deaths of workers in the country."

Clare, "This sounds a bit off to me. I'm sure there's another side to this?"

Bigsy said, "Yes. The former Prime Minister declared he would 'retain a small number of personal consultancies for my income' which included investment bank JPMorgan and a number of private individual clients according to the Financial Times. Blair's business empire is thought to have made him millions, although the structure makes it hard to tell the exact amount."

Jake, "It certainly implies that there is money to be made as an ex-Prime Minister. All the contacts and a slightly hidden soft power."

Bigsy flipped another slide, "And another one. In December 2011, The Independent newspaper reported that lobbying agency Bell Pottinger claimed to have been responsible for a variety of activities on behalf of clients considered not in the public interest including the manipulation of Google searches and Wikipedia pages. One allegation was that Bell Pottinger, acting on behalf of Dyson, used its influence with the Prime Minister and the Foreign Office to get the Prime Minister to raise concerns about counterfeit goods with the Chinese Prime Minister."

"Are we nearly there, yet?" asked Clare, "We're already on to the second bottle."

"I made it with no headers and footers, so that it doesn't show 'The Triangle' anywhere on the slides," commented Bigsy. He flipped another slide.

"That's all, folks" it said.

"Do you mind if I do some digging, too?" asked Christina, looking at Clare, "I could ask - you know - my contacts - see if they know anything?"

"Please, answered Clare, "But be aware that I am - we are all - effectively working for Amanda Miller at SI6."

"Share a cab later?" asked Christina, "Back home?"

"No, I'm going to Bermondsey, not Caroline Terrace,"

said Clare.

"But that could be a perfect alibi," said Christina, "You are out with your imaginary boyfriend and stayed over at his!"

Bigsy and Jake laughed, "Good plan! - But you'd better text the others to let them know you'll be away!"

Clare smiled, "This could work out very nicely, but I'm going to need another toothbrush!"

Christina unearths something

Christina's FSB Handler contact was codenamed Blackbird. His real name was Fyodor Kuznetsov.

Christina knew, once again, it would restart her direct dialogue with the FSB, which was something she always tried not to instigate. Still, Kuznetsov had left her alone and not cared when she had made money from a recent series of incidents.

She rang the number for Kuznetsov. A London-based car dealership answered. "I'm interested in taking one of your vehicles for a test-drive, " she continued, " A hatch back."

There was a pause on the line and then a recorded voice asked for her reference code and the nature of her enquiry.

She gave a number, and after a moment was put through to a voice.

"And how may I help you today?'

"I'm seeking a colleague, " she began.

There followed a protocol to verify security, and then Christina waited.

"Eventually a voice said, " Hello, Christina? - Or should I call you Archangel?"

"Blackbird, " she replied, " It's been a while."

"Is everything okay?" he asked, " It is so unusual for you to make the initial contact."

"Can I ask you a question?"

"Who is asking? Is it you or are you asking for someone else?"

"No, it's just me, " lied Christina, "I thought I heard someone mention something about a Medusa project and I wondered - you know - if it was linked to the old Minerva?"

"Yes I know this one. It's a precautionary tactic," said Blackbird, "Similar to how the Kremlin operates. You know how they like to monitor everyone - it's the same idea, except instead of the Kremlin running it all from around Mokhovaya Street, they can go out into the Oblast now, past the МКАД - *Moskovskaya Koltsevaya Avtomobilnaya Doroga* ring road.

"Frankly, the FSB is more cyber-aware nowadays. There's a major phishing operation using a group of hackers called CyberBerkut, targeting over 200 subjects from around 40 countries, including members of governments from Europe and Eurasia, ambassadors, high-ranking military officers, CEOs of energy companies and members of civil society. Things have move on from the days of Minerva."

"So why does the Kremlin still run Medusa?" asked Christina.

"*Дезинформация* - *dezinformatsiya* - Disinformation; we run it as a kind of placement. It is a reliable way to convince the Americans and Europeans about how much and how little we know. To be frank, I think we are even too good at it. The British don't seem to even know that Minerva was replaced, and the Americans seem to think they are running Medusa. It's incredible really, and even if it gets discovered it will only set a very out-of-date place marker on our activities. They will think we are far more primitive than we actually are. Pure disinformation. When I say 'we' run it, actually I think it has been outsourced to one of the *krysha*."

"Outsourced? To a Russian gang? What? A Bratva is operating Medusa?"

"Yes, remember *sistema*? systemic corruption? Well, the size of *blat* going to and from the Kremlin has increased. Blat are no longer just small favours; they have grown through container ports and economic sectors to now being targeted toward foreign governments. One could say it is a success of modern Russia."

Blackbird continued, "Look - I need to say something *Arkhangelsk* - You must be careful you don't wake a sleeping dragon looking at this. If the GRU get a hint, then you could have much trouble coming your way. I know you are capable operative, but they won't play nice with you."

Christina realised Blackbird's warning was friendly, but also that Medusa must be the tip of an iceberg. By creating something considered outdated, the Russians could convince the west of the Kremlin's lack of sophistication while they built new cyberoffensives. It truly was the new cold war.

The dragon from the mountains

Christina, smiling, told the others the story of the dragon from the mountains.

"Once upon a time, a famous Russian Bogatyr (Knight) Ilya Murometz was, as usually, at home. A group of old men from the village came to see him and said: 'Ilya, help us, Zmey Gorynych (the dragon) is so angry, he burnt 3 villages, he ate all the hens, we are in trouble!'

No answer from the Ilya.

Some days after they came again: 'Ilya, helps us, please, Zmey destroyed 10 villages, ate all the cows, kidnapped our wives!'

No answer.

Some days after men came again: 'Ilya, it's a nightmare. He destroyed 20 villages, he ate all the domestic animals, he kidnapped all the princesses, and he is very close to us now!'

Ilya started to get up and to take his dress. The old men were so glad!

'Ilya, you are going to help us at last!!!'

'Oh, fellows,' said Ilya, 'it's time to escape now!' "

Clare goes home

Clare was back at her flat as the sense of relief flooded over her. She sprawled across her bed and made snow angel exercises with her arms and legs. She realised that she was past flat shares and thought how, in just a few days, things had jammered in her mind.

First, the new roster had come out and Clare had been reminded of dish politics, and of night-time smoked salmon food theft. She should have realised that both Lottie and Tessa had boyfriends. The evenings were like mini parties, with the two boyfriends coming around and sometimes one of them would bring a curry-carrying friend too.

They had told Clare the tale of the competitive mess-maker - Janice - who had occupied Clare's room before Clare. If Janice put something down somewhere it would stay there until she needed it again. At first the others started putting things just outside her room, but it made no difference, so they stopped. She used to take her socks off on the sofa every night and just leave them there, she would genuinely leave them until she did laundry (which was rare).

Janice never cleaned anything, so she would cook in the kitchen and wash any item that belonged to her, but anything else would be left dirty. She would wash her plate, knife, fork etc, but if she had used someone else's saucepan she would just leave it, she also never cleaned the work surfaces or hob.

Then - for everyone's benefit - there was the 'scrunchie on the door handle' warning system - a kind of 'no entry' sign.

Or the endless trash television. Made in Chelsea, Made in Essex, Made in Gateshead, The XYZ Factor. It wasn't all as Herbal Essences as they'd made out in the advert.

And then there was that evening when someone unknown was crashing around in the kitchen at 2am drunkenly cooking 'pasta surprise' for three other visitors.

Or when Lottie's drunken boyfriend Matt turned the house into a honeymoon suite with loads of flowers and expensive boxes of chocolates. But, thought Clare, you kind of must let it happen, because this is nice, and Lottie says she has been single forever, so let her have her fun, don't be jerks. Then - as night follows day - there's the reverse: Tessa breaks up with Rick and everyone has to tiptoe around, or Tess's feelings will be hurt. Oh, she'd never say so, but you can tell from the look in her eyes. You just can.

And that was just the first week. Clare would have several more, at least. She decided that she would be seeing her imaginary boyfriend quite often.

Clare's phone rang. It was Christina.

"Glad you are back at home?" she asked.

"Christina - you can't imagine how good this feels! Thank you for persuading me!"

"You looked kind of jaded when we saw you. We all figured you needed some peace and quiet."

"Yes - it is full-on at the House, then full on at the other house!"

"Well - I bring news. A little bird has told me some things."

Christina relayed the information from Blackbird to Clare.

"There's a new project in this for Bigsy, then? To find out about the Kremlin end of things?"

"Yes - but Blackbird warned me to be very careful. Not to wake the sleeping Dragon."

"Dragon? I thought that was Chinese or Japanese?"

"No - we have many tales of Zmey Gorynych - The dragon from the mountain is in our country too!"

Another day in the House

Clare had finally got to meet Andrew Brading. It had taken nearly a week, but he seemed like a lovely person. He'd been through the mill though, because of his unguarded BAME comment. A couple of the red tops were clearly gunning for him and now that the Identity Bill Second Reading had slithered though the Commons, the news cycle were looking for something else to poke and prod.

Andrew was very aware of the 'one-liner' that Clare had provided and had shaken her by the hand by way of saying thanks.

The already crowded office was now host to another visitor, the Special Advisor named Ian Harrison.

Clare noticed that Harrison was playing his role like he was on the TV show West Wing. He kept saying things like, "Walk with me," and "Talk to me," like he was too busy to stop and think.

Clare nicknamed him M.T. - Moving Target, which was also a delightful pun on 'Empty'. She also worked out he was what she called a 'rear view mirror watcher.'

Harrison could pontificate about anything after the fact but seldom had anything new to add to the direction.

Ian has been elated, deflated, proud, over-eager and depressed in half-hour bursts since Andrew's BAME clip had been uploaded. He has also taken to stumbling into the office whenever his mood shifted to share his latest thought with his boss.

Clare could see that Andrew Brading was tolerating Ian, rather than embracing him. She wondered what Harrison's daily rate was - certainly more than a couple of grand for doing almost nothing useful. By comparison, Andrew Brading showed a no-nonsense style and independence of spirit (the libertarian), and then could flip to a common-sense embrace of difficult negotiations (the patrician).

Andrew looked up from his reading as Ian entered the room for the third time today. Clare could see that Andrew was peeved but that Harrison had missed it.

"Andrew, I've just had Wilbur Griffiths on the phone!" One of the Secretary of State for Health's special advisors. A champion of health care privatisation, free market absolutist. Not a natural ally of Andrew's. Not a pragmatic market reformer, Oh no. Off the other bloody side of the dart board, really.

'Reactive,' thought Clare.

"What did he want?'
    "He'd love to have a sit-down with you to talk through some of the provisions for shifts of the trusts to profit-creating centres.'

"That's dynamite, " thought Clare.

Andrew initials the document he is reading. Picks up the next.

"But what do you think, Ian?"

Ian sits on one of the wobbly office chairs, pulls out his phone and scans it while he speaks. "He wants to establish a relationship in case the Secretary of State gets the boot and you get his job, of course."

"Not my question. I asked what you think about the situation?"

Harrison squeezes Andrew's shoulder and lumbers off without replying.

"Idiots," mutters Brading.

Brading recollects that Harrison knows about wine, and Harrison's boss at Hayter Consulting, Jason Turner, is legendary for knowing his way around a wine list.

"They all get paid too much and take us for granted," says Brading, "Clare - don't let it happen to you."

Clare smiles across to Andrew, "I find it so hollow," she says.

"Leaning together, headpiece filled with straw," answers Brading.

"Yes, the hope only of empty men," replied Clare - also quoting from Eliot.

"Come," he says, "we should get some sandwiches, and you can tell me some more about 'The New Girl.'

"Sure," answered Clare, "But less of the girl, please."

"Oh, I am so sorry," she sees a slight blush run across his face.

"That's okay, but I don't want the name to stick," she replies.

They leave the office together.

"Look, I'm sorry about that 'girl' thing," says Brading, "This place is so damned misogynistic. What do you think of what you are seeing so far?"

"It's complicated, fragmented, interrupt driven, policy led. A few people 'in government' seem to make all the decisions. Some of it is two-faced. Some of the spokespersons are plain embarrassing. I'm amazed that anything gets done."

"That's a good and a plain-talking assessment. They told me you spoke your mind - Please continue to do so. I only ask that you don't embarrass me or the office and that I'm not asked to bail you out because of something, Otherwise, please feel free to act on any matters. Oh, and I plead to your loyalty, or that you tell me when you disagree with something I've said or done."

"That seems very fair," answered Clare, "And - in my humble opinion - you seem to do a good job!"

Brading stopped and looked at Clare.

"Now, you looked as if you meant it, unlike some!" he said.

Clare was pleased; she thought she could read Brading.

"Andrew!" called a woman's voice, "Over here!" They both looked towards Parliament Square, close to the Statue of Benjamin Disraeli.

An attractive woman was standing, waving. "It's Katherine, my wife. She is in London today for some kind of event."

They crossed the massive roundabout and greeted Katherine. Clare noticed Andrew give her the mildest of kisses to the cheek and then stepped forward.

"Katherine, this is my new researcher, Clare Crafts. She joined us just over a week ago. She was out shopping for sandwiches - but so far hasn't found any."

Katherine smiled, "Well, I think she is in luck. She could join us for lunch. I've a table around the corner at the Supreme Court."

"Great idea," said Andrew, " Let's go and be Conservatives."

They walked the few steps to the cafe at the Supreme Court.

"It's with some sadness that we walk past Roux," said Katherine. "It used to be a wonderful place, just like someone's living room and serving the best food."

"Did it go under?" asked Clare, thinking back to the virus and its consequences.

"Yes, I'm afraid so," answered Katherine.

They were soon seated at a large round table.

"When did you join?" asked Katherine, Clare thought of her interview and wondered whether she was about to have it all over again. She decided to turn the questioning around.

"Oh, just over a week ago - but tell me, what event are you attending" asked Clare.

"Oh, it's a talk about mediocrity," said Katherine, "About white men in positions of power - don't worry darling, I'll wear my dark glasses!"

"You are something of an activist too?" asked Clare.

"Yes, you could say that; I work for The Tribune, as a journalist."

"Doesn't that put you into conflict with Andrew sometimes?"

"We've worked it all out nowadays - Years of marriage, two kids and I think we've devised a system."

"Do you live in London, then?" asked Clare, "I assume you have somewhere in your constituency too?"

"We are among the MPs who haven't been on the take, over housing," answered Katherine.

Clare nodded, "Yes I heard about all the profiting from second homes and MPs staying in hotels. It was quite a feeding frenzy when one of the tabloids discovered it."

Andrew interrupted, "It is what gives we politicians a bad name, all of the ones who are on the take."

"I remember, I think it was around 160 MPs accused, including, if I remember correctly, Michael Gove. I think he was reckoned to have made £870,000 on two homes originally paid for from taxpayer sources. And didn't Maria Miller, pull in more that £1.3 million? And the respectable-looking Tory chairman Graham Brady was also implicated. Parliamentary rules meant they were entitled to keep the money.

"Entitled, says it all," muttered Andrew, "You are right Clare, the Daily Mirror investigated and found out that MPs made an average profit of £255,000 on selling their homes.

"Of the 20 who made more than £500,000 in gross profit, 14 are Tories and six are from Labour. Labour MPs made an average of £193,000 profit on sales, while Tories averaged double at around £417,000. And the politicians could reclaim thousands of pounds in mortgage interest payments under the discredited old expenses system."

"What will I be reading in your column?' Clare asked Katherine, intrigued.

"Nothing as exciting as the stuff we are discussing here," said Katherine, "I mainly deal with culture and arts - that new show at the R.A. is a case in point. And the trees wrapped in polka dots along by the river."

"Yayoi Kusama! I love her work, " said Clare, "The polka dots - the infinity rooms - her agenda - feminism, minimalism, surrealism - stylish Art Brut, pop art, and abstract expressionism. She has been said to be one of the most important artists to come out of Japan."

"I think you should write this piece for me!" smiled

Katherine, "I shall certainly keep your comments in mind when I take a look."

"I knew we'd hired a good one," said Andrew.

Calling Amanda

Another week had passed. Clare was back at her own home, expecting her weekly call from Amanda.

There was a bleep and Zoom opened.

"Hi," said Amanda, "How are you and how's things going?"

"Well, I seem to be in with everyone now, including lunch with Andrew Brading and his wife Katherine. They both seem to like me. I've also met a shifty Special Advisor named Ian Harrison, who seems to specialise it borrowing watches to tell everyone the time. And I seem to be well in with my lively flatmates, although I'm going away for a couple for days each week to spend some quiet time back at my own apartment."

"Any sign of anything unusual?" asked Amanda.

Clare relayed the information she had got via Christina.

"The Medusa Listening Station must be fairly new, " observed Amanda, "And I'm genuinely surprised that they would try an identical operation twice."

"I suppose you don't expect it the second time - but also beware that they are not just using it as a distraction. If I were you, I'd get Grace Fielding or someone at GCHQ to take a look at Cyber-attacks being mounted by the Kremlin."

"Thanks for the steer on that. I won't ask where you got it from," said Amanda.

"You might want to look out for CyberBerkut too," added Christina.

Special Advisor

Ian Harrison was pleased they had recruited him as a SpAd. A Special Advisor. He would not take the risks that Dominic Cummings had taken. He was too canny to become the story. The early history was already written of Dominic Cummings. He broke the first rule. By defending himself in the Rose Garden at No 10, Boris Johnson's chief of staff entered uncharted territory. And as senior Government figures fought his corner, the rulebook was torn up entirely.

A government aide quoted: "It is a completely bizarre situation where we've got ministers, Cabinet ministers – the Prime Minister – going out and defending one adviser. It is the complete opposite to what should be the case."

Cummings was no ordinary member of staff. Few advisers were so integral to a prime minister that they would stake as much political capital as Johnson did in order to keep them in place.

But the secret of the Tories was always about Power. How to get it and how to keep it. A few reality distortions never did any harm if it allowed one to mainline on

Power.

The charge against Cummings was that he breached lockdown rules by travelling to Durham to be near his family in case he and his wife, both with suspected coronavirus, could not take care of their young child.

Then he fanned the flames by misjudging his initial response to the joint investigation by The Mirror and The Guardian. The subsequent coverage led many to conclude he should have fallen on his sword. "That really should have been the outcome," said a former aide to another Cabinet minister.

Another ex-SpAd argued: "Your job is to help the reputation of the minister and the government of the day. Rightly or wrongly, if your coverage is damaging that, then you're not doing your job. I think most special advisors would step aside."

History showed that Cummings days were numbered. It needed an excuse, but something that would make the PM look like he was in control.

Harrison realised the Cummings saga reinvigorated the public's awareness of the cult of the SpAd. Aspersions were cast about the influence this unelected cabal have and the motivations they hold. "It's as if there are all these devious special advisers who have got this grand plan to mess things up," says one. "It often feels there's not enough appreciation that it's a load of people trying to do their very best and make what's already a difficult situation better."

Harrison knew how to keep his head down. Take the money and lie low. Or was it take the money and lie?

"I sometimes call them the people who live in the dark," Clare Short, the former Labour cabinet minister, told the New Statesman way back. "Everything they do is in hiding."

Ian Harrison was enjoying being a temporary civil servant who could now walk through the walls of Parliament. They had given him a code of conduct, which set out the roles he could carry out. This included speech writing, advising, policy development and representing the views of their minister to the media where allowed. Cummings had enjoyed power without responsibility. Harrison would accept money without responsibility.

The code also stated: "Special advisers must not take public part in political controversy, through any form of statement whether in speeches or letters to the press, or in books, social media, articles or leaflets. They must observe discretion... and would not normally speak in public for their minister or the Department."

Cummings had driven a coach and horses through that one.

Harrison was in it for the hourly rate. He could rack up a decent amount and would usually have vague responsibilities and not get involved in anything too controversial. He knew how to avoid accountability and considered himself coin operated. It annoyed him that Brading had made a comment about BAME which had swung the searchlight his way.

A rule of survival for Harrison was to always know whether the bright light was a spotlight (good thing) or a searchlight (bad thing). Harrison also knew that as a SpAd, it was most important to be liked and respected by journalists, while being trusted that you're a reliable source. Another source of income.

But right now, Ian Harrison's phone had just rung. He could see it was his boss from Hayter Consulting, Jason Turner.

"Hey Ian, How's things? I bring you news. Can we meet?"

Jason Turner continued, "Look Ian, I need to speak to you in private about some things, can we meet together soon? Tomorrow maybe? Don't panic, it's not an H.R. thing."

Ian sighed almost imperceptibly. If Turner was calling him to speak direct, then it would most likely have been a Human Resources moment. He didn't want that, not now he was well and truly comfortable in his lucrative role in Parliament.

"Sure thing, where would you like to meet?" he asked.

"How about Langan's," suggested Jason, at, say, one o'clock?"

'Hmm,' thought Harrison, Langan's Brasserie, it could only be good news if Jason was inviting him there.

"Absolutely, I'll see you there tomorrow at one!"

Langan's Brasserie

Harrison arrived at Langan's. It was one of London's traditional relaxed meeting places. Smart tablecloths and sharply dressed waiters. Parisienne cafe society brought to London by Peter Langan. He had chosen Stratton Street, Mayfair, as its location. Then Michael Caine - the actor and friend of Peter Langan, became his business partner, and the pair transformed the site with original artwork, brighter lighting with mis-matched lamps and relaxed the atmosphere of the restaurant. Everyone had visited - Patricia Taylor, Marlon Brando, Mick Jagger, Francis Bacon, Muhammad Ali, Jack Nicholson, and David Hockney, to name several, and there were discreet pictures sprinkled around of the great and the good. Not to mention the artwork, which included pieces by David Hockney, Lucian Freud and Francis Bacon,

Harrison was meeting Turner upstairs, in 'The Venetian Room' which featured murals by Patrick Procktor specially commissioned by Peter Langan.

Harrison also knew that this was the site of many a boozy evening, both back in Langan's day but also much more recently courtesy of Jason Turner.

"Hello Ian," greeted Jason. He was seated at a round table with another guest. She looked stunning as if she had just walked from the set of a fashion shoot. Claret coloured dress, blonde hair and tanned skin. Ian assumed St Tropez was her natural habitat.

"Let me introduce you to Tasha, a modelling friend of mine," said Jason. Tasha moved gracefully to extend her toned arm, and Ian wasn't sure whether to shake her hand and or to kiss it. He selected the former but thought about the latter.

"Hello," said Tasha, "Tasha is short for Natasha - Natasha Makarovna - actually, Tasha seems to go well here with the informality of London."

"So where are you from?" asked Ian, aware he was drifting into areas of questioning that could be construed as non-PC.

"I'm from Moscow originally; do you know it?" asked Tasha.

Ian shook his head, "No - I've never been there. I hope to one day." He thought his answer sounded lame.

"Yes, it is a raging city. There is always something happening. The night life can be extreme. Just don't follow the tourists around and you'll have a great time."

Jason started, "Ian, I want to bring you up to date on something. It is a delicate subject, which is why I wanted to meet you somewhere private to discuss it."

Ian leaned forward, "Is it about me?' he asked, "Only I'm getting on really well in Parliament at the moment."

A server arrived with three cocktails.

"Peter Langan's Fizz, we need to have at least one in his honour," said Jason, " I think it's vodka and Champagne, with a touch of elderflower and lime."

They clinked glasses, Ian met Tasha's eyes and was instantly befuddled.

"No, it's only indirectly about you - more what you need to do than anything."

Jason paused as if to collect his thoughts.

"We've an interesting situation that has developed with your MP, Ian - with Andrew Brading."

"He's been - how shall we say - romantically involved with Tasha here. There's a terrifically detailed audit trail of his dalliances, with hotel room receipts and a few photographs of them together,"

The server returned; they each ordered some food. Jason asked for something off-menu which sounded so good that Ian decided to have to as well. Tasha had the lemon sole.

Now Jason foraged into his small case and pulled out a some 10x7 glossy photographs.

"Here, see, a handful of the photographs."

Ian could see they were slightly blurred but there was the unmistakable profile of a beaming Natasha holding hands with Andrew Brading. In the second one, they appeared to be checking in to a hotel, which looked quite like the Dorchester. A third picture showed the two of them at a table in China Tang's. The photographer had kindly placed a menu in the foreground and the distinctive chair backs of Chinese silk were quite visible.

"Em, isn't this somewhat irregular?" Asked Ian, looking towards Tasha, "I mean - we normally see the mistress (excuse me, Natasha), but seldom get to talk to her!"

"It would be if this was an ordinary situation," answered Jason, "But for this the stakes are sky high."

"What is your angle Jason? I'd have thought Andrew was as straight as a die, and faithful to his wife Katherine and his two young children?"

Natasha spoke, "Sometimes things are not quite what they seem. You will learn this over the next few weeks. The pictures don't lie and it puts Andrew Brading into a tough position."

Jason added, "But not as difficult as the other photos. They show Brading with Shanell Kinkead from Jamaica. Here, take a look,"- Jason showed Ian a similar set of photographs, this time of Brading with Ms Kinkead.

"Kinkead by name, Kinkead by nature," said Jason rather crudely. Then he looked directly at Ian.

"That's where you come in. Ian, we want you to tell Brading that you have found this out today. Tell him privately. Tell him you were shown the photographs. Tell him that this is on the edge of circulating to the press. That you have been offered a deal to broker with him."

"He'll see it as blackmail. Pure and simple. And then he'll get the police involved."

"Ask him about his dog called Barney. He'll know what you mean."

"Barney? I didn't even know he had a dog."

" A treasured family red setter - sadly, it went missing about a week ago. One minute it was in their house and the next minute it had gone. Suffice to say it was a simple demonstration of agencies unknown and their ability to access his home."

By now they were eating. Some delicious red wine had arrived. Ian felt that his head was clouding. The alcohol. He wasn't used to what was a heady mix of cocktails plus Natasha, news about Shanell and his boss.

He finished his lunch. Natasha looked over. She placed her hand on top of his.

"You'll know what to do?" she asked, "You'll be resolute about this and report back to Jason in a couple of days when you've told Andrew?"

He felt her slightly squeeze his hand. He knew that the squeeze would be much greater if he didn't obey.

Video Conference

It was a video conference call to the Triangle office.

Grace began, "Hello everyone - Grace Fielding here: it has been a long time! Thanks, Clare for remembering me when you talked about this with Amanda Miller. It's good that we can trust one another."

Everyone said 'Hello' to Grace, who smiled back at them. Amanda was on a separate session and they assumed she was patched in from SI6.

Grace continued, "Here's what I've found out,"

"The Kremlin have been increasing their cyberattacks against military and civilian infrastructure in the West. We mark them as a persistent challenge nowadays."

"We thought you'd know about all of this, from Brexit and the various elections," said Bigsy.

Grace continued, "Yes, but we are still struggling to get a better understanding of Russia's strategy and cyber actors, particularly the growing role of the military in these issues. If we can achieve that, then it can facilitate an improvement in ours and Western governments' policies to defend against future Russian activity."

"It seems the Russians leverage western systems to help themselves?" asked Amanda.

"That's right," said Grace, "Systems like Facebook, Instagram, Parley and simple social engineering have all been used with recent significant effect. Cybersecurity is perceived as a Western notion in Russian debates, while the semantic Russian equivalent is information security *(informatsionnaya bezopastnost)*.

"The Russian military scholars and official documents present varying definitions of information warfare and information security, but it is well-established that information security is a component of information warfare, which is a term that has a technical and a psychological or cognitive component."

"It goes well beyond propaganda, then?" asked Christina, remembering her time at the Akademy.

Grace continued, "We can assert that although Russia's doctrine suggests a defensive and cooperative posture in response to threats in the information space, there is a preference stirred by Putin for offensive cyber capabilities and operations, shaped by Russia's threat perceptions and doctrine, and the institutional cultures of the departments within the military conducting them."

Grace added, "The chief of Russia's Armed Forces, Valery Gerasimov, wrote that the rules of warfare were changing, and revolts modelled on the Arab Spring presaged future wars where the protest potential of the non-military actors and the use of political, economic, and other non-military measures would be widely employed."

"Cheaper too," said Bigsy, "Than using military might"

"Gerasimov was a key driver for us, back at the Akademy, " said Christina, "He showed that warfare could be asymmetric and that - agreeing with Bigsy's point - use of cyber made it much cheaper than with conventional weapons - and potentially more far-reaching."

Grace nodded, "That's right, General Gerasimov re-emphasised the employment of mixed tactics and the maintenance of asymmetrical and classic potential at the 2019 conference of the Russian Academy of Military Sciences. He noted the changing character of war and the developing 'coordinated use of military and non-military measures' and even suggested the primacy of non-military measures over military power."

Grace continued, "Yes, so over the past two decades, Russia's military and political leadership has undergone a fundamental modification of its conception of warfare and the role of cyber operations in this developing view.
    "Some terms that Western and Russian scholars have used to describe Moscow's shifting character of warfare include 'hybrid warfare', 'new generation warfare', 'the Gerasimov Doctrine', 'political warfare', 'hostile measures', 'cross-domain coercion', and 'grey zone tactics.'"

"We were told it was 'The Information Sphere'," said Christina.

Grace node, "Yes, the so-called 'information sphere' and the concept of information warfare fits well within Russia's understanding of the changing character of war because, as General Gerasimov asserted, 'without having clearly defined national borders, the information sphere provides the possibility of remote, covert influence not only on critical information infrastructures but also on the country's population, directly affecting the state's national security.'"

Amanda said, "And the cyber influence will be wherever it can destabilise the state. They are just as likely to use Alt-Right doctrine as anything from the Communist manifesto. Their aim is to destabilise at a low cost. Get the people with easy access to guns running around shouting slogans. QAnon and Deep State theories are just as just as useful to create some chaos."

"We've seen examples of all of this," said Jake, "It is well past Crop Circles, Bigfoot and Loch Ness conspiracies - which are 'mostly harmless,' as Douglas Adams might say, and straight into 'Get Help' territory."

Amanda added, "We know that the cyber operations attributed to Moscow are not conducted in a strategic vacuum. They are enabled and shaped by broader geopolitical considerations and the institutional culture of Russia's military, intelligence, and political leadership, as well as by Moscow's evolving approach to asymmetric interstate competition that falls short of all-out conflict."

"In other words, Moscow - The Kremlin - is calculated about using cyberwarfare to support its aims," said Jake.

Grace continued, "To understand the motivations behind, and the constraints of, Russia's use of cyber and information operations against perceived adversaries, decision-makers must thoroughly study existing policy and doctrine, particularly its evolution from the immediate post-Soviet period until now, while striving to attain a more sophisticated comprehension of the actors responsible for executing cyberattacks and digital influence campaigns."

"Yes, and they have been doing it for quite some time," added Amanda, "We think there is more continuity than contrast between Russian cyber perspectives and practice. Russia's cyber posture, nested in Russia's concept of information warfare, is reflected in the offensive cyber operations launched by Russian government departments, whose institutional culture, expertise, and modus operandi have affected and will continue to affect Russia's cyber signature."

"So I'd better get rid of all of those Russian sounding anti-virus packages, then?" asked Bigsy.

Grace continued, "Such differences may have wide-ranging consequences for deterring Russia and understanding Russia's red lines, and for facilitating the creation of a long-term strategy that addresses the causes of Russia's behaviour."

Then she added, "Yes, and Russia's MoD 2011 'Concept on the Activities of the Armed Forces of the Russian Federation in the Information Space' provided a clear definition of information warfare:

"'...the confrontation between two or more states in the information space with the purpose of inflicting damage to information systems, processes and resources, critical and other structures, undermining the political, economic and social systems, a massive psychological manipulation of the population to destabilize the state and society, as well as coercing the state to take decisions for the benefit of the opposing force.'

"We get the various terms too:

- *informatsionnoe protivoborstvo* (information struggle)
- *informatsionnaya voina* (information war) and
- *informatsionnaya borba* (information fight).

"These characteristics render studying issues of preparation and conduct of informational activities 'the most important task of military science'. Considering its multi-faceted and unconventional nature, information warfare, and by extension cyber operations, may begin deploy prior to the official announcement of war and to achieve political objectives without resorting to the use of military force."

Grace added, "In line with the Soviet tradition of portraying Russia as a besieged fortress defending itself against constant internal and external threats, Moscow also views the struggle in the information sphere as unending."

Confusion will be my epitaph

The wall on which the prophets wrote
    Is cracking at the seams.
    Upon the instruments of death
    The sunlight brightly gleams.

When every man is torn apart
    With nightmares and with dreams,
    Will no one lay the laurel wreath
    As silence drowns the screams.

Between the iron gates of fate,
    The seeds of time were sown,
    And watered by the deeds of those
    Who know and who are known.

Knowledge is a deadly friend
    When no one sets the rules.
    The fate of all mankind I see
    Is in the hands of fools.

Confusion will be my epitaph.
    As I crawl a cracked and broken path
    If we make it we can all sit back
    And laugh.

But I fear tomorrow I'll be crying,
    Yes, I fear tomorrow I'll be crying.

Epitaph: Robert Fripp / Peter John Sinfield / Ian Mcdonald / Michael Rex Giles /
Greg Lake (King Crimson)

Clare gets the bug

Clare had borrowed a couple of Bigsy's little gadgets. The little Tammano gadget plugged into a USB port and was like a miniature voice recorder. All it needed was power and a sound and it would switch itself on and record everything. Even if the USB socket has been disabled, it would still work.

"It lasts around 17 hours," explained Bigsy, "Consider it around a day. Here, take two - then you can swap one for another and cycle them."

Now she was in Andrew Brading's office and had plugged the unit into a spare USB socket. She would have a recording of the whole day's events.

It was another busy day. There was further news about a big Bill sponsored by Brading and the Opposition were kicking up a storm. There would be questions asked in the House.

Clare noticed that Ian Harrison had visited their office several times. He always asked for Andrew but didn't seem to contribute anything to the Bill debate that was raging. Serena and Maggie had gone across to another building and now Clare was alone.

In walked Andrew, "Oh hello, Clare, it's a madhouse everywhere today. They don't like my Bill about Fundamental Rights.

"It is ridiculous really, because all I am doing is re-enshrining in law something that was in place anyway when we were in the EU. The tabloids have got hung up on the word 'fundamental' - as if I'm supporting a 'Fundamentalist doctrine', which is ridiculous. I'm having to fight tooth and nail to keep the Bill moving forward."

Clare scanned through the Bill's contents pages. There were around 50 separate headings. She read a few of them and they all seemed eminently sensible and protective of the populous. Some football shirt wearing twitter lobby was kicking up a fuss, and it was being magnified through some vociferous chancers on the Left.

Clare was about to reply when there was a clatter at the door. It was a sweaty-looking Ian Harrison again - maybe on his fifth or sixth sortie to their office.

"Ah Andrew, I'm so glad I've finally caught up with you. I have something very important that we need to discuss."

"Is it about the Bill? Asked Andrew.

"Bill? What Bill?"

"The one that is pushing us into overdrive this morning."

"Oh, no, it's not about that, but it is still something very important. Can we talk here? Sorry, new girl, I can't remember your name, please can we have the room?"

Clare looked across to Andrew.

"Sorry," he mouthed and used his head to gesture that she had better go.

Clare stood and walked to the door. Ian's bulk didn't move to give her an easier path.

Clare marked him down as a bad-mannered slob and a slacker.

"Good, Andrew. Look, I have something delicate to discuss..."

That was all Clare heard as the door closed on the conversation. She walked back towards the Jubilee Cafe inside Parliament. There she spotted Serena and Maggie drinking coffee with someone else. They both looked frazzled sitting next to an calm-looking black woman with dark finger coiled hair.

Clare walked over.

"Fifty headings!!" said Maggie to Clare, "That's fifty pot shots from the Opposition; they seem to think that Andrew's Bill is incredibly toxic."

"Is it because it was ex-EU or because of the word 'Fundamental' in the title?" asked Clare, "Could we change it to 'Basic Rights' or something similar? They would have a harder time attacking that and it would make it different from the EU Legislation too."

She smiled across towards the third member of the table.

"Have you met Flore Chéron, QC?" introduced Serena, "We were going to ask her about changes to the core legislation - things like the Bill's legislative titles can be difficult to get amended."

Flore Chéron smiled across the table, "Hello Clare - they have been telling me about you! Let me introduce myself, she began, I'm Flore Chéron and I work for Lion & Freshwater LLP."

"You're a silk?" asked Clare, "My uncle was a QC for a company called Deringer, I always thought it sounded a bit like cowboys!"

"Ah yes, they are not called that nowadays, they have gone triple-barrelled like many of the other firms!"

"A triple barrelled Deringer! I suppose you want that on your side in a fight!" chuckled Clare.

"You looked surprised when Serena first mentioned it. Are you surprised that I'm Queen's Counsel, or that Andrew Brading's office is concerned enough to appoint a Queen's Counsel?"

"Bit of both. You look young to be a QC and I imagined Secretary of State for Internal Affairs would have asked one of their own many lawyers to get anything fixed."

"Well thank you, but I've been doing this for many years!" Flore scribbled something into a small Moleskine notebook. She wrote it with a fine liner instead of a fancy fountain pen. Next thing she'll be typing into an iPhone. A thoroughly modern lawyer.

"What are you doing over here?" asked Serena, "I thought Andrew was in the office?"

"He is. That Ian Harrison appeared and wanted to talk to Andrew all secret squirrel. Speaking frankly, I don't trust that Harrison. He seems to be paid a lot of money to skulk around dispensing wisdom after the fact. A rear-view-mirror jock, if you ask me."

Clare thought it was better to speak frankly and create a little damage in the process.

Maggie giggled, "You should have been here half-an-hour ago. His last invoice has just arrived, and we were talking about his value to the Department."

"Who does he work for," asked Clare, "Have they got any real credentials in Government?"

Serena answered, "It's the partner system. A partner for a big, approved firm gets some work. Then they find what they call a 'floor-filler' project and backfill it with a bunch of stringers. Stringers means that the so-called employees of the partner's firm are really all freelancers. Some of them are good, but others, like Ian, have, shall we say, 'room for improvement'."

"I must go," said Flore; "It's refreshing to meet someone so forthright. It's terrific to have you working in the office of my next Department, Clare. Goodbye, all!"

"See you in the corridors," said Maggie.

There was a pause as they each collected their thoughts. Then Serena asked, " Ian Harrison - you don't know what he wanted, then?"

Clare shook her head, "He almost barged me out of the office - he wanted it to be private, just between him and

Andrew. Who does he work for then?"

"Hayter Consultants - We make a joke about them. They are a subsidiary of ISMC which stands for International Strategic Management Consultants."

"ISMC, they were connected with Brant," observed Clare, "I had something of a run-in with Brant last year."

"Intriguing," said Serena, "You do run in some interesting circles, Clare, your uncle a QC, sister in Parly and run-ins with Brant!"

"They are all very long stories, "said Clare, and then changing the subject, "So, what's the joke about Hayter?"

Maggie replied, "Hayter Consultants - slogan: 'We don't let the grass grow under our feet.'"

Clare looked blank.

Maggie explained, " Oh dear - I'm explaining jokes now - Hayter is a well-known make of lawnmower..."

The recording

Clare had listened to Harrison's discussion with Andrew Brading. Bigsy's gadget had worked perfectly and now she was about to play it to everyone, on one of her dates with her imaginary boyfriend.

She was also going to need to ask Jake to become the boyfriend because her flatmates had invited her out with their boyfriends, to a bar called Opium in Chinatown.

"I just ran out of excuses; they were most insistent that they meet you, particularly as I'd stayed away from the flat so often. But I think I will - that is we will - be able to get more information from everyone in the social setting. Both are dating other people from the Parliamentary Estate. Lottie's is another Research Assistant - Matt Stevens - and Tessa's is a Special Advisor - Robin Hunter - although he is only a PB1"

"PB1?" asked Jake.

"Oh, sorry Pay Band 1, the lowest £40k+ to £60k+. It goes up to PB4, which tops out at £145k. See, I'm learning all kinds of things!" smiled Clare.

At Clare's request, Amanda was on the call and Grace had dialled in from GCHQ.

"I think we can see something of history repeating itself," suggested Clare, "Listen to this."

She started the playback and Bigsy adjusted the volume setting so that those remote could hear it clearly.

They could hear Ian Harrison explaining about some photographs to Andrew Brading. He talked about Natasha Makarova and Shanell Kinkead.

Andrew Brading started off sounding irritated; "was this some kind of joke? Who put Harrison up to this?" He didn't really have time for the fun and games when he was so busy with the Bill."

Harrison persisted, and Brading realised that it wasn't a practical joke. His tone changed to one of annoyance. Annoyance and denial. He didn't know these women. He had never heard of them before today. He had nothing to hide. He was fully faithful to his wife and family.

Harrison explained that he had seen photographs. That on a couple Brading was holding hands with the women. Harrison had even briefly met one of the women.

"Where?" asked Brading, now angry with Harrison, "And what is it you expect to get from this - my trust and loyalty to you. Forget it. You have just crossed the line which means today will be your last day on Crown Estate soil.

Harrison played the 'Barney' card.

"Have you recently lost your dog?" he asked, "Barney,"

Brading paused, "We have actually, from inside of our home."

"Well, it was a demonstration. Of the power that certain people wield. That they can come and go to your house."

There was the sound of Brading picking up is phone, "Security, please could you come to my office to help escort Ian Harrison off-site."

Barely five seconds later, there was a knock on the office door. A brief hubbub as two new men entered, approached Harrison and offered politely but firmly to walk him from the Estate.

They heard Brading buzzing someone and a few seconds later heard Serena enter the room.

"Serena," he said, "There is something not right. That little shit Harrison has just threatened me. He says they have got something on me. Something to do with two women. Natasha Makarova and Shanell Kinkead. He implied that I was seeing these women, being unfaithful to Katherine. It's simply not true."

There was a pause on the recording. It was difficult to tell how long because of the auto-stop start when things went quiet.

"It's okay, I believe you, Andrew, of course; we've worked together too long for me to think you'd have something running on the side. And I'm sure it is the same with Katherine."

"Thank you," said Andrew, "But frankly it's the fourth and fifth estate that I'm worried about. They can make trouble out of a minor mis-speak - imagine what they can do with this!"

"Look, I've just been speaking to a new QC, Flore Chéron from Lion & Freshwater. She's not one of our usual suspects, and I brought her in to take a fresh look at your Bill. I hate to say it, but our expensive normal advisors have tackled your Fundamental Rights Bill with such little imagination. I suggest we ask her for her advice in this matter?"

Another pause, "Do you think she can be relied upon for discretion?"

"Absolutely, and, by the way, all the women in your office seem to trust her already!"

"Okay - I'd better meet her then, could you set it up without saying too much about the subject?"

"I'll try to arrange something for tomorrow."

Clear spoke up now, "The recording continues, but there's nothing of real interest; I think what you have heard sets the scene in a manner similar to the late Bernard Driscoll."

"That could be our lucky break," said Christina, "I mean if they have used some of the old moves, then I suppose they might have used some of the old players as well?"

"Good point," said Jake, "Who were those women we met before? Marion Charlotte and her friends - they all worked for the same agency too, I seem to remember - it even hired Pete Burr for that big event in London."

"We'll have to make some enquiries," said Christina, "But what is bothering me is we don't know what they are trying to influence now. It surely can't be that Rights Bill?"

Clare nodded, "I agree, we will need to see whether Andrew handles any other big Bills."

Amanda spoke, "Clare, you have exceeded expectation in the first couple of weeks. I just need to remind you to be careful. If the people involved are as strong minded as they appear to be, then the last thing we want is for them to find out about you."

Opium Chinatown

Clare and Jake arrived at Opium. They had to locate it first.

Clare said to Jake, "Well this is a secret bar if ever there was one; My instructions are to find the jade green door and head up the long dark stairway.

They emerged into a chic, hidden venue in the heart of Chinatown. Orientally themed but an element of freshness with a twist making it modern and current. Metal finishes on mis-matched Chinese furniture produced a London feel.

"Three bars - it could take us a while to find the others," said Clare, but then noticed Lottie and her extra needy boyfriend. They waved to her and Clare led Jake across to the table.

"Hooray! You must be Clare's imaginary boyfriend then?" asked Tessa.

"Oh no, I'm very real," said Jake, "My name's Jake Lambers - please to meet you all. They went around the table doing introductions. Clare finally learned Lottie's boyfriend's name - it was Matt Stevens.

"What are you drinking?" Matt asked, and signalled to a waiter.

"A Hemingway Daiquiri," said Jake, "And a Clarified Negroni, for me," said Clare.

"We are going down in flames tonight," said Matt, "Can we have six Yam Sings too,"

"Yam Sings?" asked Clare.

"Shots!" replied Matt.

"Easy, Tiger," whispered Lottie. Clare noticed Tessa was with a First Date Situation. At least Clare assumed it was because she didn't recognise him and he seemed a little swamped in the conversations.

"Hi, I don't think we've met?" asked Clare.

"Hi - yes - I've seen you around the Estate. You work for Andrew Brading, don't you? I know Maggie quite well. I'm Robin Hunter."

"It's a small world," said Clare, "I'm Clare Crafts and this is Jake Lambers,"

Matt piped up, "Well, expect 3 bars of amaaaazing Asian cocktails and a shelection of dim sum to get your appetite going."

Clare noticed that Matt's voice was a little slurred. He had ordered another round of slammers too. Jake looked at Clare signifying that he had also noticed. Clare knew Jake had the constitution of a seasoned journalist and a couple of shots on top of a cocktail wouldn't even dent him. Clare was slightly cannier and poured her second shot into the thriving tableside foliage when no one was looking.

Matt started, "So didn't you save Brading's bacon the other day? That's what I'd heard. A new girl wrote a five word sound bite, and it saved Andrew."

"Easy on the 'new girl', Matt," said Lottie. "We've all been called it, but none of us like it."

"Slorry," said Matt, slurring his words, "I meant nothing by it."

"I think we need another drink," said Jake, piling on the pressure. Clare realised what he was doing but let him, anyway.

"My shout for this round of cocktails." - Jake gestured to a server who wrote an order. "Oh, you'd better bring a half dozen of those nice shots as well and can you put this round on this card, please."

Clare could see that this would get out of control after the next round. She asked the server to bring some tap water as well.

"What are your first impressions then, Clare?" Asked Robin.

"Nothing like I could have predicted, totally frantic and interrupt-driven," answered Clare, "Or is that just because I am new?"

"Well - some things you should know, " said Lottie. Take my MP. Not Safe in Taxis. He's the slippery and wandering handed Duncan Melship, MP for Knutsford North."

"Yes," said Tessa, "We call him the Befummeler - fumbler. My cabinet minister has a different habit. It sometimes leaves white powder around his nose. The Blasenator. But he is also incredibly wealthy and has offshored most of it to the Caymans and Ireland. The public know about the Irish piece, but not the Caymans. And then there's that tittle-tattle about him and the porn-star. What did she say? She was 'happy to have helped the government through some unprecedented times'."

"And what about Andrew? Anything there for me to watch out for?" asked Clare.

A moment's silence.

Lottie spoke, "No - I think you landed on your feet. He seems to be the guiding light - all good."

"I heard something," said Robin, "It was only a passing remark. Apparently the very same porn-star is also a friend of Clive Haven."

There were groans from around the table.

"Brrr, he is a slimy toad," said Tessa. Lottie nodded.

"Well, he believes what he says, even if no-one else does, " answered Robin, "But this time he was talking about some new reform, which he wants Andrew to sponsor through the House. It is some kind of Health Passport, but Andrew seems to be refusing. It could cost him his next leg-up."

"I can't help thinking that if Haven is involved, then there must be something not quite right about the Heath Passport, said Lottie's.

"Surely that's like National Identity?" Asked Jake, puzzled.

Robin continued, "Not how you hear Clive Haven describe it. He says that the passport is for health identification only, There's Four levels - Tiers in the modern parlance - Tier 0 and 1, then 2 and then 3. They have linked it to the danger threats of the Tiered pathogens. But Andrew is dead against it. Some of you know that I shared an Oxford flat with Andrew when he was at Uni. He could be quite determined, even back then."

Robin added, "And the same flat also contained Maggie Shannon - who, Clare, you now work with. Andrew found the house through friends of his mum and dad. The owners were creative academics who had gone to teach at Carnegie Mellon for a year. Maggie already knew Andrew Brading from Oxford - I think he was already studying for his Masters when Maggie showed up - I think he was doing her parents a favour to let her in. I knew Andrew from when we were both doing a gap year in Thailand."

"You weren't at Oxford?" asked Clare

Robin feels himself bristle. "I was at Manchester. You?'

Now she looks up at him and flashes a quick smile, "Brighton - I studied Media. Communication and Cultural Politics, that sort of thing."

Robin relaxes a little, "No I was in Oxford already volunteering for the Party. We were hacking through analytics and could get undergrads to help us crunch the numbers. They could use their work for us also in their written work."

"And your job at this point, Robin? When you were sharing the house?'

"I was Head of Analytics for the local Conservative Party group.'

"And Andrew Brading?'

"As I said, he was studying for his Masters - although he was a local Officer in the Tory Party, even then whilst he worked for his PPE. And Maggie, she was just around - like as a Tory advisor. I'm amazed she went back to being an intern, but I think it was so she could work for Andrew. Although I don't think they were ever - entwined - but she has remained loyal to him, and him to her, ever since those days.

Matt interrupted, loudly. "If you spin a Chinese man around would he become disoriented?"

Lottie nudges him, "Matt. Stop. Inappropriate."

Matt says, Inn-a-prooop-priii-ate, In-app-rom-iate. Naughty. Wrong. Okay. I get the message."

Lottie smiles, "I think the cocktails must be quite strong," she looks over at Matt, who is staring at one of the waitresses.

"Hello," Matt says, "you have lovely eyes. Can you bring me and my friends here another round of cocktails?" He gestures around the table.

The server looks around the table for someone more approachable. Her eyes alight upon Jake.

"Shame again everyone?" asks Matt.

Jake looks at Lottie, who nods, "He'll be okay - he sometimes gets like this, but he'll pull through and become quite docile."

"Okay - these are on me," says Jake, offering his card to the server.

Jake has got their measure now. Well-connected highflyers, Head of this, Officer of that, Advisor. But still a bunch of twenty something political junkies, experimenting with job titles.

"Robin, you seem to know Andrew pretty well. Can you give any advice to Clare here?" asked Jake.

"I can tell you about when we backpacked around Thailand," answered Robin, "Any of the rest of you heard this before?" Everyone shook their heads.

Matt added, "Go on, tell us, dear chap,"

Robin smiled, "Good - it means I can make up more of it! - But hey Jake, if you are a journo, this will have to stay off the record. There's a muck-raking hack named Roger Slater who is digging around for dirt on Andrew. It's supposedly something to do with Brading's anti-BAME statement the other day but looks like a well-positioned hatchet job to me."

Jake said it was cool, and Clare said she would vouch for Jake's discretion.

Robin began, "Andrew and I arrived at Khao San together. It's best described as a decompression chamber between east and west. But when we arrive, it soon becomes clear that even this is a generous description; the Khao San Road actually doesn't feel like it's in Thailand at all."

"I was there once, actually" said Jake, "Gaining some life-skills! It was rammed with bars showing premiership football; Britney Spears and Coldplay blaring out; hustlers selling European T-shirts and fake British ID cards."

Robin continued, "Good description, Jake. Andrew observed straight away that this was a goldrush town. Designed to fleece the prospectors who were looking for nuggets of enlightenment."

Jake added, "And there was danger there too. We knew that a short time before we arrived 20 Thais were massacred in clashes between soldiers and anti-government redshirt protesters barely 100 metres from the Khao San Road. But it might as well have been 100 miles away: the Khao San's tourist festivities were barely disrupted."

Robin continued, "Then we met up with Jamie, a graphic designer from west London who 'took several gap years' and said that 'the Khao San just feels like home'.

"Andrew was immediately aware of the dichotomy of the well-heeled experience-dipper looking at another culture. We talked about it when we sat waiting by the roadside for a bus.

"I can see that too," said Jake, "That street was like Camden on steroids,"

"Yes, apart from the fat, bald westerners parading their suspiciously beautiful Thai girlfriends."

"Andrew and I were travelling onwards to the so-called Full Moon Party. We could have taken the overnight train or bus down the coast to the ferry terminal of Surat Thani. But we worked out it was almost as cheap to take the plane. After a couple of cramped journeys, we got to Koh Phangan, and it isn't long before we're talking to the cream of British gappers - paid for through Bank of Mum and Dad."

"At least I used my own money," said Jake sheepishly, "I travelled out with my then girlfriend and we shared our limited resources."

Robin continued, " We were sitting on the side of a dirt track near the centre of Haad Rin, the main tourist town on Koh Phangan, and venue for the next day's Full Moon Party. Tourists were whizzing past every 30 seconds on mopeds belching out acrid fumes."

"Every second shop is an internet cafe packed with tourists checking Facebook. Every third shop is a travel agent's filled with tourists plotting their next move. It's an odd place to visit if you don't like tourists. And particularly if you yourself are one."

"But Jamie- who we'd only just met - didn't think of himself as a tourist: he said he was a backpacker. 'Most of the people here are backpackers,' he insisted.

Robin continued, "Jamie explained, 'Backpackers are infinitely different to tourists. Backpackers will accept anyone. Whereas tourists are the people who back home would end up in fights. But backpackers have no interest in fighting anyone, do they?'

"Jamie directs this question at Pete, an even friendlier backpacker whom he met a few months ago in Vietnam. Pete, ear-ringed and wearing a vest, is 23, British and on a different kind of gap year; he' says he's been given a year's leave of absence from the army.

"For most the time, he has been working as a promoter for a bar in Vang Vieng, Laos, but he's back in past-its-sell-by-date Had Rin for one last Full Moon Party.

"Pete couldn't agree more with Jamie. 'Yup,' he says. 'Tourists are the people who spend their time fighting here. Tourists are people who go on holiday for two weeks. This is not a place where you can go for two weeks. This is a place for backpackers. Tourists may pay more money, but they're idiots.'

Jake interrupted Robin, "Do you know something, I wanted to get out- We - wanted to get out - Jan and I decided it wasn't a place for us at all. We'd travelled all the way there, but Jan and I only stayed overnight and then moved on."

"Maybe you were you too old when you went there?" asked Robin, "They say it is all about youth. Ten thousand people condensed into one area where they can do everything they want to, with no regrets. Back home, you get mortal and there are repercussions. Out there, you can do what you want. It's like Ibiza before it turned. It's way cheaper, too."

Matt chimed in, "Mortal? Getting mortal? Have you suddenly gone all Geordie on us, man? Way-eye-man!"

Lottie gently tapped Matt, "We're trying to listen to the

story. Shhhh."

Robin continued, "We could see that the drugs were another big draw. These guys knew exactly which pharmacies sell speed – and what to ask for when they're at the counter. They know where to go to buy weed and can name the three bars in town that list magic mushroom milkshakes on the menu.

Matt cut in again loudly, "Can't you just have Doctor Robert on speed dial? Add it into your address book?"

Lottie kicked Matt, "Shhhh - you'll get us thrown out."

Robin continued, "Andrew asked Pete, 'if everything here is all so western and familiar – and if they're spending most of the week off their heads – are they really experiencing Thailand?' - see the pattern emerging - Andrew questioning and with a moral compass?"

Robin continued, "But Pete was brutally frank. 'This isn't a Thai experience,' he admits, instantly, 'This is a party experience. Chiang Mai and Bangkok, you get a Thai experience. Koh Phangan is a party place.'

"'We've gone through the Thai experience,' Jamie clarifies. 'We've seen it, we've done it. For us this is just a nice way to cap it off and celebrate what we've achieved, all that we've been through. A lot of people just visit the Khao San Road and the Walking Street – and they're tourists. They're not travellers.'

Jake interrupted, "I don't know, I don't think Jan and I were either tourists or - in Jamie's words - backpackers?"

Robin answered, "That's interesting. It is what Andrew said, I think you reached a similar conclusion. He worked out that people passing through were not going to learn anything in Koh Phangan about Thai culture. But he thought that places like Chiang Mai- they were where you could learn so much about the Thai culture of respect"

Robin continued, "So Jamie and Pete invited us to a "shroom" session with some of their many backpacker friends that evening. A few hours later, Andrew and I rendezvous in a bar built high above Sunrise Beach (where, in 24 hours, the Full Moon Party will take place) – a bar nicknamed, for reasons which soon become apparent, Mushroom Mountain.

Jake nodded, "I remember there was an entire culture around the magic mushrooms. I think they contained psilocybin, which is a bit like mescaline and has psychedelic properties. But I also saw someone tipping some liquid into the mushrooms. I assumed it was a psychoactive drug."

Robin resumed, "So we are there, but turnout is lower than expected; Jamie and Pete are joined only by two second-year medical students from Nottingham – Hailey, who took a previous gap year, and Laura, who didn't. Laura had studied pharmacology and was worried by the mushrooms. She would not try any because she reckoned the dose was so variable. Jamie and Pete were both ready to partake and Pete went into a mad trancey kind of state. Jamie said he'd stay with him and Andrew and I decided we'd better heed the advice from Laura and chickened out; we walked down to the beach with the two med students."

"We both thought it. Andrew and me. Koh Phangan isn't really the real world, but it's still an experience. Andrew was astute even back then, he asked what the locals thought about being invaded monthly by rowdy westerners.

Jake, "Did they tell you about the other party? Jan and I found out about that too."

Robin continued, "Yes, we soon found out that the locals don't actually go to the Full Moon Party. They go to an after-party up the hill the following morning. The Full Moon's just for the young westerners."

Then, with Laura and Hailey, at four in the morning, we visited The Rock, a bar perched high above the sand at the opposite end of the beach to Mushroom Mountain. We can see a DJ booth at Paradise Bungalows, where there sits a Burmese immigrant DJ.

He'd lived in Haad Rin since he was 16 and this party is roughly his 100th. He's bored with playing the same electro-house on the same broken system to the same crowds. He stares at the thousands of Europeans who will soon be flying home and wishes he could one day go with them. But he could not afford the flight.

"Up and down the beach, young western men are peeing into the Gulf of Thailand. It was supposed to be an amazing experience, but neither Andrew nor I could tune in and drop out to it.

"That is so like my experience with Jan," said Jake.

"I thought you said your girlfriend's name was Clare?" asked Matt, looking more dissembled than ever.

"It is, this is Clare, she's my girlfriend now."

"We thought you were made-up," said Tessa, "To begin

with Clare wouldn't say your name, nor describe you. That's why we decided you were her imaginary boyfriend."

"Oh no, well, as you can see, I'm very real!" answered Jake, "So you think there really is some truth about someone gunning for Andrew Brading?"

"We had also heard about it from the lobby actually," said Lottie," I think the word got to us via Rachel Crosby - you know, the journalist. I told Maggie what I'd heard, but Crosby is either spreading a false rumour or very well-informed."

Clare decided she would keep quiet that she had also heard about it from Rachel. Otherwise, she wasn't sure where that particular winding corridor might lead.

"You all seem to know one another," observed Jake. "Yes, I even know Clare's sister Sam," said Lottie, "To be truthful, she probably contributed to the imaginary boyfriend rumour - I asked her who Clare's boyfriend was, but she said she wasn't aware that Clare was with anyone now. I guess she was being discreet."

"Here's to the sisterhood," said Clare, and everyone raised their glasses.

"We need another round," said Matt, "Hey miss waitress!"

Jake and Clare looked at one another. They sensed it was time to leave. "Early start tomorrow," said Jake.

"Brilliant to have met you all!" said Jake.

"Zàijiàn" said Robin, as they made their way to find a

black cab.

Onward to Clare's, where they had let the taxi go, because Clare's road led onto a busy thoroughfare served well with late night taxis - and there was always Uber.

"Jake, thanks," said Clare, "You made an excellent boyfriend, I'm sure they will talk about you back at the flat."

"My pleasure, as always," answered Jake, "And I think we gathered some new intel tonight. Quite a lot about Andrew Brading and about some scuzzy reporter named Roger Slater."

"Yes, I didn't say anything, but I'd heard about Slater as well. From the same source though, Rachel Crosby."

Clare leaned forward and kissed Jake gently on the cheek. He briefly hugged her.

"Hey - you can stay over if you like?" said Clare,

"Sure," said Jake, "Just like a real boyfriend!"

Politician bashing

They were both in the Jubilee Cafe, the Houses of Parliament's private cafe. Clare was sitting alone with Serena.

"There seems to be more gossip about Andrew floating around," ventured Clare, " I was out with some of the ladies yesterday evening and they were talking about what Rachel Crosby told us. Don't worry, I didn't say anything, but I thought you should know. They are talking about a hatchet job on Andrew."

"Yes, I'd also heard, although I've not done any digging on the reporter. I don't have a name yet."

"Roger Slater, that's who the rumour seems to be about. And it is linked to that fabricated story about BAME workers."

"Machiavelli at work, as usual," answered Serena, "Half virtu and half fortuna,"

"Ah yes," said Clare, "Political leadership - you touch on my friend Jake's high-horse: He sometimes quotes that Machiavelli line: when it comes to political leadership half was virtu -action oriented towards power and glory, and half was fortuna - or luck, or even 'a blind bitch goddess'."

"Or what Harold MacMillan called 'events dear boy, events'," added Serena, "Now we will need the political skill to turn circumstances we did not choose and events we could not predict to our advantage. Look - I've got a call - see you back at the office!" Serena left the cafe.

"Hey Clare!" It was Samantha.

"Hey Sam, Wow - you were right about this place. It is suitably manic. Hardly a dull moment since I've been here."

"Yes, sorry that your MP/Secretary of State seems to have a cloud over his head!"

"Fabricated. He's a lovely person," said Clare, looking into her sister's eyes.

"Oh - and if anyone asked you about me and Jake, say it's all true - although it isn't of course. He's my imaginary boyfriend so that I can escape back to mine away from the flat sometimes."

"Gottit, I wish I had one of those," said Samantha, "Only when I need them, of course."

They both laughed.

"Tell me then, what's happening?" asked Samantha. She had selected a prawn wrap and an exotic juice.

"There's talk of a hatchet job," said Clare, "But I can't understand why?"

"I expect he is being threatened by some lobbyist or another. It is fairly standard for the rags to build up a stockpile of bad news about everyone. They can then choose when to deploy it. It's interesting that there seems to be a rush to get something against Brading though. Maybe he is lily-white like they say?"

"My impression. He is."

"Well, it could be to do with that Fundamental Rights Bill he was pushing, but I reckon it is something else. Something where the Deep Tories are involved, pitting themselves against the UK heartland."

"Yes, the more I think about it, the more I think there is something we don't know about in play. Some kind of influence politics."

"Clare, I wouldn't have thought you believed in conspiracy theory?"

"I don't. But Tories who exploited the long-term disaffection of Labour's heartland voters and turned the red wall blue will need to be held to account. Globalisation and abandonment combined with the incoherence of Jeremy Corbyn offered a moment to transform the class basis of English politics, with Brexit as a flawed proxy."

"Yes, Clare, with Brexit supported by populists, the Labour covenant that endured through generations, was broken when the red wall went blue. Now, Andrew as Secretary of State for Internal Affairs finds that a lot of this lands with him. He needs a way to patch things up. But the predictable Tories will be worrying about their potential loss of power."

"Not helped when the worst of the COVID Tiers also tracked the old Red voters? Not exactly levelling up?"

Samantha added, "Those tiers didn't just track the red wall. Did you notice how they tracked the coalfields as well? Think of it. Elderly miners with breathing difficulties in most of the Tier 3 zones outside of the major conurbations. Privileged Londoners were allowed to drink expensive cocktails outside whilst Liverpool and Manchester remained in lock-down."

Clare smiled, "Yes, usually things spread outwards from London. This time it was the reverse, even as some London boroughs maxed out higher than anywhere else in the country."

Samantha spoke, "Well, they got London under lockdown in the end, making it Tier 4 before anywhere else, although the London Lockdown soon spread in a traditional way around much of the rest of the country."

She continued, "It revealed the lack of strategic clarity. Cummings was a bullying show-off, using academic sounding doublethink to befuddle the regular politicians. Most of them wouldn't know a pivot table or whether the origin on a graph had been manipulated. A full-on case of 'baffle them with bullshit'."

Clare laughed, "I would laugh about this if it wasn't so serious,"

They sat at a small table, facing one another, with their plates of wraps and fruit juices.

Samantha continued, lowering her voice, "Excuse my PPE lecture, Clare, but to unpack some of this: The inability to react strategically to events means that you become their prey, and the removal of Dominic Cummings only intensified the strategic void.

"Cummings mocked the government, yet he understood that the Government's programme could only be delivered outside of regulatory convergence and an active role for the state was required. There seems to be little understanding of any of this remaining within the Government."

Samantha took a bite of her wrap, "It is not fishing and transport but state aid that really matters; if they fold on that, then there will be no possibility of achieving their political goals. Yet the inability of Labour to renew itself as an object of affection for the working class or articulate a plausible economic plan for national renewal is allowing the Government to limp along."

Clare interrupted - "This wrap reminds me of one of those old-fashioned sandwiches, with curried chicken and fruit - what were they called? Oh, yes, Coronation Chicken."

Samantha continued, "You'll discover the Tesco Metro next to Westminster Tube soon enough."

Then she picked up her explanation to Clare, "Pretending things didn't happen are all very well, and it is obvious that some 'straight to camera' speeches have been made with an eye on historical reworking of events. Imagine the documentaries in twenty-year's time with Boris waving his arms about and pretending to be a statesman."

Samantha sipped her fruit juice, "Aside from a handful of politicians, there is no strategy, no narrative and very little energy. And they know that the next year could be worse. Instead of fixing any of those things, they are doing what Trump used to do, diverting attention with 24-hour news cycle gimmicks."

"We are all doomed!" stated Clare, smiling at her sister.

"Yes, but it does keep us all busy," said Samantha, "So what's this about Jake then - was I right the last time we met? He is very pleasant eye candy."

Bermondsey compression

Evening and back at the Bermondsey flat, Clare was in her room. A double bed with cupboards underneath, a full wardrobe and a small space where she could rest her laptop. She needed to appraise Amanda of the latest situation but wasn't sure whether she could be overheard in the flat.

Lottie was playing Taylor Swift's 'Shake it Off' loudly in the main room, so Clare decided that it would create sufficient noise cover.

She dialled Amanda on a voice line.

"Hi Clare, how has your week been?"

"A few new discoveries, but still nothing conclusive. I think that there must be someone out to get Andrew, but I don't know the reason. There's a journalist named Roger Slater who is digging around."

Amanda replied, "Yes, we know about Slater. He has run a couple of other smears on well-known people. It is the first time he's been involved with politicians though; the others were in business. He specialises in a kind of sleaze/smear of his target and gets paid well by the tabloids. I guess you'd call him a 'hack for hire'."

PART TWO

The Hollow Men

We are the hollow men
We are the stuffed men
Leaning together
Headpiece filled with straw.
Alas! Our dried voices, when
We whisper together
Are quiet and meaningless
As wind in dry grass
or rats' feet over broken glass
in our dry cellar

Shape without form, shade without colour,
Paralysed force, gesture without motion.

Those who have crossed
With direct eyes, to death's other kingdom
Remember us - if at all - not as lost
Violent souls, but only
As the hollow men
The stuffed men.

TS Eliot

Roger Slater

Roger Slater was in his home office. He lived in an apartment in the well-heeled Batchelor Street, in Camden. It was a row of almost identical terraced houses, each with a black front door and a window either side of it - like something a child would draw. He had bought it several years earlier before the extreme price hikes in London and he was certain he couldn't afford it nowadays. It was mainly luck that he'd bought a place in the area. He had wanted to be close to the Guardian's offices and had found that the area was well served with tube lines, buses and even the main line Kings Cross railway, which he could see from the end of his road.

Now he was working in Westminster, he could hop onto the Northern line and make one change at Embankment to get to Westminster or hop the Piccadilly to Green Park and work his way one stop back on the Jubilee. Either route took him around 20 minutes, door-to-door. And, of course, the rest of London was spread out before him. He didn't need a car and hired one if he needed to go further afield.

Like many journalists he knew, he was still single and had occasional dalliances with the opposite sex. More likely he would pitch up in a well-used journo-compatible watering hole like The Westminster Arms, St. Steven's Tavern or even a one-time legend like Ye Olde Cheshire Cheese - still on Fleet Street, although all the papers had moved out years ago. He knew his way around Greek Street and Soho too, and would sometimes stop at The Coach and Horses, where Hislop's Private Eye gang would convene every fortnight.

Slater believed that journalism was a drinker's game. He'd been left as something of a dinosaur since the current climate of multi-platform internet journalism (not to mention a more enlightened modern work ethic) had killed the functioning-alcoholic status of the lowly hack.

But he knew how to play the game, how to target someone and to gather information via the grape and the grain even if it meant, increasingly, using gastro-pubs and hipster dives to stalk his soon-to-be half-cut prey.

But right now he was worried. He'd been given an ultimatum by someone he'd fried in the press. A well-known and benighted businessman who seemed to have too many of the right connections. He'd been presented with a costly writ and an invitation to a meeting. He had been told that the writ would disappear if he could assist them in some small way. He still remembered the meeting inside a Chambers at the Law Courts. He wouldn't have believed the story if someone else had told it to him.

Law Courts

Roger Slater had made his way to the Royal Courts of Justice, the large, national courtroom building on the Strand. The building was acknowledged as one of the foremost examples of High Victorian Gothic Revival design. It was the 19th Century that saw the rise of Britain as an industrial and trading nation creating more litigation and forcing the construction of the new building.

Replacing Lincoln's Inn Fields, a green space which was regarded as one of the 'lungs of London', the present site was chosen; an area of seven acres to the north of the Strand of ancient and poor-quality housing. This slum property could be acquired relatively cheaply, and it was conveniently positioned close to the Temple and Lincoln's Inn.

These were the area to the north of the Courts and comprised many small offices - the Chambers of legal firms who had both the Royal Courts and the Old Bailey close at hand.

He was on his way to the chambers of a triple barrelled

firm, to try to understand how he could shake off the expensive writ.

He walked into the building, up stone steps and across panelled hallways. A smart woman asked for his name and then asked a male usher to conduct him to a large meeting room which resembled a panelled board room. There was water, coffee and tea available, so he poured himself a black coffee.

A door opened and in walked three men and a woman.

"Mr. Slater, thank you for coming, my name is Hugo Lawson-Parry QC and this is Sir Edgar Holland."

They each shook hands, and Hugo handed Slater an opulent business card and then continued, "My other two colleagues are from my practice: Emily and David. They are here to take notes of our discussion."

Roger Slater realised that Sir Edgar Holland was one of his recent hatchet jobs. And that Hugo had served the writ upon him. He was cornered.

"Now we all know how expensive these kinds of cases can become, when there is often a much simpler out-of-court settlement available," began Hugo.

"We know of your special skill and thought that simply hiring you to do something that we request might be a way to wipe clean any hint of a writ against you. So far, the only people who know of the writ are the people in this room."

Roger had been a journalist long enough to know that this smelled somewhat iffy. Was he being asked to do something illegal? Surely not from inside a QC's

Chamber.

"It is very simple; we just need you to find a few facts about a certain Secretary of State. Andrew Brading, the Secretary of State for Internal Affairs."

"But you don't know how this works," explained Roger, "I follow the smoke to find the fire. Andrew Brading appears to be squeaky clean."

"Perfect," said Hugo, " So he is more likely to go down in flames after you have discovered a couple of things about him."

He pushed an envelope across the table to Slater. Roger looked inside; it contained photographs. They were of Andrew Brading holding the hands of two women. On the back of the photo, in pencil, were written the names of the women. It presented a prima-face case of Brading seeing these two women illicitly. One of the women was black. That could also stoke Brading's recent outspoken comments about Blacks, Asians and Minority Ethnics.

"What do you need me to do?" asked Slater.

"Put the pieces together, " said Hugo, but use this information to gather other information about Brading. We would prefer to see his reputation unsalvageable."

"But why?" asked Roger, "Let's just say he is inconvenient," answered Sir Edgar Holland, "As Mr Slater, are you, unless we can resolve all of this."

How long?" asked Roger, aware that it would take time to build a case.

"You have until the end of the month, or things will

become difficult for you," answered Hugo.

"Is that everything? If I do this, will you destroy the writ?"

"You have my word," said Sir Edgar Holland.

Builder's lorry

Clare was at the office early the next morning. The short journey from the flat still took her by surprise. She had a quiet first hour before everything kicked off.

Maggie burst into the room, sobbing.

Clare leapt to her feet, put her arm around Maggie.

"Maggie, what is it? Are you all right?"

"It was terrible, and I saw it. You won't have heard yet, but Ian Harrison has been killed. It was a road accident. Terrible. Just outside of Parliament. He was on the pavement, ahead of me. I saw a bicycle swerve and hit him. Pushed him into the road and he was hit by a truck. The cyclist (all in black) was able to leg it out of the way. In fact, he crossed the junction at Parliament Square against all the traffic and shot up Parliament Street towards Whitehall. I'd say it was deliberate, but I don't think anyone would believe me."

"That's terrible. He was only in the office yesterday, talking to Andrew about something." At that moment Andrew appeared with Serena. They could immediately see that Maggie was upset.

"You've heard"" said Andrew, "about Ian?"

They both nodded. "I saw it," said Maggie, "He was about three metres ahead of me. It looked like something deliberate."

"Ian brought me some news yesterday. It suggests he was tangling with some difficult people," said Andrew.

"What news?" asked Clare.

"A smear campaign about me," said Andrew, "The details are not so important, but it looks as if there are people out to get me."

"Maggie, you'd better take today off," said Serena, "Clare, can you please go with Maggie and make sure she is alright. Don't worry about anything here. Use taxis. Go, please go, the both of you," said Serena decisively.

Clare looked at Maggie, "I think Serena's right; that's been a big shock. We don't want random people coming up to you today. It would be unbearable."

Maggie pulled herself together, "Thank you everyone, I didn't want to make a fuss, but it is so awful!"

Maggie Shannon

Clare and Maggie walked outside, and Clare hailed a black cab.

"Where to, Luv?" Asked the taxi driver.

Maggie gave an address in Agar Grove.

"I know, it," said the cabbie," the road further up past the gas towers?"

Maggie nodded, "Near to the Newmarket Ale House," she replied.

"Yes love, I've got it."

Clare and Maggie sat in the back of the taxi; Clare could see that Maggie was still upset.

"I was with him yesterday. I was only a few steps behind him today. It seems so callous. Shoving him under a builder's truck filled with bricks or something. He didn't have a chance."

"You talking about the RTA at Parliament this morning?"

asked the cabbie, "It's been all over the news. I usually drive around Parliament Square, but until I picked you two up it had been blocked off by the police. I reckon they had just re-opened it."

The cabbie went back to busily zigzagging across London. Clare and Maggie looked at London passing by. In a few minutes they were by Euston, where the cabbie said, "I'm bypassing Granary Square, we'd only get held up around there any case."

Soon, they're at Maggie's. Clare judged that it would be easy to grab another cab from that busy area, so she paid the taxi driver and then climbed the steps into Maggie's flat.

"It is so kind of you to come back with me," said Maggie, "Let me fix us some tea."

Clare decided that Maggie had settled down now. She thought she would talk about something else.

"So how did you get to know Andrew then?"

Maggie smiled, "Our families knew one another, Andrew was like a big brother to me. You can see I'm still loyal."

"Yes, I gather from some of the ladies that you'd flat shared with him when you were all at Oxford?"

"That's right. Most people think Andrew studied for a PPE Masters at Oxford, but it was actually a 2-year course to get a 2nd BA. He studied for a regular BA first, also at Oxford. But with PPE, there's a wrinkle that means if you wait five years after you get it, then it can be upgraded to an M.A.(Oxon)."

"I was studying there too, but I took the three-year PPE to get a regular BA. You can probably do the math to work out that Andrew helped me get into the house - er - flat in Oxford, mainly because our parents knew one another. I guess you'd say that 'I know where the bodies are buried' with Andrew, but - you know something - there really aren't any. Katherine and he both went to Harvard and by the time I'd finished Oxford he was married, in Parliament, and looking for an assistant. I jumped at the chance!"

"What is this strange campaign against him about?" asked Clare, "You must know about it?"

"Yes, he told me and Serena that there is someone trying to discredit him. He didn't think it was anything to do with the Right Bill, nor the BAME statement. He thinks that the BAME disruption has just become a convenient stick with which to flog him."

"I don't think he has told Serena, but Andrew thinks that the situation that someone wants to stop him on is the passing of the Vaccines Bill."

"Vaccines Bill?" asked Clare, "I'm not familiar with it."

"No, it has been kept quiet and has another title in the House, something about 'Protection of Healthcare Rights' or something similar.

Maggie brought the two teas across.

"Milk, no sugar?" she asked, and Clare nodded.

"It's builder's tea, I hope that is okay?"

"Perfect," answered Clare.

"Remember the Tiers that were used when the pandemic virus was at its worst? Tier 1, 2, 3 and 4 where 4 described the worst restrictions and 1 was originally for places like Cornwall which had very little early deaths?"

"I remember all too clearly," said Clare.

"Well, there' a consortium who are trying to use the Tiering as a blueprint for medical reform. They want different levels of vaccination and healthcare applied to Tier 3 and 4 people, compared with, say, Tier 1 and even a Tier 0."

"That sound bit like something out of Philip K. Dick!" Said Clare.

"Understand now why Andrew's favourite quote is from Bladerunner. You know - that piece where Rutger Hauer is on the roof in the torrents of rain.

"Yes - 'Attack ships on fire off the shoulder of Orion. I watched C-beams glitter in the dark near the Tannhäuser Gate'..."

"Well, imagine if they get your Protection of Healthcare Rights Bill passed. It becomes a licence to manage humanity. Decide who gets the good stuff - Tier Zero and who gets the life-shortening Tier Three or Tier Four protection." Forget about killing replicants - this is management of the human livestock.

"It always worried me when the politicians started talking about herd immunity, like the population were some form of cattle."

"Andrew told me he was concerned about this around

three weeks ago - just about when you arrived, Clare."

"He also reminded me of another scheme the had happened previously. It showed that Big Pharma or Big Chem could generate money-making schemes."

Transgenic

"You must have heard of the Monsanto cases?" asked Maggie, "Transgenic wheat?"

"I'm a little hazy on it, I remember it was something to do with Genetic Modification?" asked Clare.

"Oh, there was more to it than that. It opened an entire line of ethics questioning. Along the lines that the wheat crop was licensable - just like having to rent your Microsoft Office licenses every year, they invented something capable of forcing farmers to renew their license to grow their crops every year."

Clare asked, "So what did they do?"

Maggie answered, "It is something of a high horse of mine. In March 2015, the EU Patent Board granted patents for two plants which had been bred conventionally, not genetically engineered. These were a tomato (which had low water content) and a broccoli (which had enhanced glucosinolates). This set a precedent for patents to be granted on conventionally produced plants, and their seeds.

Clare asked, "Why is this a problem?"

Maggie continued, "If a patent is granted on a plant, the breeder not only 'owns' the plant, but gets subsequent rights on all its genetic traits. This is logical if applied to genetically engineered plants, as those plants are defined by the specific trait present only in that species."

Clare asked, "So they could then grab the rights to all apparent derivatives?"

Maggie nodded, "Yes, if patents are granted on the results of an open cross-breeding process, there will be many traits within the new plant which exist in other plants of the same species."

Maggie added, "So you are right, Clare; a single patent, say on a simple cross-bred tomato plant, can de facto cover hundreds of tomato varieties. The patent could also cover its seeds, and potentially the seeds of other varieties. This could ultimately lead to one patent owner having legal rights to all tomato plants and seeds, for instance."

"For the organic grower this raises the risk of a legal challenge when saving and swapping seeds. In effect the seed could come with a User Agreement, similar to one on a piece of software. "

"It means that plants and seeds can be patented if they are defined by a single DNA sequence that has been individually created. For example, a genetically engineered plant which has a gene inserted to make it herbicide resistant."

"This is like trying to patent all of nature?" asked Clare.

Maggie nodded, "Yes, then we get to patented seeds and plants. They can be considered the property of the patent owner – who can restrict their use and distribution. This puts our food supply in the hands of breeders, such as large agribusinesses, rather than the growers."

"All of this is happening while European patent laws are changing. It used to be that the results of conventional breeding processes were not patentable, but as of that ruling in 2015, they now are. This negates the whole intention behind the patenting process (known as Article 53b) and opens a wider pathway for patent granting.

Clare asked, "But who grants the plant patents?"

Maggie answered, "It is another comfortable little club: The European Patent Office (EPO). It is funded by the fees from patent applicants... wait for it... such as Syngenta and Monsanto and it is not answerable to the EU justice system.

"Instead, we have a closed shop system, where the EPO benefits from applications. Indeed, it is in its own vested interest to invite and grant patents."

"We can foresee a time when not just plants, but the very DNA of a seed could be patented – leading to control of our heritage seeds by the large agribusinesses.

Clare queried, " But that would affect farmers, small plant breeders, and ultimately the food supply chain."

Maggie nodded, "Yes. So that is precisely how biodiversity gets licensed. If the EPO continue to grant patents on seeds and plants bred by conventional processes, there are four important consequences:"

"Firstly, increased prices for farmers and consumers through the monopolisation of the seed market. That way small breeders will be edged out and the large agribusinesses will be free to determine the prices for their seeds, at the costs for farmers, and ultimately consumers. The three biggest companies Monsanto, Dupont and Syngenta already control around 50 percent of the global proprietary seed market. They are the ones who will decide which plants will be bred, grown and harvested - and how much they will cost."

"Is this a copycat strategy?" asked Clare.

"Not at all - each of the seed manufacturers jealously guard the way the create their proprietary seeds," replied Maggie, "And Secondly, contrary to the intended purpose, patents on seeds substantially hinder innovation. These patents can be used to block access to the biological diversity needed by other breeders and farmers to breed and grow. If permission is granted, a licence fee must be paid to the patent holder. And no further breeding can take place without permission of the patent holder. It would be like building an Office software product extension. You'd still have to pay Microsoft for the licensing rights."

"Wow! licenses to plant crops and vegetables!" said Clare

Maggie continued, "Third, As the patent owners spread their control, there will be less access to diverse agricultural varieties for breeders and farmers. Growers will have restricted choices and gradually the diversity of species and genome types will decrease.

"I can see that," said Clare, "Like stopping natural selection."

Maggie added, "Exactly, we can predict endangered food security. Given reduced diversity, crops are less capable of adapting to diseases or changing environmental conditions (such as climate change). High agricultural biodiversity is essential for our food security.

Maggie paused, then added, "That's not all though. There is the matter of the transgenic wheat monopoly that you referred to, Clare. Monsanto's MON 71800, which was made glyphosate-resistant via a CP4/maize EPSPS gene was the furthest developed. Monsanto received approval from the FDA for its use in food, but withdrew its EPA application in 2004, so the product was never marketed.

"But then Monsanto faced class action lawsuits after its genetically modified wheat was found in areas it was never approved to be in. Monsanto still claims it is mystified and that all its experimental GMO wheat was destroyed.

"The search for the rogue wheat is still ongoing. The GMO wheat, labeled MON 71800, was field tested by Monsanto in 16 US-states from 1998 to 2005.

"Monsanto had engineered 71800 to be resistant to glyphosate, the active ingredient in its herbicide Roundup, which it also manufactures. It had conceived the seed as a companion product to the herbicide. But it discontinued 71800, the company says, to focus on corn, cotton, and oilseeds.

"But now 71800 appears to have migrated from one of Monsanto's test plots. But how? And were there other farm fields pocked by GMO wheat? Had seeds of 71800 taken a ride on a container ship across the Pacific?

"Not exactly comforting to American wheat consumers

or producers. The American wheat export business is worth $8 billion and neither Europe nor Asia is interested in accepting GMO crops grown outside controls. This, along with Monsanto's political power, perhaps explains the secrecy around the story.

"So we still don't know where the abandoned mutant genetically adjusted wheat came from and Monsanto isn't talking. If MON 71800 escaped the lab then what other abandoned experiments could? If the planting was deliberate, who did it and why? Is it safe to eat the wheat?"

Maggie paused.

"So can you see how this could be applied to the Tiered vaccinations? A matter of 'Rights'."

Clare nodded, "Yes, similarly a few global conglomerates grab the 'Rights' to production and then build out a Tiered licensing vaccine model.

"But who are the people that want to support this, then?" asked Clare.

"It's a spinoff company, we think that are a subsidiary of Brant Industry. They are called the ever-so-friendly-sounding Elixanor."

Clare asked Maggie, "So what are we saying, then? That Andrew is fronting a Bill to push through the Vaccine licensing? That the UK Government can see it as a way to subtly manage the population? That somehow, some vested interests are trying to manipulate this?"

"No, to the contrary," said Maggie, "Andrew would not do such a thing. He would stand against it. Of that I am certain. That's what this Protection of Healthcare Rights Bill is supposed to be about.

"It is why they are trying to remove him, to put in place someone who will support their cause. That's why the allegations of mistresses and of inappropriate choices of words have surfaced. And back to Ian Harrison, he was the one sent to warn Andrew about all of this. My guess is that Harrison knew some of the upstream players and was considered too dangerous."

"It looks as if they could get away with this!" said Clare.

"We will need some pretty powerful players to stop them," said Maggie.

"Look," said Clare, "Both our cups! The tea leaves have formed the shape of a Triangle! You know something, I might be able to help you some more!"

Red Light District

I've seen all your qualifications
You got from the Sorbonne
And the painting you stole from Picasso
Your loveliness goes on and on, yes, it does

When you go on your summer vacation
You go to Juan-les-Pins
With your carefully designed topless swimsuit
You get an even suntan on your back, and on your legs
And when the snow falls, you're found in St. Moritz
With the others of the jet set
And you sip your Napoleon brandy
But you never get your lips wet, no, you don't

But where do you go to, my lovely
When you're alone in your bed?
Won't you tell me the thoughts that surround you?
I want to look inside your head, yes, I do

Your name it is heard in high places
You know the Aga Khan
He sent you a racehorse for Christmas
And you keep it just for fun, for a laugh, ha-ha-ha
They say that when you get married
It'll be to a millionaire

But they don't realize where you came from
And I wonder if they really care, or give a damn

Peter Sarstedt

Marion Charlotte gets minted

It was mid-evening by the time Clare got back to her own home in Caroline Terrace. She phoned Amanda to tell her about what Maggie had said.

"Hi Amanda, Clare here...A few more pieces of the jigsaw."

"Oh Hi, Clare, I'm in a hotel now, in Milan, actually. I'm with some people. Can I call you back in a while? Say around 10 o' clock Milan time?"

"That's fine," said Clare, "It'll be 9pm here. Ciao"

"Ciao Ciao," replied Amanda.

Clare decided to call Christina, to get some ideas.

"Hi Christina, I think I've found out some more."

Clare told Christina about Andrew Brading and the Protection of Healthcare Rights Bill and explained that she had found out that Maggie Shannon had known Andrew Brading from a flat share in Oxford, long before he became an MP, and even before he married Charlotte.

Katherine commented, "There's nothing particularly suspicious there, although the Protection of Healthcare Rights Bill is probably a camouflage for something else."

Clare went on to describe the two women now interlinked with Andrew Brading. Shanell Kinkead and Natasha Makarovna.

"Tasha?" said Christina, "I think I know her - from my time in Bulgaria. She was another one of the Russians sent there to play with NATO equipment. They had a nickname for us - *Kifla* - which means 'loaves' but was their slang for selfie models. It implied that we were there to get selfies of ourselves standing by Bulgarian scenes. Tasha was one hot loaf! This changes the game though. It tells me that there are Russians involved.

"What about Shanell Kinkaid- I think she is Jamaican?"

"No idea, but I know someone who might have an idea...Marion Charlotte. Why don't I call her?"

"That would be great; and I think you know Marion better than I do from that Raven business."

"Okay - let's talk again later," said Christina, "Maybe about 9 pm?"

"I can't then, I'll be talking to Amanda, but I could call you back when we are done?"

"That works for me...Speak later!" said Christina.

Christina looked through her phone to find Marion Charlotte's number, and called.

"My god," says Marion, "I was only thinking about you the other day. How are you? I can guess what this is about. It's all started up again. Minerva the listening station. They have moved it and given it a different name. I'm quite worried actually, in case they want to call me up."

Christina spoke softly, "You don't need to worry from us, but we noticed that the listening station was running again. You know it is in a different location?"

"Yes, it is near to the American Embassy now, in one of those blocks of apartments. London is crazy. You can buy a whole floor of an apartment block and no-one bats an eye-lid."

"Yes, we thought that is what they have done. Lessons from the money launderers, I suggest."

"That's right, the oligarchs have bought so much of London that a mere splash on a luxury block goes almost unnoticed."

"I'm interested in couple of people. Shanell Kinkead and Natasha Makarovna?"

"I know them both. I think you've met one of them too, Christina - Don't you already know Natasha?"

"That's right, we go back a long way."

"Well, the other one, Shanell, is Jamaican and described as an actress. Her main specialty is honey trap, though, and she has caught a few men in her time. She works through the Jennifer Sussex agency - Miel Doux Artists, just like I did."

"Did?" asked Christina, "You've stopped?"

"Yes," said Marion, "After that scrape at the Lanchester, with the guns and all, I decided I'd better find another pursuit. I'm married now, to Lord Edgar Hinton of Gloucestershire."

"Wow, that sounds impressive! So are you a Lady?"

"I am! Lady Hinton of Gloucestershire. I know what you probably think, and I'm sure most of it is true. But Edgar is both dashing and kind and seems to have a very good supply of money from his hardware manufacturing business. I am settled now, and thankful for it."

"Congratulations!" said Christina.

"Thank you," answered Marion, "Now how else can I help you today before we part company again for a long time!"

Christina smiled; she knew that her call had brought back bad memories for Marion.

"Do you know whether the two ladies have ever been around an Andrew Brading?"

"I doubt it, " said Marion, "Brading is well known as totally loyal to his wife Katherine. Anything I've attended in the past when Brading showed up, he was always alone or with his wife. I place him as steadfast and not easily swayed."

"So why would there be photos of him with other women?" asked Christina.

"I expect they have been manipulated; see if you can get

the original digital copies; I'm sure your friends Bigsy and Clare will be able to spot any irregularities. Trust me, there will be some!"

"That's brilliant, so you are telling me that the compromising photographs are probably fakes. That's very useful to know."

"Sad to say, deepfakes were becoming increasingly a way that the old Minerva operated, when it was trying to compromise MPs in the past. Some things don't change."

"Okay and who was running the old Minerva?"

"It was set up to look like the Americans, with all those Junior CIA agents, but it was really the Kremlin looking for ways to grab power. But I thought you realised that when we last met?"

"You know it is called Medusa now?" asked Christina.

"No, I didn't actually. I haven't kept up with all of that business!"

"Marion, Thank You. Er - I should say Lady Hinton, Thank You; I hope I won't need to bother you about this anymore!"

Marion said, "Thank you, Christina and *Paka-Paka*."

Christina laughed; Marion had just said 'bye-bye' in perfect colloquial Russian.

Amanda is not shopping

It was 9pm and Clare reached for the phone call from Amanda.

"Hey, so why are you in Milan?"

"I had to meet someone. They were a little bit shy about giving out information. Don't worry - it's nothing to do with your case, though."

"London, Paris, Milan... Are you sure you're not just on a giant shopping expedition?"

"Well, it is Fashion Week here now. It's amazing how Milan goes over entirely to fashion, whilst in London the whole event can be swallowed up in a couple of major venues!"

Clare replied, "Okay, well I found out a few things. Let me summarise."

Clare flipped open a small black notepad.

- Brading is under pressure
- They are trying to discredit him over his misinterpreted Black Asian Minority Ethnics statement two weeks ago in the House.
- As Secretary of State for Internal Affairs, Brading is trying to pass a Fundamental Rights Bill that is at least as good as the one passed by the United Kingdom.
- Someone has sent in an investigative reporter to trip him up
- Someone from an aggressive lobby has also sent him threats via the now deceased Ian Harrison, a Special Advisor who was deliberately killed by a cyclist outside Parliament.
- Someone is starting rumours that Brading has been seen cheating on his wife.
- There are photographs, but Marion Charlotte suggests they may be manipulated.
- One of the women implicated has links back to the FSB.
- Minerva is active again as Medusa, to corrupt and then blackmail MPs and other key figures
- The next Secretary of State for Internal Affairs Bill is for the Protection of Healthcare Rights but Brading is against it
- The Protection of Healthcare Rights Bill introduces the so-called Vaccine Law and Healthcare Passporting - Brading considers both to be immoral and unethical.
- The Vaccine Law can become a huge money spinner for a ruthless corporation.
- There are rumours that Brant and Elixanor are lobbying to pass the Protection of Healthcare Rights Bill.
- Brading's co-workers, Maggie Shannon and Serena McMillan are extremely loyal. Everyone else (such as Lottie and Tessa) only have good words for Andrew Brading.
- His wife, Katherine, is lovely and does not suspect anything amiss.

Amanda smiles, "Wow - that is comprehensive, Clare, you and the folk from the Triangle have been busy. Now, do we know more about the leverage over Brading?"

Clare answered, "No, but I assume it links to the two women and becomes a simple blackmail. Getting the Bill passed with its innocuous title then gives an unscrupulous Corporation a carte-blanche to manufacture and ship the vaccine. From a politician's point of view, it can also bring about tiered response to vaccines. It could make huge sums of money."

Amanda answered, "Yes, but think about a Russian angle on this too. I suspect they will be up to their usual tricks of money laundering. Think about it. Fast Moving Consumer Goods can be a mechanism for operating money laundering. Remember when car washes and then, later, apartments were used to launder? Now it is FMCG that provides the opportunity.

"Waste goods was so 1980s as exemplified with The Sopranos and then Breaking Bad with the car washes in the early 21st Century. Later a few property developers in Miami, London and West Coast America became stained by one man's laundering reputation. We all know who I am talking about.

"There still has to be ways to move the big money around and to clean it in the process. Hooking into the supply chain of FMCG related to vaccines makes an easy option, especially because it is being handled in such large quantities. I guess you'll tell the others about this?"

"Tomorrow night, answered Clare, I'll be visiting the Triangle offices again."

Balls Brothers, Bishopsgate

Roger Slater had arranged to meet Matt Stevens at Balls Brothers, in Bishopsgate. There were several Balls Brothers to choose from, but he wanted it to be one away from the usual hubbub of Parliament. This was more an Institute of Directors alternative hangout and Slater felt at home here.

He knew that Stevens was fond of his drink but needed to be somewhere he could keep up without it looking too obvious. The wines topped out at around £50 per bottle and he could probably pick a nice mid-range red - something like a La Galiniere Merlot, du Donjon, Languedoc, which would do nicely and could be replenished at will.

Going to a cocktail bar ran the risk of alcohol overshoot, with Matt whizzing his way through a row of slammers. This could look respectable, but Matt could also get gently pickled and thus better able to answer Roger's questions.

A few minutes after the appointed time, Matt breezed into the bar. Roger had already ordered and was sitting with the first bottle of red wine. He poured Matt a hefty glass.

"Hey, Cheers, Roger! How are you anyway? I had a bit of a binge yesterday with a few of the lads; we finished in Parly late and then headed over to Soho. Things got a tiny bit out of control and I ended up sleeping it off on my friend's sofa. He'd a supply of fresh brand-new shirts so I showered and put one on. Look carefully; it's still got the 'you pulled' lines on the front." He pointed to the remains of some sharp creases where the shirt had been folded into a packet.

Roger smiled and thought of the story he would need to tell Matt to get him to open up. He decided to talk about tax havens.

"Your MP has been busy recently with a few foreign flights? I noticed he'd been to The Caymans and then to Luxembourg. I'm not telling you anything that isn't already out there, but there's those who do and those who don't. I sometimes get a queasy feeling that something has gone badly wrong with the world economy and that's why these moves are necessary, but I'm never sure."

"Don't let it slip through your fingers, is what I say, " replied Matt, "I mean I've seen it all since I've been in Parly. I studied tax and tax havens before I came here. But if I once thought some of it was dubious, I can understand now why powerful governments don't just close them down. Apart from anything else there's the whole eco-system to consider,"

Roger poured another glass of wine, "Yes the byzantine world hosted – only on paper, you understand – by the Grand Duchy of Luxembourg, where Amazon has located its European headquarters, slashing its tax bills around the world. Remember how in 2011, Amazon revealed that the US Internal Revenue Service was chasing it for $1.5bn in back taxes."

Matt nodded, he gestured with his wine glass and Roger

noticed the red wine slide nearly over the edge of the glass, "I know, it's amazing how these stories flicker in and out of the press, but little gets done. There must be too many people dependent upon it now for the threats to have any real impact. It's similar with Google - The most famous phrase in Google's corporate philosophy, 'Don't be evil,' was been almost entirely removed from the technology giant's code of conduct."

Roger agreed, "Yes, when Google restructured into Alphabet in 2015, it replaced its simple language with vague and less specific wording such as "ethical business conduct". "The Google Code of Conduct is one of the ways we put Google's values into practice," the updated guidelines begins.

"Snore," said Matt, "It's been deliberately made to sound bland."

Roger added, "And then there was Apple - achieving in 2013 what Senator Carl Levin called, the 'holy grail' of tax avoidance, setting up offshore corporations legally incorporated in Ireland and the US – but for tax purposes, not resident anywhere. Apple shifted $74bn into one of these subsidiaries between 2009 and 2012, paying just 2% in tax on it."

"A bit more wine?" asked Roger and signalled to the nearby barman, who walked another bottle of the La Galiniere over to their table. He quickly uncorked it and poured two even handed glasses.

"Thank you," said Roger, grateful that he had Muesli for breakfast that morning.

Matt continued, "Tax havens' defenders say they smooth the flow of capital around the world, removing roadblocks and red tape. But what are those roadblocks? Taxes, regulation and democratic laws. Havens are places where you can put your wealth in order to escape the rules at home. Those rules might be around tax, or criminal laws, or rules about transparency and disclosure, or financial regulations. You don't have to put your wealth itself in the tax haven. It is the legal structure that owns the wealth – the shell company, the trust, or whatever – that usually matters."

Matt paused, took a glug of wine and then continued, "The asset itself – the thing you own – can be anything, anywhere. It could be a painting or a Learjet or a Swiss bank account, or a luxury home in Mayfair that the owner – let's say a Ukrainian oligarch – is currently using for the benefit of his daughter. Instead of owning the house directly, the oligarch owns the house via an intermediate structure in a tax haven. The land registry records won't list the oligarch's name, but the name of some anonymous offshore shell company. And when you go to find out who owns that company, you'll come up against a brick wall."

Roger noticed that Matt had now acquired red lips from the wine, "Yes, This can all take a bit of getting used to, even for people with wealth."

Matt added, "A few years ago, when Hurricane Ivan headed towards the Cayman Islands it sent a stream of light aircraft racing to Miami. They contained computer hard disks, relating to a large slice of the world's Cayman-held wealth. (Banking assets in Cayman account for nearly a 15th of the world's $30tn in banking assets.) When the storm passed, they flew them all back again."

Matt questioned Roger, "You know how transfer pricing

works?"

Roger wasn't sure, "Go on, explain," he said.

Matt began, "Well, there are many tricks used to shift money offshore, and a pinstriped army of accountants and lawyers to help people do it. The commonest technique is one called transfer pricing, employed by pretty much every multinational. Let's say MyCorp picks and packs a container-load of bananas in banana-capital Ecuador, and it costs the company $1,000. It sells them to a French supermarket for $3,000.

"The obvious question is: Which country gets to tax the $2,000 profit – France, Ecuador? The answer is, 'Wherever the multinational's accountants decide.'"

Matt continued, "So MyCorp sets up three companies, all of which it owns: EcuadorCo, HavenCo (in a zero-tax haven) and FranceCo. EcuadorCo sells the container to HavenCo for $1,000, and HavenCo sells it on to FranceCo for $3,000. That's basically it. (The bananas themselves don't go anywhere near the tax haven: this is all just paper shuffling in New York or London.)

Matt paused, sipped his wine and then continued, "But it's a shell game. Blink and you miss what happened. It cost EcuadorCo $1,000 to pick and pack the container, and they sold it on for $1,000. So EcuadorCo records zero profits, meaning no taxes. Likewise, FranceCo buys it for $3,000 and sells it to the supermarket for $3,000. Again, no profits, and no taxes. HavenCo is the key to the jigsaw. It bought the container for $1,000 and sold it for $3,000 – a $2,000 profit. But it is based in a haven, so it pays no tax. In short, all the profits have been stripped out of France and Ecuador and shovelled into the haven. Whoopee!

Then a decent slug of the red, "Of course, it isn't that shimple, defences have been erected against this kind of sharp practice, but the lawyers find 'legal' waysh to get around them, in a constant game of cat and mouse. This all transfers wealth away from taxpayers towards corporate shareholders. A kind of wealth extraction scheme. "

Roger noticed that Matt's speech had started to slur. He was also waving his arms more furiously.

Roger added, "But let's not forget all the criminality that tax haven secrecy facilitates. When multinationals use these platforms, they provide these places with immense political cover. If you are a tiny bit illegal you can hide inside the well-fortified shelter. A case of who gets the cream and who doesn't."

"Or who getsh the wine, here let me pour us both some more," said Matt.

"Have you heard about poor old Andrew Brading?" asked Roger.

"Oh yes, I think I know that one. As a matter of fact, we were all talking about him the other day," continued Matt, "About his time in Thailand."

"Oh, I don't think I've heard that one," said Roger.

With a slurred voice, and another glass of red wine, Matt continued his recollection of the conversation they had all had in the Opium bar in Chinatown a few days earlier.

Emily Karankawa

Pete Burr's phone rang.

"Jake Lambers," he read.

"Hi Jake, I thought we'd seen the last of one another?" joked Pete.

"Don't panic, I think we have," answered Jake, "But I was hoping you could make an introduction to one of your friends for one of our group."

"Go on..." Asked Pete, "But I'm not going to be surrounded by gangsters or soldiers, am I?

"No this is cool. I was hoping you could ask one of your contacts - preferable an American - to invite Bigsy to the new setup, however briefly. You could say he was an expert in surveillance or something."

"And why would I do that?" asked Pete, good-naturedly.

"We'd like to take a quick peek around inside Medusa station, and an invitation is quicker than us doing a breaking and entry kind of thing. Look - I seem to remember you telling me that you'd once dated someone there - Emily something?"

"Emily Karankawa - yes she's American but I think would like to be thought of as a native American. Her people lived in Texas for many centuries. She's the real deal."

"Pete, I detect a hint of longing there! Do you think you could run an introduction for Bigsy?"

"Phew, I'll have to walk across that burning bridge again," answered Pete, "Honestly - I've got some butterflies at the thought."

"Right then, that's settled - We'll have to put in some good words for you too, with Emily. Not too many good men get a second chance!"

Pete smiled, "Oh - I guess I can do it - and if Bigsy or you can get me another date with her, then that's a bonus," he said wistfully, "Come on; give me the details!"

"They are in a email. I'm just pressing Enter," answered Jake, "And Pete, 'Cupid' is The Triangle's other name. Although, come to think of it Bigsy would make a better tooth fairy."

eMail chain

On XX XXX XXXX, at 14:37, Pete Burr <pete.k.burr@hot_mail.com> wrote:

Useful Contact: D. Barlow

Hi Emily,

Long time, eh? I hope you are well.

I thought your workplace might be interested in this guy who I met. He's a security specialist named Dave Barlow and he seems to know everything about surveillance.

I've attached his details below, but I can fix an introduction at your office if that's okay?

He's said he's prepared to travel although he lives in London in any case.

Best wishes,

Pete x

Peter Burr

\<Attached Dave Barlow.Vcd\>

On XX XXX XXXX, at 15:05, Emily Karankawa
<emily.karankawa@XXXXXX.com> wrote:

Re: Useful Contact: D. Barlow

Hi Pete,

I still have visions of those shorts.

Thanks for the tip off. I'd like to see him. Can you send an invitation to both him and me for a get-together, say next Tuesday at 13:00 at my offices?

You are welcome to also attend.

Best wishes,

Emily

Emily Karankawa

On XX XXX XXXX, at 16:18, Pete Burr <pete.k.burr@hot_mail.com> wrote:

Re: Re: Useful Contact: D. Barlow

Hi Emily,

Meeting arranged for Tuesday. Dave has confirmed.

See attached.

Best wishes,

Pete x

Peter Burr

<Attached Dave Barlow(Bigsy)/Emily Karankawa meeting.iCal>

Bigsy fails the interview

Tuesday at Riverside Quay. Bigsy and Pete Burr arrived and asked the concierge to buzz through for them to Emily Karankawa. The concierge looked like any other for an apartment block, and there were other bustlings of package deliveries, laundry and even car hire returns being processed.

They were both photographed, given a visitor lanyard and told to wait by the elevators.

"This isn't quite like a regular apartment block, observed Bigsy. Photographs and Lanyards?"

"I havn't ever visited before," said Pete, "I've only seen the outside."

The elevator door pinged, and Emily peered across to them both.

"Welcome to Riverside Quay," she said, gesturing for them both to get into the lift.

There was then what Bigsy judged to be an awkward moment whilst they all stood looking at the doors on the way to Emily's floor.

"It's right at the top," she said, "We can see parliament, the American Embassy and flights coming in along the Thames."

"Ideal spot for a listening station," thought Bigsy. He was working out that it looked as if Emily and Pete would like a few minutes alone to talk out some things. This could play to his advantage.

"We've got CR07 booked," said Emily, "Any coffee or water before we get started?"

They came out onto a busy floor. Bigsy was aware of the all-around windows and that the area had been partitioned into a series of pods. There was a corridor close to the main supporting wall and there, inset, were several glass fronted meeting rooms. The adjacent pods were filled with people wearing headsets and with either one or two monitor screens. Busy could see that some of them displayed text, but others showed picture in picture videos. Unlike some noisy 'help desks' that Bigsy had visited in his technical line of work, this was a fairly hushed environment, which gave Bigsy the impression of more incoming than outgoing calls.

"They were soon seated and Emily brought in one of her surveillance specialists to interview Bigsy. Bigsy knew he needed to be 'good, but not that good' in the interview. He wanted the interviewer to say that he was okay, but not exceptional. Bigsy dialled back his knowledge as he fiddled with the conference room's projector mouse.

The interview started and Gavin, the specialist asked a few framing questions to calibrate Bigsy's knowledge.

"I couldn't find much about you on the Internet - I tried the usual places; Facebook, LinkedIn and Twitter..."

"No, I prefer to go dark," answered Bigsy.

"Not too dark?" asked Gavin, referring to the Dark Web."

"No, I steer clear of anything with an x or a z in it," answered Bigsy.

They both laughed. Bigsy added, "or anything with pictures of bears, however fancy."

Gavin remained quiet at Bigsy's last remark which was an oblique reference to Russia's security initiatives codenamed Fancy Bear and Cozy Bear.

Gavin began asking Bigsy specific questions about security protocols, which Bigsy found straightforward enough to answer.

Bigsy made a quick reference to a fired director from the Cybersecurity & Infrastructure Security Agency (CISA) after the election beset with Russian hacking rumours and he could see that Gavin was somewhat deflated.

"It's all got so confusing, said Bigsy, "One simple little thing like the GRU Unit 26165 gets given so many different names. Fancy Bear, APT28, Pawn Storm, Sofacy Group, Sednit, Tsar Team (by FireEye) and STRONTIUM (by Microsoft). It's too much - but I guess everyone needs to have a proprietary name for the hackers?" Bigsy decided he would blow up the next question. He fiddled with the white Apple mouse some more, flicking it from hand to hand as if agitated. When he stopped, Pete quietly removed it from Bigsy's arm range.

"So, what do you think of Guccifer?" asked Gavin.

"Goosy Fur? how do you spell that?" asked Bigsy, knowing that Guccifer 2.0 was a well-known faux-Romanian hacker.

"No, Guccifer 2.0 That's G-U-C-C-I-F-E-R," replied Gavin, now certain that he wouldn't hire Bigsy.

"Nope, I'm drawing a blank, said Bigsy, "Unless it's a code name for Dimitri Badin, the GRU officer and suspected member of APT28. He's the main suspect for the cyber-attacks on the Bundestag?"

Gavin looks at Emily, he was wondering who was interviewing whom.

"Emily, I think we are more or less finished here. Dave Barlow shows a great deal of promise, but I think still needs some more comprehensive depth before he would be able to help us."

Bigsy decided to put up a small amount of resistance, "I hope you can see I'm keen and fairly well informed? It would be great to work for you, and I'm sure I could learn quickly."

He decided to wreck his chances, "I'm sure I could help you stand up some significant resistance to those damn Russian hackers."

Emily stood, "Dave, Pete, thank you both very much for coming in today, and at such short notice too. We can let you know soon after this meeting of our final decision."

"Er, I can take it. I don't think I've passed, have I, Gavin? Don't worry, I just really appreciated the opportunity."

Gavin could not play poker and shook his head, "Sorry, mate," he said.

Bigsy looked suitably crestfallen.

"Look - no hard feelings, if I could walk out with Gavin so I can get some feedback and maybe, Pete, you could be escorted by Emily?"

Bigsy wicked slyly at Pete and suggested that he and Gavin remain in the conference room for another five minutes. Emily and Pete walked to the door and Bigsy could see that they were pleased to have a minute alone.

"I realised I'd blown it on that Guccifer question," said Bigsy, "Were there any other things you didn't like?"

"Honestly, not really, you were almost too good to be true, like you knew what I was going to ask you," answered Gavin.

"Well, keep me in your address book, you never know when I might come in useful!" answered Bigsy, "It's been a privilege to meet you!"

Gavin smiled, "I guess the others will be downstairs by now. You can't keep your colleague Pete waiting."

They had walked back to the elevator. Bigsy had successfully swapped the Apple mouse in the conference room with the one in his pocket. That should give them some ability to hack into the system.

Street level. Gavin and Bigsy shook hands. Bigsy walked back over to Pete, eyebrows raised, "Well?"

"Yes," beamed Pete, "A date, this Friday! Thank you,"

Straight Ahead

Have you heard baby what's the wind blown round?
Have you heard baby?
A whole lot a people comin' right on down

Communication, yeah, is comin' on strong
It don't give damn baby
If your hair is short or long

Jimi Hendrix

How long will that watch battery last?

Bigsy was back at The Triangle's offices. He used a computer to call up the mouse he had left in Medusa and sure enough; it appeared on his screen. He had adapted it with a small computer placed inside. It was enough to get onto the intranet of Medusa and to send packets of data back to The Triangle.

Jake and Christina were looking over his shoulder and looked impressed.

"I used an Apple Watch to make a computer small enough to fit inside the Mouse," explained Bigsy, "That mouse can even tell the time!"

"And the weather I expect," said Jake.

"Let's see what we can find then?" said Bigsy, and he started up a primitive looking 'green on black' session on his Triangle office computer.

Within minutes, he was browsing some useful looking report abstracts. Let's see what we've got," he said.

"Ahah, here's one about Facebook: 'Following Facebook's announcement that it would give Congress the details of 3,000 advertisements bought by a Russian agency to sway the US election, Russia threatened to ban the company from the country during its upcoming election.'"

"Well, that's a turnaround if ever I saw one," said Jake.

Bigsy continued, "The special services have always played a crucial role in the Soviet Union and in modern Russia, and nowadays deploy 'active measures', from propaganda, espionage to actual violence."

"That's exactly what we were taught in Akademy," said Christina.

Bigsy looked at another one, "How about, in its new report, the Bellingcat server suggests that the Russian Federation is attempting to influence European politics by reaching out to youth organisations of European political parties?"

"Ha!" said Christina, "Some of the instruction given is so primitive. I remember from our training. They explained to us what a cocktail party was like, but it seemed to come from a 1950s textbook! I don't think the west has much to fear from that!"

Bigsy said, "Here's another one: A London-based think tank says Moscow's bid to establish a bloc of four neutral or pro-Moscow Balkan states has experienced major setbacks in Macedonia and Montenegro."

"I'm not surprised by that one," said Christina, "The old USSR was always territorial. I'd say Russian plans could be broken if they don't get this under control. Two pinch points. The Balkans and the Adriatic."

Bigsy added, "Russia could be on a mission to restore its Soviet or imperial glory and to prevent liberal democratic values from taking root in the Russian political system. Yet the tools used are precisely the ones that emerged during the liberal '90s and until recently were not subject much to government interventions: the online media and tech sectors. Nowadays, the Russian government builds up many sophisticated tools of online propaganda."

"Dreams of old men," said Christina, "The new guard took over Russia after the fall of the USSR. They took over the banks and then bought up all the state industries at knock-down prices. If powerful old-guard people were in the way, they got pushed out of windows. That's why there's so many gold-encrusted young oligarchs with model wives and a string of mistresses. Russia had to reinvent the Mafia to run everything. VV said, 'I'll give you this thing,' (like an oil refinery) 'you go figure out how to make money.' And if anyone won't play along, there're dozens of hungry young people waiting to grab everything that's on offer, backed up by the Kremlin. Do as you are told, pay your tithes and don't step out of line."

"VV?" asked Bigsy, "Vladimir Vladimirovich Putin," answered Christina, "or Vova"

"Here's one about leak spinning," said Bigsy, "The Citizen Lab group at the University of Toronto's Munk School of Public Affairs published a report describing a new case of the so-called "tainted leak;" stealing, doctoring and then publishing data presenting them as authentic."

"Yes, always make more out of a leak, use it to support your agenda, said Christina, "Akademy 101."

Bigsy said, "Here's one we already know about: 'A study reveals a major phishing operation of the group of hackers called CyberBerkut, targeting over 200 subjects from 39 countries, including members of governments from Europe and Eurasia, ambassadors, high-ranking military officers, CEOs of energy companies and members of civil society. Although the Citizen Lab group does not demonstrate a clear link to the Kremlin, it shows in the report that it has key links to Fancy Bear or APT28, previously accused of the attacks on the Democratic National Committee and the campaign of Hilary Clinton by the US intelligence agencies and cybersecurity firms.'"

"We really should go to that site and have a look around," said Jake.

Bigsy added, "It goes on, 'Russia's hybrid challenges continue to threaten security across the Euro-Atlantic community, which is why there is such a need for a comprehensive, coordinated strategy that will engage both the nations of NATO and the EU, and the institutions themselves. Four key categories of hybrid threats can be laid out together with corresponding recommendations; the categories are: low-level use of force, cyberattacks, economic and political coercion and subversion, and information warfare.'"

"A lot of this stuff is since Putin came to power. He is a great believer in asymmetric warfare and the use of lies," said Christina, "They gave us extra sessions on some of this near the end of our training. The media used to support it was in a different league from the old 1950s and 1960s textbook content of a lot of the stuff."

"This one is quite amusing, " said Bigsy, "Pot calling the kettle black: 'The United Russia party issued a report investigating whether and how the United States tried to influence the elections in Russia. Leonid Levin, the chair of the State Duma's committee on information technologies, presented the report in the Parliament. According to him, media outlets like CNN (which does not broadcast in Russia), Voice of America or RFE/RL were part of an attempt to interfere with the domestic electoral process in Russia'"

"Hilarious," said Christina, "Great use of mis-direction."

"Whoa," said Bigsy, "What about this one, then? 'In the NATO Strategic Communications Centre of Excellence official journal, James Rogers and Andriy Tyushka describe the Russian anti-hegemonic offensive seeking to desynchronise political developments in the regions close to Europe, to distort European perceptions of reality, split the Atlantic democracies from the European continent and saturate the vacuum with false and fictitious narrative. There are also chapters analysing the influence of Russian academic, political and public spheres on the politicisation of information warfare or examining the role of botnets in propaganda dissemination.'"

"And I thought it was Trump that was using reality distortion and Fake News! It looks as if everyone is at it!" said Jake.

"And one that strikes to the core regarding Medusa," said Bigsy, "Look, they say: 'Russia is the only country to date to have definitively combined cyberwarfare with conventional warfare. As far as the Kremlin thinks, geeks and hackers now rank alongside soldiers and spies as weapons of the state.'"

"I have to agree," said Christina, "The West needs to have

zero tolerance for cyberattacks. Where there is evidence that individuals or countries are behind cyberattacks, they should feel the full force of the law. That would not only send a political message, but also deliver a blow to these activities."

Bigsy added, "Her we go, 'It is necessary to adopt an integrated approach to cybersecurity. At present, the various aspects of what constitutes 'cyberwarfare' are not being addressed together, which could lead to gaps in security. Western countries should increase funding for cybersecurity education programmes, especially when we consider Russia's cyberattacks succeeded several times because individuals fell for phishing scams via e-mails.'"

"Yes, it's like socially engineered attacks, still relying on human frailties," observed Jake.

Christina nodded, "Yes, we were taught that civil and military contingency planning should include scenarios on which access to the Internet is limited and the internet infrastructure should get at least as much defence and protection as other strategic assets."

"Oh yes, and something else," said Bigsy, "I managed to intercept a couple of emails to Emily. One of them had copies of the original photographs of Andrew Brading as attachments. I'll be digging into them soon."

"How long will that watch battery last?" asked Jake.

Love nest scandal

Andrew was awake early. He'd heard the early news on the World Service, before Radio 4 had re-awoken. He seemed to be the main story of the morning. Someone had leaked a lot of information about him and then restitched it in a most unrealistic manner.

He glanced down towards his phone. There were some missed calls and a few texts from Serena and Maggie. He knew that they must have heard the story.

Now he needed to see it written before he responded.

He started his laptop and selected The Echo's home page. There was his photo, from yesterday judging by the suit and tie he was wearing. And there were a couple of old photos too. One he recognised and another he didn't.

He worked out that one of them was from someone's Instagram but the other one wasn't anything he recognised. It showed him with a slim dark-haired woman. They were crossing a street into what appeared to be a hotel. They were holding hands. Characteristically, the Echo had done two blow-up circles from the photo. One was of the hotel sign and the other of the hands linked together.

He decided he would need to read the story. The headline ran as:

Brading BAME Beauty break.

MP-shocker as BAME-critic in love-nest scandal.

He read the story. It was densely packed with lies. He had never met this woman. He had never visited the hotel described. The article further described him as a free spirit (true) who didn't mind the occasional magic mushroom (not true). The photo he recognised was of him with an old girlfriend - Jan - with whom he had backpacked to Thailand. It was unimaginable that Jan would tell tales about him, when they split, they were still fond of one another and it was mainly because Jan had been offered such a fantastic job in L.A. That caused them to part company. And anyway, Katherine knew all about Jan, so there was no angle there.

Andrew decided he'd better alert Katherine to what was happening. She was away on business, in Brussels, but he knew she would be awake and probably already at work. The hour was later in Europe in any case.

He called, "Hi Katherine,"

"I've seen it. I didn't call you because it was so early. I don't believe any of it, by the way."

"Thank you, Katherine, I was just going to reassure you of that. It's someone's idea of a vendetta. Let me tell you it won't work. There are three pictures. One of me (yesterday). One of me with Jan - many years ago and another of me holding hands with a woman I've never seen before, allegedly going into a hotel."

"Can you sue?" asked Katherine, "Defamation, Libel? I mean it must be a hatchet piece, I'm going to use my contacts to find out who wrote it."

"No need. I'm pretty certain it was a Roger Slater; that was the rumour going around here, anyway. He's a freelance hack and well-known for hatchet pieces, usually on businesspeople. He must be branching out. By the way, the woman is Jamaican, so I expect they will link this up with the BAME stories."

"Don't worry - remember I'm media trained," said Katherine, "And in the business, so to speak. You should get someone to warn that woman that she becomes an accomplice in the Libel if she says anything more, by the way. I'll only say we are in love and that I don't believe a word of the story. I'll also say that there is no other story. I suggest you get legal advice as well, so you don't accidentally ruin any case against the Echo. Love you, gotta rush, Bye."

Andrew breathed a sigh of relief that Katherine was so instantly understanding and also so practical about the situation. He had one less thing to worry about now and some useful suggestions about what to do when he got to the House.

He called Serena back.

"Hi Serena, I've seen it now. Don't believe a word of it. Katherine knows and will support me. She suggests I get a lawyer to help build a case against the Echo."

"Okay, Andrew, I'll inform the office that it's a made-up story and tell everyone to stay tight-lipped. It begs the question though, what do they want to get you for?"

"I know, I guess it's one of my current string of Bills," answered Andrew.

Deepfaked

Clare was back in Parliament. She noticed the additional reporters hanging around and the media teams setting up across on the grass across from Victoria Tower. She realised that they were all interested in following the Andrew Brading story now and she was quite pleased that they still didn't recognise her.

Then she caught Rachel Crosby from the corner of her eye.

"Hello, Clare," began Rachel, "It looks as if my prediction has come true. That Slater is ruthless. Where do you think he dug out that story from?"

Clare looked at Rachel and tried to assess if she was genuinely quizzical or just fishing for some quotes.

"Off the record," said Clare, knowing that would give her a few sentences which Rachel couldn't attribute.

"Well played," said Rachel, "I don't believe the story, so I'm interested in getting to the truth."

"None of the allegations in the story are true," answered

Clare, "I'm going to try to get to the bottom of this. How about we cut a deal?"

"Sharp for a 'new girl!' answered Rachel.

"Yes, I've played with media before. I know how it works. You stand by for an exclusive that counters the allegations against Andrew. I know the moves, but we're not there yet."

"You sound confident?" queried Rachel.

"Oh, very!" said Clare, knowing that to waver now would diminish her position.

"Okay, you've got my number. Come to me first and I'll splash it across the paper!" said Rachel. "But every day the story loses value,"

"I know," said Clare. In her bag she had a memory stick containing the photographs which Bigsy had filtered from Emily Karankawa's email. Bigsy had looked at them on his computers and shown Clare how to prove to Serena and Maggie that they were fakes.

She moved towards Andrew Brading's office, ready to reveal the photographs. She wasn't even sure whether Andrew had seen them all.

Inside, Serena was looking despondent.

"Hi Clare, we had had so much bad coverage today. The photograph clinched it. They are now saying that Andrew is hypocritical. Seeing this woman - Shanell Kinkaid a Jamaican - with Andrew and yet him allegedly saying anti BAME statements in Parliament. My head explodes.

Clare smiled, "We should look at the originals then - it is part of a set of photographs. There are plenty of things wrong."

Clare placed the memory stick into her laptop. "Don't ask me how, but I've managed to acquire the originals of the photographs. There are two of Andrew with Shanell and three others of Andrew with another woman, Natasha Makarovna,"

"Who?" asked Andrew, "I have never heard of this woman,"

"So we will soon be able to prove," said Clare, "My friend Bigsy has been busy with some analysis software. Nothing fancy, just Adobe Lightroom. He imported the pictures and then showed me how to look at the hidden information. Here we are:

Clare showed the five photographs as if they were a little film strip on her laptop. To the right was displayed a series of numbers and other information.

"This other data is called the EXIF information. It stands for Exchangeable Image File format and it is recorded by the camera taking the picture and includes the lens, the shutter speed and so on. Let's look at your photos, with the two different women."

Clare dialled up the pictures one at a time on the Lightroom display, which showed a big picture surrounded by data.

"First, there's the two of you crossing the street with hands held together. Isn't it strange that the two incidents should only be around five minutes apart? You must have been busy, Andrew. Now let's look at the two of you outside of the hotel. Here's one with Woman A, and five minutes later, here's one with woman B."

Now, the final picture of you with Natasha at China Tang's. That's along Park Lane and maybe a 20-minute cab ride from the hotel shown here. But look at the timestamp. Another 5 minutes later. You must have used a motorcycle. According to this, you used the same camera, see, the serial number!"

Serena shook her head, "This is great Clare, but it would be difficult to disprove any of this in the press with an explanation about date stamps, camera data and locations."

"I know, but my colleague Bigsy found something else. In the rest of the EXIF data is a log of any amendments made to the picture. Usually, it covers cropping the picture or, say, boosting the brightness. Well, on all of these it also shows that there have been further edits made - with Photoshop."

"That's more like it!" said Serena, "If we can prove the photos have been doctored!"

"It is what Bigsy did next," explained Clare, "He used another piece of software - ForensicPhoto, which looked at the whole image and then found areas where there had been manipulation. For example, the spacing of the pixels changed or there was a change in the blurriness of the photograph."

"What did he find? " asked Serena, looking excited.

"He showed me that the road crossing and the approach to the hotel was accurate. It's just that the person, allegedly Andrew - is someone else. The photos have been posed and then had Andrew's face blended in - like a deep fake. That covers all of the photos of Andrew crossing the street and checking in to the hotel."

Maggie chipped in, "So the pictures of Andrew have been doctored to place him with the two women!"

"Precisely," answered Clare, "And it is easy to prove!"

"That's better, " answered Serena, "And it can be captured in a single headline too! - 'No cheating here, Brading exposes fake photos!' " said Maggie.

"Brading deepfaked by enemies," said Clare, "That'll give use the high ground again."

"Yes," smiled Serena. Andrew looked relieved.

Andrew goes on the offensive

Andrew asks from his office "Okay, so do we attack?"

Clare added "Serena, I know you might think it is playing with fire, but I've made an arrangement with Rachel Crosby."

"You learn fast, " said Serena, "What did you discuss?"

"Well, I knew she didn't believe the hatchet piece, and so I agreed with her that if I could get some evidence to disprove it, then she would run it - but we must move fast before the story times out."

"Impressive, Clare," said Serena, and Maggie nodded.

"It will be so good to clear Andrew from all of this mess," she said, "But I'm wondering who leaked the stuff about Thailand?"

"I can rule the list down to six or so people," said Clare, "Including me - but it wasn't me!"

"Well, who then?" asked Maggie.

"You know we went out for that ladies' night in Chinatown?" said Clare, "It was me, my boyfriend Jake (It wouldn't be him), Lottie, Tessa (my flatmates) and their boyfriends - Robin and Matt."

Maggie said, immediately, "Not Matt Stevens!" and looked at Serena, "You see I know Robin really well, but Matt is a walking legend of indiscretion. Everyone knows that (sorry Serena) he can't hold his drink and that he blabbers every rumour he is ever passed. If you want to make sure a news story leaks, pass it to Matt. He's an idiot."

"He was rather drunk the night we met him," said Clare, "and kept ordering rounds of tequila and other shorts. To be honest, I'm amazed if he could remember any of it."

"No, Matt is a hardened drinker," said Maggie, "He has a reputation around these parts."

Clare was intrigued that Maggie had said, "Sorry Serena," and wondered why.

Serena started to speak, "Yes, it was me that originally sponsored him into a role. I was under some pressure to find him something a few years ago, but I've regretted it ever since. But Matt Stevens is a two-year man. A year to mess things up, and then a year on special disciplinary measures before he gets moved. Then it's the same thing all over again."

Clare said, "Well I think Lottie should know and perhaps we can prepare something 'special' for him!"

Andrew smiled, "Clare, thank you for being such an instant asset to our team. Now we need to think through what we are going to do about this situation."

"Okay," said Clare, "I'm going to call Rachel Crosby and also one of my friends who might help with Roger Slater. Right now."

Clare stepped outside. There was so little private space inside the main offices and outside all the corridors were busy. She decided to go outdoors and to contend with the traffic noise. Rachel picked up.

"Hi Rachel, I bring you a story!" announced Clare.

"Wow, that was quick!" said Rachel, intrigued that Clare had been so busy, "You must have already known something when I saw you this morning!"

"Let's meet!" said Clare, "Outside of Parly - somewhere quiet if they is even possible!"

"Okay," said Rachel, "Across the river? - How about the Marriott?"

Clare smiled, it was the very venue she had chosen with Bigsy and Jake when they had first met Chuck Manners.

"That's perfect," said Clare, "How about at 3pm?"

They agreed to meet, and Clare then called Christina, "Hi Christina, how do you fancy playing a strong-arm tactic towards a reporter?"

"Tell me more..." Answered Christina, "I assume this is the reporter who has tried to destroy your MP - Andrew Brading? Where are you tough? It sounds so noisy!"

"You're right about the reporter and I'm staining in one of the Parliament car parks, looking across to place barriers," Clare explained the evolved situation to Christina and gave her a free hand to 'frighten' Roger Slater without causing any actual bodily harm.

Then it was time to cross the River Thames to the Marriott's cocktail bar. A haven of tranquillity just behind one of the main tourist drags.

Brant Shareholders' Meeting

Jake, Bigsy and Christina went along to the Shareholders' Meeting of Brant. It was at the Elizabeth Hall, almost opposite Parliament.

"We'll get some refreshments at the event, they will want to ensure everyone is in a good mood," said Bigsy.

They were shepherded through industrial airport scanners and made to put their phones into little pouches.

"It stops the signal to the phone, like a Faraday Cage," explained Bigsy. They are doing it more frequently at pop concerts nowadays."

"We must bring back the Zippo lighters to make the candle effects then," said Jake, "Instead of holding up our phone torches."

Jake and Bigsy scanned down the list of presenters. Aside from a major bank, there was Miller McDonald, a Texan MVP at ISMC. He was hosting the event. Jake, Christina and Bigsy all recognised him from prior Raven events. He seemed to be a Raven Corporation fixer. It was his company that had facilitated various celebrity events, including the ill-fated one when everything kicked off at the Lanchester.

"I'm amazed he is still able to do any of this after the Lanchester," said Jake.

"He must know where an awful lot of bodies are buried," added Bigsy.

"I remember Chuck called him a tanned, drive-by handshake," said Jake.

Then there was Trudi Hartmann, Chief Executive Officer, Brant, who they remembered as a close ally of McDonald.

"She used to work for ISMC," said Christina, "That's an interesting change as she is now the CEO of Brant. I seem to remember there were rumours about Hartmann intertwined with McDonald too."

"Yes, there was quite a lot of collateral damage around them, I recall," said Christina,

"Remember Bernard Driscoll- that rude idiot of a Minister who was compromised by the efforts of ISMC, acting on behalf of Raven. We think he was killed by the Roslavl Bratva run by Tima Maximovich. If so, that would have been orchestrated by Vassily Turgenev."

Jake said, "How could we ever forget that."

Christina added, "Then Sir Charles Frobisher - also threatened by Turgenev. He disappeared after saying he was going on a helicopter flight to Nice airport from

Monaco. A likely death at sea caused by Vassily Turgenev."

"Oh yes," said Bigsy, " That was when we were investigating Brant."

Christina continued, "And Gerhard Schmidt - who I met at a Raven event - later blown up, with seven others on a yacht off Monaco. Almost certainly an American smart mine attached to the vessel. The suspect was Vassily Turgenev."

"Maximovich and Turgenev were both killed, too, in that helicopter explosion outside of London," said Christina.

Jake added, "And then, I see Michael Tovey, MP is attending this meeting. He has sailed through everything relatively unscathed. Amanda's people believed he was duped until they unearthed a significant Foundation Fund in the Caymans. Tovey had made the same stupid mistake as Driscoll and was funnelling money into it via a well-known bank. Amanda thinks Tovey is further up the decision tree than he is letting on."

Jake added, "And there's a Norwegian who we've never seen before: Arne Holstad, Ph.D., Chief Science Officer, Elixanor, who seems to be the new kid on the block. He's sitting on the intellectual property that Brant wants to acquire."

Raven Corporation was a complex company. It had spun off another company in the last two years called Brant and then through Brant it was in the process of acquiring a further pharmaceuticals research company, named Elixanor.

They were presenting a press release about their latest

strategic acquisition and it appeared to turn Brant from a sell-off afterthought company into a strategic asset of Raven.

Jake, Bigsy and Christina watched the glossy shareholder show from some seats near to the back. The presentation glittered with the best and probably the most expensive Event management.

Brant and Elixanor Pharmaceuticals, Inc. (Elixanor) have entered into a definitive agreement for Brant to acquire Elixanor.

Elixanor shareholders will receive $60 in cash and 2.1243 Brant American Depositary Shares (ADSs) (each ADS representing one-half of one (1/2) ordinary share of Brant, as evidenced by American Depositary Receipts (ADRs)) for each Elixanor share. Based on Brant's reference average ADR price of $54.14, this implies total consideration to Elixanor shareholders of $39bn or $175 per share.

The boards of directors of both companies have unanimously approved the acquisition. Subject to receipt of regulatory clearances and approval by shareholders of both companies, the acquisition is expected to close in the next three weeks, and upon completion, Elixanor shareholders will own c.15% of the combined company.

Trudi McDonald, Chief Executive Officer, Brant, said: "Elixanor has established itself as a leader in complementary biology, bringing life-changing benefits to patients with rare diseases. This acquisition allows us to enhance our presence in immunology. We look forward to welcoming our new colleagues at Elixanor so that we can together build on our combined expertise in immunology and precision medicines to drive innovation that delivers life-changing medicines for more patients."

Arne Holstad, Ph.D., Chief Executive Officer, Elixanor, said: "For nearly 30 years Elixanor has worked to develop and deliver transformative medicines to patients around the world with rare and devastating diseases. I am incredibly proud of what our organisation has accomplished and am grateful to our employees for their contributions. This transaction marks the start of an exciting new chapter for Elixanor. We bring to Brant a strong portfolio, an innovative rare disease pipeline, a talented global workforce and strong manufacturing capabilities in biologics. We remain committed to continuing to serve the patients who rely on our medicines and firmly believe the combined organisation will be well-positioned to accelerate innovation and deliver enhanced value for our shareholders, patients and the rare disease communities."

Both companies share the same dedication to science and innovation to deliver life-changing medicines. The capabilities of both organisations will create a company with great strengths across a range of technology platforms, with the ability to bring innovative medicines to millions of people worldwide. The combined company will also have an enhanced global footprint and broad coverage across primary, speciality and highly specialised care.

Brant's mixed portfolio includes a growing scientific presence in healthcare. Brant has developed a broad range of technologies, initially focused on small molecules and biologics and with a growing focus in precision medicine, genomics, oligonucleotides and epigenetics. More recently, Brant has increased its efforts in immunology research and the development of medicines for immune-mediated diseases.

Elixanor has pioneered complement inhibition for a broad spectrum of immune-mediated rare diseases caused by uncontrolled activation of the complement system, a vital part of the immune system.

Elixanor's franchise includes nano-engineering solutions as well as blood management solutions including the Tropus (a managed vaccine and healthcare delivery mechanism), additionally a first-in-class anti-complement component 5 (C5) monoclonal antibody. The medicine is approved in many countries for the treatment of patients with paroxysmal nocturnal haemoglobinuria (PNH), atypical haemolytic uremic syndrome, generalized myasthenia gravis and other related spectral disorders. More recently, Elixanor launched Tropus and TiC(Tropus-in-Cartridge), a second-generation C5 monoclonal antibody with a simple and convenient licensed monthly dosing regimen.

Elixanor's immunology expertise extends to other targets in the complement cascade beyond C5 as well as additional modalities, with its deep pipeline including Factor D small-molecule inhibitors of the alternative pathway of the complement system, an antibody blocking Fc receptor (FcRn)-mediated recycling, and a bi-specific mini-body targeting C5, among others. The FcRn extends the half-life and hence the availability of pathogenic immunoglobulin G (IgG) antibodies.

Brant, with Elixanor's R&D team, will work to build on Elixanor's pipeline of 11 nano-machine enhanced molecules across more than 20 clinical-development programmes across the spectrum of indications, including tiered-licence support for healthcare remediation.

Elixanor's leading expertise in complement biology will accelerate Brant's growing presence in immunology. The Elixanor acquisition adds a new technology platform to Brant's science and innovation-driven strategy.

The complement cascade is pivotal to the innate immune system. It plays a crucial role in many inflammatory and autoimmune diseases across multiple therapy areas, including haematology, nephrology, neurology, metabolic disorders, cardiology, ophthalmology and acute care.

By licensing the solutions on a tiered basis, the healthcare solutions become affordable to national governments and can be cost-effectively targeted across wide populations.

In contrast, Brant's capabilities in genomics, precision medicine and oligonucleotides can be leveraged to develop medicines targeting less-frequent diseases. Combining Brant's capabilities in precision medicine and Elixanor's expertise in rare-disease development and commercialisation will enable the new company to develop a portfolio of medicines addressing the large unmet needs of patients suffering from rare diseases.

The combined companies will bring together two rapidly converging, patient-centric models of care delivery with combined strengths in immunology, biologics, genomics and oligonucleotides to drive future medicine innovation. Brant has already established Bodø, Norway for its research centre for nano-engineering and is examining London for its corporate Headquarters, capitalising on talent in the London medical research arena.

Brant's acquisition of Elixanor, with its strong commercial portfolio and robust pipeline, will support its long-term ambition to develop novel medicines in areas of immunology with high unmet medical needs.

Elixanor achieved impressive revenue growth over the last few years, with revenues of $5.0bn in the last year (21% year-on-year growth). Elixanor has exhibited skilful commercial execution in building its 'blockbuster' C5 franchise. The success of the franchise is demonstrated by the effective transition of over 70% of patients from tradition medicines to Tropus-based dispensation of medicine in less than two years from launch in its key markets, including the US, Japan and Germany, as well as the strong pipeline of additional indications for Tropus and TiC.

Brant intends to build on its geographical footprint and extensive emerging markets presence to accelerate the worldwide expansion of Elixanor's portfolio.

The acquisition strengthens Brant's industry-leading growth, underpinned by its broad portfolio of medicines, which will enable the new company to bring innovative medicines to a broad range of healthcare practitioners in primary, speciality and highly specialised care. The combined company is expected to deliver double-digit average annual revenue growth across each of the next five years.

The end of the presentation arrived. There was loud music and the lights twinkled across the stage.

"That was some show, topped off with a Muse track. I'm surprised they didn't hire the band," laughed Jake, "Management and Science buzzwords supreme. I bet most journos just copy the Press Release into their articles!"

Bigsy laughed as well, "Yeah! A right portfolio of medicines convergant, patient-centric models of care delivery with combined strengths in immunology, biologics, genomics and oligonucleotides, yet wholesomely addressing the unmet needs of patients suffering from rare diseases."

Jake and Bigsy both laughed, and several people turned their heads to see who was making the noise.

"Boys! Shhh! They are playing down the other activities of Brant," said Christina, "For example, how it builds military bases and stocks them with contractors."

Jake nodded, "Well, they seem to have struck lucky with this situation, but I guess they need to get it through Parliament. That must be why they are pushing the lobby processes."

"And leaning on Andrew Brading," said Bigsy.

Chumocracy

Rachel Crosby wrote her commentary for The Post about Andrew Brading.

It blew the scandalmongering out of the water. The next day Katherine Brady did her own opinion piece about the Red Tops in The Tribune. It had enough retaliatory firepower to make the very printing presses shudder.

Andrew Brading also went on the attack about self-interests in Parliament. He knew that the lobbying against him was being done to further the creepy self-interest of a few MPs.

Brading stood in the House of Commons.

"They used to call it 'jobs for the boys'. But times have moved on. These days, well-connected insiders securing plum government contracts to resolve Government difficulties are as likely to be women as men. The Tory establishment is no longer simply an old boys' network. It's a chumocracy at the heart of government

"Barely a week goes by without another revelation: the vaccine chief who went to school with the prime minister's sister and is married to a treasury minister; the test-and-trace chief married to an MP (who happened to be the UK's official anti-corruption champion); the string of well-connected firms granted six- and seven-figure contracts to supply, consult, research, poll.

"Another scoop about a man who lived near to the health secretary and pulled him pints in the local village pub. Surprisingly, he then wins around £30m of work supplying plastic vials to go into medical test kits even despite having no prior experience of manufacturing highly regulated medical products.

"Nice work if you can get it.

"Of course, denials were issued at first, until, ridiculously, a bouncy castle manufacturer said it had been asked to make an inflatable clean room for the medical test supplies.

"I wish it would stop there. Now I see that a Founding Partner and Chief Executive of Tribalistic Capital Management, a $7bn Global Emerging markets specialist investment company has been appointed to the Department for International Trade. I note that Tribalistic moved from onshore to offshore ahead of Brexit and has made additional arrangements with the Cayman Islands to protect assets on behalf of its bond holders. I could comment further that I see a member of our very own government is involved with this company, but I realise that this will do neither me, nor the country any good.

"Instead of scurrilous hatchet jobs, the free press of this country should turn its eyes towards proper investigative journalism. Media scrutiny of the contracts I mention and the placements I describe and whether they are efficient and value for taxpayer's money?

"Such scrutiny is vital because many are awarded without the normal competitive tender.

"Proper scrutiny safeguards against cronyism and corruption."

There was silence. Several people looked towards the Prime Minister.

Then a hubbub.

Too many MPs had realised that this could turn into the early 21st Century expenses scandal all over again.

They could be caught out.

Yes, that agreeable lunch at Rules. That trip to Royal Cheltenham, escorted by those lovely ladies. The modest loan of a holiday home in Tuscany. Of course, it was lobbying. Lobbying fair and square.

"Order, Order," called The Speaker, several times whilst motion papers fluttered to the floor.

Plate glass corner office

A quiet, well carpeted corner office. A view across the entirety of London. Plate glass.

Trudi Hartmann was expecting visitors.

"Hello Michael, I expect Miller will be here in a minute. We have something to discuss."

She beckoned to her assistant, Nicole, who came into the middle of the office.

"Nicole, could you get us both coffees, please."

Michael Tovey acknowledged the courtesy, "Thank you, Nicole,"

Just at that moment Miller arrived, "I'll make that three," said Nicole, as she walked past Miller McDonald.

"You decided to stay on, then?" asked Tovey.

Miller's voice carried its distinctive Texan drawl, "As a matter of fact I live in London nowadays; at least for half of the year," He looked towards Trudi and Michael all at once remembered that Miller and Trudi were 'an item'.

Nicole reappeared with a dainty tray, with three bone china coffee cups, a milk jug and a silver pot containing more coffee. Miller gently lifted the tray from Nicole and continued with it towards the oblong coffee table at the meeting-room end of the office.

They all moved across and sat in the comfortable chairs, whilst Nicole moved to the outer annex of Trudi's office, "Call me if you need anything," she stated quietly.

Michael found himself seated between Trudi and Miller.

"Well, what are we going to do about Andrew Brading, then?" asked Miller.

Trudi and Miller both looked expectantly toward Tovey.

"Em, he seems to be making more noise of late. I think that scandal shook him up," said Tovey.

"Yes, but he is capable of stopping our plans," said Trudi, "The point of Brant taking over Elixanor was to monetise their products. To deliver tiered healthcare support to the UK population."

"It's why we put through that narrow bill about licensing of healthcare products a few months ago; we needed to position the main Bill," continued Miller.

"There's a whole group of interested parties waiting for this. Michael, you should know that after you presented at the Healthcare Research Group session a couple of months ago," Trudi looked at Michael Tovey with something that could only be regarded as an icy stare. Tovey noticed that she pronounced his name as Mik-a-el.

"We have provided you with considerable funding for your Tovey Healthcare Research Trust and the separate funding that goes directly into your Cayman Islands investment," said Miller.

"It's about time we had a little something in return," said Trudi.

"Tell me what you need," said Tovey, sipping his coffee and trying to look unruffled.

"Neutralisation," said Miller, "Neutralisation of Andrew Brading. There are various ways but if he were to lose his spot in the Cabinet, whether by scandal or by some other means, then we could move someone more - er - patriotic and sympathetic to our cause."

"Me?" asked Tovey.

Trudi spoke, "Well you are a good example, a moderniser, well liked, connected, photogenic, and as far as we know with little back-story beyond those slightly awkward funds in the Cayman Islands."

"But you will need to move swiftly," said Miller, "We want that Protection of Healthcare Rights passed, so we can capitalise on the initiative."

"You can't become a direct stakeholder this time, either;

we will have to invest on your behalf and put the funds into Tovey Healthcare Research Trust. It will be untraceable that way."

Yes, but lose the Tovey, from the name, change it to Tovarich or something," said Trudi.

Miller smiled, "That's quite an ironic name! Maybe something that sounds scientific, Psidium - maybe?" said Miller.

"But how can I 'neutralise' Brading, as you put it? They are his Bills, and I can't stand there from the same side of the House and critique them?"

"No need, we can drop more innuendo into the lobbies," said Trudi, "Brading may survive one critique, but he won't survive a second loss of trust."

"Let us introduce you to a specialised colleague of ours, Anatoly Yaroslav. He has been most helpful in other situations requiring speedy results," said Trudi, "I took the liberty to pass on your contact details but did ask him not to be in contact until after our session today."

Tovey's brow furrowed, "I assume with a name like that, he is Russian? I'm not sure that it is a good idea to be seen with Russians around the House."

Miller said, "Don't worry, Boris Johnson was doing it all the time, remember that the Russian-born billionaire newspaper proprietor Evgeny Lebedev was nominated for a peerage on Johnson's watch. Come to think of it, so was his brother Jo Johnson. The Evening Standard and Independent owner Lebedev held a party in Italy attended by Boris Johnson when he was foreign secretary, Lebedev was said by many to be a surprise name among Boris Johnson's life peerage nominations granted, which have led to accusations of "cronyism" against the prime minister.

Trudi added, "Boris Johnson showed 'fearless leadership' when giving his friends peerages, but most importantly signalled that the Tories had no wish to reduce the size of the House of Lords."

Miller added, "Yes, we couldn't get away with anything so blatant in America. That Johnson could get away with it shows what a private member's club your House is. The Lords was already the largest second chamber in the world. Now, with over 800 unelected peers, voting on our laws for life and The Lords is stuffed with party loyalists."

Tovey said, "I supposed I can see what Brading was alluding to in his 'chumocracy' speech. I can also see his speech was disloyal to the government and that his waves disrupt getting his own Department's Bills passed. Yes, I'll talk to Yaroslav."

Killer Genie

Michael Tovey decided he'd better check out Yaroslav before he met him. He was dismayed when he saw his history. It was that of a Russian Mafia thug.

When the Southern District Court of New York had attempted to prosecute Anatoly Yaroslav on charges of racketeering and conspiracy he was acquitted when the case against him fell apart.

Yaroslav, was depicted as a stocky, five-feet-four frame and wrinkled face which belied his jaunty personality. He had been in a scuffle whilst on detention. Among his fellow detainees at one point were Martin Shkreli, the snarky hedge fund manager and pharmaceutical CEO, and Vincent Asaro, the elderly Bonanno family mobster whose life served as the inspiration for the film Goodfellas.

Yaroslav had nothing to do with the initial altercation. It began as a verbal dispute between a fellow Georgian named Giga Gakharia and some Latin Americans.

Only after it escalated into a brawl did Yaroslav enter the picture, rushing into the fray to give his outnumbered compatriot a hand.

Gakharia, of course, was more than just a countryman to Yaroslav. As a *vor y zakone*, or 'thief-in-law,' a high-ranking honorific given to select members of the ex-Soviet criminal underworld and whose usage is thought to have originated in the gulags of the 1920s, Gakharia was the kingpin behind a vicious Brooklyn-based Russian mafia (or Bratva) for which Yaroslav allegedly was a key henchman.

Thus, Gakharia was effectively Yaroslav's boss. Whenever a problem emerged with the rank and file, say, with a messenger who was late on a payment or an employee who did not offer sufficient *obshchak*, or 'tribute,' Gakharia would allegedly summon Yaroslav to mete out a disciplinary solution. But there are clues that their relationship was not purely transactional.

Gakharia was star-crossed from the moment he set up his US operation. The FBI had wiretaps and informants homed in on Gakharia, recording what would amount to several years' worth of evidence. Headquartered in Brighton Beach, Brooklyn, where Gakharia ran an illegal poker house above a restaurant, the group had bases in at least six other states.

Gakharia ran his lines of business as a dizzying array of criminal schemes, in which blue-collar rackets coexisted with ostensibly white-collar ones. The scams included the sale of contraband cigarettes, the defrauding of casinos by hacking into slot machines, identity theft, credit card fraud, murder-for-hire conspiracies, and using femme-fatales to seduce well-heeled victims and later drugging them with traditionalist chloroform.

Gakharia's eclectic, high-minded ambitions for his enterprise were in line with his villainous heritage. Indeed, the *vory*/*vor y zakone* as a subculture had been making inroads in the US since the early 1990s, back when the FBI had not quite smartened up to their dealings. From the outset, though, the *vory* were noted for their special brand of ruthlessness. Even John Gotti is reputed to have once said of the *vory*, "We Italians will kill you. But the Russians are crazy—they'll kill your whole family."

Gakharia's fledgling criminal outfit, however, would never get a chance to flourish into the kind of interstate empire of which he dreamed. Gakharia, along with more than twenty-five of his alleged associates, was arrested in a sweeping federal roundup. That included Yaroslav, who was charged on two counts: one for participating in RICO conspiracy, the other for participating in wire fraud conspiracy.

Unlike many of his co-defendants, Yaroslav did not strike up a plea deal with the government.

If there can be said to be a crucial difference between the Italian American mob (La Cosa Nostra) and Russian organized crime, it is that the Russians have a culture of "flipping".

Clearly, Yaroslav didn't share this sentiment. Indeed, Yaroslav's refusal to cooperate was a source of frustration for one of his previous lawyers, who later resigned, citing his client's supposed stubbornness.

The government believed it had a watertight case against Yaroslav, arguing that as the "primary enforcer" for Gakharia's group, Yaroslav someone whose role was "breath-taking and extraordinary."

In other words, the prosecution contended that Yaroslav wasn't just kept in the dark and then trotted out for a routine beating; he was a valuable member of the Gakharia dynasty, privy to the larger conspiratorial designs of the group.

According to court documents, Yaroslav's defence lawyers briefed an account of at least four key errors made by the trial judge.

It explained why some of his peers received sentencing below federal guidelines but Yaroslav was the only one not issued with a sentence. By comparison, Gakharia, who was facing life, received forty-five years.

Five months later in an interview conducted and translated by his previous counsel over email, Yaroslav was asked to describe his detention surroundings. "I have never been in such a company before," he wrote. "Murderers, terrorists, fraudsters."

"The genie is out of the bottle," thought Tovey, "A killer genie."

Don't look back

he not busy being born is busy dying

Bob Dylan

blow your harmonica, son

Christina was at the Triangle offices when Clare appeared for her next debrief and update to Amanda Miller.

"You have got trouble," said Christina, "I just heard something from Blackbird. He says that the Kremlin are interested in what happens next in the UK and that Andrew Brading is at the heart of it."

They were on Clare's weekly conference call with Amanda Miller. "Yes," said Amanda, "I don't know specifically about Brading, but I have heard that Anatoly Yaroslav has come into the UK on a diplomatic passport."

"Yaroslav?" asked Christina, "He was the one who saw off Turgenev and Yegorin, when we were trying to ship them back to Russia. He used a Pechora SAM - a surface-to-air-missile - in Surrey! - and blew their helicopter out of the sky. We think he was working for Maximovich, who was working for the Kremlin.

What do we have?" asked Amanda, "It looks as if The Kremlin are trying to remove Brading. That their soft power approach with innuendo didn't work. Brading was too clean for the mud to stick. Now they want to use a Kremlin enforcer. We'd better upgrade Brading's security."

"Remember if this is some kind of Kremlin inspired threat, that they simply don't care and won't uphold any of the niceties of international law," said Christina, "Think of the Salisbury poisonings or even back to Litvinenko and the Polonium in a teapot. The Kremlin will use what it takes and simply lie about their involvement to everyone."

"What is the driving force behind this? The motive?" asked Bigsy.

"They want Andrew Brading or his replacement to support the Protection of Healthcare Rights Bill otherwise there'll be trouble coming every day" explained Amanda.

Clare nodded, "Yes, it is one of the Bills in Andrew's 'hopper'. He has to pass the Fundamental Rights Bill first. They were interfering with that one, but I think the bigger game was to tarnish his reputation in the House."

"There are too many vested interests," added Jake, "If they can lose Andrew Brading as the Secretary of State for Internal Affairs then they could put a tame puppet in place instead."

"Who are contenders?" asked Clare, "There is no-one obvious"

"We should wait to see which names start to gain currency one the next few days. I expect it will be someone new and probably a little less well-known," said Jake, "It's standard play."

"But what is their game?" asked Bigsy.

"It's what Andrew has referred to as the chumocracy at work," explained Clare, "If they can get the Protection of Healthcare Rights through, they have an open route to bring in as much 'tiered' healthcare as they like."

"I see," said Christina, "Couple that with the recent acquisition of Elixanor by Brant, and it is like a licence to print money."

"And the icing on the cake is that the vaccines they would produce can be classified as FMCG - Fast Moving Consumer Goods - That is also music to the Bratva's ear. They can mix their tainted money into the cash stream and cleanse it all together. A new source of money laundering is born."

"There are so many aspects to this," said Jake, "Is Andrew Brading aware?"

Amanda spoke, " We should brief him. I really think it should be at SI6, here at Vauxhall Cross, where we can provide the necessary 'Theatre' around it. We can also stress how much danger Brading is in, with his resistance to passing the Bill."

"But do we know who else is involved?" asked Jake, "Aside from the likelihood that Yaroslav has been activated?"

"Our best guess is that it is some of the people we saw at that recent Brant/Elixanor Shareholders' Meeting," answered Bigsy.

"And that points back to some of the same people that

were involved with Raven the last time," said Christina, "Miller McDonald, Trudi Hartmann and that MP - Michael Tovey?"

"Tovey, the backbencher?" asked Amanda.

"Sorry, we didn't mention him previously, because it didn't seem significant. It does now though," said Jake.

Christina looked pensive, "I'm worried by that. The usual move by Yaroslav is to do a substitution. The conventional Bratva tactic would be to destroy Brading and replace him with one of their own - in this case it could, perhaps, be Tovey."

Jaffacakes and regulation

Clare was seated back in Andrew's office in Parliament. The office was busy. Andrew Brading was there, as were Serena and Maggie. Maggie was opening a packet of Jaffacakes, which she had bought in the nearby Tesco Express.

"I'm going to sound callous when I say this, but I've not noticed a single difference since Ian Harrison's demise," said Andrew Brading.

"I was thinking the same," said Maggie, "You'll have to make me into your Special Advisor!" She offered the Jaffacakes around.

Maggie smiled across to Clare. They were both surprised when Serena said, "Andrew, that's not such a bad idea! You would have someone you trusted acting as your Special Advisor!"

They all looked across to Clare, "What would you think if Maggie becomes a Special Advisor?"

"I think it would be terrific!" said Clare, "I mean, if Maggie is in for the long haul then it has to be a good decision."

Serena said, "Okay - we can start the process, but we mustn't be caught out by the 'chumocracy' that Andrew spoke up against in the Commons the other day." She was delicately holding a Jaffacake and nibbled at its circumference.

Andrew smiled, "We've some other fish to fry at the moment. I need to get the Fundamental Rights Bill passed, and then we can concentrate on what we intend to change in the Protection of Healthcare Rights Bill. It is like the European Research Group - The title of the Bill has little to do with its implied objectives - remember ERG - it was totally opposed to Europe and quietly manoeuvred by Jacob Rees-Mogg."

"Yes, but I suppose the Fundamental Rights Bill is the umbrella one under which the individual Bills get proposed?" asked Clare.

"That's right, and actually it means we in the UK are more or less tracking what the EU is doing on these topics," reiterated Andrew.

Maggie spoke again, "The topics, again, are: Dignity, Freedoms, Equality, Solidarity, Citizens' Rights, Justice and General Provisions."

"But they've not been 'polarity adjusted?' " asked Clare.

"No - they are what they say they are," answered Andrew," Simple Rights, and simply expressed."

So why are the lobbyists after you, then?" asked Clare, perplexed.

Andrew began, "They don't like where it may all lead. No business organisation other than the lobbyists, has such an extensive network of contacts with government ministers, MPs, civil servants, opinion formers, and the media.

Clare said, " But surely lobbying is the means by which big businesses seek to influence politicians in order to increase their profits?"

Andrew nodded, " There is some truth in this, of course: businesses lobby politicians in order to increase their profits."

Clare nodded, "Yes, I suppose high profile business scandals like the collapse of Enron and Arthur Andersen only add fuel to the fire."

Andrew interrupted, "Precisely. However, many other groups and individuals engage in activities aimed at influencing politicians, building relationships with the media and other stakeholders, and raising political issues with policy-makers."

Serena said, "We see it all the time. The British policy-making process is dynamic, fragmented, and subject to a great many influences from a diverse range of organisations hoping to shape policy decisions by communicating with Parliament, government, and one another in the interests of promoting (or resisting) change.

Andrew again, "Yes. Direct or indirect lobbying of policymakers and other stakeholders is widespread and deeply ingrained in our democratic system. Indeed, it is symbolic of a healthy pluralist democracy."

Serena answered, "But we all know that the size and shape of the contemporary lobbying community and its techniques have been influenced by wider social and political change; changes within government and Parliament, and the growth of supranational institutions which have affected the locus of decision-making."

Andrew was looking riled," Yes, so the effective communication of political issues and agendas to policy-makers has come to involve a great many disparate and diverse activities which are not about directly approaching government or Parliament at all – activities as varied as government relations, grassroots campaigning, stakeholder management, partnership building, branding, reputation management, strategic planning, legal advice, media strategy, and corporate social responsibility initiatives."

Clare asked, "Which kinds of organisations are in the business of influencing and shaping policy in Britain?"

Serena continued, "Corporate lobbying in the UK is big business, although public affairs professionals working in the consultancy or corporate in-house sector have long worked under a shadow of mistrust and scepticism.

Maggie added, " Yes, it is very difficult to get a clear idea of the number of people involved in private sector lobbying and how big the industry is, giving the impression that it is secretive and, therefore, unsavoury.

"But isn't there a list?" asked Clare. She plucked a second Jaffacake from the packet.

"No, that's part of the problem," said Maggie, "There is no official register or list. And even if there was, the main obstacle is the fact that the precise forms of activity which constitute 'public affairs' are ambiguous and diverse, and hence, the number of people engaged in it is blurred and difficult to find out."

Clare asked, "But could there be other agencies at work? We know about the Russian click-farms. What about other more clandestine forms of influence?" She was thinking about the original Minerva station and now about the newly discovered Medusa station but didn't want to let on to the others.

"It can be an expensive business," said Maggie, "Any figures do not take into account the enormous number of other consultants, advisers, and experts in other professions and sectors who provide public affairs support in one way or another.

Serena nodded, "Yes, many PR agencies which specialise in the corporate and financial sectors offer strategic advice to companies on a range of issues such as brand reputation and crisis management, which involve many of the kinds of activities commonly associated with public affairs, but which are not always labelled as such."

Maggie added, "Then there are the management consultants who also offer advice in areas and on issues which often overlap with those dealt with by public affairs specialists. Investment banks, in offering advice to clients on mergers and acquisitions and such like, often advise on how to deal with the complex legal and political issues which surround financial markets, crisis management, perceptions management and corporate relations. All of which is entirely or peripherally covered by the term 'public affairs'. Law firms regularly provide counsel to companies and individuals on a range of issues to do with legislation and the changing nature of UK and EU regulatory frameworks, which again fit directly within the ambit of public affairs."

Andrew spoke, "Yes, there area a lot of fingers in the pie. The picture is complicated even further because on top of all these consultants there is also a huge and thriving community of in-house public affairs practitioners, legal advisers, corporate communications specialists, financial advisers, public relations experts, and strategic planners who work throughout the private sector on issues which can in be termed 'public affairs'. Finding out the number of people employed in these positions poses an even greater challenge than working out the size of the consultancy sector. "

"But it is one thing to use direct statistics and science to drive a point of view, quite another to use moral suasion against an MP or Minister," declared Clare.

Andrew nodded, "Exactly. The second reason lobbying and public affairs activity within the corporate sector remains controversial stems from a wider scepticism about the role and influence of business in public life more generally. Lobbying on behalf of big businesses who want to increase profits for their company shareholders and expand their market share seems, for many, qualitatively different from lobbying on behalf of, say, endangered animals, and feeds easily into widespread worries about the power of business to usurp government and dictate policy for its own ends."

Serena added, "The increased globalisation of international markets and the increased fragmentation of the policy-making process have led to a growing fear that it is becoming easier and easier for corporations to find their way into the policy-making and decision-making process and use their commercial might to influence global political decisions away from the public interest and toward their own interests and the interests of their shareholders."

Andrew nodded, "That's what George Monbiot called the 'corporate takeover' of Britain. He said that the growing dominance of big business on the national and supra-national stage has meant that conventional democratic institutions are being squeezed out. As he puts it '...seizing powers previously invested in government and using them to distort public life to suit their own needs. The provision of hospitals, roads, and prisons in Britain has been deliberately tailored to meet corporate demands rather than public need. Urban regeneration programmes have been subverted to serve the interests of private companies, and planning permission is offered for sale to the highest bidder.'

Clare spoke, "That's like the old song 'Selling England by the Pound'. It is also reminiscent of what happened in Russia after the collapse of the Soviet Union. A chosen few could buy up the state's assets at knock-down prices and then make huge profits from them. The natural resources were a classic example, oil, energy, refineries, mining. Systems that had long run-rates upon which to capitalise."

"And that is my worry," said Andrew, "we introduce our Fundamental Rights Bill but then see it get hijacked by a few sneaky additions, like that new Protection of Healthcare Rights. The Bill has been drafted to do the exact opposite of what it says in the title. It externalises the run-rate of medicines and vaccines, making them ripe for monetisation. There is a great pressure being brought on me to move it forward, although I am resisting."

"But how can that be?" asked Clare, looking bewildered,

"Surely you run this Department?"

"I do," said Andrew, "But it is a complex mechanism. There are permanent Ministers and many units within the Department who are under other influences. Fundamentally, I suppose we are seeing corruption because of corporate lobbying. People in the Department get lobby-sponsored trips to Wimbledon, The Races, best seats at the ballet. 'Just delete a sentence from the Bill, could you?'

"Think who owns the debentures, the corporate boxes? The reputation of the lobbying industry in Britain has been hand in glove with high-profile scandals which have led many to assume that underhand tactics and nefarious practices are endemic among lobbyists. They always seem to have 'something' on people in power or influence."

Serena said, "Yes, there are the old examples: I'm thinking of the famous 'cash for questions' scandal in which an established lobbyist (Ian Greer, of Ian Greer Associates) was accused of paying MPs to table parliamentary questions.

"Then Derek Draper's all too public claim that he was on intimate terms with the most important people in the Government and that he could, for a fee, approach them on behalf of clients. Together, the scandals that surrounded these two events brought those who worked in public affairs under the intense and hostile glare of the UK's media."

Maggie said, "Yes, and so the industry responded by setting up the Association of Professional Political Consultants. It's a self-regulatory body for public affairs professionals. It requires members of the APPC to publish the names of their clients, the names of any paid staff who are involved in the provision of public affairs services and are bound by a statutory code of conduct aimed at improving transparency. Firms are not legally required to join, and so they need only sign up if they think it will be in their commercial interest to do so.

"There is a concern that any code of conduct which seeks to restrict the activities of member firms in the interests of transparency will cause those firms opting out and pursuing their commercial interests more effectively outside the code. This is exactly what some big public affairs agencies have done."

Clare asked, "But what about state actors, for example, the Russian, Chinese or even the Americans?"

"And even the Europeans nowadays, ever since the UK left the EU," said Serena.

"It could lead to a systematic form of corruption," said Andrew, not realising how much Clare already knew, "We are defending against major and clandestine players."

Serena said, "You know what...I think I feel a speech about Regulation is required!"

The others nodded their agreement.

Old fashioned tactics

Clare was back in Bermondsey. Lottie and Tessa were both home and Tessa's boyfriend Robin Hunter was also sitting on the sofa in the lounge.

"Hi Clare," he said, "Tessa and I are going out in a while - to The George - to meet up with a couple of friends - as a matter of fact I think your sister Samantha will be along as well. You are welcome to come along if you'd like?"

"No, I'm zeroed out," answered Clare, "I've done so much today!"

"Okay - I get it - first few weeks can be tough on anyone!" answered Robin, "Er - by the way - it wasn't any of us that gave the Brading story to that journalist."

"I'm less sure," said Clare, "It has to be one of the 'Opium' group, judging by the fidelity of your story, as described in the press. I expect it was someone 'under the influence,' you know."

She could see Robin's brows furrow and then ping back as he worked out - suddenly - who had probably done it.

"Your office is remarkably unlucky, what with leaks and that SpAd killed - Ian Harrison - wasn't it? I heard he was run over by a builder's truck outside Parliament?" he added as if just remembering.

"A terrible accident," said Robin, "But he's not the first SpAd to meet his fate either," he added.

"No?" asked Clare.

"A couple of years ago, a friend of mine, Stan Daly was helping a Minister resolve sort of security situation, when he O.D'd on LSD."

"I didn't think LSD killed you?" asked Clare.

"Not directly. But he stood on a balcony ledge and then toppled off, straight onto a car roof six floors below. I knew him quite well but didn't even know he did drugs."

"Unless someone spiked him?" asked Clare.

"I know, we were all trying to work it out at the time. And the rumours were that the Minister was mixed up with the Russians."

"Who was the Minister?"

"It was a Minister called Bernard Driscoll. Come to think of it, Driscoll was killed too, in a road crash maybe a year later."

Tessa appeared in a tight-fitting dress.

"Wow! Hot!" said Robin, "Okay - shall I say Hi to your sister if I see her?"

"Yes, do, you can say that you've met Jake too, if you like!"

Imaginary Boyfriend Day

It was one of her 'imaginary boyfriend' days again, and Clare was back at the Triangle offices.

Amanda was dialled in on a video link and Bigsy, Christina and Jake sat with Clare as she described the situation.

Clare spoke, "Andrew Brading admits he is under pressure. They want him to push through the doctored Protection of Healthcare Rights Bill which will derestrict the ways that vaccines and other health care are provided. He seems to be pressurised by vested interests. He knows that the photos used to blackmail him had been faked and can prove it.

"He intends to come out all guns blazing in the next few days and to make a speech in the commons about Regulation."

"Does he know about the Listening Station and the dirty tricks being deployed?" asked Amanda.

"He's on the receiving end, but I don't think he knows just how well orchestrated it all is," answered Clare.

"Plausible deniability, that's good," said Amanda, "But I've arranged for his security status to be uprated. He gets the same treatment as the PM around Parliament now. Black support vehicle and a couple of outriders to clear the route. I want to send a signal that we are on to them."

"What? A signal to Yaroslav? I don't think he'll mess around; you know. He seems to be totally ruthless."

"I know; the one thing we can't defend against is a broad daylight attack with guns - but I'm afraid that's what he might attempt."

"Well, he used a Surface to air missile when he was in Surrey, can't we just arrest him?" asked Clare.

"Unfortunately, not. He's on a Dip. Passport and travels around on CD plates. Like a bubble of protection around him. We'll have the Embassy shouting about diplomatic rights if we try to pull him in."

Christina smiled, "Classic, textbook stuff, just like we were taught at the Akademy. But you must pay particular attention because he is likely to go dark, and that is when he will most likely strike."

"He won't break cover though, surely?" asked Amanda.

"No, you are right, he will hire a crew to do whatever he is planning. He might even use Brits or another country's nationals to throw you off the trail. And as for hardware. I can remember being in Paris when my flatmate Galina had a Swiss Arms 511 sniper rifle delivered by courier. It could fire a .50 around 3 kilometres."

"Interesting..." said Amanda, "I always wondered about that G8 working party in Paris."

"No comment," answered Christina, archly.

Clare looked at Amanda on the Screen, "Amanda, we've found out a lot for you now. We know that Andrew Brading is under a threat. We've found the Minerva replacement and potentially uncovered the Protection of Healthcare Rights Bill's commercial purpose. We even know that it could involve Raven and Brant, via the new Elixanor company. What else do you want from us?"

"Honestly. You've done great. And you are undetected in all of this. That is the beauty of the approach. If I send in regular SI6 employees, they will be identified very quickly, whereas you go completely under the radar. Having these sessions is also a clever idea, and the fact you can bring in extra people from the wider team is excellent. I really think you need to stick with this now. We could uncover the whole conspiracy."

Christina nodded, "Amanda is right - It has the hallmark of Russian involvement, with the direct links back to the old Minerva and also to Raven. I always thought that Raven Corporation was like unfinished business. This could be a way to tie it off. And Amanda's right, you are still a clean skin, so very valuable!"

"Hmm. Clean Skin... I'm not sure I like the sound of that," said Clare, with twinkle in her eye.

"How about squeaky clean?" asked Jake, laughing.

"Stop!" said Clare, "You may be my imaginary boyfriend, but that doesn't give you any special rights!"

"Ahem, no, certainly not," Jake coughed.

"Okay? We continue then?" asked Amanda.

"Okay - let's keep going, but from here on I'll reserve the right to bail!" said Clare.

Backhanders

The House of Commons chamber was packed. Andrew Brading was just standing to make a speech on the subject of Regulation. It occurred to him it could be his last. They could take away the whip if he was too disloyal. Or perhaps even worse. But he needed to send a signal that he was not being played.

He started, "Britain likes to delude itself that it is better than the rest of the world. That the 67 million citizens of this cluster of islands are somehow a little bit elevated from the billions living elsewhere on our planet."

There were mild shouts of bafflement from both sides of the House.

"Order! Order!" bellowed The Speaker.

Andrew continued, "This strain of self-defeating exceptionalism is especially noticeable when it comes to the issue of corruption."

There. He had said it. Corruption.

There were further shouts and a few coughs. The Prime

Minister shot him a glance as if to say - "Take great care"

He continued, "Our leaders preach about the sanctity of democracy, sneer at dodgy elites in developing nations, hold summits to promote transparency and pose as protectors of probity in politics. They are right to rail against the curse of corruption since it is 'one of the greatest enemies of progress,' as David Cameron once said."

Now there was a loud shout from his side of the House. This was irregular. He would expect the kerfuffle to come from the Opposition benches.

"Order! Order!"

"We are fortunate that we do not have to grease palms every time we deal with officials; in some nations, this has been shown to account for about one-third of salaries. Yet what a shame that successive prime ministers failed to practise what they preach, instead presiding over a business and political culture riddled with corruption."

"Order! Order!" Andrew could sense the walls closing in on him.

"Britain has passed tough anti-bribery legislation and measures to combat money laundering. Yet it does little to clamp down on tax havens under jurisdiction of our flag that enables wealthy people and major firms to avoid contributing to the public purse. Now that "Singapore on steroids' is being bandied about, it becomes a clear sign that Britain is to become a deregulated business playground.

Brading continued, "Governments even hand huge contracts to the shameless corporations that encourage and benefit from such disgraceful practices. Note also how often thieving autocrats and their allies stash stolen assets with the help of our accountants, bankers, estate agents and lawyers.

"Order! Order! Will the Right Honorable Gentleman please make his point?" asked The Speaker.

"At the root of this problem lies a political system that sanctions corruption. Not the overt plundering seen in some places with politicians taking vast backhanders for deals and contracts. The expenses scandal showed Westminster was engaged in lesser but similarly tawdry practices. Instead, it is the constant drip-drip of corruption."

"It is the world of private dinners, party donations, lobbyists, favours and questionable relationships."

"As we put forward our Bill of Fundamental Rights, we should clarify that these are not self-serving for our political and chattering classes. That instead, we are doing something for every citizen of this glorious land. And we should not try to dilute the Bill by substituting clauses from further Bills, which attempt to trump the statements in this Bill."

"Trump!" shouted someone.

"He'll be wearing a baseball cap next!" shouted someone else.

"Order! Order!" barked The Speaker, attempting to bring proceedings under control.

Andrew Brading continued, "Corruption, whether personal or systemic, is a cancer that eats away at the body politic. It destroys public faith. It fosters a system of patronage that benefits the elite and disempowers those lacking the right connections. It fuels state capture by powerful corporate interests while disadvantaging challengers.

"It is wrong on moral, economic, political and social grounds. When will Britain finally accept that even our nation is not immune to this disease and demand the disinfection of a tainted political system?"

The House of Commons had erupted. There was paper throwing, loud shouts and the fury of many MPs from both sides of the House. How dare this MP - admittedly a senior member of Cabinet - challenge their integrity?

"Order! Order!" once more called The Speaker, "I will close this session if we cannot behave in a more moderate and courteous manner."

Brading knew he had made his point. He also realised that it had been deflected by the huffing and puffing of other members. The playground bullies. He caught an eye from the Prime Minister. He could see the PM was not happy.

Take a ride

Outside the Chamber was chaos. There was a phalanx of MPs from both parties attempting to get to Andrew Brading. He felt someone sidle close and then a woman's voice whisper in his ear, "You want a platform? I'll give you one." It was Rachel Crosby.

Serena noticed and pulled Rachel from Brading. She turned towards Serena and spoke, "I'll help Andrew make his case through my column. It will be good counter to the obvious swipes he will get from the red tops. Let me help you."

Serena nodded, "Our office will be in touch. Right now, is too busy to handle this but we are interested."

Rachel looked Serena in the eye. "Okay - we have an agreement."

The security detail attached to Andrew Brading was now hustling him towards the Category 1 area where his car was parked. His driver was waiting, and they were soon outside the Estate, escorted by the outriders and a black Range Rover with an added security detail.

Andrew Brading was alone and could feel the adrenaline rush subsiding in his body. It was like feeling gravity suddenly pulling him back into the leather seat. A few moments of respite from everything and no-one talking to him, not even a phone call. He pulled the palm of his hand over his eyes and let it rest there for a few seconds.

So peaceful.

Suddenly he felt a bump and the car lurched to the right. He opened his eyes and looked out of the window. There, to the right, at eye height, he could see a small drone. He wondered if it was trying to take his photograph and he thought that someone was breaking the rules around the Parliamentary Estate, which had a strict no-fly zone policy toward drones.

His driver called out, "Danger, Sir, Lay down in the car,"

To begin with he felt sluggish and slightly embarrassed to do this, but then the driver called a second time "GET DOWN!"

He pulled himself flat along the seat. So much for a peaceful day. He could hear a metallic thump on the roof of the car. Surely it wasn't a bomb?

There was a loud crash and he felt himself tumbling. The roof of the Jaguar car had gone, and he could see daylight. He was aware that he was being flipped over and he gripped at the other seatbelt to steady himself. As he looked down he could see a huge amount of blood. His driver also appeared to have gone. There were a couple more thumps and he could only see grass and a kerbstone. He lay where he was, unsure if the car was about to explode, but unable to move to free himself from his own seatbelt.

He realised he was still conscious and as his hearing returned, he was aware of blue lights and shouting, "Stay Clear, Stay Away!"

Then he blacked out.

St Thomas Hospital

Brading awoke. He was in bed. He looked around the room and could see two bulkily armed policeman talking to one another. He noticed the paraphernalia of monitoring equipment.

One of the policemen noticed him awake. "Mr Brading? Mr Brading? We've just called through for a doctor. They say you are okay, Sir."

He could tell as a doctor approached the bed. "Mr Brading? You are in St Thomas Hospital. Can you hear me? The doctor was shining a light into his eyes. She looked over towards the equipment.

"Your vital signs are good. Can you tell me the month?"

He realised he was being tested for his level of recall. He tried to answer the questions but could not speak. He gestured.

"That will be because we had to intubate you when you first arrived. We had to stick some pipes into your mouth and down your throat," she explained, "We were worried about your breathing and potential loss of oxygen supply to the brain."

Brading nodded again. He understood.

He could see the two policemen looking towards him. The second one looked like he was going to faint. Brading realised he might not look too pretty at present.

"The policemen are here to provide protection. You have a mild concussion from the explosion.

The doctor continued, "It will take you one to two weeks to recover. You will need to get plenty of rest and avoid stressful situations. Have someone stay with you for the first 48 hours so they can look out for problems such as changes in your behaviour or difficulty concentrating or understanding. Take the medication we provide. Increase your daily activity very slowly. Don't return to work or drive until you feel you've recovered. Avoid sport or strenuous exercise."

"I'm telling you this so that you realise that it is not as serious as it looks. These policemen are contacting your wife right now."

Brading felt the scene slipping away. He was so darn tired.

"It's okay," said the doctor, "The body is a marvellous system. Right now, it is trying to recover and is telling the patient it will be quicker if he sleeps."

Serena and Maggie were already on their way across to the hospital, but Clare had said she would stay in the office. She decided to phone Christina to get an external viewpoint.

"Yes, I saw it come up on my phone, as Breaking News" said Christina, "It looks as if a drone was used to deploy a bomb directly onto Brading's car. They could have steered it from anywhere in the vicinity. My guess is from across Parliament Square. It gives a great view and has many routes of escape. I guess the drone would only need to be in the air for less than five minutes."

"Do you think this was Yaroslav?" asked Clare.

"Almost certainly he will have arranged the hit, but would not be nearby, on purpose. He will have paid others"

Clare could see an incoming call - it was Amanda. She added Amanda to the call with Christina.

"Hi Amanda - I'm talking to Christina at the moment."

"Hi Christina, Hi Clare. We've seen the footage from Parliament Square - it was a manually operated drone. It looks as if someone in the Square was operating the drone and made their escape as soon as it exploded on the roof of the car.

"Andrew Brading survived although his poor driver was decapitated by the blast. Andrew Brading is in a secure ward at St Thomas' Hospital now. He can't speak but that is because of short-term intubation. He has concussion but they reckon he'll be functional again in a few days. His wife Katherine knows. The drone and explosive showed a middle eastern origin. We've got some footage from across the Square of a couple of Arab-clothed men hurrying away from the area."

"I'll guess this is simply laying a false trail," said Christina, "It's how we were trained in the Akademy.

Confuse your pursuers."

"Yes, that's what we thought too. They both hopped into a cab in Great George Street and headed toward Birdcage Walk."

"That's toward the Palace," said Clare.

"Yes, but it is also toward plenty of tourists," said Christina, "They are going to melt away."

"You are right, Christina," said Amanda, "That is exactly what they did. Disappeared."

Singapore

We sail tonight for Singapore,
We're all as mad as hatters here
I've fallen for a tawny moor,
Took off to the land of nod

Drank with all the Chinamen,
Walked the sewers of Paris
I danced along a colored wind,
Dangled from a rope of sand

You must say goodbye to me

Tom Waits

Ideology

Back at the Bermondsey flat, Tessa and Lottie were very interested in Clare's latest gossip.

"That's three or four headline events in your office since we've known you!" said Tessa, unscrewing a bottle of crisp, chilled Chablis.

Lottie added, "Yes Brading has been all over the papers. There was that BAME comment first, then the fake indiscretion with those two ladies - One could say the 'cheating on his wife scandal'..."

"Then, Andrew Brading's SpAd gets knocked down in the street outside Parliament and then, barely 100 metres from the site of that happening, someone tries to blow up Andrew Brading! What is going on?"

Tessa poured some generous glasses of wine, "Don't panic - there's another one in the fridge," she said.

"...Neither of the slurs about him were true," said Clare, "The BAME story was manufactured from nothing and then the photos of the two women were proved to be fakes,"

"Something you'll come to realise in this game is that it is not whether it is true, it is whether it is perceived to be true!" said Lottie, "Take the Boris Johnson as an example: With one throw of the dice, he broke the Brexit interregnum. After three years of frantic inertia, he resolved the impasse through transforming the class basis of the Conservative Party. A conjuring trick."

Tessa added, "Yes, but so effective. His sleight of hand renewed his party for a generation and ripped into the Labour heartlands by aligning Brexit with national renewal and exposing the class divisions within Labour by siding with the poor. Remember all the Red Wall narrative? As a political strategy it was brilliant - less so when the 'wall' turned blue and became kind of neglected."

Clare smiled, "Hmm - Levelling Down instead of Levelling Up!"

Lottie continued, "Although the Conservatives led across every social class, their lead in the skilled and unskilled working class was particularly emphatic. It was similar to Thatcher's 'Cortina Man' strategy. Boris had no equal in the cabinet. There was also no coherent opposition, his majority was impregnable, and all his MPs signed up to his agenda. Hail Caesar. Meet the new King of Merry England. Implausible 'Good King Boris.' "

Tessa added, "Now we in the Party are all being told that the Tory goal is to make domination hegemonic through two measures. The first is to identify the Tories with the working class and the country towns and to distance them from London and finance.

"But surely that is class polarisation against the ruling

financial and cultural elite?" asked Clare.

Lottie agreed, "Yes, it is, but it is even more subtle because of all the places you won't get blow-back. Remember the Conservative vote went down across the home counties, and especially those areas nearest London. The party concentrated entirely on the towns and villages of the North and the South, the country shires and the post-industrial working class, the basis of what was the Brexit coalition. The Conservatives positioned to be more northern and proletarian. Watch the skeezy PM drink beer with his new MPs in the many bars in Parliament.

Clare smiled, "It's a case of the Cavaliers lording it over the Puritans."

Tessa nodded, "Yes - It is a SpAd powered strategic Power Grab. Nothing to do with Party politics or conventional ideology."

Lottie sipped the wine, "The second step is a break from fiscal orthodoxy and to embrace the activist state. Expect to see cynical propaganda around the country lanes of England in partnership with local government. Expect a chummy house building boom. Expect to see the state sell-off whatever it can get away with. It's the Russian model, but with a state better equipped to manage financial matters. It's 'Liege and Lief' - from the Middle English as 'loyal and ready,' a pledge made by peasants to the lord of the manor. The peasants' fealty will be to the Cabinet. A group of nouveaux lords presiding over the riches, or spoils of state. 'I can give you the means - you must make the money,' as Putin would say.

Tessa poured into each wine glass, "And make no mistake: The government will violate EU rules on state aid and competition law with relish. 'Singapore ne plus ultra,' as it has been described."

"Out of the mouths of Etonians," said Lottie, "electi videntur ius hereditabunt terram."

Tessa laughed, "Die Elite glaubt, ein Recht zu haben, die Erde zu erben - The elite think they have a right to inherit the earth!"

Clare added, "I think there should be a phrase about show-offs too!"

Lottie sipped again, "They say it is an era of change. No. It is a change of era. Jumping the S curve. The old era and consensus were defined by four shared assumptions: that the nation state, democracy, the working class and conservatism would matter less. The dominant forces were the educated middle-class, globalisation, written constitutions and liberalism."

Clare asked, "But what about the Opposition?"

Tessa walked towards the refrigerator, "They Lost. Big Time. The family from hell. The responses of blame, avoidance, denial, anger, displacement, and depression are all both shocking and predictable. Labour is full of hate and blame and unable to understand how it got sidelined. With a few exceptions, it is no longer a tribe and has lost its homeland."

Lottie looked at her empty glass, "Now, glimpse a future where a progressive mind can only be reactionary, nostalgic and backward looking. The left can't see that the decisive role of the working class will be in ironic assertion of national sovereignty through its democratic vote. The consequence? To renew the ancient institutions of Parliament and the common law. This new era will be a foreign country for those who thought the arc of history was with them."

Clare asked, "Okay, so I see the Conservatives positioned to sell off the state. Where does Andrew Brading fit into this?"

Tessa had unscrewed the second bottle and was pouring more wine for everyone, "He doesn't. That is just it. He wants to stand up to this flagrant rip-off. That is why he is fronting the Fundamental Rights Bill. To give the populous a say in their own rights. It is also why he wants to curtail the Protection of Healthcare Rights Bill - which was cynically selling healthcare rights to the highest commercial bidder."

Clare asked, "And who is behind the Protection of Healthcare Rights Bill?"

Lottie answered, "That's just it. We don't know. But I think there will be a Big Pharma Corporation poised somewhere to make the government an offer which will put the Big Pharma onto a gravy train."

Clare decided she should keep quiet about Raven and Elixanor, although speculation was already rife.

"So, should we all invest in Big Pharma?" she asked instead.

Beauty and the Devil are the same thing

Christina was on her way to visit Roger Slater, at his home in Batchelor Street. She knew it would have more of an impact if she visited him on his own doorstep, rather than in a venue that one of them had selected.

She knew he would be in. When he was between stories, he seemed to be a creature of routine habits and would usually be back by around seven 'o clock in the evening.

She rang the bell. She'd decided to wear a leather overcoat, for maximum threat level, but had unbuttoned it so that he would see her vivid red dress when he answered the door. She carried her Mulberry bag on her shoulder.

There was a clunk as the door opened. Before her stood the noticeably quiffed Roger Slater.

"Oh," he said, "I was expecting someone else."

"Roger Slater?" asked Christina, "My name is Alya. I have some news for you. May I come in?"

Christina smiled and she could see Slater melt in much the same way he melted his targets with a concoction of alcohol and probably rohypnol to get the information he required.

She took in the room.

'Mapplethorpe/Rodin' said a large poster of a male nude next to one of Rodin's almost identical sculptures. Then the stairwell contained a cropped picture of leather trousers. And another wall contained a picture of Debbie Harry in a white vest sitting in a leather chair. Big clues about Slater's penchants everywhere.

She resumed her pace, "Yes, I have some news for you. My name is Alya Sokolova. I'm from the GRU. That's Russian intelligence. I've been asked to give you a warning. You are playing with fire, writing that hatchet piece about Andrew Brading. I don't think you know how much trouble you are in."

Slater looked amused, "Look, love," he said, "I think you'd better turn your tight little cheeks around and leave. I don't know what you are talking about."

Christina pulled something from her pocket, "Look, I don't want to be more demonstrative than I need to,"

Slater was staring at the blackened cobalt vanadium blade of a Russian Spetsnaz Predator knife, held by his unexpected visitor.

"Yes, 17 centimetres of blade, with the last four serrated, stab and rip... Love, " she explained, "Now I'm going to need a little information from you today, but my knife is very clean and I really don't want to mess it up."

She could see that Slater was entirely out of his depth.

"Okay, okay..." He said, "What do you need to know."

"Simple enough really. Who put you up to the story about Brading? I want names and the organisation."

She could see that Slater was thinking quickly about ways he could fob her off with lies. He did the obvious 'tell' of looking up and to the right to seek creative inspiration.

"No. Don't try to lie to me, or I'll have to show you what's in the Mulberry," she said.

Slater changed his mind quickly. She could see his eyes move down and to the left, he was accessing facts now.

"Okay, it was a routine assignment. They just paid me well. It was a company who asked me to do it. Something to do with lobbying. ISMC, they were called, but I think they were working for someone else. My main contact was Miller McDonald."

Christina stiffened as she heard this name. Miller McDonald had worked for ISMC supporting the incentives to tarnish MPs when she had been investigating Raven all of that time ago.

"Okay - but anyone else?" she asked.

"A woman...Trudi something or other, I seem to remember," he answered, "and an MP... Michael Tovey was his name. Oh, and someone from Elixanor - Arne Holstad."

Christina looked at Slater. He had folded quickly but he

seemed to be telling the truth. She thought about whether a grand reveal was necessary.

"Thank you, Mr Slater, you have been most helpful. Let's just think about this for a moment. If you were to mention this to your employers, or to the police, about our little meeting, there is every chance that word would get back. That means you might suffer reputational damage as a journalist who can't protect his sources. But worse than that, some of the people who have employed you would carry a grudge. Let me show you something."

She opened the Mulberry and lifted its content into view. A SIG Sauer Copperhead sub-machinegun.

"Pretty isn't it? It is surprisingly quiet with the built-in noise suppressor, more of a rattle than a bark. Now I'm not the one you should worry about. It's the men in Mapplethorpe leather jackets who come in through your doors and windows at night if you were to spill our little secret."

"I get it; I won't say anything. Will you be leaving now?" he asked, weakly.

"Yes, thank you for our little chat."

Christina walked back to the front door and let herself out. She had secured the weapon in her bag and the knife in her coat and was almost skipping along the road. Sometimes it was good to let the training kick in.

Bodø

Christina and Jake were on a plane bound for Oslo.

They had followed up on Slater's information and Jake had positioned himself as a journalist prepared to write a largely puff-piece about the technological breakthroughs occurring at Elixanor, fronted by Arne Holstad. To do this, they had to travel to Oslo and then on another plane to Bodø, which was on the west coast of the Nordland peninsula, and within the Arctic Circle.

"I suppose this feels like going home to you?" asked Jake.

"Not really, the Norwegian landscape might be like Iceland, but their language is different enough. We kept the old Norse in Iceland, but the Norwegians decided to adopt other words and phrasing from Germany. I can usually work out what they are saying, but it is much harder for a Norwegian to understand me talking in Icelandic," answered Christina.

They had both looked up the facts about Bodø, including the climate and were prepared for snow underfoot and nights to be light, but when they finally arrived it was almost as temperate as London.

"It's not like Reykjavik at all," observed Christina, "We'd have pretty consistent snow at this time of year. This seems to be quite an anomaly."

"Maybe it has something to do with global warming?" hazarded Jake as they both climbed into the back of a taxi-van and were whisked lite-night into the town centre and down to the town's harbour where their hotel was located.

"It's late," said Jake.

"Yes, see you tomorrow morning!" said Christina.

In the morning Jake and Christina met in the lobby of the hotel. Christina had ordered room service for breakfast, whilst Jake had taken a breakfast in the restaurant. Christina was carrying a canvas khaki bag with leather straps and Billingham written on the front. She looked the part, like an artsy photographer.

"You know how to use those things?" checked Jake.

"Do you know how to operate a Kalash?" she replied, "How complicated can it be?"

"Point taken, and we don't really need the pictures in any case."

"Maybe not. Although we can get some useful ones of the surroundings."

A car arrived to take them to the Elixanor facility. They had been told that it was far easier to go in a company car than to try to get into the secured facility in a taxi. They also knew about not discussing 'business' in the company car, which could well be recording them both.

They were soon in the Visitor Suite of Elixanor. Someone came to greet them.

"Hello, my name is Runar Teig, I'm here to accompany you around the building so you won't get lost," he explained, "First, we have a small annex with breakfast, just in case you haven't eaten."

He escorted them to a room with a beautiful view across the water and several hotel-style hotplates with a variety of 'help-yourself' breakfast offerings. Next to it were some altogether more Norwegian-looking items. Scrambled eggs mixed with smoked salmon served on breads and toast, a distinctive brown cheese, some dainty rolled pancakes, and a large flask containing a dark, black coffee.

Christina helped herself to the coffee and a small pancake and looked around for the butter.

"You have some cinnamon butter?" she asked.

"Ah, someone who knows how to eat a lefsa," smiled Runar, "Here - although I also like them wrapped up with Gravlax. Here- try this - it's gravlax with treacle and dill."

Christina smiled and as she bit into it felt a rush of her childhood in Iceland. They were just like her Pabbi used to serve for breakfast in the cold months.

At that moment another person arrived.

"Thank you Runar, I'll take it from here. Could you wait for our guests in the office annex?"

He strode forward and shook Jake's and Christina's hands. A handsome chiselled man, Christina decided he didn't have much body fat and looked as if he spent a lot of time in the fresh air, probably climbing mountains and running.

"Yes, I'm Arne Holstad," He continued, "I'm pleased to welcome you both to Norway and to our little facility here in Bodø. Let's go on through to the meeting area. Will you want me anywhere in particular for the photograph?"

They walked into the next room and Christina could see it was set out like an informal lounge, with an enormous plate glass window looking out toward the sea. It screamed Scandinavian design and looked effortlessly cool.

"There will be places here for us to photograph you. I'll probably take several pictures," she said, "Although it would make more sense to have a picture of you in one of the labs. You know, it will go with the cutting-edge science theme of the article."

"Ah - I hadn't allowed for that. We would need special permits to go into the laboratories. I'll ask Runar to see what he can do. I guess it doesn't matter what you have as the background science?" he smiled.

"No," said Jake, "Although something fancy with dials and screens always looks impressive. Ideally with lots of white walls."

"I think we can provide that without too much trouble," smiled Arne.

"Now, what would you like to know?"

Jake asked some questions about Arne's background and how he got into science. Arne's well-rehearsed replies could have come from a Wikipedia article. Then Jake changed tack.

"What about the recent action with Brant?" he asked, "I'm sure our readers would love to hear about life in the fast lane."

"If I speak directly to you, I will need your word that you won't attribute it back to me," Arne said.

Jake nodded, "Of course, we can show the article as coming from a number of sources. I could even stop the attribution after your background bio."

"To be honest, I think I am due to be replaced here," Arne continued, "No-one has said as much but at the last couple of strategy meetings it was abundantly clear that I was against the hasty monetisation of our recent discoveries."

"How so?" asked Jake.

"We have designed a vaccine here and a distribution mechanism which was to reduce the inconvenience of regular injections. We created a small cartridge delivery system, like the cannulas that are used in routine surgery."

"I know - those little inserts that they can plug drips into!" interrupted Christina.

"That's right, except the ones we designed were smaller and had a nano-engineered component. The nanobots could control the flow of vaccine and literally count the number of drops dispensed. It makes for a very fine and granular delivery system."

"I see, but can you control the nanobot system as well?" asked Jake.

"Yes, that was the latest addition to the system. The bots can read a tiny marking on the cartridge to know how much to dispense and over what period."

"That is an incredible breakthrough," said Jake.

"Yes, but the unintended consequence is the ruthless ways that it can be monetised," explained Arne.

"What do you mean?" asked Jake.

"Well, suppose that you identify a pure form of vaccine. The dose can then be regulated at various degrees. A higher quality dose for the rich and a lower quality for the poor. The 'bots can also turn off the dose at intervals, requiring more of the vaccine to be supplied. It is like the recipient has a short-term usage licence. It is like seed licensing all over again, but this time the crop is human life."

"But surely no-one would do this?" asked Jake, "I mean it is so immoral!"

"Quite," said Arne, "But consider the revenue flow. Millions or billions of people requiring regular top-ups of the vaccine."

"Why would you tell us this?" asked Jake, "And surely you do so at some risk to yourself and the company?"

"Yes, but I'm really worried. We have invented something so dangerous if it falls into the wrong hands. Think also of the implications of vaccine tampering. Too hideous to contemplate."

Christina took a few photographs, "You know, I think we'll need some from the lab too. And with you looking a little more upbeat."

Jakes looked across at the ashen-faced Arne, "So why are you telling us this? Do you want us to do something?"

"I really want the whole thing stopped. I have made my feelings known to the company and to Trudi Hartmann, but Miller McDonald and Ms Hartmann are more intent on replacing me now. Sometimes I fear for my life, although they keep saying they are going to pay me off."

Runar re-appeared, "Hello again," he said "I have arranged for you to visit one of our low security facilities. They are taking a couple of pieces of scientific equipment across as we speak, to make a good background for the picture of Mr Holstad. We have transportation outside."

The four of them walked down to where a Volkswagen bus was parked outside the doors of the briefing centre. They all climbed aboard and were driven to another building, which said Lab Facility 12 on the signage.

"L12 - Here we are," said the driver, punching a button for the side door of the bus to open it. They all climbed out of the VW bus. "It is usually faster to travel around the site on the buses than to call for a car, even when I'm the CSO," said Arne.

Runar handed out some new badges on lanyards. "You will need these inside or otherwise you won't be able to move around. Please don't lose the pass and give it back to me afterwards."

They walked towards the main entrance to the lab. Christina readied her camera and took a couple of exterior shots.

Then they were inside. Christina could sense the air pressure inside. The room was set to expel air, and she assumed that somewhere else there would be an air-scrubber for incoming air.

"You will soon get used to that hum," explained Arne.

"It reminds me of being on a plane," said Jake.

"Ah - it is actually considerably quieter. It runs at around 46 dB, which is just above home noise but lower than background music," explained Arne, "You are simply attuned to it when we first enter the space."

Christina could see a couple of men shifting a new piece of shiny white kit into position. She noticed they were talking in Russian.

"Just plug it in anyhow, they only want it for a photograph. Let's make a few lights come on," one was saying to the other. A third person appeared with a smaller piece of equipment, "Hey Dmitri, put it over there, but leave it so that it can be wheeled around!" called one of the Russians, still speaking Russian.

Arne spoke to the three men, in Russian, "Thank you all, we can take it from here!"

They moved away leaving the group of four visitors to be arranged by Christina.

"Mr Holstad, if you could stand so that we can see the dials on that piece of kit, please, and then Jake, if you could be talking to Mr Holstad..."

Christina took a few photographs and then said she was finished. Runar called for another security guard to escort them back outside. Christina noticed that the security guard also spoke Russian.

Code Words

By the next evening, Christina and Jake were back at the Triangle offices. They had invited Clare along and had called up Amanda for the briefing. Amanda had also called Grace Fielding from GCHQ.

"This must be serious!" joked Jake, seeing Grace appear on the Zoom call, "Now we have GCHQ as well as SI6!

"Hello Jake," smiled Grace, "it's been a while!"

"Yes, and we've just arrived back from Bodø, in Norway," said Jake, "But no snow on our boots!"

"No, it is surprisingly temperate in that part of the Northern peninsula," replied Grace, " I spent a few months further north in Svalbad - that's the separate islands off of northern Norway. We were making some adjustments to a satellite array for tracking unusual movements in the Arctic Circle. We had the snow but somehow they managed to keep the main routes cleared."

"What did you find out?" asked Amanda.

Jake and Christina explained that Arne Holstad had seemed on edge when they met. That he'd told them about the designs of the vaccine dispenser and how it could be operated by nanobots. He had expressed his misgivings about the way that Miller McDonald and Trudi Hartmann planned to monetise the patents through licensing the limited use dispensing of vaccines and other healthcare products.

"And we know that Michael Tovey, the MP is also involved," added Christina.

"And you may not know the latest news," said Grace. "In the Financial papers today, it states that Elixanor is holding an Extraordinary General Meeting."

"That is unexpected," said Jake, "I could understand if we'd published the article about Arne Holstad, but otherwise..."

"Not really unexpected," corrected Christina, "He said he was likely to be replaced and that McDonald and Hartmann were already lining things up. Do we know who his replacement will be?"

Grace shook her head, "No - there's only rumours, but nothing definitive. A couple of names in the frame are a well-qualified Russian scientist named Belochkin Mitrofan Timurovich or possibly a Norwegian scientist named Mikael Bjornstad. My money is on the Norwegian, simply because I think they would draw too much attention to themselves with a Russian fronting the scientific efforts."

"That's a good point," said Christina, "There seemed to be many Russians working there. I saw three from the science facility - all Russian-speaking and then a security guard - who was also Russian fluent. Even Arne Holstad spoke Russian to the other workers."

"We'd better check the FT tomorrow to find out what has been happening then," said Bigsy.

"There is something else," said Grace, "Someone has found a way to hack some of the information. It could be a leak, but I suspect it is someone monitoring our communications. We have traced one end of it to Medusa, but the other ends seem to terminate somewhere in Whitehall."

"What was the leak about?" asked Jake.

"It was about Yaroslav. They seemed to know that we knew he was here in London. There have only been a couple of direct references to him - he is usually a code word - Besheny."

Christina giggled.

"I see you like the irony," said Amanda, "*beshenaya sobaka* - rabid dog. It seems appropriate for Yaroslav.

"That's right, but they also referred to Q in Whitehall as their source."

Bigsy was intent, "Q? I know that code. It's an old BT code. I used to work in comms with an old fella named Albert. He retired, but before that he was fond of talking about the good old days as a British Telecomms engineer.

"He and some others wired up a series of tunnels under Whitehall with loads of comms gear. There were also situation rooms built. I guess the most famous is the Cabinet Office War Room behind Downing Street. But there's supposed to be miles of tunnels. He referred to it as 'Q.Whitehall.' I always remembered it because of the James Bond character named Q. You know - Desmond Llewelyn, then John Cleese and then Ben Wishaw."

Amanda interrupted, "That's right - Pindar was the official code name. It still is, as a matter of fact. Pindar was the house left standing after Thebes was razed in 335 BCE. The space under Whitehall is still a crisis management and communications centre, principally between the MOD headquarters and the actual centre of military operations, the Permanent Joint Headquarters in Northwood. It is connected to Downing Street and the Cabinet Office by a tunnel under Whitehall."

Bigsy said, "I can remember Albert saying that the tunnels were long, too. He used to get about in them on a bicycle. One end was at the Horseferry Road Barracks and the other end was right up by Trafalgar Square. The tunnels took in The Treasury, Downing Street, The Foreign and Commonwealth Office, Minister of Defence and went right up to the Admiralty Citadel. You can still see access points as anonymous doors on the side of a few buildings along that route, as well as rotundas and even still functional lift shafts."

Amanda nodded her agreement, "You are quite right, Bigsy, and there's even more than you describe."

"I always assumed that the big underground complex at Kingsway was tapped into the system," said Bigsy, "And there were rumours that the cable routes went all the way out to Bethnal Green."

Amanda nodded, "Correct, Bigsy, although this hasn't been a state secret for many years. It is, however, pretty galling if someone has applied an old-fashioned wire-tap to it."

"That's my guess," said Bigsy, "With so much wire to select, it wouldn't be difficult for someone disguised as a telecom engineer to get in and tap into a few of the cables - literally a wire-tap."

Jake added, "But it will be damned difficult to find now. It's around 1.5 miles of cable run and presumably a rat's nest of wires. An immense amount to trace."

"Albert knew a thing or two about tracing faults," said Bigsy. "He taught me a few golden rules. One was that 'the causes of 95% of faults were in the access boxes'. The second thing was to 'never forget the need for power' - and that's beyond the 50 volts DC carried on the phone line. Another thing I remember was to 'find the cleanest line and work down.' - For tracing a fault that is. Oh, and a last one, 'look for the handprints' - he reckoned that many faults were the consequence of human intervention."

"I reckon we could chop the problem into smaller pieces. We'd still need a bunch of technicians, but we could scan for a Wi-Fi signal to the outside, trace the lines for both faults and ultra clean lines, and inspect the access points for signs of tampering."

Jake and Christina looked at one another, "This still sounds like a lot of work! And its based on the theories of long-retired telecoms technician," said Jake.

"Get me a bicycle, and a torch," said Bigsy, "I'll start the hunt!"

"No offence, but we can do better than that," said Grace, "We can send you a team from here, GCHQ's finest, with some modern scopes too. That should speed things along. But do tell them Albert's rules!"

"We have a plan then, to find the source of the leak."

"It's not enough," said Amanda, "I want to bring this thing down. Enough is enough. We need to destroy both Medusa and Elixanor and bring whoever is running this to justice."

"Would you like me to dig into Elixanor?" asked Grace, "I'm sure we can find some dirt."

"Please go ahead," requested Amanda, "I'll clear all of this with Jim Cavendish. He'll be pleased to know that we are finally stopping all of this noise in the system."

Extraordinary General Meeting

The Elixanor EGM was scheduled for London, in a headquarters building of Brant. Arne Holstad arrived and noticed several other people waiting in a lobby area outside of the meeting room.

He entered and could see Trudi Hartmann, his CEO, as well as Miller McDonald from ITMC and Michael Tovey as well as a few people he didn't recognise.

"Let me introduce one another," began Miller McDonald and started to go around the table. Two names stuck in Arne's mind. Anatoly Yaroslav and Mikael Bjornstad.

Arne knew what was coming.

"Yes, we invited you here today as part of our restructuring plans," explained McDonald.

"We have decided that your extensive and highly credible record inside Elixanor has earned you a place as a special member of our Board. Arne Holstad, it is with our deepest thanks that we have designated you as a Special Scientific Advisor to the Board, with a one-off payment, in fully vested shares of 200,000 shares. You will also qualify for an immediate payment in money of US$1.2 million the moment you walk out of here, and an annual retainer for as long as you work as SSA of $100,000. None of this will affect your pension rights and you can consider this to be a per diem of $25,000 - in other words, four days' work per year."

Arne looked shaken by the sum. His quick calculation meant that he would never have to work again. They were buying his silence. He could also see Yaroslav in the room, smiling. He knew of Yaroslav's reputation and realised that if he was difficult about any of this, then Yaroslav would arrange something unpleasant for him. Truly carrot and stick, a large carrot, and an even larger stick.

"I assume you will want me to accept this straight away?" asked Arne. Trudi nodded, "Yes, we can vote you off of the Board, but this seems like an altogether more gracious and fitting way for you to leave. See, I have arranged for our attorneys to be present to witness the event."

Arne thought for a moment. Selective witnesses and a fait accompli.

"I accept," he said, "But you will need to give me time for my lawyers to process the paperwork."

"We took the liberty to invite them also," said Trudi, "They are waiting outside the meeting. I provided them with advanced copies of our agreement. I believe they found everything was in order."

Arne thought for a moment, 'what was the English phrase - ah yes Stitch-up' - he had been well-and-truly stitched-up on this occasion.

"Let me ask Mr Yaroslav to escort you from the room."

Yaroslav stood and Arne could immediately see the intimidatory nature of the way that he moved, like a huge, coiled spring, ready to release.

Yaroslav crossed to Arne and gently pressed his palm into Arne's back: "Here, let me show you the way. You should be pleased; you are a very lucky man, on any number of counts."

Arne was now outside of the room $1.2 million wealthier. Well-recompensed but muted under the threat of who knew what, if Yaroslav was unleashed. Yaroslav spoke softly, in Russian, to Arne, "I suggest you take the money and then we will never need to meet again." Arne recognised it as a threat.

Inside, as Yaroslav returned, there was more discussion. "Okay, so how do we move Michael Tovey into Andrew Brading's role?"

 "You want me to finish it?" asked Yaroslav, "I have people in the hospital. One word and it is done."

They all looked towards Miller McDonald.

"No. We can finish him another way. Politically. Expose his Cayman Funds."

Tovey looked confused, "But Brading is squeaky clean?"

Miller McDonald replied, "Not if he has your funds. You didn't make the name change from Tovey, so I arranged for our lawyers to do it. The new name of your accounts isn't Tovarich. No. It is Andrew Brading."

Tovey looked crestfallen, "But that was my money!"

Miller continued, "No. It was money you fronted. Your payments start when we have positioned the new company and started up a few government contracts. You will be rich beyond your wildest imaginings."

Miller explained, "We have leaked the story about Brading's Cayman investments to the UK tabloids, with documentary evidence. After all of the other noise and disinformation about Brading, he is finally finished. Any denial by Brading will just dig him a deeper hole."

Trudi addressed Tovey, "And in the meantime, Mr Tovey, you can quietly assume his position in Cabinet, with responsibility for his Fundamental Rights Bill and Protection of Healthcare Rights Bill."

Trudi looked Yaroslav.

"Did Arne Holstad seem in agreement?" she asked.

"I don't think he will be making any fuss," said Yaroslav, " I think I can head back to Moscow."

"Before you go, there is one other small thing," stated Trudi.

"Oh yes? What's that?" asked Yaroslav.

"I'd like you to make a visit to Roger Slater. He is the reporter who helped us with the Andrew Brading situation. Nothing difficult, just to remind him who paid him for the work and of the need to remain silent"

"Just a friendly visit?" asked Yaroslav, "Can't you get one of your local people to do that?"

"Not really, I think you have some compelling ways with people."

"You want me to encourage his co-operation?" asked Yaroslav.

"You and maybe one other person?"

"What to hold him while I talk to him?"

"You seem to have the measure of it," answered Trudi, "Just be 'unforgettable' with him."

One-way ticket

"This isn't a ride you can take again,
but one, I'm guessing,
that is simply impossible to get off."

— *Scarlett Thomas, The End of Mr. Y*

Rachel Crosby

Clare had phoned Rachel Crosby to arrange a meeting. They sat in a small cafe across Westminster Bridge from Parliament.

"You said you'd be interested in stories about Andrew Brading?" asked Clare, sipping her coffee, "I think I've got you one."

"Hmm, Brading is becoming toxic now," observed Rachel, "You've seen the stories about his Cayman Island accounts, no doubt?"

"Seen it, but don't believe it," said Clare, "The real story is that he has been comprehensively framed."

"You'll have to give me more than that," asked Rachel, looking into her flat white coffee.

"Well let's go through the sequence of events. He gets mis-quoted on a BAME matter."

"I'll agree with that," said Rachel.

"Then he gets put into a faked photo or two with various

women."

"I'll go with that too - he has always been such a goody-two-shoes. And I assume you can prove the photos were faked?"

"Yes, naturally. Then he gets bombed. By unknown, presumed Arab parties,"

"Yes, although the Arab connection was never proven. But I agree he could have died like his driver did in that low-tech drone attack."

"But he didn't die, and then a story emerges about him having money offshore in the Cayman Islands."

"I agree it doesn't seem very likely. There are other MPs I'd place higher on the list than him."

"Quite. We did some digging. Brading's company in the Cayman's had a recent name change."

"Interesting."

"Yes, from Tovey Holdings to Brading Holdings."

"Surely no-one would be that stupid?" asked Rachel, "To put real names on the company."

"Unless the whole thing was a setup," Clare passed a paper across to Rachel, "See the name of the legal firm that facilitated the transfer? They have to be worth an investigation."

"I'm not going to print anything without more proof. I've stayed away from the original story. I'd need to come in with hard evidence to change this around. Like the organisation that the legal firm were acting for."

"Okay, but suppose they are trying to damage Brading. They have knocked him off the games board now. Who will his replacement be? Michael Tovey? Tovey who is linked with Brant?"

"Interesting. You think someone acting for Brant has tried to tarnish Brading and to conveniently substitute Tovey?"

"That's about the size of it," said Clare, "And we think that Brant's fixer firm ITMC is also involved - through a Miller McDonald, who seems to be -ahem- romantically linked with Trudi Hartmann from Brant. As a matter of fact, Trudi used to work for ITMC."

"This is getting somewhere now," said Rachel, "This has more of a Sunday papers exposé about it! Double page spread with diagrams and pictures!"

"Excellent," said Clare, "You'll have to let me know what else you need!"

"Coffees are on me," said Rachel.

Due diligence

In the Triangle offices, Bigsy smiled," Look what has just come up on the Internet!" - He routed the link to Clare, Christina, and Jake.

"Wow," replied Jake, "I think Grace has excelled with this one! Why Brant wouldn't pause when they uncovered some of this. Next we must show it to Rachel Crosby."

The Triangle office fell quiet as they each read the due diligence about Elixanor that Grace had identified.

Elixanor due diligence

Elixanor is a privately held health technology corporation. It was initially touted as a breakthrough technology company, with claims of having devised blood tests that required only very small amounts of blood and could be performed very rapidly using very small, automated devices the company had developed. The use of nanotechnology to achieve this was revolutionary and paved the way for the subsequent refinement of vaccine technology.

However, the original blood test claims later proved to be false. Founded fifteen years ago by 19-year-old Patricia Watson, Elixanor raised more than US$700 million from venture capitalists and private investors, resulting in a $10 billion valuation at its peak some six years ago.

Elixanor was hyped to its investors and in the media as a breakthrough in the blood-testing market, where the U.S. diagnostic-lab industry posts annual sales of over $70 billion. Elixanor claimed its technology was revolutionary and that its tests required only about 1/100 to 1/1,000 of the amount of blood that would ordinarily be needed, and the cost of testing was far less than existing tests.

A turning point came around five years ago, when two medical research professors and an investigative journalist questioned the validity of Elixanor's technology.

The company faced a string of legal and commercial challenges from medical authorities, investors, the U.S. Securities and Exchange Commission (SEC), Centers for Medicare and Medicaid Services (CMS), state attorneys general, former business partners, patients, and others.

Four years ago, it was estimated that Watson's personal net worth had dropped from $4.5 billion to virtually nothing. The company was near bankruptcy until it received a $100 million loan from Leningrad Associate Bank secured by its patents.

Elixanor received sanctions from the CMS, including the revocation of its CLIA certificate and prohibition of Watson and other company officials from owning or operating a laboratory for two years. A new Chief Scientist was hired: Arne Holstad. He announced Elixanor would work on research into miniature medical substance dispensing machines. Three years ago, Elixanor said it had reached a settlement agreement with CMS related to the blood testing.

Then, Elixanor, Watson, and former company president Yagovkin Lavro Kirillovich were charged with "massive fraud" by the SEC. One section of the complaint says Watson falsely claimed that the company had annual revenues of $100 million, a thousand times more than the actual figure of $100,000.

Elixanor and Watson agreed to resolve the charges against them, with Watson paying a fine of $500,000, returning the remaining 20.9 million common stock that she held, relinquishing her control of the company, and being barred from being an officer or director of any public company for ten years. It was at this time that Elixanor was taken over by Brant, itself a subdivision of Raven Industries.

According to the Brant agreement, if Elixanor were acquired or otherwise liquidated, Watson would not profit from her ownership until more than $800 million was returned to investors and other preferred shareholders. Elixanor and Watson neither admitted nor denied the allegations in the SEC's complaint. Kirillovich did not settle. Then, less than a year ago, the U.S. Attorney for the Northern District of California announced the indictment of Watson on wire fraud and conspiracy charges. Kirillovich was also indicted on the same charges.

....

"Wow, a hundredth to a thousandth the normal blood amount for testing is almost homoeopathically small quantities!" observed Clare.

"Tropospheric!" Jake added, referencing the Scarlett Thomas book - The End of Mr Y.

"It seems suspicious that Patricia Watson was so young," added Bigsy, "I know that VCs often start young, but raising $700 million at age nineteen seems way off the scale."

"She has to be a front," said Jake, "An unwitting name put forward.?"

"I think Rachel will be pleased to receive this," said Christina.

"Pleased," said Bigsy, "Ecstatic, more like."

They all paused in thought, looking out of the window at drizzly grey skies freeze-framed like TV-static hanging in the air.

weasel words from a professional

Clare and Serena were sitting in Andrew Brading's office. Serena was fuming.

"That shit of an MP Michael Tovey has moved into Brading's position. He's also done a Gove and denied stabbing Andrew in the back."

"Ah yes," said Clare, "I seem to remember Gove's doublespeak at the time. He denied betraying his former ally Boris Johnson when he stood against him for the Conservative leadership, saying his weasel words that he believed the Tories had made the right decision by making Theresa May prime minister.

Clare continued, "What a slimy line in defence too, I remember him on maybe World at One saying something along the lines: 'I wouldn't say I stabbed him in the back but I certainly came to the judgment in the immediate aftermath of the referendum campaign that, while I had originally thought he was the best person to be prime minister, for a variety of reasons that I won't go into, I didn't think he was the best person at that point.' - Nothing like convoluted doublespeak, is there?"

Serena nodded, "Then he went on to attempt to cover it up with the priciest of reasoning, 'It's not treachery. I explained my reasons at the time. The water is under the bridge.' Do you see how he did that? A forward reference to the reason and then a backward reference but with the actual reason conveniently missing!"

Serena looked more annoyed, "Well, he came out into the open later, when he ambushed Boris by bidding against him for Premiership. Do you remember when he stunned Johnson and the rest of Westminster by announcing just three hours before nominations closed for the Conservative party leadership – that he had reluctantly concluded his old chum Boris was not up to the job? Truly a twist of the knife."

Serena continued, "Well hold that thought about Gove. It's tantamount to what Tovey has just done to Andrew in this latest move."

"Look at Tovey's egotistical statement, 'Now with the benefit of hindsight and the opportunity to spend time on the backbenches reflecting on some of the mistakes Andrew Brading has made and some of the contrary judgments that I concluded, I think I am the right person at the right time,' "

Serena grimaced, "If ever there was a clumsily scripted speech then this must surely be it."

"Is there anything you can do?" asked Clare.

"I think there is. I met Flore Chéron from Lion & Freshwater a few days ago. She was introducing herself to Andrew and Katherine. She's a Queen's Council and seemed very positive toward Andrew and offered her card for services. I think she'll be interested in this situation, which is most unconstitutional lobby placement."

"I guess you'd better tell Andrew and Katherine what you are thinking," observed Clare, "I mean the whole womanising thing is mixed in with this and could get messy."

Serena smiled at Clare, "You know something, Clare? Andrew and I have worked together a long time and know how one-another tick. Trust me, he'll be pleased to know I'm working the system for him. You know what? You should come along when I get the meeting."

Fielders Court Chambers

Clare and Serena were sharing a taxi to Fielder's Court Chambers, where Lion & Freshwater were based and where Flore Chéron had an office.

"Have you ever met a silk before?" asked Serena.

Clare was bashful in her response, having known various members of the legal profession because of her father and her uncle, who was a QC himself. And then there were a couple of scrapes that The Triangle had been involved with, where legal cover had proved useful. Clare decided to answer blandly.

"I've met a couple of Legals before, but I can't remember how 'high up' the system they were. But I know that a silk is a big deal!"

"Flore's the real deal. Looks the part, and very quick witted; reminds me of you, actually!" said Serena.

In a few minutes they were in Flore's office, which looked like something one would expect to find in a Charles Dickens novel about the legal profession.

"Nice panelling!" greeted Clare they shook hands.

"Oh, I know! We have two offices actually. This is the one for private clients - they usually expect a legal office to look like this and be all quill-pens and wig powder. The other corporate office is completely different - Plate glass and steel. But I thought it would be more convenient to meet here, rather than traipse over to Canary Wharf."

Serena smiled, "Thank you for seeing us, I didn't take the decision to call you lightly. And I also admire your reputation and the standards you drive."

"Well thank you," said Flore, "Let's see if we can make some sense of this. Actually, you remember that you did set up a brief meeting for me with Andrew when he was considering what to do about his Fundamental Rights Bill?"

Serena gathered her thoughts. She tried to turn them into things which Ms Chéron's yellow pad could handle.

"Yes - I remember. It's been a whole catalogue of recent events. We suspect a covert campaign to discredit Andrew and substitute Michael Tovey. We believe it will have been lobby inspired."

Flore looked up from her pad.

"I'll need to stop you there. I'm not sure I can handle a case that might be based upon innuendo?'

Serena nodded. "Andrew is like most politicians. He humanly screws up sometimes. First, it was a mis-reported quote about him being anti-BAME. Then an accusation of womanising via a rogue reporter. Then the bomb. And to top it all, the fraudulent banking receipts apparently showing him with Cayman Island interests. I've known Andrew a long-time, and this is too much to conceive and entirely out-of-character. Someone wanted him moved out of the way and was prepared to stop at nothing to achieve it."

Flore had been taking more notes, "You present it all as a conspiracy, which might work in a John Grisham novel, but I'm afraid won't work in a regular court case. There is too much supposition involved. Let me take your story to pieces."

She walked across the wall to the panelling, pressed one of the panels, and a whiteboard appeared behind a hinged door.

"There is a secret door as well," she said, smiling.

"What about a cocktail bar?" asked Clare.

"You are looking right at it, said Flore, "But it is a bit bloke-ish, filled with men's drinks and some token wine. Come on, we'll open it."

Flore pressed a different panel and a small bar appeared, with a mirror behind it.

"Personally, I find it a bit like a James Bond set," said Flore, "But at least the wine is chilled,"

She picked up a marker and wrote down the four items.

1) Anti BAME quote
2) Womanising
3) Bomb
4) Cayman Tax retreat.

"I'm ruling out getting involved with the bomb - which should go to the anti-terrorist squad. Cayman Island - you need a forensic accountant. It leaves two and I'd say the most straightforward to pressurise is the rogue reporter attempting to implicate Andrew in womanising."

Serena and Clare stared at the whiteboard. Clare felt that this was usually her role when they were planning something at a Triangle meeting.

"With the reporter, we can get him on Libel - if you say he has manufactured the allegations and passed them on, then it would be damaging to Andrew's reputation and there is the basis for a case."

Serena said, "Frankly, it is too late to rescue the situations that Andrew finds himself in. They have done too good a job, but I'd be interested in trying to understand who has been doing this to Andrew."

"Well, there's a couple of things you could try," said Flore, "Look you don't need to hire me for this - and my Chambers would cost you a pretty penny. I can, however, give you some informal advice here and now. I like Andrew and can see that the government will need other help over the coming years. I'm more interested in getting Lion & Freshwater onto the approved list than trying to make up a case based upon what you have told me."

"That is remarkably honest and forthright of you," said Serena, "Let me thank you now, before you have even given me the advice."

"Okay - let's see. Who did you say the reporter was, and who does he work for?"

"It's Roger Slater and he is a London-based freelancer."

"Okay - we can assume he is a hired gun then. No newspaper to leverage; you will have to make this personal. You don't have good grounds for any form of police action either. Under PACE - that's the Police and Criminal Evidence Act 1984, you can't even legitimately search Slater's home or office. He can play the journalism card to prevent access to anything."

"What can we do then?"

"Legally, you could request an injunction against Slater. To stop him from hounding Andrew Brading in the future."

"That's a good idea," said Clare, "It would show Slater that we are on to him and could be reputationally damaging to him as well. People won't want to hire him for further shake-downs!"

Serena looked pleased, "Flore - I think you have cut to the quick of this. We can alert Slater and see where he runs for cover. It doesn't require the police to rattle him either. It is certainly a start."

Flore smiled, "I'm only sorry that I could not be of more service, and may I please remind you to look kindly upon Lion & Freshwater for your next public interest situation!"

Flore closed her notepad. Serena and Clare noticed how she had stayed scrupulously polite throughout their meeting, but some of her pointers made them both uneasy. If she could break it down into a few words on the whiteboard, then whoever was running the vendetta could just as easily add additional steps. It wasn't over yet. The troublemakers could be back, but the bomb the next time could have a touch more explosive. This situation would still require some significant steps to dismantle.

Ship and Shovell

Matt Stevens is rattled. There seems to be rumours going around that he was the leak who passed the information about Andrew Brading to the reporter. Even his girlfriend Lottie had told him he had been found out.

Matt was meeting meet Roger Slater again to tell him that he was not, under any circumstances, to reveal his source. It would cost him his job, and he'd only been paid in wine for what he had let slip.

They were meeting at a Victorian pub, The Ship & Shovell in an upstairs area, which was enough of a walk from Parliament to mean they could be private. The pub was also unique, being split in half by an alleyway which ran through the middle.

Matt had not dared tell Lottie that he'd spilled the beans about Andrew's background because of the trouble that Andrew Brading had been involved with. He was sitting in a corner, sipping a glass of beer when Roger Slater arrived.

"How much time have you got?' Roger says as soon as the 'hellos' are out of the way.

"I've a ton to do, but no meetings till later,' Matt replies. Slater is looking calm and carefree, as if his expenses budget could run for the entire afternoon.

"I'm in trouble," says Matt, "And I think it's because of what I told you when we last met. To be honest, I can't remember what I said - well not all of it anyway."

"You are fine," says Slater, "There's nothing you said to me that I didn't already have from another source."

"Will you protect your sources though?" asks Matt.

"Of course, even if they subpoenaed me, I'd still be able to claim a journalist's right to protect sources."

"But you are close to Parliament with this story," says Matt.

"The story is over. There is no follow up, I've been paid and will walk away."

Another man enters the upstairs bar, carefully carrying two glasses of wine on a small silver tray. Slater lowers his voice, "You have nothing to worry about,"

There is a minor crash. The new man who has entered the bar sees his wine flip around and smash onto Roger Slater.

"How clumsy," says the man, "But I'm not sure whether I'm the one who should be sorry?"

Roger Slater stands looking toward the darkly tanned man. To Matt, the man looks as if he can carry himself. You'd want him on your side in a fight, that's for sure.

The man glances across to someone else, who neither Roger nor Matt had noticed sitting in another corner of the room.

Now, Corner Man stands and walks across to the scene of the accident.

"That didn't look like an accident to me," he says, in a heavy accent,

"No," says the other man, "It wasn't - it was for Slater,"

Roger Slater looks alarmed that they have mentioned him by name. He appears confused, dripping with red wine in his ruined shirt. Matt wants to be somewhere else. He is not sure whether Slater has somehow brought this on, but it doesn't look as if it will end well.

"Here," says Corner Man, "Take my handkerchief. I don't care if it goes red."

 Roger Slater takes the handkerchief and turns back to Wine Glass Man.

"I think you'll find a message on that handkerchief, " says Wine Glass Man.

Slater still hasn't said anything but now asks, "Who are you?"

"We are friends of your employer," says Corner Man, "They have asked us to remind you about confidentiality."

"Silence," says Wine Glass Man, "One way or another."

"Goodbye now," says Corner Man and the two of them

walk downstairs without looking back. The silver tray and the glasses are on the table where Slater sat talking to Matt.

"My god," says Matt, "That was intense. Were they people you knew? Or what did you do to upset them?"

Roger Slater was looking at the handkerchief, now red stained like his shirt.

On the handkerchief was written, "Spilt wine before spilt blood."

"Are we finished?" asked Roger Slater, "Only I need to go now, and don't worry, I won't be saying anything."

Matt sat surveying the damage as Roger exited towards the stairs.

Superinjunction

Slater was back at home. He was thinking about the last few days. First, a mad woman threatens him at home with a knife and then he gets a warning treatment from two men in a bar. He has so much red wine on him that the first taxi driver refused to take him as a passenger.

Now he was back at home. There is a sudden knock on the door.

"Damn," he thinks; he's still not got a security camera installed.

He puts the chain across the door, opens it a small amount and peers outside.

A slight man dressed in a suit and tie stood outside.

"Mr Slater?" he asks.

"That's me," says Roger Slater.

"Well, here is a court order, served to you in person," says the man, handing over a buff-coloured envelope. Too startled to reply, Slater took the envelope.

"You have a pleasant evening," said the thin man as he turned and was gone.

Slater looks at the envelope, then picks it open by a corner.

It was a court order. A damn injunction against him. He read it quickly. It was plainly to stop him publishing anything about Andrew Brading, yet it had been "anonymised" – using initials apparently plucked at random – so that no one could tell who was bringing the action. The claimant was listed as "KJS" rather than Brading.

No one searching any court list could ever guess that this was a well-known politician going to court. Further defendants were listed as "persons unknown" because the lawyers didn't know who leaked the information to Slater. Slater realised he was obligated to inform the paper that had published his article about this injunction. He also realised that it was reputation limiting. He would be bound up in legal red tape and unable to function as a journalist.

The order began by warning of the possible penalties for infringing the breach of a court order.

He looked through the wording for the key features:

1A: Slater agrees not to publish any further part of the KJS Report, or cause or authorise anyone else to do so.

1B: The publishing newspaper has to keep any copies of the document it may have. This can be significant if the claimants want to try to have the document returned or if, for instance, they want to see if they can identify the source who leaked it.

5a: Here the judge worries about the possibility that publicity about the injunction could "unfairly damage the interests of KJS." He therefore orders that the court hearing must remain a secret: no one is allowed to describe it, or the claim.

5b: The judge orders the "alphabet soup" approach to naming the case. No one will be able to see KJS has been to court.

5c: Just in case there's any doubt about the total secrecy of the proceedings, there can be no reference to any "persons or places" related to the case.

6: All the papers relating to the case will be sealed. That means no one (snooping journalists or MPs, for instance) can inspect any of the witness statements or any other papers to do with the case.

7: Having effectively put a wall of secrecy around the whole affair, it moves on to the injunction itself. It says that everything about the KJS article and further investigations is secret and nothing about it can be published.

10: Then more blood-curdling clauses about the secrecy of the proceedings. Neither Slater, nor newspapers, must publish any papers, documents, witness statements or letters to do with the case.

13: Costs. The order makes no specific order about costs at this stage - this is because the judge is not able at this point to decide where the overall merits of the case lie. Slater realises it was like a bottomless pit of costs.

18 The order was directed at Slater, but through him to newspapers. This clause warned that anyone who was aware of it and knowingly breached it would also be in contempt of court and could be locked up or have their assets seized.

...

Slater throws the paper onto the table. He realises it was a gagging order. More than that, it was worded like a superinjunction. And worse of all he would be obligated to tell newspapers he dealt with about being served with the injunction. But he could not tell them the basis. No-one would want to give him work after this.

Three things, the woman with the gun, the two heavies with the red wine and now a super-injunction. He couldn't even talk about his own tribulations.

Well, maybe one answer - to turn to the crown and provide evidence. Instead of water into wine, he could turn superinjunction into supergrass.

But first, a bottle of Lagavulin's finest.

Bigsy and the Tunnels

Bigsy had made it to the tunnels. He felt a mild excitement that he was now in the very area where his old work-buddy Albert had once worked. Albert had been old school, already close to retirement when Bigsy met him, but he always seemed to have practical ways to solve problems, many of which were not in the official manuals. "RTFM" was for Albert a last resort. "Read the flippin' manual" as it might politely be considered.

Now, Bigsy was with team organised by Grace from GCHQ and they were inspecting the miles of cable-run inside the tunnels of Pindar, looking for something that shouldn't be there. Bigsy remembered another one of Albert's little phrases - "New wires", which was another fast way to diagnose a problem. Albert reckoned that most of the cables which lay undisturbed would not go wrong unless a workman put a digger through them or something else, like a flood occurred.

So Bigsy was less intent on scouring every inch of the grubby tunnels to locate the wiretap which had been added. He tried to think about it logically. Where were the main switching centres in the tunnels? Where was a good supply of power and even a way to get a Wi-Fi signal to the outside world?

He decided it would be in a control centre close to a lift shaft. Maybe even one with some kind of public access. It narrowed the search somewhat. The Cabinet War Rooms were open to the public. They were also close to Downing Street. It seemed like a likely spot. Bigsy fired up 'The Lollipop' which was a small gadget that he had used for some years to detect spook signals around his offices.

It composed a bright orange dome underneath which was a slim handset with a few buttons and a LCD display. Although simple to look at, it could scan for all signals between 50MHz right the way through to 3.5GHz. It was easily enough to locate a rogue Wi-Fi or other encrypted signal and was a high-tech version of the units used by spies in James Bond movies.

To his amazement, when he switched it on in the Cabinet War Room, he was greeted with a couple of signals - one was for Wireless Internet Direct - which was the Wi-Fi which reached across much of the Parliamentary estate, the second one was for chibis, which Bigsy initially though was a fast food joint. Closer inspection revealed its signal strength to be much too high for such a purpose and he also noticed that the signal had been set as 'hidden', although his PCE-29 Electromagnetic Field Meter was picking up the signal clear as a bell.

He gestured to one of the technicians from GCHQ.

"Look, I think this is the signal. His colleague soon triangulated it and they found a small wiring closet in the main corridor. It was surrounded by a clock, fire extinguisher and even a kind of fire hose in a glass cabinet.

"Plenty to distract the eye around here," observed the GCHQ technician. They opened the wooden fronted cabinet and could see the cabinet had a distinct left side and right side.

"Oh my god," said the technician, "Rats' nest!"

Bigsy was less phased by the interior of the cabinet. He had seen early wiring closets and knew that the wires ran in on the right and were then clipped together in the left-hand side of the cabinet. Sure, enough in the middle was a kind of ruler marked from 10 to 90 repeating and with 100, 200, 300 marked at where the hundred marking would be.

"It's the individual extension markings," explained Bigsy, "See the twisted pairs of red and white wires going to each terminator point?"

The technician looked and Bigsy pointed, "Do you notice anything else? See that? A blue and white twisted pair. I wonder where they go? Let's see. The main buss of the cabinet. This is a wiretap."

The GCHQ technician looked and pointed to the base of the unit. A dusty small black plastic square was visible.

"Oh look!" said the technician, "A raspberry Pi! I wonder how that got there?"

He shone a torch on it and Bigsy could see a couple of small lights were on. The card-deck sized device was active.

The GCHQ technician made as if to unplug the unit. "No wait," said Bigsy, "We should consider this carefully before we remove it, we might want to send some new signals along it first!"

The technician smiled, "Have you worked with us before?"

Get it On

"for meanwhile, I'm still a thinkin' "

Marc Bolan

Meanwhile, back in Bermondsey

Clare was back in Bermondsey. She was listening to Lottie telling a story about her boyfriend Matt.

"He was in the bar with Slater when he was approached by a heavy thug. The thug tipped a bottle of wine over Slater. Matt says he tried to intervene but was blocked off by a second even more intimidating thug. Matt says they looked as if they had come from central casting and were dressed like a couple of Russian gang members. Matching leather jackets, shaved heads, lots of tattoos. They roughed Slater up a bit and then left. Matt isn't even sure what caused it , but he is rattled now."

"Why was Matt with Slater anyway?" asks Clare, "Wait. Was it Matt who leaked the information about Andrew?"

Clare sees Lottie is embarrassed.

"Clare - Please don't tell anyone - Matt is an idiot sometimes and does get rather drunk. I'm sure he didn't mean anything by what happened."

Lottie adds, "Funnily enough, there's no love lost between my MP Duncan, and Roger Slater. Slater exposed Duncan's wandering hands a couple of years ago in a similar hatchet piece. Duncan never forgave him."

"But was it true?" asks Clare, "About Duncan Melship?"

Lottie shrugs, "Oh yes, we all used to warn one another about him. He didn't get the nickname "Handyman" for nothing!"

Tessa added, "Nor the Befummeler!"

"Handyman! Befummeler!" Clare laughs and then shudders, "So maybe Slater had his uses?"

"He would only ever do anything for money," says Lottie, "Maybe now it has backfired upon him?"

"What does Melship think? Will he support the new man?" asks Clare.

Lottie answers, "Yes, I think so; He's under the whip and so he will do what he is told."

Tessa adds, "You have to remember my MP is Labour so we have to think differently."

"Oh yes, I was almost forgetting - The beloved two-party system!" replies Clare.

That secret entrance

Andrew Brading was making his way back to Parliament using the Tube. He decided that his first day back after the bomb would need to be cloaked in some secrecy. At the top of the deep escalators in the grey caverns of Westminster underground station, most passengers either make for the exit straight ahead on to Westminster Bridge or duck right to come out on Whitehall.

But Andrew Brading headed left before taking a sharp right along the underground walkway and disappeared through a badly lit revolving door, on the inside of which is a police guard.

He was using one of the lesser-known ways into the bubble that contains the British parliament.

Having shown his green and white striped security pass, and passed through the security gates, he avoided the hassle of bag-searches or x-ray machines that visitors have to endure at the main entrance.

Then he was on another underground walkway. Turn left and he could walk through a tiled passageway between a stone unicorn and a crowned lion, to a colonnade to take him towards the main House of Commons debating chamber.

To the right is New Palace Yard and the MPs' underground carpark or the other side is Speaker's Green and Speaker's Court.

On most days, this walkway is crammed with people walking purposefully in both directions. He could blend in here and would have avoided the theatre of a re-appearance in front of the media.

Recognisable by their security passes, if not always by their faces; some MPs seem to find coming to Westminster a bit of a drain on their time and prefer to stay away.

Other MPs still look bewildered and lost, because they are.

"It takes about a year for them to find their way round," one of the many machine-gun-carrying policemen remarked. "You can tell, because that's when you become invisible to them. At the start, they are always friendly, saying hello and holding doors open. Then it stops. I'm sure they are not bad people, but they just become part of the bubble."

The police recognise the nuances of the badges.

The peers by their red and white striped passes. The media are identifiable by their brown badges, the Palace staff by their grey ones. Lords' assistants and researchers are issued with straight reds, green and white stripes are the MPs but the most terrifying species of all are those with straight green - Commons advisors.

Now Brading needs to find out a few things - but he would do so from the covert area of his office. He turned the corner and slipped in. There was a muffled cheer. Serena ran to greet him. Maggie and Clare stood back and watched him take his seat.

"Well, they've bombed me, although I feel terrible about Derek, my poor driver- and his family. The experts said if it had been a few inches further back it would have taken off my head, instead of leaving me with terrible headache. Thank you all for the wishes and chocolates and everything. My visitors polished off most of the chocolates, although I did manage to hide the Toblerone bar."

Serena smiled, "We thought flowers would be a little bit -er - final in the circumstances."

"I understand; now we need to come up with a plan to get the bastards!"

Vauxhall Cross and the Plan

Amanda had called Jake. She had asked for a further meeting, but time it was to be at Vauxhall Cross instead of over a video link.

"I'm concerned that we don't get overheard this time," explained Amanda, and I'm bringing Grace in for the session as well.

Jake alerted Clare and all of them piled into a couple of taxis around to the dramatic-looking building housing SI6 and overlooking the Thames and Vauxhall Bridge.

"It's like Gotham City has been given a good clean," commented Jake.

As they approached the building, Jake said to Clare that it was bringing back all kinds of awkward memories. He had been locked away in an adjacent building while Bigsy, Clare and Chuck Manners had been touring Arizona on an earlier adventure.

"It reminds me somehow of a post-modernist Aztec Temple," observed Clare, looking over the structure, "And considering it is supposed to be secret, it is interesting that every taxi driver in London knows where it is."

They heard the taxi driver chuckle. He came onto the loudspeaker in the back of the cab. "Luv, I was already driving when they built this place. The one before it was at Century House, near Waterloo and was just as well-known. I dunno what we'd do if we ever really had a cold war. They put this up really quick, though when Mrs Thatcher told them to look sharpish."

"They say that there's almost as much underground as there is above ground?" said Clare.

"Yes, there's a lot below surface." answered the taxi driver, "Its somewhere to lock up all the spies. And did you know there's a tunnel under the river too? It goes all the way to Whitehall."

In the other taxi there was a similar conversation, but in this one Christina was telling how the Russians had, in 2000, supplied an RPG-22 anti-tank rocket to some local dissidents who had fired on the building from the adjacent Spring Gardens.

"All it did was help justify the cost of the triple glazing," said Bigsy, somewhat drily. "Yes, but it also showed how vulnerable most of London is to unsolicited attack," added Christina, "And I remember, we used to think of the Netta - RPG-22 - as a disposable asset. The firing tube was made of fibreglass. Truly fire and forget."

After complex security procedures, they were inside the building, albeit without their locked-away cell-phones. Amanda had appeared and was to escort them to the room.

"We are in the Dick White Room," she announced, "It's quite a big deal to be on that floor."

Christina smiled, "Dick White? Wasn't he a founder of SIS?"

"Not exactly," answered Amanda, " He helped the move of MI6 to its previous building and was also the head of both services - MI5 and MI6. The floor is the only one to have the rooms named instead of numbered - There's Mansfield Cumming - he was the founder, Paul Dukes, one of the first superspies, Hugh Sinclair - from when we were at 54 Broadway - which we outgrew. Oh and a few others too."

"But not a James Bond room?" asked Jake, "You are not the first person to ask that question," said Amanda, evasively.

They arrived at the floor. It was like an office executive suite, with its own receptionists and coffee stations. Amanda led them to the meeting room. Jake caught a glimpse of another door, "James Bond Suite," it said, printed onto official-looking signage.

Inside the room, Grace was already seated, everyone exchanged greetings and then Jake asked, "I've just got to ask, that James Bond Suite. Can I look inside later?"

Amanda and Grace both smiled, "I think you will be very disappointed; it's a storage cupboard which someone had the wit to name. Nothing to see there, except cleaning materials."

"Or is it?" said Bigsy, also smiling.

"Okay, to business," said Amanda, "I wanted this to be

face to face to avoid any unnecessary security exposures."

"First, some new developments: Roger Slater has turned himself over as State evidence. He says he has been threatened and hounded for long enough and he now wants to declare everything he knows."

"That is consistent with something I heard from one of my flatmates," said Clare, "Lottie - who is the girlfriend of Matt Stevens, said that Slater was threatened by two Russian-looking gentlemen when they were in a pub."

"And why would your flatmate's boyfriend be with the reporter?" asked Grace, confused.

Clare added "Well, it's a long story, but we flatmates all went out together with a chap called Robin Hunter, who was dating Tessa. Robin told some stories about Andrew Brading, which Matt then drunkenly passed on to Slater. To be honest, I get the impression that Matt is somewhat rattled too after the Russian encounter."

Clare looked a little guilty, 'I must come clean too about another one of the threats to Slater. Serena and I visited a well-known QC who suggested we should serve a court injunction on Slater to stop him from pestering Andrew Brading. By the time it had been written it had turned into a very heavy-duty super injunction."

"No wonder Slater wants to run for the hills!" said Amanda. Christina decided she would keep quiet about her encounter with Slater. The piece of the story about the sub machine gun might not play too well inside SI6.

"Another very interesting facet is the discovered back-channel - based upon a wire-tap inside Whitehall. We can thank Bigsy here for helping track it down and for preventing it from being decommissioned. Now it could be a useful asset for us to send false information to whoever is listening."

"We should also remember the findings from our trip to Norway," said Jake, "Arne Holstad, The Chief Science Officer of Elixanor was to be replaced. He told us that the nano-delivery of the medicines didn't work, yet we know that the system is about to be sold to several governments."

"And it isn't even the first time that Elixanor has been caught being economical with the truth," said Grace, "They lied about a blood testing system once before and were caught and fined by the U.S. Securities and Exchange Commission."

"There's something else," added Christina, "I received a phone call yesterday from Marion Charlotte - except she's Lady Hinton nowadays!"

Amanda looked interested, "Lady Hinton - married quite recently to Lord Edgar Hinton of Gloucestershire?"

"Yes, but we all knew her in a previous life when she worked for an escort agency. It turns out she knew the people that framed Andrew too, both Natasha Makarovna and Shanell Kinkaid."

Christina decided to edit around her own knowledge of these people and the agency. It could otherwise get too complicated to explain, especially to the British Security Services.

"Well, Marion called me yesterday. She said that as I'd been asking about Tasha, I might be interested in the latest gossip. That Tasha was now dating Michael Tovey."

"That's hilarious!" said Clare, "Have you seen Tasha, and then Tovey? Tasha's a model - slim, fashionable, delectable and a head turner. Tovey is - how shall I say - someone you'd cross the street to avoid."

Is it another set-up?" asked Jake, "Like the time that Raven and Brant were plying MPs with all manner of experience to get their way."

"I'm beginning to see why you have called us all here," said Clare, "and to this fancy meeting room!"

"I want this whole situation to stop, and we are the people who can do it." answered Amanda, "And with that in mind, I've asked some others to meet us here, " Amanda pressed a button, "It's okay, you can show them in."

A door opened and they could see one of Amanda's assistants, ushering someone in.

It was Andrew Brading.

"Oh, a whole roomful of people," he said startled, "Which one of you is Amanda?"

Then, Serena followed him into the room. She looked around the faces.

"Clare?" she said, looking surprised.

Andrew now looked more closely, "Clare?" he repeated.

"I have some explaining to do to you both," started

Amanda, "And I must apologise for the clandestine way we brought you here. We did not want there to be any security leaks."

Grace had turned the earlier discussion into a chart, which she now displayed on the room projector.

Andrew and Serena still looked baffled.

"Clare, I'm confused. Are you part of SI6 or something?"

"No, not at all, I happen to know Amanda and she asked me if I could assist with something,"

"It certainly accounts for your quick-wittedness," said Serena, "I knew you had an above-average IQ - just the way you fixed that first problem for Andrew..."

"Pure luck," said Clare, modestly, "Although I have been in somewhat similar situations before."

"So Samantha is really your sister?" asked Andrew.

"Oh yes, although Jake here isn't exactly my boyfriend!" smiled Clare.

"Hello, yes, I'm Jake. A co-worker of Clare's"

"And I'm Christina - another co-worker,"

"And I'm Dave Carter - call me Bigsy - we all work for a small outfit called The Triangle."

"Well, I'm pleased to meet you all, but I assume you are some sort of security consultants?" asked Andrew.

"They are a mixture of security consultants and other

capabilities," answered Amanda, "And this is Grace Fielding, from GCHQ."

Grace started to stand, sat down again and smiled.

"GCHQ, SI6, Vauxhall Cross, Security Consultants...You are pulling out all the stops," said Andrew, "I hope it is worth it!"

They all looked back toward the image that Grace had projected. Amanda explained everything for Andrew and Serena.

Brading

- Brading reputation damaged by Slater innuendo
- Brading bomb perpetrators (unknown?)
- Brading Unconstitutionally replaced by Tovey
- Slater turning State evidence

Elixanor Deal

- Elixanor a sham company with bad technology
- Arne Holstad replied by Mikael Bjornstad
- Tovey to push through the Healthcare Bill to facilitate Elixanor deal
- Tovey associates are Miller McDonald and Trudi Hartmann working for (unknown?)

Dirty Tricks

- Medusa listening station in use
- Wiretap discovered
- Yaroslav as suspected enforcer on behalf of (unknown?)

Clare looked at the list and had a secret pang of envy that Grace had summarised everything so well. No wonder Grace was an information officer at GCHQ.

"So what do you expect to do about the situation?" asked Andrew, "I'm kind of resigned to being outwitted by the scourge of the media."

"I have several plan objectives," answered Amanda, "Let's list them, Grace!"

1) Find out who is running Medusa
2) Stop the Protection of Healthcare Rights Bill in its current form
3) Discredit Elixanor
4) Capture McDonald and Hartmann and identify their bosses.
5) Curtail Yaroslav and his gang.

"I'm not sure we can guarantee to put you back in position, Andrew, but we'll give it a shot as well."

Andrew and Serena both smiled. Serena asked, "Look, can we tell Maggie about this? She would otherwise be the only one of our office out of the loop?"

Amanda considered, "She is trustworthy? The Triangle people have worked together for a long time, as have Grace and I. We also know the Triangle organisation very well. It would be important to have a similar trust in Maggie?"

Andrew spoke, "I have known Maggie since she was a teenager - let me rephrase that - since she was eighteen. She is determinedly loyal. I would have no reservations about having her included."

Serena nodded, "I have to agree. And it would be more difficult to work around her. She is very capable and would soon work out something was going on."

"Okay, then, it'll be this group, plus Maggie and my boss Jim Cavendish."

Serena looked surprised, "Jim Cavendish - wasn't he one of Clare's referees for when she got the job?"

"Oh yes, it was better to decouple Clare from me," answered Amanda.

"So now all we need is a plan," said Bigsy.

"Grace and I might just have an idea about that!" declared Amanda.

PART THREE

Politicians

"Politicians were mostly people who'd had
too little morals and ethics to stay lawyers."

George R.R. Martin, Ace in the Hole

Identity Bill, Second Reading

Once again, the Commons is crowded. It is to be the second reading of the Identity Bill, over which Andrew Brading has unwittingly become the headline news ever since the first reading was sneaked through the House. He hopes that Amanda's Plan will work.

Andrew Brading takes to the floor and launches the first part of the Plan:

"They have done it. The right wing of the Conservative party has won its historic victory."

"The UK has become a sovereign 'third country', with its limited trade deal with the EU. The UK, right-wingers believe, has been reconciled to its true history as a nation of offshore islanders. We have our own sandcastle upon which we can fly our own flags and create our own policy. We have taken back control, so long as it doesn't irritate anyone else, nor impinge upon the scallywag plans of the elite."

There is scuffling and rustling of papers.

A quiet "Order, Order," issues from The Speaker.

Andrew continues, "But those same right-wingers have also failed, according to their own terms. Theresa May's 'red, white and blue' nation is long dead, and a hastily-patched hustler deal turned out to be better than no deal at all."

 Andrew hears muttering from behind him. His own backbenchers are getting ruffled.

"Order, Order!"

He continues, "Of course, our EU friends will not be supplanted by a great new Europe where British trade flows unimpeded; there are now frictions and barriers, not least in services. Witness our lorry queues. The strange absences of tomatoes, the difficulty of selling sausages abroad. Confused fishing legislation connected to a time-out in a few years creating landed catches which cannot be sold. But that's not all, the same confusion applies to components and to large items stored in containers. Deregulatory moves by the UK are already being met with EU retaliation."

"You say Tomato," bellows someone.

"And I say Tomayto," shouts someone else.

"Order! Order!," calls The Speaker.

Brading continues. This would get him into the papers, that was for sure, "In short, the UK has repatriated economic sovereignty and discovered that, far from allowing it to humble the EU, it has harmed itself. Our Leaders who supposedly stood up for the greatness of the renewed British nation have been revealed as 'champions of free trade' who only understand the underbelly of the modern economy and as boastful flag-waving nationalists who don't realise that great British rulers once looked down on such tinpot antics."

"Tinpot speech," shouts someone from his own party.

"Listen!" shouts a cross bencher.

"Order! Order!" beckons The Speaker, now raising his voice.

Brading resumes, "As things now stand, the UK has made its pointless gesture, a politics of headlines in which sovereignty is performed by bleating world-beating absurdities. We have a promise without a plan. We have a selection of political tinkerers, intent on adjusting the table to their personal advantage. We have broken out of one regime of international relationships into a holding pattern worse than that which came before, but with a blind hope of redemption although, more likely, stagnation or damnation."

"Order! Order!" shouts the Speaker, just to make sure that the speech could conclude,

"Will the Right Honourable Gentleman please consider reaching a conclusion,"

Brading smiles, "Yes, Mr Speaker, I will make a point and list some pertinent though vulgar considerations. We might end up with a renewed plebiscitary and parliamentary democracy in which the people take back control, but not just from Brussels."

The speaker looks intrigued at where Brading's argument may lead.

Brading continues, "Now it is cronyist faux Tories making the EU's bureaucrats look like models of honest and transparent politics; our politicians use systematic mendacity, abetted by a loyal red-top press and unconstrained by a whip-controlled parliament. The game can be revealed. The pie was in Brussels. Our politicians want it closer to get their hands into it. We've seen Russia drift from oligarchy into kleptocracy. Now our moneyed and ruling classes want the same for Britain."

"Vulgar," shouts someone.

"Sermo Vulgaris," shouts someone else.

"Give way," calls a third.

Brading continues, "No. 'Nemo mortalium omnibus horis sapit.' - Of mortal men, none is wise at all times - And so, in their failure as champions of free trade, Britain has repeated a failure of the 1950s, an attempt to create a western Europe-wide industrial free trade area that led instead to the UK seeking entry to the European Economic United Kingdom in 1961. Perhaps they might reach back even further into history, to the aspiration of an earlier generation of Tory press lords, who pushed for 'empire free trade' in the 1920s and 1930s. These people – who had 'power without responsibility', in Baldwin's famous phrase – also failed, as India and the dominions remained protectionist.

"Ironically, the imperialists and press lords of that era wanted to create a trading bloc to rival the United States; today's politicians would prefer a deal with the Americans, handing control to Washington rather than Brussels. But the US, even after scurrilous Trumpism, is still protectionist and deeply committed to exporting hormone-enriched science-project foods."

"Chickens!" someone shouts.

"Fried Chickens!" calls another.

"Order! Order! You must let the Right Honorable Gentleman continue and desist from these childish cat-calls." says The Speaker.

Brading again: "We could develop a Cayman Islands model: merging the UK with an archipelago of tax havens run from the Caribbean, to create an even bigger tax-avoidance paradise than the one we already have.

"Don't be fooled, we could give up on the rest of the world, and focus on national renewal, on so-called levelling up of beyond the red wall. But we already have some indication of how this is going."

Brading pauses and looks around the House. He could see the Prime Minister giving him the same look that he'd been given for his speech about the Fundamental Rights Bill. This time he could also see the red-faced whip standing behind the Speaker and looking about as angry as it was possible to be without hitting someone.

Brading continues, "The creation of new national

business is, in reality, contracts for cronies - even shamefully through the national emergency of a pandemic - and dodgy startups angling for subsidies, while chummy businesses actually invest overseas. We should hardly be surprised that "levelling up" turns out to be a cynically small pork-barrel fund for financing better bypasses.

"Yet this ideological maelstrom gives an opportunity to abandon old nostrums and re-energise with a new national mission.

"We should disabuse ourselves of the cosy and outdated notion that Britain's ills are caused by imperial hangovers and a consequently incompetent upper-class elite. We should wake up and offer an alternative future to contest the rich-boy narrative – one that amounts to more than just better welfare and more administrative competence.

"We need a revised agenda: of greater equality, of common purpose, of rising wages, of meaningful work. We could embrace the idea of a refreshed democracy, of really taking back control, of an anti-elite politic rather than a reheated technocracy.

"We should speak in realities, not celebratory fantasies, and seek to create a truthful democratic politics, which is essential to any real programme of progressive change. The bonfire of national illusions may have only just started, and current circumstances force an essential understanding of Britain's place in the world.

Brading gestures slowly with his hand, no fingers outstretched lest they look like daggers, "We are no longer a potentially 'top nation'. Britain will not escape the orbit of Europe; it never did, even at the height of its power. It must imitate far more than it innovates.

Inserting 'UK discovery' and 'UK first' into the illusory Premier speeches fools no-one, not even Gogglebox.

"Understanding these truths is crucial to a genuine national reconstruction, which should aim to create a real better country, not to fake being the best."

"Gogglebox!" someone shouts.

"Order!" commands The Speaker, adding "You are so predictable."

Brading continues, "And so, Mr Speaker, I conclude. A policy of national reconstruction, for the foundational economy, for the support of better everyday life, needs to be built on a double critique: of the failed policies of the past 40 years, and of the ultras seeking an even more disastrous turbo-Thatcherism. If we think about this properly, we can instead write a new history for the British nation."

He stops. Looks around. Silence. A solitary clap from the Visitors' Gallery.

Someone passes him a small piece of yellow paper. "See me in my office," it reads. Signed by one of the Whips.

Truth to Power

The next morning Andrew Brading used the same route to work via the Tube entrance to Parliament.

He slips quietly to his office, where he is greeted by Serena, Clare and Maggie. They had a bottle of Dom Perignon ready and Serena asks Andrew to open it.

"Uh, I'm a bit bleary after last night's TV circuit!" answers Andrew, "But it was amusing to see the Pomps chasing around after me."

"And the short, ultra-pompous, terminally slippery, bespectacled headmaster was on the radio this morning at around 8 o'clock trying to explain the philosophy behind your remarks. It was priceless."

"Take a look at the papers, I bought physical copies this morning, I think the assistant in WH Smith was quite bemused," says Clare, "Look!"

She spreads the headlines around the desk.

BRADING SPEAKS TRUTH TO POWER
(The Guardian)

RIGHT DEFENCE
(The Telegraph)

GOGGLEBOX MENTIONED IN BRADING
PARLIAMENT DEBATE
(The Mail)

BRADING SPEECH IN FULL
(The Times - full transcript behind paywall)

DIANA'S ORIGINAL PLEA TO END CRONYISM
SUPPORTED BY BRADING
(The Express)

MODERN LIFE IS RUBBISH - SAYS BRADING
(The Star)

BRADING BLAMES TOMATO SHORTAGES ON EU
(The Sun)

"Well, Part One of Amanda's plan seems to have worked rather well. Now we need to send that invitation to Tovey."

Fashion

Michael Tovey was having a hectic week. Now that Andrew Brading had self-destructed in Parliament, his way getting the Protection of Healthcare Rights Bill out seems assured. He had felt like celebrating and then, boom, out of nowhere he'd received an invitation from a supermodel to go to London Fashion Week.

He'd met Natasha Makarovna a couple of times with Miller McDonald, and she'd always seemed to like him, but now she'd asked him to accompany her to London Fashion Week. Well, not to the whole week, but to a couple of events on Wednesday.

"It is always good when we go with someone. Usually, I turn up with a couple of other models, but sometimes it is good to be seen with a politician or racing driver. You know the kind of thing, I'm sure."

Michael was delighted at the prospect and even asked Natasha (call me Tasha) what he should wear.

"D'you know, I don't think it will matter, but I can suggest you go classic politician. Dark suit and maybe some braces for a hint of classic. Then remember a funky tie and a different nonmatching pocket square. You could bring a hat too. And dark glasses!"

Michael had written it down into a shopping list and headed over to Saville Row to get something that fitted the bill. He'd been told to go to Armani when he'd blinked at the prices and sure enough the Emporio in Knightsbridge had fitted him out with a suit, shirt and some accessories for under £3000, which was less than half what he'd have spent in Saville Row.

"And trust me," said the assistant, "The fashionistas will recognise this as Armani, and you'll be thought of as one cool politician."

Michael decided that it was probably expensable in any case as working attire.

London Fashion: Wednesday

Another day in Andrew's office. Clare was more interested in the online and social media today. She'd been looking around Facebook, Instagram and a couple of fashion magazines and found several closeups of Michael Tovey with Natasha Makarovna.

Some of these were syndicated press pictures too, so they were all properly captioned with the event and the people in the picture. Michael Tovey was well-and-truly seen with Natasha.

The Daily Herald - Jasmine Richards - Fashion Editor

FOR ALL THE DEDICATED FOLLOWERS of fashion there has been only one place to be in recent days. The annual London Fashion Week has put aside the sale signs and recession fears dominating the industry and got people talking about clothes and designs again.

WEDNESDAY MORNING: The British influence on the global stage is at an all-time high. Our home-grown designers are at the helm of some of the biggest luxury brands in the world and our designers are shaping trends and making a huge impact on the global catwalks.

I dragged my man Carlton with me. It was clearly going to be a chore for him to spend the day watching 5ft 11in models strut their stuff on the catwalks.

We stopped at the 18th Century Spencer House first, it's the historic home of Princess Diana's family and venue for a new designer Edith Sparrow showing off her personal brand. Before that, Sparrow had worked on Giorgio Armani's Black label for five years. Sparrow had launched her collection last year in Milan and it was intriguing to see the interest generated.

Fleets of people-carriers ferried VIPs to the venue. Cameramen, photographers and the all-important fashion editors were arriving. We immediately spotted so many big hitters.

Among them were editors from the main fashion press and our back-stage pass meant we caught a glimpse of Edith in action manoeuvring the models and clothes. It's where we caught the stunning supermodel Tasha dressed by Edith Sparrow. Tasha explained she was taking a rest from modelling on this occasion. Her beau for the day was political man Michael Tovey, who had got the memo and was dressed in an Edith Sparrow designed piece of Armani suit, although he claimed it was 'pure luck' that he was in the right attire.

We were ushered upstairs to three gilded rooms, with high ceilings and priceless artworks lining the walls. The regal setting was fitting for this luxurious collection and being one of my most favourite designers, Sparrow did not disappoint.

The statuesque creatures displayed flashes of feathers, fur, crystal studs and beaded linings. Hand-painted cashmere and prints onto stretch cotton and duchesse satin provided an entirely opulent collection from Sparrow.

As the audience cheered and when Edith Sparrow took the customary walk round, you could see the relief across her brow. This was a huge success, and she could tell by the audience's face that they loved it.

A select few were invited for a glass of champagne - of course. I bumped into Edith's mum, who had come down for the show. Air kisses and congratulatory words were fired across the room while cameras were trying to grab the main lady for a few words. I was accosted by a photographer. How exciting I thought, she wants to take my picture. Well almost - she was doing an accessory feature and wanted to take a picture of my shoes. Oh well. However, on our way out another photographer asked if she could take a picture of the Edith Sparrow dress that I was wearing. You see, loyalty pays.

MID MORNING: Onwards with the style pack to the British

Fashion Council tent. I had been invited to meet Charlie Dassault, fashion god.

We had been asked to join her at the Jonathan Bryht show. We stood in line to collect our passes and I couldn't help but notice this wonderful array of colour from the crowd.

There were no recession blues in sight.

There was a big Eighties revival thing going on and girls were wearing neo-orange lipstick, which incidentally I also saw on the catwalk too.

Interesting.

Before the show we bumped into Natasha Makarovna again, still with her MP in tow.

Makarovna said she was particularly interested in a smaller pre-show collection, inspired by what were referred to as ladies of the night. In fact, that was her tame reference to what were a well-cut and edgy collection from Londoner Amy Slice. There was a couture feel in the weight and structure of the garments. The highlight of this collection was the innovative rucksack dress. A little bonkers but remember where you heard about it first.

AFTERNOON: Then it was front row at the packed-out Jonathan Bryht show. Magnificent fabrics and textures with pronounced shoulders and seriously padded hips. Nude chiffon flapper dresses. Then time for a dash to Soho House where Ellie Yellow was exhibiting her new collection. Ellie is a hand embroiderer who studied at Central St Martins College in London. Known for her vibrant colours, contrast and craft, Ellie produced her most refined collection to date. A colour palette of ginger, hard pink and her signature electric blue formed the core to this season. There were biker jackets, mohair coats, sheep skin miniskirts and mirrored denim bodices.

My 6in platform shoes were beginning to irritate me, although good exercise for my calf muscles. My assistant Julie also didn't let the side down, directing and filming in her 5in red suede heels. We even got some of our tame MP closely admiring Tasha's outfit.

Upon reflection, we all agreed that the feeling here in London was uplifting. Yes, there was plenty of talk of tightening purse strings, a certain downturn in consumer spending, but most designers feel that these shows are a critical part of their marketing campaigns.

EVENING: Dom P. What else can I say?

Slater's interview

Roger Slater knew that turning State's evidence was effectively ratting. He would technically be a criminal defendant giving testimony to prosecutors about other alleged criminals.

He'd want a deal though. Immunity from prosecution.

After all, he was helping to ease the caseload, and prosecutors could get on with successfully prosecuting the most pernicious of criminals.

He called in his intentions a few days ago and been given an appointment to attend Islington Police station to make a statement. It all seemed remarkably civilised.

He'd gone by taxi. The parking restrictions around the outside of the Police station were legendary.

He'd also called up his usual solicitor and explained the score. The article, the injunction, the threats. Charles Hardy, his routine Brief, had agreed to meet him at a nearby Italian, before they go on to the cop shop.

Roger Slater walks under the sign for Chapel Market and

toward the small Italian cafe which serves a great breakfast with all the trimmings.

Charles is already there, suited and booted, "Hi Roger, This is a bit off-piste for you, isn't it? Super injunctions and so forth?"

"Yes, I'm afraid I've got myself in rather deep this time. I took some very generous fees but forgot the rule."

"What rule?"

"If it looks too good to be true, it probably is too good to be true."

Hardy adds, "There's some other news too. They have informed me that there will be a Home Office observer at the interview. You are shaking some trees, that's for sure."

"I hope the right apples fall down," answers Roger.

"We are due to be there in ten minutes, we'd better press on."

Roger pays the bill for their coffees and they leave.

Walking toward the Police Station, Slater has a sense that he was being watched from a parked car. He thinks he sees a flash of glass from a telephoto lens. They turn the corner to the right and walk along the edge of a yellowish 90's brick building without any ground floor windows. Then around the corner they see the blue light. Police Station. They walk inside for processing.

They are soon escorted to a tiny interview room. There is a glass wall - which Slater assumes contains a one-way mirror - and a panic bar around the room about a metre from the floor. A recorder is bolted to the interview desk and seems to include DVDs rather than the more conventional cassette tapes used by many police forces in TV dramas.

Slater couldn't help wondering whose bright idea it was to move from one outdated technology to another one. Still, it said 'Made in Luton' on the front of the unit.

"Good Morning, Mr Slater, I am Detective Inspector Evan Davis, and this is Constable Lillian Grant. We are being joined today by an observer from the Home Office, given the nature of your statement. This is Alex Smith."

They sit across the table from one another. Slater decides that the combined age of the three of them interviewing him would be less than 100. Alex, in particular, brought the average age right down.

Lillian starts the recorder, which consists of placing three individual DVDs into separate slots, then pressing a cassette-tape deck style record button. Slater decides that the specification for the new system must have been to make it as much like the old one as possible.

DI Davis leads the questioning. He seems to write a lot onto his notepad.

"It's for the transcript of the interview," he explains.

Slater describes the situation he'd been placed in. To be offered above average fees to get some dirt on Andrew Brading. That the people he was working for had provided him with the women, and the photographer. He'd written the piece, published it but then the trouble had started. He'd been warned first by a mad woman with a knife and gun, then by a couple of Russian gangsters and finally by the threat of a super-injunction.

"My client wishes to make it clear that he is a victim of circumstance in all of this. Had he known that the photographs had been faked, then he would not have written the piece," explains Charles Hardy.

"Yes, but now I'm concerned both for my innocence but also because the people harassing me seem to know where I live. The red wine they spilled was a warning. They left a message along the lines that next time it would be my blood. Look, I've told you the names of the people involved - Hugo Lawson-Parry QC and Sir Edgar Holland. I've still got Lawson-Parry's business card actually, I put it in my wallet."

He fumbles with his wallet, then hands DI Davis the card, as if by way of proof. Then he continues, "I admit I did an expenses scandal piece on Holland a year or so ago, and that he served me a writ. I seriously didn't expect it to escalate."

Slater notices Alex Walker writing something down.

"And I'll need protection," says Slater. "Ian Harrison was the SpAd to Andrew Brading. He was literally pushed under a truck. Brading was bombed. If I leave here without a deal to protect me, then you'll be reading about me in the papers next week. It'll be on you."

He sees DI Davis squirm in his chair. It was too rich for him. To his surprise, the Home Office 'girl' pipes up. "We can fix this. But you'll need to grow a beard. Come with me after the interview, I'll arrange something."

Slater looks at Charles.

"Too good to be true?" asks Charles.

"No, to the contrary, this is Slater's one big lucky break. It is a one-time offer. Come along or take his chances. When I am gone, I am really gone."

Charles looks at Slater, who seemed to be having a minor meltdown. "You want my advice? Go with the lady."

"You can both come along if that makes you feel any better," says Alex, "I have a car waiting outside."

The two police look at one another. This interview has gone sideways. They were uncertain of what to do.

"I have this, also," says Alex, "It's a warrant for the removal of all evidence of the interview, the DVDs, your notes, that business card."

Alex produces some paperwork.

"This is highly irregular," says DI Davis.

"Not where I come from," says Alex. She looked in her bag and produced a second identity card and a smaller card with phone number printed upon it.

DI Davis looks at the identity card: Alex Smith, Secret Intelligence Services, Police Liaison Officer.

Then he asks, "That's not even a proper phone number, beginning with 333?"

"Trust me," says Alex, "It works and will put you through to my controller. Oh, and here is my Warrant Authorisation for the Removal of Evidence."

She opened a slim envelope and flattened the paperwork onto the desk.

TOP SECRET - the paper was headed and then went on to authorise the removal of all evidence of the interview with Roger Slater.

"I'll need to check this with my superiors," says Davis.

"Check away, but please don't take too long. The car is waiting outside to transfer Mr Slater and his solicitor to somewhere safe."

Davis leaves the room, leaving Lillian seated and in charge of the interview.

"I've never had anything like this happen before. But I suppose you are going to say I can't tell anyone?"

"That's right, I'll remind you of your commitment under The Official Secrets Act (1989). And I'll even add that means you can't tell 'just one other person.' We all know where that leads. And I'm afraid the people we are dealing with don't mess around. Guns and bombs; we've already heard about it from Roger, here."

DI Davis returns, "It's pukka, Lillian. I don't know how you've managed it, but I hope you are doing something worthy to protect the country. My boss tells me I've got to sign something as well?"

"That's right, both you and Lillian need to sign this Official Secrets Act addendum. It expressly forbids you from referencing this meeting... Forever."

They both scribble signatures onto the beige-coloured

forms that Alex produces.

"Thank you," she says, "You have both been most co-operative. Now I'll leave with Mr Slater and Mr Hardy and we'll be out of your lives in a matter of moments. Put the last hour down to an extended coffee break or something."

Alex ushers the two men out of the interview room and along a corridor, which leads to a green metal side door exit from the Police Station. A black SUV is waiting. They all climb aboard.

"Let's go," says Alex.

Slater hears the driver on his radio, "Package, plus one, collected."

"I think you are my plus one," he says to Charles Hardy.

They crossed town, the driver skilfully weaving through traffic and around little-known back roads. Suddenly they were on the Embankment, heading west. Slater had, by now, assumed they would be going to the SI6 building south of Vauxhall Bridge, and he was surprised when they pulled up along Millbank by a slightly grubby looking garden railing topped with high security fencing and large overt CCTV cameras.

"Welcome to MI5," says Alex, "This is where we will process you."

"At least it's not a deserted car park with a gang of men in leather coats!" says Charles.

They all walk in through a wide entrance and to a small desk, surrounded by plate glass. The security appears to start more overtly behind them, through what looked like a kind of airlock chamber.

"You must get some temporary badges to go any further," explains Alex, "But note that they will time out in 12 hours."

They were each processed, noticing that Alex didn't receive the same treatment. They walk through the airlock system and were inside. The air seems fresher inside the system and Roger Slater realises it must be treated and cleaned.

"We are going to meet a couple of the bosses," says Alex, "Behave and look respectable if you want to get what you need."

She takes them to a meeting room on the first floor. Out of the windows they can see the River Thames. There are two people in the room.

"Hello Alex," says the woman, "Any problems?"

"No, it went like a dream, Amanda,"

The man speaks, "Let me introduce ourselves, Amanda Miller and James Cavendish. We both work for the security services. We were most interested in what Roger Slater knew from his interactions, and as importantly, who sent him to discredit Andrew Brading."

"I've told the police all that I know. Barrister Hugo Lawson-Parry and Sir Edgar Holland commissioned me to write the piece and even supplied the photos and evidence. I should have thought more carefully about diligence. Look, I asked the police about doing a deal. I think I am in danger now - I've been threatened a couple of times and am also under a super-injunction."

Amanda keeps quiet that she had brought the super injunction to flush Slater out.

"Well, in the capable hands of Alex, we can find you another identity. It will literally be today and you will have 48 hours to move your assets around. You won't be able to tell anyone where you have moved or of your new identity. As a safety feature, we will, if you wish, advise one other person - your solicitor - of your new identity. But you must be very sure that you trust Charles and his ability to keep secrets.

Roger looks at Charles, "Oh yes, I trust Charles implicitly"

Amanda states, "In which case, we will have considerable processing of you to do. We have arranged for you to be kept in a secure apartment in Dolphin Square until the end of the week. You won't be able to leave, but we have the fastest and securest internet access so that you can set your affairs in order. And you'll be moving to another part of the country. We will sell your property in London through a third party and pass the funds to you."

Amanda adds, "I wouldn't come back to London for at least three months and alter your appearance somewhat by that time. After a month we will withdraw all protection and you will be on your own. You can move around freely, but it would be plain stupid to revisit old haunts. And every person you tell of your identity change, beyond Charles here, will further increase your chances of discovery. After three other people know, those looking will certainly find you."

Charles looks at Roger, "Are you sure you want to do this, old chap?"

Roger looks back, "It's this or being blown up or gunned down."

Chocolate Paradise Peachtree

Amanda had called the meeting of the Triangle. Clare was seated with Christina, Jake, and Bigsy in the Triangle offices. Grace was on a link from GCHQ. Bigsy was staring at a big blue box of chocolate covered biscuits.

"Well, so far we are running to plan," says Amanda, "Slater folded easily enough and we are relocating him now. He gave us a couple of unfamiliar names, one of which was a Queen's Council with a tainted reputation: Hugo Lawson-Parry and Sir Edgar Holland."

Grace replies, "I looked through the usual places, but Lawson-Parry has a huge question mark by his name for helping a client who later turned up in a Serious Fraud Office report. Slater says the meeting was in the Chambers of Lawson Parry, but I've tracked it down to a rentable meeting room in Chambers."

Bigsy cracks open the box of thick chocolate-covered biscuits.

Amanda asks, "So what is the story with Lawson-Parry?"

Grace explains, "The SFO secured convictions against

three former oil executives who conspired to give corrupt payments to secure contracts in Iraq. The contracts were scripted by Lawson-Parry."

"In the years of reconstruction following the overthrow of Saddam Hussein, three men conspired with others to pay bribes to public officials at the Iraqi South Oil Company and, and to the Iraqi Ministry of Oil, to secure oil contracts for the oil company and its clients.

"Making profits from the reconstruction work. That's like what we heard Brant was doing when we looked into them?" asks Jake, finding a round biscuit covered in orange tin-foil.

Grace continues, "The post-occupation Iraqi government commissioned the oil company to run projects as part of a 'Master Plan' to rebuild Iraq's oil industry and thereby expand the country's oil export capacity. It seems that middlemen were expected and paid off, in a number of cases the transactions were certified by Hugo Lawson-Parry."

Bigsy smiles, "Lawson-Parry claims he has clean hands?" Bigsy had stacked several of the biscuits in front of him in case the box went out of range.

Grace adds, "Yes, 'a clean skin'. Lawson-Parry said his role was purely to ensure that the contracts for installation of offshore mooring buoys and new oil pipelines were drafted comprehensively. He claimed no knowledge that the oil company benefitted from these state-run projects, nor that the defendants conspired to bribe public officials at the oil company and Ministry of Oil to secure contracts with the oil company and its offshore counterpart."

Clare interrupts, "Well, he would say that, I suppose, although I'm sure it must have damaged his reputation?"

Grace replies, "Less reputational damage than you might think. Now Lawson-Parry is on the radar of crooks and money launderers, because he can possibly draft them a good deal."

Grace adds, "The SFO case became almost like free marketing for him. The bribes totalled over $6 million to secure contracts worth $800 million for the supply of oil pipelines and offshore mooring buoys. Two of the co-conspirators were found guilty of paying over $500,000 in bribes to secure the $55 million contract for the offshore mooring buoys. The curious thing is, I found Lawson-Parry, by referencing 'solicitors', but couldn't find him listed as a barrister or QC."

Amanda adds, "What despite Lawson-Parry effectively setting the peg rate for bribery?"

Grace adds, "Yes, afterwards, the SFO Director said: 'These men dishonestly and corruptly took advantage of a government reeling from dictatorship and occupation and trying to reconstruct a war-torn state. They abused the system to cut out competitors and line their own pockets. It is our mission to pursue and bring to justice those who use criminal means to weaken the integrity of business.' - Think about it. If you were like these men, wouldn't you like a lawyer like Hugo Lawson-Parry?"

Grace explains, "And Sir Edgar Holland isn't exactly untarnished either. The most interesting references were in the Paradise Papers. That's a huge set of documents that show how the world's biggest businesses, heads of state and global figures in politics, entertainment and sport have sheltered their wealth in secretive tax havens.

It's a case of Sir Edgar Holland sheltering his funds in Britain's offshore empires."

"I can remember the Paradise Papers, but not so much of the detail," says Bigsy, noticeably well through his chocolate biscuit pile.

Grace continues, "It was a leak of 13.4 million files that exposed the global environments in which tax abuses can thrive – and the complex and seemingly artificial ways the wealthiest corporations can legally protect their wealth. Nowadays, even terabytes of data can become exposed. The Paradise Papers were around 1.4 Terabytes, which is only a single hard drive."

"The material, came from two offshore service providers and the company registries of 19 tax havens, and was famously obtained by the German newspaper Süddeutsche Zeitung and shared by the International Consortium of Investigative Journalists with partners including the Guardian, the BBC and the New York Times.

Grace pauses to catch her thoughts and then continues,

"These so-called Paradise Papers revealed:

- Extensive offshore dealings by Donald Trump's cabinet members, advisers, and donors, including substantial payments from a firm co-owned by Vladimir Putin's son-in-law to the shipping group of the US commerce secretary, Wilbur Ross.

- How Twitter and Facebook received hundreds of millions of dollars in investments that can be traced back to Russian state financial institutions.

- Extensive use of Cayman Island trust funds as money protection vehicles.

- Aggressive tax avoidance by multinational corporations, including Nike and Apple.

- How some of the biggest names in the film and TV industries protect their wealth with an array of offshore schemes.

- The billions in tax refunds by the Isle of Man and Malta to the owners of private jets and luxury yachts.

- The secret loan and alliance used by the London-listed multinational Glencore in its efforts to secure lucrative mining rights in the Democratic Republic of the Congo.

- The complex offshore webs used by two billionaires to buy stakes in Arsenal and Everton football clubs.

"Well, that is pretty comprehensive stuff, but what about Sir Edgar Holland?" asks Jake.

Grace answers, "Yes, there's details of a previously unknown $450 million offshore trust that has sheltered the wealth of Sir Edgar Holland. And of course, Sir Edgar Holland has been a leading donor to the Tory Party."

Grace adds, "Here, we can see the information."

Grace shares her screen with everyone.

She reads it:

'Sir Edgar Holland, 68, one of the Conservative party's biggest donors, faces fresh questions over his offshore affairs after the Paradise Papers revealed a previously unknown trust sheltering his vast overseas wealth.

'Scores of emails and financial statements chart the inner workings of the Bermuda-based Sullivan Trust from its creation just after he became knighted.

'The documents show the offshore law firm Peachtree, acted as trustee but terminated the relationship, a decision questioned at the time by Holland's representatives.

"I remember Peachtree," says Jake, "The source of much press gossip when it was first discovered, although it seems all but buried nowadays,"

"Exactly; the power of the press to manipulate events," says Bigsy, "I guess there were too many cronies likely to become exposed?"

Grace continues reading. 'The value of the Sullivan Trust fluctuated, but a leaked financial statement recorded it as having assets of $450.4m (£341m) in 2006.

Grace adds, 'Intriguingly, several emails show concern being expressed by Peachtree about the way the Sullivan Trust was being run. The concern was that Peachtree, as trustee, was in effect being asked to rubber-stamp decisions it believed it should have been informed about in advance.

'A senior lawyer for Peachtree wrote in an email: 'There

have been very large sums of money involved and I am very concerned that there has been inadequate supervision of both transactions and distributions ... To put it bluntly, we seem to be told nothing, whereas we carry the responsibility of acting as trustee.'

Grace continues, 'Then we see that Sir Edgar Holland is a former party treasurer and deputy chairman who has given millions to the Conservatives, including £800,000 towards the party's most recent campaign. He is influential in British politics through his polling company and the website GoTory, a centre-right blog aimed at grassroots party activists.

'Holland's spokesman, Quentin du Barry, said the peer had never engaged in tax evasion, abusive tax avoidance or tax avoidance using artificial structures, and "any suggestion or implication that he has will be vigorously challenged".

Grace smiles, 'Balance that with Holland being turned down for a knighthood twice because he was a tax exile in Belize. He gained his title after saying he would take up permanent residence in the UK again.

She adds, 'Then there was a political storm when he confirmed he was still a "non-dom" and did not pay tax in the UK on his earnings abroad. Holland then promised that he would abandon his non-domiciled status to comply with a change of law.

'The Sullivan Trust was set up whilst he was a "non-dom", with his three children named as beneficiaries. Ashcroft was named as the settlor and a beneficiary, the only one entitled to income for life.

Grace continues, 'That's when the trust became the focal

point for a series of multimillion-pound capital distributions, loans and share transactions. A typical example of trust activity is a document saying the trustees agreed to forgive a loan of $29.5m to Ashcroft.

'Oh, and to cap it all, the original trustee was the Brant (Offshore) Trust Services Company, which was taken over by Peachtree Services (Bermuda) Ltd.

"Oh my god," says Bigsy, "My head will explode! Did you say Brant, Grace? There's a direct link from Peachtree to Brant?"

"Only 'kind of'," answers Grace, "This is a takeover of Brant by Peachtree, not the other way around."

"I'm not so sure," says Christina, "Ever heard of a reverse takeover? Raven are good at that. When they took over Brant, instead of calling it Raven, they kept the Brant name. I wonder if they have done something similar with Peachtree. A friendly name hiding Brant underneath, as well as a vehicle for all manner of backhanders?"

Amanda comments, "Yes, I suspect you are right, Christina. It would be useful for Raven/Brant to have something like Peachtree for quartermastering."

Christina bit her tongue to decide not to correct Amanda. In the Russian Army the quartermasters were conventionally considered to be responsible for intelligence operations.

The Burma Road

Serena was back in the Houses of Parliament. She was on a third-floor corridor, known as the Burma Road. To reach it, she had to walk up a rather bleak, stale-smelling, winding staircase. The press organisations are based along this corridor. Politicians seldom visited the Burma Road in person. But their spin doctors, policy advisers and press officers are an almost daily distraction, attempting to portray events to their leaders' advantage. Serena knew she would be in competition with others as she started to spread her news story around.

It's a dance that is generally played out with good humour and politeness; many party press officers are former hacks themselves, hired because they understand the system and know the characters involved.

Unlike outside Westminster, everyone really is in it together. There's no point falling out with people you've got to work alongside every day, unless it's really worth it. Serena was typical of Conservative spinners who were, without fail, polite; it's as if finishing school was part of their training.

If the news is not good, the spinners' task is to try to

minimise the damage by telling anyone who will listen that down is up and not everything is quite as bad as it seems. In 2001, Jo Moore, a spin doctor in the Department of Transport, was forced to resign after sending out an email on 9/11 that said: "It's now a very good day to get out anything we want to bury." Her mistake was to put it in writing.

Trying to bury bad news is still standard practice. If a government has good news, it will usually try to make sure that dominates the headlines for the day, so other good news may be held back. Having two pieces of good news on the same day is a waste of good news. Bad news, however, is best dealt with wholesale. If the government releases several reports on the same day, it is odds-on that there is something it doesn't like in at least two of them.

Serena knew she had something confusing to put out and so carried it around as printed sheets of almost copy-ready material. She also had a fall-back position. She would give a supercharged version of the story to Rachel Crosby, with enough exclusive material in it to make sure that Rachel won the battle of the headlines.

Mistaken Identity

Michael Tovey exposed as Brading imposter
By Rachel Crosby

Tovey's love tryst with supermodel Natasha Makarovna is exposed during scenes at London Fashion week. Tovey is seen all over London with model Tasha including photographs of the couple returning to their bolthole at The Dorchester. Speculation abounds that earlier photographs of Tovey were doctored to implicate Andrew Brading in Tovey's lustful grab for power.

Michael Tovey recently took over Andrew Brading's role as Secretary of State for Internal Affairs, after a silent and bloodless coup during which Brading was implicated in an almost identical love triangle.

Katherine Brading, Michael Brading's journalist wife, commented, "I have never been in any doubt as to Andrew's loyalty and fidelity."

Margaret Tovey, wife of Michael Tovey was unavailable for comment.

Critics of Brading's replacement noted that Tovey was appointed in secrecy, by the Prime Minister, without a normal Cabinet selection process.

Background sources close to the Prime Minister revealed that a significant Conservative party donor directly influenced Tovey's selection.

Further shock revelations show that Tovey had a Cayman Island fund later credited to frame Michael Brading. Named the Tovey Fund, it was renamed to the Brading Fund, via a series of meetings at Peachtree Services, George Town and represented by Hugo Lawson-Parr, QC.

When asked about this, Andrew Brading commented, "I'm very surprised if my colleague Michael Tovey would go to such lengths to take over my role. If these allegations are true, then he must be suffering from a mental illness and we should offer him our sympathies. I am only pleased that the truth has finally come out and that the situation no longer places any strain upon my marriage."

Michael Tovey has a keen interest in the promotion of the Protection of Healthcare Rights Bill, a Bill for which Brading wanted substantial reforms to before publication. Sources close to Brading indicate that there may be commercial interests associated with the Bill in its current form.

Shake it off

'Cause the players gonna play
And the haters gonna hate
Baby, I'm just gonna shake
I shake it off, I shake it off

Heartbreakers gonna break
And the fakers gonna fake
Baby, I'm just gonna shake
I shake it off, I shake it off

Shake it off, I shake it off
I, I, I shake it off, I shake it off
I, I, I shake it off, I shake it off
I, I, I shake it off, I shake it off (Whoo-hoo-hoo)

Hey, hey, hey Just think while you've been
gettin' down and out about the liars
And the dirty, dirty cheats of the world
You could've been gettin' down
To this sick beat

Taylor Swift

The Globe Tavern

Michael Tovey surveys the messy traffic-clogged street at the borders of London Bridge station and London Bridge itself. A stumble from the Barrow Boy and Banker onto the stairs down to the Borough Market. Street food and French country cheeses. Across the way he spies the pub. The Globe Tavern. Used by and lived above by Bridget Jones, at least in the movie.

He enters the surprisingly quiet pub and Tasha is waiting, hair pulled back and in a dark trench coat. She is with a man and another woman, in a leather coat with military-styled epaulettes. He senses this will be a war council.

Tovey has already spent the morning in the Westminster trenches and is ready for some hand-to-hand combat if that is what it takes. With a short smile, Natasha disarms him.

"Who has been a naughty boy, then," she says, and looks first towards him and then to her companions.

"This is Hugo Lawson-Parry QC and Shanell Kinkead,"

Tovey looks at the stunning black woman, who smiles back at him.

"Weren't you also a friend of Andrew Brading?" he asks.

"No, I've never met him," answers Shanell, "But I'm pleased to meet you."

"Look, dear chap," says Lawson-Parry, "You seem to be in a bit of a pickle now. In fact, I've been asked to give you some advice. You need to drop the current plan and even relinquish your position in the House. It's time to fall on your sword dear chap, and that way, with modern politics, you can be up and running again in - oh - I daresay two years. Tops. Probably back in Cabinet."

"But what if I'm happy to tough it out?" asks Tovey.

"I think there's another sword involved as well. A very Russian one and I think you know who carries it." Lawson-Parry was referring to Anatoly Yaroslav, and Tovey knew it.

"But it is not all bad news, the fund in the Cayman has been redesignated to you. I know it has because I personally supervised it. Call it carrot or stick. Take the money - or run. And even better, Brant has just finished its takeover of Elixanor and both shares have benefitted- You should be substantially better off. Now if you don't mind, Tasha and I will leave now, but I think Shanell has something else for you. Oh, and I nearly forgot."

He hands Tovey a small carrier bag containing a bottle. On the bag is written, 'Cayman Islands Airport Authority.' Inside is a bottle of Seven Fathoms Premium Rum from the Cayman Spirits Co. Tovey places the bag on the small round table.

Tasha and Lawson-Parry stand to leave.

Tasha whispers "Goodbye, and be careful, *Lyubimaya*!" And quietly kisses him on the right cheek. Tovey realises he will never see her again.

Then Lawson-Parry shakes his hand, "Think carefully, dear chap, it's not worth getting hurt over this."

They both leave, leaving Shanell, who then leans forward so far that he could feel her hair brushing his cheek.

She whispers, "They have all decided to go along without you. You'd best play their game." She delicately kisses him on the same cheek as Tasha, then stands and leaves the bar.

Tovey fiddles with the bag containing the liquor which he absentmindedly stands it on the bar table. He'd just received a double, or even triple warning.

"Excuse me, Sir, but you can't drink that in here," comes a strident and somewhat amused tone from the barman.

Tovey decides to leave and was soon outside in the brightness of daylight. He feels his twice caressed cheek but decides he's really had several rounds in a boxing ring.

Surprise pizza

That evening, Clare was back at the Bermondsey flat. Tessa and Lottie had been asking her for more information about Brading and Tovey.

"It's such a complicated story. Why would Tovey want to take over Brading's life - and his lovers, come to that!" says Lottie.

"It's been one intrigue after anther since you joined the flat," says Tessa, "We've never had such excitement nor mystery!"

"Pure coincidence," says Clare, "I didn't even know Andrew Brading a couple of months ago! And I've never met Michael Tovey."

There was a buzz at their front door. Lottie presses the entry phone.

"It's a pizza for you, Clare? From Domino's?"

"I didn't order one," says Clare, confused.

"More mystery?" says Lottie, "Here, I'll go get it, so long

as I can have a slice!"

Lottie disappears downstairs and comes back with the pizza.

"Mmm, it looks delish, Veggie Supreme, with slaw and wedges! Are you sure you didn't order it?"

Clare shakes her head.

"Look the guy gave me this envelope - maybe it'll show who made the order then? Could it be a strange love token from Jake?"

They open the envelope. It contains three photographs. A pub somewhere. Michael Tovey, being kissed by Tasha the model. Then one of him being kissed by a very attractive black woman. And a third one of them sitting around the table with a small carrier bag on it. The words Cayman Islands Airport were clearly visible on the carrier.

"Wow, wow, wow!" says Tessa.

"You never disappoint," adds Lottie.

Clare looked a little surprised, "Erm, I don't know where these are from, nor how they got my address."

"Do you think they have been sent anywhere else? Like to the press or anything?" asked Lottie, "I mean, these pictures are dynamite and just about corroborate that story from Rachel Crosby."

"Do you think she has got the pictures too?" asks Lottie, "I mean they could do a lot of damage."

"I need to call someone," says Clare, "This is most unexpected."

She walks across to her room and dials Jake.

"Jake, guess what I've just received? - Only a set of incriminating pictures of Michael Tovey with Tasha and another woman. Just like the Brading set-up, only I get the feeling these will be real rather than photoshopped."

Jake pauses, "We should call Amanda and let her know - My guess is that Tovey is being ditched by his previous accomplices and they want to make sure it is comprehensive. I'll call Amanda and the others and tell them of the development. Can you photograph the pictures, please, and send them to me in an email?"

Clare did as she was requested.

"Expect to hear from me later," says Jake. Clare walks back to the living room, where Tessa and Lottie were already two thirds of the way through the pizza.

"Mmm - Great pizza - Any news?" asks Tessa, "You should have more mystery callers bearing illicit photographs!"

Two separate women

Amanda answers Jake's call. She listens whilst Jake explains.

Then she says, "They are dumping Tovey. This is just to make sure. I'm guessing the pictures have gone to Tovey and a member of Brading's office - They probably picked Clare as the most lowly - even if she technically outranks Maggie, they know that Maggie and Brading are good friends.

"I imagine that if Tovey doesn't take these strong hints, then they will go after him. Another tragic road accident, probably. Other than the two women, who seem to be 'paid extras' there doesn't seem to be any trail leading back to anyone.

"But there is a man's suit on the edge of the 'carrier bag' shot," says Jake, "I think there were four people at that rendezvous, not three."

"Well spotted," says Amanda, "Shall we pull in Natasha Makarovna?" We could ask about the meeting. She can hardly deny it."

"Do you think they have sent it directly to the papers?" asks Jake.

"I doubt it. They are showing the players what they know. And they have considerable leverage over Tovey before it gets published. He's a lost man after it goes to press. They must know that."

"Very good!" says Jake, "I compliment you on your knowledge of how these things work!"

"I've been involved in enough of these situations," says Amanda, "The only unusual thing about this is that the two women appear separately most of the time. I suggest we have a video meeting tomorrow evening. We should wait to see how things play out."

Kensington Gardens

Michael Tovey was not used to being given such an extensive security detail. Now, as he walked home across the Kensington Gardens, he had two concealed armed men in front of him and a similarly armed man and a woman walking behind. He was the dot in the middle of a five on a dice.

Tovey had started to use the walking route during the pandemic. It meant he could spend less time on public transport and the route gave him space, air and exercise. He could also people watch with impunity and yet he would quickly be back in his pied-a-terre in Bayswater, all at the taxpayers' expense.

Tovey didn't expect any trouble. He'd been given a gentle warning - well three gentle warnings when he was in The Globe Tavern and had no plans to open his mouth about any of the business.

He would do what was suggested by Lawson-Parry. Fall on his sword and yield control back to Andrew Brading, who he assumed would be ready to take over again.

He paused as if to consider his route. Today, he'd go directly from West Carriage Drive in a diagonal fashion to the little gate that came out by the traffic lights on the Bayswater Road.

As this blew over, he could quietly retreat to the back benches, having also moved the small number of millions of dollars from the Cayman Islands to somewhere else secure.

He'd been reading the Offshore Financial Center report, which described jurisdictions providing corporate and financial services to non-resident companies on a scale that is incommensurate with the size of their economies.

Traditionally, OFCs were assumed to be small, low-tax jurisdictions in remote location - like The Caymans. More recently, The Netherlands and the United Kingdom were edging up the rankings. The current government was good for this financial re-engineering, even if it did only affect a small portion of the population.

He looks across the park. A red-setter is running at break-neck speed, and he assumes it was off the leash. He hears a whistle, and it turns and bounds back to its master. Then a metallic click. Behind him. He turns towards it just as a man falls from his bicycle to the ground. The four security detail are running to the man. Tovey can see a weapon laying on the ground. One of the security detail kicks it into the grass by the side of the path.

The woman speaks to him urgently, almost a shout,

"Come with me now!"

He sees a black SUV driving from the road inside the park and bumping across the grass toward him. The woman bundles him in and then climbs into the front passenger seat herself. Her colleague clambers into the other passenger door and pushes his head down.

"Let's get him away from here," she barks to the driver. Tovey suddenly realises he had taken on more aspects of Brading's life than he expected.

Not a bomb this time, but a cold-blooded shooting attempt in the middle of a public park. Heck, it was a Royal Park. The gunman was on Royal property.

The BMW SUV was revving hard. It skitters back from the grass onto the road and starts a siren. Tovey was aware that a blue light was flashing from somewhere as it picked out the cars around him. He marvelled at the ease with which the driver slid through the London traffic and how quickly he was back along the Embankment. He had a feeling that he would be going to see the security services.

The black vehicle approaches some formidable looking security gates. There are two large, yellow-and-black chevron-painted metallic barriers in the road looking like two giant bulldozers, yet the driver hardly slows as he approaches them. Sure enough, they fall away, and they enter an internal road, then turns sharply left down a ramp and into an underground car park. Only then does the vehicle slow and appear to be following a light system like planes use at Heathrow airport. He taxies to a bay and everyone gets out of the SUV.

Immediately, several soldiers surround him, and they all are escorted into an underground bunker-like structure, where it was clear they were to be processed like so many drunks on a Friday night.

The woman walks over to Tovey. "Hi, I'm Alex Smith, I'll

be your case officer while you are here. The man on the bicycle in the park was attempting a hit. Lucky for you, his gun jammed. A failure to feed. He must have been practicing the hit and not noticed when the magazine became dislodged. A rookie error actually. You were very lucky."

"I want to thank you all," says Tovey still somewhat disorientated, "And where exactly am I?"

"You are under SIS, in one of our hidden levels. Before you can go any further, we will have to process you. Then we can take you to my boss, Amanda Miller."

The meeting

Amanda had set the call for the evening. She has a lot to tell.

She notes the full turn-out from the Triangle and asked Grace to link into the session. Amanda is seated next to Alex Smith, who has been particularly busy, first with Roger Slater and then with the aftermath of the attempted hit on Michael Tovey.

"Hi everyone, we have had a busy couple of days - mainly thanks to Alex Smith here, our plan is still on track."

She looks towards Alex, who waves at the screens.

"Bigsy muttered, "Alex Smith? That's gotta be a made-up name?"

Amanda says, "Bigsy, you of all people would know how sensitive these microphones are!"

"Oops, sorry," says Bigsy, "Sorry too, Alex Smith!"

"Well, thanks to your discovery, Bigsy, we have been able

to trace the monitoring of the Whitehall communications. As we suspected, it goes right the way back to the listening station. Thanks to Grace, we've also been able to add in a little trick of our own, which means we have been able to pick up some of the chatter from Medusa."

Grace chips in, "Yes, and fascinating it has been. We suspected that Miller McDonald and Trudi Hartmann were running things, and it transpires that they have been, but also using Antanov Yaroslav as an enforcer. Yaroslav is linked to the Roslavl Bratva, which is run by Tima Maximovich.

"We brought Tovey in after the attempted hit, He folded up like a Chinese lantern. The hitman did most of our work for us. We even had to buy Tovey some new trousers. Although I expect the pair he was wearing were at the taxpayers' expense."

"What did Tovey tell you?" asks Jake.

Alex answers, "Well, he was quite shaken and emotional actually. He didn't want to die, nor for his family to be implicated. When we'd calmed him down, we asked him who he'd been with and he told us that he had been manoeuvred into the new Cabinet position by Miller McDonald and Trudi Hartmann. He said that Anatoly Yaroslav was their enforcer, and McDonald and Hartmann had used Yaroslav to encourage him to take on the new role."

"That's pretty much what we'd all suspected," says Jake, "But it's good to get it corroborated."

Alex continues, "Well, Tovey told us how he had been threatened. He'd been set up by Natasha Makarovna and been in pub with her and the other woman in the photographs - Shanell Kinkead, although he said there was also another man present - A Queens Council named Hugo Lawson-Parry."

"Ah, the suit in the photo," says James, "That makes sense!"

"Not actually," says Grace, "Lawson-Parry turned up earlier in this investigation, but when I looked for him the records, I couldn't find anyone with that name. Tovey said that Lawson-Parry was definitely a Brit, but I'm less convinced."

"Whoever he is, he mixes with some hardball company," says Jake, "I mean Yaroslav - wasn't he Maximovich's enforcer when we were investigating Raven Corp?"

Christina nods and then chips in, "Maximovich used Yaroslav to terminate Yegorin and Turgenev when they were due to fly back to Russia. But I seem to remember that you, Amanda, were trying to install Maximovich as a mole?"

Amanda nods, "The law of unintended consequences again, I'm afraid. We let him run and then, after his symbolic violence in the UK, he simply melted back in with his compatriots. But now, we need to deal with Yaroslav."

"I thought Yaroslav had already left the country?" asks Jake.

"We did too, initially, but then picked up some chatter from Minerva. Miller McDonald asked him to stay longer, as an insurance policy linked to Michael Tovey."

"Well, based upon the Medusa messages we intercepted,

it looks as if Yaroslav is finally going back to Moscow. He used a 'stunt double' to exit the country the first time, so that we would think he had already gone. This time he is using 'Terminal Six'.

"Terminal Six?" asks Jake, "That used to be a nickname for Northolt? It was where all of the well-heeled and well-connected used to fly from during the pandemic. Fewer questions asked."

"Correct," says Amanda, "It still functions as a quiet way for civilians and military and Royals to enter and exit the country from close to London."

"How the other half live!" says Bigsy.

"It got rather busy during times of lockdown," says Amanda, "although there's still a cap of 12,000 civilian flights a year on it."

"I remember, it's officially a military airport," says Jake, "Plenty of the people I interviewed for my old magazine 'Street' used it. It even had concierge parking arrangements, and who wouldn't mind having their Lamborghini guarded by military? I seem to remember the runways were resurfaced a while ago and it caused an uproar because the well-heeled couldn't use it and had to make do with Heathrow. But the new runway can take massive planes like Hercules and Dreamliners. Then to have a Bentley waiting to whisk you away. What's not to like?"

"Yes, Boris Johnson's Uxbridge constituency running an airport using the same services firm as City Airport, with maybe only a fifth of City's number of flights, but all of them VIP. It would make for some fascinating reading."

"It's been done," says Bigsy, "But if you add 50% to cover the military manoeuvres, you still only get to 18,000 - or maybe 20,000 flights per year. That's only a quarter of, say, Bristol or Newcastle."

"But highly lucrative, I daresay," says Jake, "All the politicians, posh people and oligarchs."

Amanda interrupts, to keep the meeting on track, "Well, Yaroslav is to exit there tomorrow. He's due to be on a Ukranian private jet to Moscow."

"Will you require anything special?" A new voice cuts in. Jake recognises it as Jim Cavendish, Amanda's boss at SIS.

Amanda speaks, "Hi Jim, yes, I think we should prepare a special reception for Yaroslav."

Amanda looks as if she is considering what to say next, "Yaroslav ran the hit on both the Special Advisor Ian Harrison and on Michael Tovey. Yaroslav was just lazy and used the same cyclist as a hitman twice. We pulled him after the attempt on Tovey. The hitman was wounded but we kept it secret that he had survived. His name is Stefan Kostyantynovych Tarasenko, a Ukranian in London on a Canadian passport. He speaks with a very passable Canadian accent and claimed to be Steve Wheeler, which proved to be about as convincing an alias as that of those two Salisbury Cathedral enthusiasts."

"What, the two who went after Skripal?" asks Bigsy, "Hilarious when they started reciting Wikipedia."

"Not so hilarious for the brutal poison they spread around Salisbury," says Grace.

"No; point taken," says Bigsy, "but 'Wheeler,' a cyclist assassin?"

"That's where we had to get a little more creative with the interview technique," says Alex, "They patched up Steve Wheeler aka Stefan Tarasenko and we did a little digging. It turns out he was, despite his bungling, something of a big deal. He was what's known as *novyy afganskiy*, brutalised by the aftermath of the original Russian/Afghan war.

Alex continues, "He wasn't even involved in the original conflict, but only in the last few years, when Russia has been running strategies to recover its position."

She adds "Tarasenko was one of the coverts sent in by Russia which was betting that the situation in Afghanistan would be stabilised leading both to the withdrawal of Western forces from Afghanistan, and more importantly, from Central Asia.

"This would have opened up the possibility of Russia's economic expansion and the overall growth of its influence in Afghanistan. At that time Tarasenko was a serious player."

Christina chips in, "I knew a couple of people - *afgantsy* - both edgy and they both died young in normal jobs in Russia."

Alex continues, "With the deteriorating security situation and the expansion of the Western presence in Afghanistan and Central Asia, Russia became more interested in maintaining the Western presence inside Afghanistan itself.

Alex continues, "They still needed a pot-stirrer. That's where Tarasenko came in. He was sent into increasingly wild and dangerous situations to engage the US and NATO's forces, resources, and political attention in that country, thus weakening them by default.

"Asymmetric," says Christina, "Use a few to distract many."

Alex adds, "It gave Russia an additional tool, by means of transit services and transportation, to obtain political and economic benefits from them. Tarasenko was like a match being used for his bright flame, but also cynically being burnt down."

"It reminds me of the ten classifications for FSB agents; he'd be near to the bottom, " says Christina, "Always expendable, if only he knew it - How the mighty fall."

Alex nods, "Correct. Russia increasingly sought to exploit the problem of Afghanistan, in order to increase its presence in Central Asia and strengthen its cooperation with the countries in the region. Tarasenko was still a player in that increasingly concealed conflict, but he'd have been living on the edge of his nerves. It probably gave him the PTSD we can see in him since he has been captured by us.

Alex continued, "Tarasenko came back raw, shocked and angry, either bursting with tales of horror and blunder, or spikily or numbly withdrawn. He did what people usually do in such circumstances: Adapted, coped. His nightmares were less frequent, the memories less vivid.

"I see," says Jake, "Then Yaroslav meets him. Wiry, intense and morose, Tarasenko has that brittle and dangerous quality that Yaroslav needs. Give him money, at a time when most were eking out the most marginal of lives, even living with parents and juggling multiple jobs.

"Yes, make him a torpedo!" says Christina, "'torpedo' – a hitman," she explains, "Excuse my Moscow slang."

Amanda nods, "Yes, we see a once mighty player reduced to a war victim and then falling into the pay of the mobsters. Not even as a bodyguard, but as a straightforward killer. Car bombs, drive-by shooting and knives in the night."

Alex adds, Yes, but with the rise of the kleptocracy, even the gangsterism had reached its end. No wonder a somewhat sketchy hitman arrives in London on an e-Bike."

Clare speaks, "He was still lethal though. Have you matched him to the traffic cam footage from outside Parliament yet? To see what happened to Harrison?"

Amanda speaks, "We have. It positively identifies Tarasenko. Too arrogant to even wear a face mask and sloppily using the same e-bike and bike helmet for both hits."

Jim speaks again, "It is instructive to think of the Russians when we see what is happening in London now. Commentators have dubbed Russia a "mafia state". It is certainly a catchy epithet, but what does it actually mean? "

Jim continues, "It means, I think, that the Kremlin rather than being under the control of the criminals, is a shadowy puppeteer making the gangs dance on its strings. But the truth is more complex."

Jim adds, "The Kremlin does not control organised crime in Russia, nor is it controlled by it. Rather, organised crime prospers under Putin, marching in time with his drum. Putin has publicly acknowledged, time and time again, that corruption is widespread. However, after many years of his rule, we have seen little evidence that he has ever intended more than a public show of resolve and a periodic purge of officials fallen from favour who serve as disposable scapegoats."

Amanda speaks, "So we can see the early signs of this behaviour now in the UK?"

Jim again, "We can, but it is uncertain from where it originates. It could be simply the well-heeled elite of Britain, out for quick money, or it could be a leveraged attempt from, say, Russia or China, to infiltrate and divert Big Business."

"Now let's think how we can stop all of this," says Amanda, "We need to stop Raven and its chain of subsidiaries for once and for all."

"Okay," says Clare, "We can ask Andrew to help, Andrew Brading. He's made himself unpopular in Parliament but is probably about to be re-awarded with the post of Secretary of State for Internal Affairs. After all, he was cheated out of it by Tovey and now there is proof."

"Yes," said Jake, "And we know their plan was to introduce a Bill which would open the way towards tiered medical support. The richer you are, the better medicine you receive. Tier 0 for the politicians, Tier 1 and 2 for the well-heeled and elite. Tier 3 and 4 for the rest of us."

"Andrew can simply expose that, in another one of his

inflammatory speeches. We can have Rachel Crosby pre-briefed too!"

"But what about the actual company - Elixanor?" asks Amanda.

"We can use Arne Holstad to help with that. He can speak against them."

"And the capture of McDonald and Hartmann?"

"I've a feeling that when this plan unravels, someone else like Yaroslav will be sent to tidy things up. We should simply be there first and get McDonald and Hartmann to tell us what they know."

Jim's voice cut in, "It sounds, Amanda, as if you have the start of a plan. Call me if you need anything, but otherwise I'll assume Amanda is running things, goodbye, all."

There was a click on the broadcast and he was gone.

PART FOUR

How to execute a plan

A goal
without a plan
is just
a wish

The Little Prince - Antoine de Saint-Exupéry, 1943

PLAN 01 – Remove obstacles

Dusted

Yaroslav was dusted. He'd taken some of that Guyanian cocaine from a meeting in Docklands yesterday. Dealing with the Cali cartel was just about at the edge of his comfort zone. The Cali were highly leveraged through their calculated attempts to legitimise their business. It meant if he was dealing with them, they could look all friendly and business-like, with respectable people in business attire, yet have rented the whole floor of the conference suite and have other men with guns sitting ready to deploy.

He'd been supporting the negotiation of a new route using the "gancho ciego," or "rip-on rip-off," method in which full-size containers are tampered with at sea or as they await export. The route was from Guyana to Rotterdam, but the cargo was supposed to be coconut oil. The people he was supporting were keen to see it extended to Guyanese timber export or something bulkier to increase the size of the shipments.

So now he'd lost his mind on some of that white powder. He was on his way to the airport and knew he could sleep it off on the flight back to Russia.

They enter the gates of the airport, which looks like a

military compound. Northolt, it says on the sign. He's not been here before although he has heard that Maximovich and several others from the top had all been through the so-called Terminal Six. The car stops and the driver speaks with a smiling woman in the control booth.

"Yes, you can drive the car up to the doors of the plane, but you know we have to put our own driver in? Airport safety protocol. Or you can transfer to one of our cars, or simply wait in the VIP lounge? - It's your choice?" she smiles at the driver.

The driver turns and in Russian asks Yaroslav which he would prefer.

"Let them drive us in the Bentley, " Yaroslav answers. It means they don't need to transfer the luggage and he could soon be asleep in the comfort of the executive jet.

Another liveried man jumps into the driver seat of their Bentley. "Hmm," he says, "Mulsanne extended wheelbase. Very nice. I had a go in a Flying Spur the other day, but this is much nicer. I've to watch out for all the plane lights as well as the normal traffic signals. See that amber light? it means that the AN-32 wants to taxi. We have to wait on this line so that it doesn't hit us with its wings."

Yaroslav looks over. He notices the plane's registration is EW, which he recalls was the old Soviet Union.

"Belarus plane in today, they come from all over, " said the driver, "I've got to look out for a Lunajet Challenger 350 - They don't usually fly from here - they are usually from Farnborough."

He pauses at another white line with traffic lights. A

military jeep pulls up alongside and then an untidy looking green Volvo saloon behind.

"These aren't like normal lights," explains the driver, "Sometimes an aircraft manoeuvre takes much longer than you expect. It's one of the reasons we have to drive you around the airport. Also it'll stop you from taking a wrong turning at the runway."

By now there was a short queue of traffic, including an airport bus, which looks as it if was ferrying a few soldiers to a military plane.

Then a gentle tap on the side glass of the Bentley, almost unheard inside through the double glazing. Yaroslav and the driver both look around. It is an SA80 combat weapon. The driver slides the window down.

"Freeze," says the soldier holding the gun, in a very polite tone.

"Now will the driver and front seat passenger please leave the vehicle."

"Nice to meet you gents, and this is a first, too," says the exiting driver, as he is escorted away. Jaroslav's driver reaches behind his back for a pistol but gets clubbed to the ground by another soldier.

A bulky, camouflage-dressed soldier takes the driver's seat. He is wearing a green beret.

"Welcome to my world," he says, and slams the car into drive, accelerating rapidly across the airport to where the shape of a military Hercules could be made out. He races up the back ramp and into the plane, where he gracefully stops the vehicle.

"Now for a ride, but only after we've disabled the Bentley's tracker and your cell phone."

Another green-bereted man steps forward with something resembling a metal detector.

"The tracker is behind the heater ducts. Yaroslav has two cellphones and there's another one in the glovebox. The car also has a built-in SIMM."

A woman in camo-gear gestures for Yaroslav to hand over his cellphones, finds the one in the glovebox and the slot for the SIMM in the inside of the Bentley. The soldier with the metal detector prises off some trim and reveals a large grey battery and a small device.

"It's the tracker - It was the tracker," he says, clipping off the battery's wires. Then he re-tests everything with his scanner.

"Clear now, no signals," he declares.

"Such a waste to make it fish food," one soldier remarks as he looked at the Bentley.

They manoeuvre Yaroslav forward in the plane and take him to a row of uncomfortable -looking red webbed seats. This was not what Yaroslav had planned.

"Bumpy ride ahead," says one of the soldiers.

Yaroslav notices that they all have tags over their names. He makes out the red dagger patches on their battledress. Royal Marine Commandos. He sees that the grubby Volvo saloon has boarded the plane and is secured behind the Bentley, away from the rear hatch.

The commandos take a row of red-webbed seats and strap themselves in. Yaroslav is being accompanied by a whole squad of marines. He does not think they are taking him to Moscow.

The rear hatch raises and the judder of four turboprops signals the start of a flight.

He felt the queso blanco drifting around his brain.

Disappearing

Yaroslav's plane's engines change tone. He senses they are low, but he has an intense pressure in his ear. He's not sure whether it is from the descent, or from the white powder. By the angle of the plane, they have been flying in a circle. He wonders if they are due to land. Then a bang. The rear hold door is opening. After his eyes adjust, he can just make out the sea. They are flying low. Over the noise of rushing air, he hears another sound. It is a winch. He sees the Bentley moving towards the open hold.

Then, a bang and the car lurches forward, over the end of the plane, into the sea.

Yaroslav realises he is being 'disappeared'. He has done this to enough other people to know the moves. Disappeared without trace. The rear door of the plane is closing again. The marines had cheered when the Bentley rolled into the sea. The plane had skipped up in the air, but he reckoned it must have been the release of a couple of tonnes of metal, so no wonder.

Then a second reduction in the plane's engine sound. He heard another clunk sound from underneath. Wheels down. They were going to land. It had been around a ninety-minute flight. Paris? Too close. Amsterdam or Brussels, also too close. Frankfurt, maybe? But they were near to water. Hamburg then, or Bremen.

The plane does a navy landing, all wheels down onto the tarmac at once. Like a carrier landing would be. So different from an air force landing which rotates the nose down after the back wheels are all on the ground

He looks out of the plane's hold. His eyes fix upon the vehicles. They still have UK number plates. He has not even left the U.K. Unless this is a very elaborate set-up.

The woman marine walks up to him.

"You are in Prestwick, Scotland. We have a few questions for you here. Answer them and we'll keep hold of you. Fail to comply and you'll be transferred to the plane over there."

Yaroslav sees the white plane. It looks like a Boeing 737, but he recognises it as a C-40 Clipper. Along the side of it is written 'United States Navy'. Yaroslav realises he could be transferred from the UK government to the US. Extraditioned through Prestwick.

The woman adds, "Oh, and don't mistake the outside of that other plane for anything familiar. The Americans strip out the seats and install cargo webbing. Our Hercules is far more comfortable. You can come with me now."

She guides him toward the green Volvo car and into a back seat. A camouflaged driver takes the driver's seat, and she sits in the front passenger seat.

The driver reverses the car at high speed, off the plane and onto the tarmac. Then he selects forward, and they race off towards a hangar along the perimeter of the airport.

They drive inside and Yaroslav can see a single small plane and the rest of the hangar is taken up by a large concrete structure.

"This will be your home for a while. I recommend you talk. It will make things so much more pleasant for you."

Yaroslav weighs his options. They are between this woman Devil and the deep blue sea where his Bentley is already residing. He looks at his watch. He'd been on the road into Uxbridge 3 hours ago.

Red line around

Yaroslav is in what he considers to be an interrogation suite.

"What do you want from me?" asks Yaroslav, displaying a certain arrogance.

You were brazen in arranging those attacks," answers the first interrogator - a tanned well-set man with long dark hair - he could advertise tobacco on television if it was still allowed - "First, Ian Harrison and then attempts on Michael Tovey,"

"But I thought another man was responsible for both of those situations?" asks Yaroslav, "If he blames me, he is simply trying to save his own skin."

The second interrogator is an athletic blonde-haired woman - power dressed in a dark trouser suit, "He does blame you, and furthermore he showed us pictures of you with him and even of you passing him money - twice actually. Once £10,000 for Harrison and then £20,000 for Tovey."

"I see, a Special Advisor is worth less than a Member of Parliament?" says Yaroslav.

"The bicycle technique is hardly original either," says the male interrogator, "Just like Zelimkhan Khangoshvili in a Berlin park on his way home from midday prayers at a local mosque.

The woman adds, "Someone on an electric bicycle shot Khangoshvili twice in the head and once in the shoulder. The assassin was arrested by German authorities within a few hours of the murder, ridiculously having been spotted throwing his gun and wig into a nearby river."

"Neither that, nor the Harrison and Tovey events have anything to do with me," says Yaroslav.

The man continues, "On the contrary, it fits neatly into a broader pattern of international attacks perpetrated by Kremlin agents in recent years. Targeted assassinations are nothing new in the intelligence world, but the air of plausible deniability exhibited in the past seems to have disappeared today."

The male interrogator adds, "What's more, killings like the Berlin attack or the bike rider in London fly in the face of Russia's international commitments and cause significant damage to the Russian government's credibility. Despite that, the death toll continues to mount."

The woman adds, "These murders show the Kremlin's readiness to hunt down foes across the globe with little regard for the laws of host countries."

"I have told you. None of this has anything to do with me," answers Yaroslav.

The man continues, "These attacks allow Russia to intimidate perceived traitors while sending a chilling message of defiance to the country's international adversaries and reflect the increasingly hostile dynamic between Russia and the West since the 2014 invasion of Ukraine.

Yaroslav adds, "Victims of Putin's assassins serve as symbols of what happens to anyone accused of betraying the Kremlin. I don't want to be on that list."

The woman begins, "Sergei Skripal, who survived being poisoned by two Kremlin agents during an operation in Salisbury, England, had earlier been imprisoned by the Russian government for slipping state secrets to the West. I think you are finding yourself in a similar situation now."

Yaroslav is determined to stay calm, "I am no spy, certainly not working for the Russian government."

The woman continues, "Maybe not, but your employers have direct links with the Russian State - they employ you, so you are consequently an agent of Russia - and blundering around, typical of the kind of errors that they make."

She adds, "For example, the poisoning of Bulgarian Emilian Gebrev was linked to his role in the arms trade, where he frequently foiled Russian attempts to make deals in Africa and Asia."

The man grins and says, "Both Skripal and Gebrev survived, as have numerous other targets, suggesting a decline in professionalism as Russia seeks to deploy greater numbers of assassins abroad. We think, Mr

Yaroslav, that you are one of them."

Yaroslav replies. "Maybe there's an element of sticking two fingers up at Western countries here, as if Russia is saying 'we don't even really care if this works or not,' - but remember, I'm not involved."

Yaroslav was having difficulty working out who was the tough one between the two interrogators. That Columbian cocaine was still strong.

The woman continues, "Soviet hit squads were a routine feature of the first Cold War. Following a brief lull during the 1990s, President Putin reopened the door to Kremlin assassinations on foreign soil when he backed a new Russian law allowing extrajudicial killings abroad under the guise of "combating extremism and terrorism."

The man adds, "Then we saw the troubling nature of this Putin law raised early on by London-based Russian defector Alexander Litvinenko, who warned that it could target Putin's personal enemies."

The woman again, "Within months, Litvinenko was dead. Using rare radioactive polonium to poison Litvinenko turned his death into a protracted public execution that served the Kremlin's purposes admirably. It left exiled opponents of the Putin regime in no doubt of the fate that might await them, while allowing Moscow to protest its innocence."

The man speaks again, Yaroslav thought that the two of them made a strong tag-team, "I guess he is probably preparing something for you now, Putin... His use of international assassinations has escalated significantly. The Russian seizure of Crimea and subsequent military intervention in eastern Ukraine are watershed moments in the history of Moscow's post-Soviet relations with the Western world."

Yaroslav replies, "You are clutching at straws. Putin isn't interested in me. There are huge traitors to pursue; just pick up a copy of Pravda and you'll see."

The woman answers, "You are right, of course, it is not what Putin thinks that counts here. It is what those who commissioned you think. If they are trying to develop new business, which links back to Russia, or to develop new secret service tactics to corrupt our political structure, then they will be most upset if you tip up their apple-cart."

Then the man, "The Kremlin engages in an escalating campaign of hybrid hostilities against the West. Targeted assassinations are only part of this global confrontation, which also includes everything from cyber-attacks and disinformation campaigns to election meddling. You know it is being unpicked slowly, but Putin is pleased because for the Kremlin it is a cheap way to conduct warfare."

The woman again, "Russia has already paid a price for its increasingly aggressive actions, with its spree of Kremlin-linked killings proving particularly damaging to the country's international standing. The US government expelled 60 Russian diplomats and closed a Seattle consulate in 2018 in response to the Skripal poisoning. That had a serious effect on the capabilities of Russian services to operate abroad. When your name is properly linked with British diplomatic actions against Russia then I suggest your card will be well-and-truly marked."

"No-one in Russia will believe it," says Yaroslav, "Least

of all Putin. He won't even have heard of me."

The man smiles, "It's irrelevant. You've done this at exactly the time when the US and its partners need to increase the pressure on the Kremlin. What does that mean? We can simply hand you over to the Americans. Hop on their nice white plane for an extraordinary journey and give thanks to Barack Obama for his law ceasing rendition torture. Then pray that you don't end up in Egypt or earmarked as a terrorist."

Yaroslav smirks, "You don't have the power to hand me to the Americans, anyway. And it would create a huge diplomatic incident back in Moscow."

The woman speaks again, "That's your opinion. Now that the Kremlin's use of assassins throughout the Western world is in danger of becoming the new normal, fresh options should be explored that will introduce escalating costs on Putin's regime while also galvanizing public opinion.

"You could, Mr Yaroslav, become very famous. With the Russians as a botched hitman and a killjoy for their business development. Or with the Americans as a ruthless enactor of the Kremlin's asymmetric threats."

The man adds, "You could wind up as famous as the Russian opposition's man Navalny. Poisoned, taken to a Berlin hospital where he was in a coma. Then, recovered, he went back to Moscow. "

"Yes, to serve time in Matrosskava-Tishina prison."

The woman says, "You are well informed about the political opponent who exposed Putin's Winter Palace in Gelendzhik. Was that poisoning another one of your commissions? This time, Mr Yaroslav, it is different. You are not a provincial insurgent but a connected member of the Roslavl Bratva. Try as you might to decouple these London incidents from the Kremlin in policy terms and in the public imagination. But given the futility of sanctions or expelling diplomats as means of punishment towards Moscow, the only face-saving alternative seems to be your disappearance.

"Heck, you might get the powers-that-be drawing their own red line around you."

Yaroslav goes quiet. He wishes he could clear his mind. The residual cocaine magnifies the threats against him and gives him jitters.

PLAN 02 – Enrolment

Garrick

The business card Lawson-Parry had handed to Tovey had made him easy enough to contact. Alex had taken the card and then called him directly.

"Mr Lawson-Parry? Hello this is Alex, the Personal Assistant of Sir Stafford Peters. He has recently been passed your name related to membership of the Garrick Club. Apparently, you have been on the waiting list for some time?"

"Er, Gosh, I can't say that I even remember, although I am certainly interested in joining. I know that many of the legal profession are members and that it can provide a helpful way to liaise with one another."

"That's just what Sir Stafford Peters said. Apparently, over 100 QCs are members of what must be one of London's last remaining gentlemen's clubs."

Alex continued, rather sternly, "Speaking as a female, I'm not so certain that I agree with the Garrick's men only attitude, but I do understand it is a forum where senior members of the legal profession socialise with each other.

Sir Stafford Peters says that men get a unique opportunity to form connections with senior legal practitioners to support their professional aspirations."

"Well, Alex, thank you for contacting me, I would certainly like to follow up on this most courteous invitation. Where would Sir Stafford Peters like to meet me?"

"Why, at the Garrick, with you there as his guest!" says Alex, "I'll send you an invitation. I believe I have your correct email address on this business card?"

They continue for a few minutes to arrange the meeting.

Alex smiles as another part of Amanda's plan has now been set.

Lawson-Parry now relishes a comfortable leather chair inside the Garrick waiting for Sir Stafford Peters. Instead, Michael Tovey and James Cavendish approach him. Tovey identifies Lawson-Parry and now the two of them sit down beside him.

"Oh, Michael, I hadn't expected to see you here," said Lawson-Parry, taken aback.

"We're here to see Sir Stafford Peters," said James Cavendish, "My name is Jim Cavendish, I've some things in common with a few friends of yours."

James gestured to a steward, who appeared and looked quizzically toward Lawson-Parry.

"Single malt, dear chap? The Garrick's Club Single Malt is pretty good stuff and you can't really get it anywhere else. Smokey and peaty. It must come from Islay and it reminds me of an Ardbeg or a Lagavulin."

"Yes, please, I'll have one then, thank you."

"A gentleman's full measure?" asks the steward.

"What, oh, yes please," stutters Lawson-Parry, trying to regain his composure.

"You'll probably need the drink, when we've finished this little conversation," says James Cavendish.

"You see, we had a delve into your records. We found you listed as a solicitor, but there didn't seem to be anything about barrister, nor, for that matter, Queen's Council."

Lawson-Parry looks flustered, "I can explain. My original barrister listing was in the Register, but under the name William Clark. I changed my name, but the Bar has had difficulty keeping up. Look in the records for William Hugo Clark and you'll find me." He takes a gulp of the whisky.

"But why would you want to practice under another name?" asks James Cavendish. He notices Michael Tovey looking similarly intrigued.

"It was those damned Panama Papers. I'd help draft a few of them, and it was only a matter of time before the system would catch up with me. It was altogether easier to adopt another name, which worked out well for me as it happens." Lawson-Parry took another slug of the whisky.

"Another name where you also promoted yourself to Queen's Council?" asked James Cavendish.

"It seemed so easy at the time. I had to fill in some forms and tick some boxes, I didn't intend to practice as a QC, but I thought it would give me some additional gravitas when dealing with certain clients."

"Until you were discovered, anyway," says Cavendish. He notices that Lawson-Parry has downed the whisky.

"Another?" asks Cavendish gesturing toward the empty tumbler.

"Oh, yes please, you are right, it does seem to be having the required numbing effect."

"Okay, well I haven't fully introduced myself," says Cavendish.

"You're from the Service?" guesses Lawson-Parry, "There was a word that you were getting close, I've been waiting for something like this to happen."

"Correct," says Cavendish, "SI6. And we take a dim view of a gunman in the Royal Parks shooting at a Member of Parliament."

"I wasn't involved in any of that, nor on the hit against Harrison," says Lawson-Parry.

"But you know the people that were?" asks Cavendish.

"It depends...I'd need protection to give away any information. You can see they don't mess around."

"Well, that's what we have in mind. For you to assist us but for your colleagues-in-arms to be unaware that you've done anything."

"What - a double agent?"

"In a manner of speaking. Frankly, it's your best chance now. Think about it.

A.   You are exposed as a fraudulent barrister and dozens of contracts come crashing down, creating many angry enemies.
B.   Your colleagues get wind that you've been talking to SI6 and seek their own punishment for you - perhaps invoking Anatoly Yaroslav.
C.   You help us; we get what we want (which isn't you, by the way). It keeps you clear of any wrongdoing and then you go back to your current life.

Tovey chipped in, "I'd say it was an easy decision really, wouldn't you Hugo?"

Hugo pauses, twisting the second, now half full glass of whisky in his hand.

"You know, half full is better than half empty. What will you want me to do?"

"You'll have to come with me, to join a few others and be briefed," answers Cavendish.

Rolling

Amanda's briefing room is almost full. They have Grace, Alex, Lawson-Parry, James Cavendish and the people from The Triangle present.

"I want to thank you all for coming along," says Amanda, "The first part of our plan is working well. We have Yaroslav captured and now Mr Lawson-Parry has agreed to assist. Next Andrew Brading must expose the Protection of Healthcare Rights Bill for what it is and implicate Elixanor and Brant Holdings. After that, we can let nature run its course. A television interview with Arne Holstad and then we can let the stock market decide the fate of Brant and Elixanor."

"We'll need Andrew to make another one of his inflammatory speeches?" asks Clare.

"Correct," answers Amanda, "and with Rachel Crosby well-briefed, we should be able to get Arne Holstad and also you, Mr Lawson-Parry onto the evening's 'News in Focus,' TV show."

Amanda adds, "A few well-placed questions and I'd expect Brant Holdings to want to call an emergency

Summit with Elixanor, in London."

Lawson-Parry interrupts, "You realise this could finish Elixanor. They have only just completed their takeover by Brant. Their stock is worth more now because of the Brant investment, and Brant's stock is now more dependent than ever on the fortunes of Elixanor. A double whammy of a broken product and a refusal by the UK Government to pass the Protection of Healthcare Rights Bill would ruin many months of plans and many millions of dollars of investments."

Amanda smiles, "Exactly."

PLAN 03 – Light the Touchpaper

Brading on Corruption

House of Commons. The Chamber was packed. Andrew Brading was to give another speech about his Fundamental Rights Bill, which would pave the way for the Protection of Healthcare Rights Bill. Several pundits were expecting fireworks when Brading stood up.

Madam Deputy Speaker:

"We now come to the Fundamental Rights Bill Committee statement. Andrew Brading will speak for up to 10 minutes, during which no interventions may be taken. At the conclusion of his statement, I will call Members to put questions on the subject of the statement, and I will call Andrew Brading to respond to those in turn. I call the Chair of the Fundamental Rights Bill Committee, Andrew Brading."

Brading speaks:

"We set up the Fundamental Rights to protect the citizens of this country. We may have based it upon the work of the United Kingdom, but that is no bad thing. It is paving the way for universal and Fundamental Rights for everyone and to prevent some of the scurrilous behaviour we see today."

"A Remainer's speech!" someone call from the Opposition.

"Order! Order!"

Brading continues, "A recent case springs to mind, related to housing and a planning deal. It is the stuff of television drama and yet it is still rife in our economy. Our housing minister is typical of the current crop of Cabinet ministers, an insipid character rising without trace and doing what he was told by that unelected and bullying Special Advisor to whom the Prime Minister reported."

A rustling of papers.

"This hapless Minister was most notably headlined for breaching the demand for people to 'stay at home whenever possible' during pandemic lockdown. He sat gloriously at a Tory fundraising dinner next to the former owner of a national newspaper who was being challenged by a London council over a £1bn housing redevelopment at an old newspaper print works in London. The Minister had been called to approve the scheme."

"Hear, hear!" called from the Opposition benches.

"That Tory donor texted to say: 'We don't want to give Marxists loads of dough for nothing!' Oh, no, he wanted to avoid paying any citizen related levy for the redevelopment. A case of 'don't let them eat cake'. Not even bread.

"This isn't Bake-Off," yelled someone from his own party.
    "Order! Order!"

Brading continued, unabashed, "Then, the following month, the donor sent another text urging hurried consent to avoid paying £45m in a new community-benefit levy. The Minister caved in, gave permission, even overruling officials in his own department and councillors hoping to spend their windfall on education and health in one of the country's poorest boroughs."

"Disgraceful," comes a shout from the Opposition.

"Order, Order," calls Madam Deputy Speaker.

Brading continued; he was used to this type of treatment when he made speeches, "Two weeks later the ex-newspaper owner handed £12,000 to the Conservative Party, small change compared with the huge sum he had sidestepped paying. The decision was challenged by the London borough, then the minister agreed to a court quashing his move after admitting it looked "unlawful by reason of apparent bias"."

An unexpected silence from the Chamber.

"There. That's an example of the bypass of Fundamental Rights. Go to the right dinner parties. Lobby the right people and suppress any levelling-up payments. A small 'bung' at the end should round things off nicely."

Huffing and puffing from both sides of the House.

"Order, Order!"

"Meanwhile, pictures have emerged of the Prime Minister with his arm around his grinning donor. The saga stinks from start to finish. It reveals the hypocrisy of a government that claims to be on the side of ordinary people while doing the bidding of billionaires."

Brading notices, once again, the steely glare he is receiving from both the PM and one of the whips.

"There is nothing surprising about this scandal (except perhaps the rather small size of the magnate's donation-more like a tip than a fee).

"It shows again the sleazy nexus of money and power that lurks behind the doors of Westminster and Whitehall, one in which rich people can buy access, favours, knighthoods and even seats in the upper house of our parliament, plus a planning system that is woefully open to abuse. Every party knows the problem and has been stained by similar scandals. They are happening all of the time."

Cries from the Opposition benches, "Get your own people in order!"

"Order, Order!"

Brading continues, "Let's wind back. Think of Tony Blair and the Bernie Ecclestone affair, when the motor racing tycoon switched support from the Tories, bunged Labour £1m and lobbied successfully for his sport to be exempted from a tobacco advertising ban. Or Cameron's party treasurer Peter Cruddas resigning after being embroiled in a cash-for-access row.

"Blair even admitted in his biography that party donations were 'prima facie buying influence', adding that 'once in government no one believed a big donation could be made from the goodness of heart'."

Brading paused and looked around the Chamber.

"Many politicians loathe the need to suck up to rich hustlers. But it a cost of staying in power. And yet nothing gets done, even as Britain slides in the global ranking for transparency.

"The disagreeable whiff is not helped by a prime minister failing to release a report about Moscow's penetration of our political system.

"Disagreeable whiff - hot air more like," shouts someone.

"It highlights once more how the corruption bedevilling Britain is not just about money. It is about access, accountability and influence in the shadows of Westminster. These scandals flare up repeatedly. Sometimes they lead to resignation, but never to real reform. Any actions are tokenism."

Brading looks around again, "Yet corruption, whether personal or systemic, is a rot that erodes away at the body politic. It destroys public faith. It fosters a system of patronage that benefits the elite and disempowers those lacking cash or the right connections. It levels down, fuelling state capture and rent seeking by powerful corporate interests while disadvantaging challengers. We are building a kleptocracy."

"This is wrong on moral, economic, political and social grounds. That is why I launch and promote the Fundamental Rights Bill. But I resist the attempts of saboteurs to derail it in its later stages."

"There have been overt attempts to interfere with and influence the Protection of Healthcare Rights Bill. To subvert its purpose and to nullify its effectiveness. A powerful lobby exists to attempt to couple it together with the Identity Bill and then to tier citizens into strata according to heaven knows what 'science and fact-based criteria'."

"The real purpose? To monetise healthcare, and to place it in the hands of the elite. To structure healthcare so that those deemed Tier 0 and Tier 1 (Politicians and Elite) get the best products and this further down the tiers the Tier 2 - professional and middle classes and Tier 3 and 4 - everyone else, gets delivered with an economised and less effective form of treatment. It is the danger of building the castes of Brave New World, the Alphas to the Epsilons. The population has already been indoctrinated with ideas of Tiers from the times of the global pandemic. Now they can be levelled down - not up - by the disgraceful reforms being smuggled through by lobbyists in this new set of Bills."

Silence.

Brading continues, "I may preside in some futility over the Bills and the process by which they are created. I cannot control the ways that the individuals are influenced to adjust and tarnish the intention of the original offering. When I have intervened, I have been attacked, not with words, but with bombs. Someone has uttered something facile about taking back control. Well, 'they' have. They - the elite and power hungry - They - the fat cats - now have more access through closeness to the pie and the trough. We are being levelled down and it is by our own government."

Now, the Chamber erupts, with cries of "seize control!" and "Order, Order!"

Serena, Clare and Rachel Crosby are watching from the Visitor's Gallery.

"That should get the headlines tomorrow!" says Serena.

News in Focus TV show

With Rachel's assistance, Serena had managed to get a slot on the evening news programme, "News in Focus," for both Andrew Brading and Arne Holstad. John Morden from the Labour Party Cabinet is also present. Now that Andrew Brading is hot news again for his third inflammatory speech in Parliament, there was even talk of him creating his own new party.

They were all seated in the studio with Victoria Ford. They had been introduced and now a TV package of Brading speeches was playing, with a voiceover.

"Ahead of Tuesday's votes on the Fundamental Rights Bill, attention has focused on the rights and wrongs of the House of Commons seeking to 'seize control'."

The voiceover ran along the lines that there was nothing unusual about a democratic parliament controlling its own procedure and business. Indeed, the core principle of parliamentary sovereignty already gives the Commons control by default.

Victoria starts: "Well Andrew Brading, you stirred a hornet nest with your remarks about Parliament and corruption earlier today."

"Yes, Victoria, I did, but now I'm concerned that even this usually balanced programme is being influenced by an external agenda. This is NOT - I emphasise - NOT about anything to do with seizing control or creating a new party. I see those lines of questioning as deflections, something this government is very good at."

Brading continued, "No, I want to return to the principle of Fundamental Rights. That a Newcastle shop-assistant should have the same basic rights as someone in Uxbridge who happened to go to Eton or Oxford."

"And furthermore, that the follow-up Protection of Healthcare Rights Bill should not use the Identity Bill to classify strata of the population and determine different heath regimes according to which stratum a citizen is deemed to belong in."

Victoria cut in, "But your accusations in Parliament were quite cutting. You implied that there is a level of corruption running through the place, influenced by the lobbying activities of big business."

Brading smiled, " Yes, that's exactly what I implied, and – let's be straightforward here - all of those examples I cited have been well-exercised in the media. It is just that nothing gets done. An occasional paper tiger is stood up, but then, like the Russian interference paper, it gets kicked into the long grass."

"John Morden, what do you have to say about this?"

Morden, middle-aged, dark-suited, edged forward in his chair,

"That hidden report refers to Britain 'welcoming oligarchs with open arms'. However, it says the UK government's building of links with major Russian companies has been counter-productive."

Brading interrupts, "Yes, in that it offered ideal mechanisms by which illicit finance could be recycled through what has become known as the London 'laundromat'. Their money was also invested in extending patronage and building influence across a wide sphere of the British establishment. PR firms, charities, political interests, academia and cultural institutions were all willing beneficiaries of Russian money, contributing to a 'reputation laundering' process."

John Morden tried again, "But Andrew, won't this make you a laughingstock? A major conspiracy theory, and the threat of toppling your own party?"

Brading replies, "The media are already calling London 'Londongrad' implying that Russian influence in the UK is 'the new normal', and there are a lot of Russians with very close links to Putin who are well-integrated into the UK business and social scene and accepted because of their wealth.

"This level of integration, in 'Londongrad' in particular, means that any measures now being taken by the government are not preventive but make up damage limitation."

Victoria interrupts again, "Mr Holstad, welcome to the debate. You were the Chief Science Officer for Elixanor, a company implicated in the Protection of Healthcare Rights Bill. What do you have to say about Mr Brading's allegations?"

Arne Holstad begins, "Well, I know less of your British Parliamentary system, being from Norway, but I do understand how the suggestion for tiered healthcare, as suggested by Mr Brading, might work. We attempted to build exactly such a drug dispensing system in Elixanor. It was for the graduated care of existing patients, rather than to create a tiered healthcare structure. It just wouldn't be the Norwegian way. Unfortunately, the law of unintended consequences came along when some foreign investors monetised the invention."

Victoria asks, " So who were these people? Was it, as Mr Brading implies, lobbyists trying to affect a political outcome?"

Arne replied, "Well, as a matter of fact, it is an academic question, because the truth is, we could never get the invention to work properly. Inside the drug dispensing used nano-machines but they were inherently unstable. It means we had a good idea, but no product."

Serena and Rachel were watching from the control box in the studio, "This is great," whispered Rachel, "He's just blown the lid off the whole proposition - and it is the second time that Elixanor have been caught misrepresenting a product."

Rachel wrote something on a piece of paper and handed it to the show's producer.

"Ask about Patricia Wilson..."

The producer looked at Rachel, then whispered something to someone miked into Victoria's headset.

"Ask about Patricia Wilson."

"...Thank you, Mr Holstad, you seem to be suggesting that Elixanor may have exaggerated their claims? It's not the first time is it? Can you remind us about Patricia Wilson?"

Arne Holstad paused and looked back at Victoria.

"It's probably a long story, I'm not sure I can tell it here."

"That's perfectly fine, Mr Holstad, you can go ahead."

Holstad begins, "Well the original founder of Elixanor was Patricia Wilson, who raised US$700 million to start the company. Unfortunately, in its enthusiasm, Elixanor faced a string of legal and commercial challenges from medical authorities, investors, state attorneys, former business partners, patients, and others. It looked as if powerful interests were stacked up to acquire the company after devaluing its stock."

"Elixanor received sanctions from the regulatory authorities, including the revocation of its Clinical Laboratory Improvement Amendments certificate and the prohibition of Pat Watson and other company officials from owning or operating a laboratory for two years. That's when I was hired to run things and I announced a new direction for Elixanor working on research into miniature medical substance dispensing machines. It was the start of the new nano-engineering direction for the company. But Elixanor had to pay off some serious lawsuits and fines to recover its position."

"Thank you, that was a great summary for us all," said Victoria, now being fed information about Elixanor into her earpiece.

"And I believe Patricia Wilson was only 19-years-old when she started the company?"

"That's correct, although she did have seasoned backers for the original company formation."

Brading cuts in, "It illustrates my point though. Here's a company which has already misrepresented its offering once now attempting to link with a government Bill on Healthcare. In effect to monetise its product."

Victoria nods, "And Mr Morden, any concluding thoughts?"

"Yes, with a Labour Party in power instead of the current government, there would be stringent Party rules to prevent such abuses of power."

"Well, thank you all for joining this debate; now we must move on to another topic. Britain's roads have long been pothole-ridden and now a scheme to keep the potholes as a means of speed management has been proposed. More on this after the break!"

Rachel looked towards Serena, "I think that will have clinched things. We should call Amanda and tell her what just happened. And it is, of course, on the back of Brant's recent acquisition of Elixanor. I suspect the market will open lower for both companies tomorrow."

PLAN 04 – Reaction

Stock Market

Clare was back at the Bermondsey flat.

"You've done it again!" says Tessa, "Another day of headline grabbing for Brading!"

"I've just come from that very TV studio," replies Clare.

"What - were you there when Brading and that scientist were talking? - on 'News in Focus?' - it was great telly!" says Lottie.

"I reckon it will crush the share price though, of - what were they called? - Oh yes - Elixanor!"

Robin appeared from the direction of Tessa's bedroom.

"I overheard you talking! - Hey Clare - good to see you - I've just taken a look at the price of Elixanor. It's tanking, down more than 30% and still heading south. And the financial papers are saying it will pull down Brant too; quite a disaster!"

Clare smiled, "Andrew is quite principled. He could tell that something was amiss and I think his speech this afternoon in the Commons has flushed it out. The thing is, we still don't know who is pulling the strings."

Robin looks thoughtful, "Well I guess you could follow the trail back into Elixanor. See if there are any other interesting people loitering on the edges? They are bound to have a pow-wow after that lot has gone down."

Clare's phone rings, Amanda speaks: "Tovey has been invited to a meeting tomorrow. It's at the London boardroom of Elixanor. He's asked for some backup. We are sending Lawson-Parry and as his assistants Alex Smith and Christina."

"I can understand Alex, she's one of yours, but why send Christina?"

"She asked to be included. She'll also be able to keep track if there are any Russians involved. If there's any trouble, she'll also be quite useful and perfectly deniable!"

Clare smiled; she would want to check with Christina for herself.

Dubious funders

Clare was in the Triangle offices. She walked over to Christina.

"Hej,"

"Hey, so what's the I heard about you supporting the Elixanor meeting?"

Christina answers, "Yes. Have you seen their share price today! It has crashed and taken Brant with it!"

Bigsy looked up.

"Yes, it's true, Amanda asked me to go along."

Clare asks, "She said you volunteered?"

"In a manner of speaking. I'm working off a couple of situations with British Intelligence. It's all good humoured, but I do really still owe Amanda until after this."

"You sure you'll be alright?"

"Yes, and I think I can provide good back-up for Alex and even for Tovey, you know something? I think that Russia could be behind this. When I heard that Yagovkin Lavro Kirillovich was involved in the funding of Elixanor, it started to make sense. Lavro Kirillovich is a well-known Bratva member, quite close to Prigozhin, actually."

Bigsy speaks, "Is that Prigozhin, the same one that set up the "troll factory" which used fake internet accounts and fake news to influence US voters in the 2016 presidential election?"

"According to the US intelligence services, yes, from St Petersburg," answers Christina, "He was indicted by a US Grand Jury over that election interference. Prigozhin famously shrugged off the indictment, saying: 'Americans are very impressionable people; they see what they want to see. I'm not at all upset that I'm on this list. If they want to see the devil, let them see him.'

Bigsy reads something from his screen, "It says here that Prigozhin, his family and associates keep their luxuries, like yachts registered in the Seychelles and Cayman Islands offshore tax havens.

"US individuals and firms are now prohibited from doing business with him or providing services for his jets. Although his jets have flown many times to destinations in Africa, the Middle East and Europe in recent years, the US statement says."

"It sounds as Prigozhin is above the law," said Clare, "or at least laughing at it."

"So, what is the Kirillovich link with Prigozhin?" asks Bigsy.

"Good question!" says Christina, "but still a mystery!"

PLAN 05 – Execution

Elixanor Business Strategy Meeting

It was the time of the Elixanor Business Strategy Meeting.

Michael Tovey, Hugo Lawson-Parry, Alex Smith and Christina Nott arrive in an SUV driven by MI6, and a further group of five SI6 people wait outside at ground level.

"Remember," says Alex, "If both my hands go up in the air, hit the floor," she looks around at each of them as if to check they have understood. She demonstrates - with a small gesture more like a surrender rather than a goal has been scored at Wembley. Alex is in a black business dress, looking for all the world like she is about to give a PowerPoint presentation.

They all look towards a glass windowed tower block in London. It has a prestigious city address, but nowhere on the building does it mention any of the names Elixanor, Brant or Raven.

"Nothing so tame for the people from Elixanor," says Christina looking towards the sky. A red and blue civilian helicopter is landing on the roof of the building.

"H-130," says Alex, "Pretty helicopter,"

Christina is impressed that Alex seems to know so much about hardware, "I used to ride around in H-145s," she said, showing she was also knowledgeable.

"That's serious kit, military, twin engined; suitable for light attack. What were you, some sort of black-ops commando?" asks Alex.

"This and that," smiles Christina.

They pass through security, which was reassuringly lightweight after some of the situations they had all been in. 'Bags and beeps' said Christina quietly and Alex smiled.

Then they are escorted to an express elevator and onwards to the top floor.

There's an outer lobby and a group of men sitting around.

"Security," hisses Alex.

They walk through one set of double doors to the meeting room. It breathtakingly shows off its full-length plate glass windows looking out across the City of London and toward the river and Tower Bridge.

 Already seated inside were Miller McDonald, Trudi Hartmann, Sir Edgar Holland, Mikael Bjornstad as well as a six other thick-set tattooed but suited individuals.

"They must be the bankers!" jokes Christina to Alex.

Christina and Alex scope the room on entry. Two exits and the tats were marking them. Altogether six security people in the room. Odds were against if it turned difficult.

Alex put two fingers on her face and ran them up and down. She was signalling that the security was armed. Christina quietly nodded.

Then the doors at one end open and in march another two strangers. Christina recognises one as Lavro Kirillovich and whispers it to Alex. Kirillovich looks tanned and at ease in the situation, more like someone that has just spent a week vacationing on a yacht than about to enter a hard-ball meeting. The other guy looks like a flustered bagman - probably the accountant, and they are surrounded by another six-security people, this time four men and two very attractive women.

Alex says to Christina, "Odds are stacked, we'll need to use my tag. Wait for my signal."

Alex fingers her security lanyard. Attached was a attached slim ATEX - which was a military version of a lone-worker alarm. A sophisticated device, it provided a high-performance GPS tracker and Active Response Center pings in case of emergency. It also contained amber alert mechanisms which would detect sudden increases in activity, like running or diving for cover.

Alex was trained to use the device such that she would not create false alarms and its slim format meant it looked like just another security card on her lanyard.

Christina and Alex could see what they assumed to be Kirillovich's dark blue-black helicopter clearing the building and flying away towards docklands.

Christina recognises it as a Kazan Mil Mi-38. Unmistakably Russian, but one of their less clumsy looking designs. Most Russian helicopters looked as if they had been designed by a child with some tin plate toys and a few crayons.

Kirillovich moves to sit at the head of the table, offset from Miller McDonald who looked as if he was to chair proceedings.

Miller starts to speak, "I want to thank everyone for coming. This is one of the gravest situations we have faced in a long time, and I want to ensure that we give it our fullest attention. The main board is unaware of this meeting. But right now, it is better to light a candle than to curse the darkness."

"Stop," says Kirillovich, quietly, "Brant is down 35% and Elixanor nearly half its previous valuation. This has all happened in a day. Where I come from the candles would be used for other purposes than to shine a light. My *derzhatel obshchaka* - bookkeeper - says we have an unrecoverable position. The Tambovskay Bratva have run out of patience. Someone in this room is accountable and must pay the consequences."

Kirillovich stands. "You allowed rings to be run around yourselves. First, the Member of Parliament makes damaging speeches. Then you substitute him for the man seated over there. He points to Michael Tovey. You can't warn him off nor get the Bill positioned in Parliament. You bodge the bomb attempt."

Kirillovich grimaces and his gaze moves from Tovey back to McDonald.

"Then, to finish it all off, you provide a broadcast on live television which destroys the credibility of the new company. We created this to operate as a new money-making machine, supplying legitimised drugs to the health service. It didn't matter whether they worked, as long as people believed in them."

He looks now at Trudi Hartmann, "And you, Trudi understood the nature of them as Fast-Moving Consumer Goods. We could mix other Bratva money streams with them and cleanse most of our money. Was it too much to ask? That you'd follow the plan?"

"I've lost one of my main operatives during all of this too. Anatoly Yaroslav has disappeared. He'd approve of our current plan; of that I am sure. I've decided that you are all to pay for this. It is the only way that I can recover the situation with the Tambov clan. Putin will pay a particular interest and I don't want him thinking that I don't rebalance after a failure."

Christina could hear another helicopter outside the building.

Kirillovich smiles, "Yes, I've got another transport for you all. You'll be out for a replanning session that I've booked for us all in Rotterdam. You'll go there by Mil-26. It's one of the strongest helicopters around. It has even rescued Chinooks from Afghanistan.

"Only, this time, it won't be able to cope with all of you. I've arranged for a short one-way flight for you all. To somewhere in the North Sea.

"Sadly, there will be a rotor failure and the copter will crash into the sea. It will be tragic. My security detail here is from the 16th Special Purpose Brigade, its a Spetsnaz Brigade, based in Tambov. They are perfectly used to jumping out of planes into the sea and for this assignment are getting very well rewarded. Four years' salary for this single mission for every man. He spoke some Russian which Christina understood.

"Round them up, I can hear the helicopter approaching."

Alex raised her hands in the air. Christina pushed Andrew Tovey to the floor and saw as Alex did the same with Hugo Lawson-Parry. There was a huge explosion as the plate glass windows crashed into the room. The Spetsnaz pulled out firearms, but Christina kicked one of them and his submachine gun slid across the floor towards Alex. She racked it back, but at that exact moment there was a further crack as two smoke grenades ignited. The meeting room was filled with dense purple and green smoke.

"Stay down," shouts Alex, as she slithers on her elbows though the smoke.

Christina realises the grenades were civilian rather than military and the smoke was less choking than she was used to. It was the type of effect used in a film rather than in a conflict situation.

She hears loud voices and a short rattle of suppressed sub-machine gun fire. It could have only taken five seconds for the new troops to gain control of the room.

The gunfire sounds like warning rounds rather than a firefight.

Christina hears the Spetsnaz commander stand down his men, barking instructions in Russian upon seeing they were massively outnumbered by people in full combat gear.

Military under Alex's command have reached the building and rounded up the meeting occupants. The dozen Spetsnaz surrender, having brought small arms to a full-fledged war zone. Christina looked at them, idly wondering if there was anyone she would recognise.

Christina is impressed at the way Alex carries herself, emotions ran ice cold in Alex. She's also instructed that Christina, Hugo and Michael were moved to another part of the room.

Then a bulky, dark-combat dressed man hands a gas mask to Christina. "Here, it's got comms and IR too," he said as she donned the Mira CM-7M mask. Suddenly she could breathe better, as well as hear commentary on what was happening.

The Spetsnaz had been rounded up and she could see that there were additionally around 20 commandos in the room. They had blown the glass with Brisant - a form of high explosive with a good shatter profile. Then they had swung into the room just like in the movies, throwing a few colourful smoke grenades around.

The Section Commander from the commandos spoke to Christina, "I expect you could hear our chopper outside. We had drop 20 men on the roof, without landing. We intercepted their Mil-26 with a couple of Typhoons from Lincolnshire. I think some residents will have heard the sonic boom over Cambridge. The Mil pilot surrendered immediately he saw the two combat planes."

The smoke was clearing quickly, aided by the new open-plan look of the floor, with its missing windows and a very long drop to the ground. Noisy fire alarms ring out and Christina wondered what the story would be about this building's sudden damage. Instinctively everyone was standing on the other side of the room from the open air.

Christina sees Tovey and Lawson-Parry. She'd heard about Tovey's change of trousers after the assassin incident and thinks he'll need a whole suit this time. It looks Armani, as well.

Lawson-Parry is pale but lightly covered in tomato and chilli dips from the refreshment table. She assumes that it had tipped over on to him. Alex is standing with another of the commandos, quietly chatting. Christina notices she is carrying an SA-80 rifle. Christina realises that a commando must have passed it to her.

Alex borrows this commando's radio and is clearly talking to the operations Commander. Then she flips out her iPhone and calmly calls Amanda.

"We're all safe and everyone has been rounded up. They were going to put us on a helicopter and drop us into the North Sea," she quietly explains, "It's more like something out of a James Bond Playbook." Christina realises Alex must now appear how she herself once did when she was just starting out. Young, unruffled, and as tough as nails, yet with command over a conflicted situation.

"Nicely done," says Christina, to Alex.

"Yes, thank you. I wasn't sure whether the troops were already in place when I pressed the button, but I realised it was just about the last moment that we could contain everything inside the building. A roof-top firefight would have been more difficult - probably we'd have had some casualties too, especially if we'd had an HC-4 chopper up there." She presses her business dress back into shape as she adjusts the weight of the gun's shoulder strap on her shoulder.

Christina admired Alex's logic. Alex Smith was one cool customer.

"I was just speaking to Amanda," says Alex, "It seems the other half of the plan has worked as well!"

"And what might that be?" asks Christina.

"Let's save it for the debrief," suggests Alex, "We can update Clare and the others too!"

VIP check-in

It was time to visit Amanda's office once again. Clare, Bigsy, Jake and Christina made their way by taxi and expected the long security clearance procedure.

This time Alex greeted them and whisked them into a separate VIP check-in where they were sent through security clearance swiftly, and the Alex showed them to a meeting room, less impressive than the last one, but still a decent size and kitted out with modern projectors and other office trappings.

"Hello," says Amanda, "I think all of our plans turned out rather well!"

"What was the other mission that you were doing while some of us were at Elixanor's meeting?" asks Clare.

"Well, we though that the Minerva and Medusa operations had gone on long enough, so we had a go at shutting them down. It was indirect, however."

Jake looks as if he had worked it out, "You used the Americans, didn't you?" he asks, "They were running it and could put a stop to it!"

"That's right," says Amanda, "We told the Americans that we'd discovered that Medusa had been bugging Whitehall and they folded almost immediately. It could cause a diplomatic incident if they were seen to be spying on their allies. Five Eyes and all that."

Amanda referred to The Five Eyes intelligence alliance comprising Australia, Canada, New Zealand, the United Kingdom and the United States. These countries are party to the multilateral UKUSA Agreement, a treaty for joint cooperation in signals intelligence.

"Did you give them any form of proof?" asks Bigsy, "I mean the hack to the wiring closet was pretty plain to see."

"Yes, actually, I escorted one of the American chiefs to the same spot in the Cabinet War Rooms and showed him what we had discovered. He knew about the tunnels, obviously, but had no idea that the cables were being used for spying."

"The whole Medusa operation has been closed down," says Grace, "They simply left and then a couple of days later some removals vans pulled up and took most of the kit away.

"It was a massive embarrassment being almost outside of the American Embassy.

"They have left behind a perfectly usable telephone call centre. I'm wondering if we can use if for GCHQ, actually."

"And what happened to the staff?" asks Clare, "How was that handled?"

Grace answers, "Well, most of the staff were Londoners, with a few American controllers in place. The Americans have returned to Washington and New York and the Brits have generally been relocated to other forms of call-centre.

"A few people left the organisation, and we think they may have been the plants arranged by Moscow. Altogether it has been a productive few days."

"So, what have we achieved?" asks Clare.

"I'm glad you asked," answers Grace, firing up a wall projector.

1) Andrew Brading reinstated as Secretary of State for Internal Affairs
2) The Fundamental Rights Bill prepared as legislation
3) The Protection of Healthcare Rights Bill stopped in its current form
4) Elixanor products exposed as sham
5) Brant and Elixanor diminished in the marketplace
6) Key lobby blackmailers captured including Miller McDonald and Trudi Hartmann
7) Enforcers Anatoly Yaroslav and Lavro Kirillovich captured. Both with strong cases against them.
8) Medusa spy listening station closed down.
9) An entire Spetsnaz section captured and to be used in diplomatic trade.

"That's a pretty good set of outcomes," said Bigsy, "However you look at it."

Amanda adds, "Yes, although I see that Raven is launching another Bio-engineering company now called Biotree. I guess it has at least put their plans back some years."

Grace added, "Not to mention the minor players like Roger Slater the tilted reporter, that fake barrister Hugo Lawson-Parry and the medium-sized corrupt politicians like Sir Edgar Holland and Michael Tovey.

"When the debrief gets written the Serious Fraud Office will have a field day!"

Amanda looks towards Clare, "I guess you'll be out of this now?"

"Yes, I've been thinking about that. Mainly what I'll tell my sister Sam; she'll think I've wimped out of the life, yet it is a life that she enjoys. And I have to decide what I'll tell my flat mates. They already think I have a raucous lifestyle."

"You should invite Samantha to meet you with your flatmates. Tell everyone together, then get out a 'Men In Black' gadget and wipe their minds!" says Bigsy.

"Not such a bad idea, actually; have one story for everyone and tell it once," says Alex.

"Yes," says Clare, "The trick will be to somehow make it believable!"

"I've an idea!" says Jake.

Corrupt

Now choose your next Ed Adams novel!

Triangle Trilogy		Link:	Read?
1	Triangle	https://amzn.to/3c6zRMu	
2	Square	https://amzn.to/3sEiKYx	
3	Circle	https://amzn.to/3qLavYZ	
4	Ox Stunner	https://amzn.to/3sHxIgh	
		(all feature Jake, Bigsy, Clare, Chuck Manners)	
Archangel Collection			
1	Archangel	https://amzn.to/2Y9nB5K	
2	Raven	https://amzn.to/2MiGVe6	
3	Raven's Card	https://amzn.to/2Y8HLgs	
4	Magazine Clip	https://amzn.to/3pbBJYn	
5	Play On, Christina Nott	https://amzn.to/2MbkuHl	
6	Corrupt		
		(all feature Jake, Bigsy, Clare, Chuck Manners)	
Now the Science Collection			
1	Coin	https://amzn.to/3o82wmS	
2	Pulse	https://amzn.to/3qQIBvL	
3	Edge	https://amzn.to/2KDmYOW	
4	Now the Science	https://amzn.to/3iG5Nc2	
Edge of forever Trilogy			
1	Edge	https://amzn.to/2KDmYOW	
2	Edge Blue	https://amzn.to/2Kyq9au	
3	Edge Red	https://amzn.to/2KzJwjz	
4	Edge of Forever	https://amzn.to/3c57Ghj	

Ed Adams

CPSIA information can be obtained
at www.ICGtesting.com
Printed in the USA
LVHW052007220321
682109LV00023B/1590